EARTH WAS GONE—AND IT WAS THE RING THAT HAD SENT IT AWAY

The Ring of Charon was the most powerful machine ever built by human hands. It had crushed Pluto and Charon to nothing at all, down into a black hole. The Ring's beauty was a fearful thing.

Sondra stood next to the Autocrat, staring out at the Ring. "There it is," she said. "Our one hope for finding Earth."

"How long will it take?" the Autocrat asked.

"If we can get our singularity resonating with a Charonian black hole, it will cause a wormhole between the two. The trouble is that there are millions, maybe billions, of combinations. So how long? We don't know."

"Could you induce a wormhole if you got the pattern match?"

"Oh, yes. God yes. We've learned a tremendous amount about manipulating gravity in the last five years."

"Is there any hope at all of finding Earth?" the Autocrat said.

"There is more than hope."

Books by Roger MacBride Allen

The
Shattered Sphere

Second Book of the Hunted Earth

Roger MacBride Allen

A TOM DOHERTY ASSOCIATES BOOK

NEW YORK

This is a work of fiction. All the characters and events portrayed in this book are fictional, and any resemblance to real people or incidents is purely coincidental.

THE SHATTERED SPHERE

Cover art by Boris Vallejo

A Tor Book
Published by Tom Doherty Associates, Inc.
175 Fifth Avenue
New York, N.Y. 10010

Tor® is a registered trademark of Tom Doherty Associates, Inc.

ISBN: 0-812-53016-0

First edition: July 1994
First mass market edition: September 1995

Printed in the United States of America

0 9 8 7 6 5 4 3 2 1

To Eleanore Maury Fox—
Home is where she is.

Contents

Contents

Illustrations

Author's Note

"Have you finished *The Shattered Sphere* yet?"

That is the question I have been asked more than any other since *The Ring of Charon* came out. Readers, friends, editors, agents, and all sorts of other people have wanted to know. I am more pleased than you can know that the answer is now "yes." Here it is.

To everyone who has been patient—and impatient—for this book, let me say thank you. I hope that the results have been worth the wait.

Special thanks are due to my editor, Debbie Notkin, and to Beth Meacham, Patrick Nielsen Hayden, Tom Doherty, and the entire staff at Tor Books. Now, at long last, I can stop hiding from them. Thanks also, once again, to Linda Silk, whose artwork graced the advance reading copies. Thanks to my parents, Tam and Scottie, for their comments on the manuscript.

And finally, thanks also to Eleanore Maury Fox, to whom this book is dedicated. She read the original manuscript and provided a great deal of firm and much-needed advice. There are, needless to say, a lot of other reasons for me to say thanks to Eleanore, but that's another story—one that isn't anywhere near done yet.

—Roger MacBride Allen
London, August 1993

Dramatis Personae

The Autocrat of Ceres. The absolute ruler of Ceres, and de facto hegemonic leader of the entire Asteroid Belt. By tradition, the holder of the office renounces his or her name and all links to his or her previous life upon entry into office.

Joanne Beadle. Operations technician at Kourou Spaceport, South America. She acts, rather reluctantly, as Wolf Bernhardt's personal assistant during his stay there.

Dr. Wolf Bernhardt. Head of the U.N. Directorate of Spatial Investigation (DSI) and Director of the Multisystem Research Institute (MRI).

Dr. Sondra Berghoff. Director of the Ring of Charon Gravitics Research Station at Plutopoint.

Canpopper Notworthit. A rather inefficient cargo handler on NaPurHab.

Dr. Selby Bogsworth-Stapleton. A "Leftover," that is, a citizen of Earth stranded in the Solar System by the Abduction. The only trained archaeologist on the Moon, she heads the exploration of the Lunar Wheel and the Wheelway Tunnel system.

Sianna Colette. A young woman, orphaned as a teenager by the pulsequakes of the Abduction. As the book opens, she is a graduate student working at the Multisystem Research Institute (MRI) in New York.

Dr. Larry O'Shawnessy Chao. Formerly a youthful and very junior researcher at the Gravitics Research Station, Pluto. Chao accidentally activated the huge Charonian being, the Lunar Wheel, and thus inadvertently set in motion the events leading to the Abduction. As the book opens, he is working on the *Graviton* project.

Lucian Dreyfuss. Once a technician at the Moon's Orbital Traffic Control Center, he was captured by the Charonians in the Rabbit Hole. He is presumed dead.

Eyeballer Maximus Lock-on. A rather moody and forceful woman, she is head of navigation and guidance on NaPurHab.

Dr. Ursula Gruber. Director of Observational Studies at MRI and a key adviser to Wolf Bernhardt.

Dr. Gerald MacDougal. Second-in-command of the *Terra Nova*. He is married to Marcia MacDougal. A born-again Christian, he is a trained exobiologist.

Dr. Marcia MacDougal. Once a planetary engineer on Venus Initial Station for Operational Research (VISOR), now a researcher in Charonian symbology. She escaped from the Naked Purple Movement in Tycho Purple Penal as a teenager. She returned to the Moon when VISOR was mothballed. As the book opens, she is based at the Lunar North Pole and involved in research into Charonian language and behavior there.

Wally Sturgis. An expert in computer modeling. As the book opens, he is employed at the Multisystem Research Institute.

Ohio Template Windbag. The Maximum Windbag, or leader, of the Naked Purple Habitat (NaPurHab).

Tyrone Vespasian. Director of the Lucian Dreyfuss Memorial Research Station (a.k.a. "The Rabbit Hole") at the Moon's North Pole.

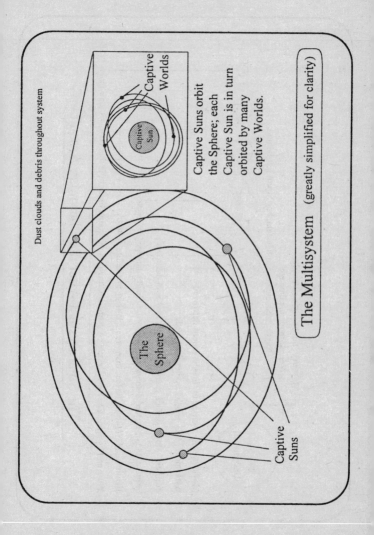

Dust clouds and debris throughout system

Captive Worlds

Captive Sun

Captive Suns orbit the Sphere; each Captive Sun is in turn orbited by many Captive Worlds.

The Sphere

Captive Suns

The Multisystem (greatly simplified for clarity)

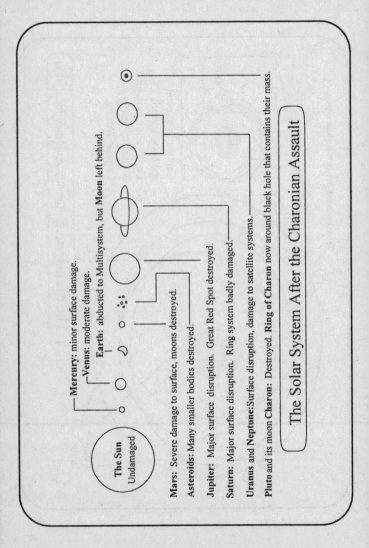

The Sun
Undamaged

Mercury: minor surface damage.
Venus: moderate damage.
Earth: abducted to Multisystem, but Moon left behind.

Mars: Severe damage to surface, moons destroyed.

Asteroids: Many smaller bodies destroyed.

Jupiter: Major surface disruption. Great Red Spot destroyed.

Saturn: Major surface disruption. Ring system badly damaged.

Uranus and Neptune: Surface disruption, damage to satellite systems.

Pluto and its moon Charon: Destroyed. Ring of Charon now around black hole that contains their mass.

The Solar System After the Charonian Assault

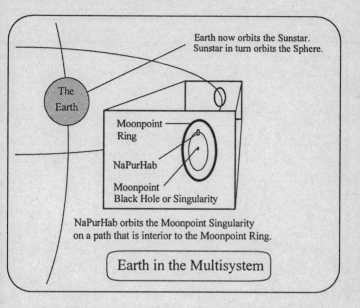

Earth now orbits the Sunstar.
Sunstar in turn orbits the Sphere.

The
Earth

Moonpoint
Ring

NaPurHab

Moonpoint
Black Hole or Singularity

NaPurHab orbits the Moonpoint Singularity
on a path that is interior to the Moonpoint Ring.

Earth in the Multisystem

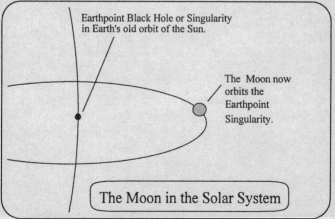

Earthpoint Black Hole or Singularity
in Earth's old orbit of the Sun.

The Moon now
orbits the
Earthpoint
Singularity.

The Moon in the Solar System

One

Boarding Party

*Others called it the Adversary, but it had no name for itself,
or even a sufficient awareness of self for a name to be meaningful. The distinction between individual and group was as
meaningless to it as it would be to a volume of water that
happens to be divided and then recombined. The Adversary
could divide itself, and merge itself, to whatever degree it
chose. But the Adversary was, ultimately, one.*

*It lived in the warm, slow, soft recesses of heavy gravity,
of gravity fields powerful enough to slow time down to a reasonable rate of speed. As seen from out in the cold and dark
distortions of fast-time space, the Adversary was deep inside
a truncated wormhole aperture, seemingly unheeding of the
outside universe.*

*But it was not so, even if the slowed passage of time inside
the ruined wormhole might make it so appear. It was aware
of its surroundings, even if it was slow to react to them.*

And it had detected a vibration in the fabric of the gravitic links. Some time past, as measured in the cold and dark of fast time, there had been a series of disturbances. As a series of lightning flashes might briefly illuminate all of a darkened landscape, and so serve to guide one across it, the gravitic vibrations made much that was hidden suddenly visible. The Adversary could see the path to new sources of power, of energy, illuminated across the expanses of wormhole links and fast-time space.

Slowly, oh so slowly as seen from fast-time space, it began to move.

"The *Terra Nova* was, of course, built to be the first starship. In the parlance of the time, she was a sleep-ship. Her passengers were meant to be frozen before departure, and to sleep away the long years and decades between the stars, then thawed and decanted on arrival at the target star system. However, budget restraints forced the mothballing of the great ship a few months short of completion. She was never launched toward Alpha Centauri, as intended. Instead, she sat in a parking orbit of Earth.

"As chance would have it, the *Terra Nova* was swept up along with Earth when the planet was abducted into its new surroundings in the Multisystem. The *Terra Nova* was immediately set to work studying Earth's startling new environs.

"The ship's designers named her for a famous British exploration ship of the early twentieth century. No doubt they would have chosen a name of better omen had they examined the history, rather than the myth and romance, surrounding that namesake vessel. That *Terra Nova,* Commander Scott's ill-fated command vessel on his fatal trip to the South Pole, was a rather ordinary ship, a whaling vessel pressed into Antarctic service, quite ill-suited to exploration or Antarctic conditions. As a result, she found herself in the greatest of difficulties on many occasions, putting her crew in great and needless peril. Her unsuitability was a contributing factor in the expedition's disastrous failure.

"Our *Terra Nova*, on the other hand, was built for the sole purpose of exploration—but found herself forced into virtually every other role instead. By turns a mothballed hulk, a military craft, a rescue ship, a lifeboat, and many other things besides, she earned fame for doing all the things she was never meant to do.

"In one of the great ironies of the history of exploration, the ship built to search for and colonize new worlds trillions of kilometers from Earth instead found herself among any number of new and fertile worlds a mere stone's throw away from Earth—and yet she dared not approach any of them, let alone take up orbit or send down landers."

—*Earth in the Multisystem: A Chronicle of Exile,*
Jose Ortega, Central City Press, 2436

Aboard the *Terra Nova*
Deep Space
THE MULTISYSTEM
June 4, 2431

"*Hijacker* now five kilometers from the Close-Orbiting Radar Emitter." The tracking officer kept up her steady, monotone reports. A half million kilometers away, the long stern chase was drawing to its close. *Terra Nova* might have built and launched *Hijacker*, but the mother ship was nothing but an observer now. There was nothing she could do to help. Captain Dianne Steiger stared at the main bridge screen, at the huge lump of rock that was the CORE, straining her eyes for the dim, tiny dot that was *Hijacker*, the frail, tiny ship that had departed the *Terra Nova* nearly a month before.

Her hands gripped the arms of her command chair hard, her fingers dug deep into its fabric. She longed for a cigarette, but she had smoked the last one on board two years before. The CORE and *Hijacker* might be hundreds of thousands of kilometers away, but that didn't make the little ship's mission any less important. *Hijacker*'s crew had to succeed. They *had* to, or else it was time to change the *Terra Nova*'s name to the *Flying Dutchman* and be done with it.

The damnable COREs, the endless thousands of COREs, had prevented Dianne's ship from approaching any planet for the last five years. The *Terra Nova* could not even return home to Earth, for Earth had been surrounded by its own swarm of COREs.

But this CORE was out in the depths of space, nowhere near a planet, all by itself, traveling between worlds on some unknowable task of its own. Maybe, just maybe, this one the men and women of the *Terra Nova* could take on.

"*Hijacker* now three kilometers from the CORE," the tracking officer reported.

Dianne stared harder at the screen. Ah, there she was, just coming into view of the long-range infrared cameras. Even with all the enhancers cranked up all the way, *Hijacker* was nothing but a dim brown dot crawling into the picture frame. Staring at the image made Dianne's eyes swim. She blinked to clear her vision, and found she had lost track of the hard-to-see blob of color. Then the Artificial Intelligence system, the ArtInt, running the display system threw a yellow target circle centered around *Hijacker*. Much better.

No need to throw any such circle around the CORE, of course. The alien ship was the size of an asteroid, and all too easy to see. In fact it *was* an asteroid. Perhaps even calling it an alien ship was a bit misleading. Dianne glanced to her left, where Gerald MacDougal was sitting, staring at the screen himself.

Gerald always argued, quite plausibly, that the CORE was as much crew and captain as it was ship, one semi-organic whole. Certainly the CORE was alive. More or less. Unless you chose to regard it wholly as a machine. Dianne sighed and gave it up. Nothing was ever clear when you were dealing with the Charonians. And even if they were the most deadly enemy that humanity had ever faced, and even if the Charonian's utter failure to notice that humans existed was the one thing that kept humanity from being destroyed, there was something damn mortifying in the arrogant way the Charonians steadfastly ignored everything human. Cockroaches got more attention from humans than humans got from Charonians. Sometimes Dianne thought it would be a victory just to get the other side to acknowledge the existence of humans.

"Any change in radar emissions?" Gerald asked. Any shift in radar could be a warning that the CORE had spotted *Hijacker*. The *Terra Nova* was not putting out any radar herself, but the ship's passive detectors were tuned and focused, watching the CORE's emissions for any changes caused either by the CORE's beams being deflected or by the CORE changing its active search pattern.

"No, sir. No change in radar emissions, no target-induced shift in outgoing beam. No new activity that we can detect."

That was good news, or at least the absence of bad news. *CORE* stood for *"Close-Orbiting Radar Emitter."* This one was not in close orbit of anything at the moment, but it sure as hell was emitting radar like crazy.

The radar was meant to detect any object large enough to threaten whatever planet the CORE happened to be protecting. If it detected a threatening meteor, the CORE would shift course and smash itself into the incoming rock, knocking the rock off course, if not smashing it to bits.

Such protection was necessary. Earth's new home, the Multisystem, was full of spaceborne debris and clouds of dust, thick enough in places that comm lasers would not work. *Terra Nova*'s lasers had not been able to punch through to Earth for weeks. The ship had been in radio silence for all that time as well, for fear of attracting the CORE's attention.

The best estimate was that there was between fifty and five hundred times as much skyjunk as in the Solar System. Dianne shifted nervously. As if she needed something else to worry about, something else she could do nothing about. There was no real way to know that the Solar System had survived, and plenty of reason to fear that it had not.

But best to focus on the problem at hand. Counting the Earth, there were at least 157 planets in the Multisystem, and every last one of them was surrounded by a cloud of COREs. The COREs were a first-rate defense against asteroids, but the damned things went after ships and landing craft just as relentlessly, swarming out to smash into any craft whose projected course intercepted a planet. The *Terra Nova* dared not get within three hundred thousand kilometers of any of those 157 planets. There was no danger of starvation, of the ship dying, of course: *Terra Nova* was designed to cross the dark between the stars, and Earth could still send the occasional outbound resupply ship. The COREs did not seem to care about objects moving out from a planet—most of the time. Something like half the outbound supply cargoes made it through.

No, survival was not the issue—the question was one of the ship's usefulness, of its meaning. What was the point of a starship that could not get near a planet? *Terra Nova* had long since learned all she could about the Charonians from 300,000 kilometers away.

But *Hijacker* might be the key. If the small, stealthy ship could land on this CORE undetected, if her crew could make use of the tiny scraps of information that were all humanity knew about the COREs specifically and the Charonians generally, it was just possible they could take over the CORE, learn how to control it. Then maybe, just maybe, they could find a way to make all the COREs back off, find a way that would allow the *Terra Nova* to send landing craft to explore some of those worlds. Earth could launch new spacecraft, and humanity would have a chance to rebuild the orbital facilities that had been destroyed.

Maybe, just maybe, getting a prize crew aboard a CORE would be the first step toward humanity's reclaiming control of its destiny. The second stealthship, the *Highwayman,* was nearing completion, down in the *Terra Nova*'s massive holds. If this first attempt worked, they would be ready to capture another CORE almost immediately. *If* the first stealthship worked.

Hijacker was supposed to be invisible to radar, built with every possible trick of stealth technology that the crew of *Terra Nova* could manage. But no object could be made completely invisible at all detection frequencies, and the closer *Hijacker* got to the CORE, the more likely it was that the CORE would spot her. In fact, never mind radar. If the CORE used visual or infrared, it would be all over. There was no evidence that COREs had any sort of infrared or visual sense—but there was no proof they didn't, either.

Hijacker was painted matte black to make her hard to spot visually, but there was damned little they could do to hide the fact that *Hijacker* was warmer than empty space. After all, if the *Terra Nova* could track her on infrared from a range of a half million klicks, there had to be some chance that the CORE could spot her three klicks away.

Dianne wished to hell she knew how things were going on the little ship. But *Hijacker* had to maintain radio silence, and she was not large enough to carry the sort of pointing and tracking gear required to keep a comm laser pointed accurately over long range. There was no way to know more than what the screen and the tracking officer could tell her.

Now came the worst part, the most dangerous part. *Hijacker* was moving slowly in relation to the massive CORE, but she still needed to match velocities with the behemoth. That meant firing some sort of reaction thruster. Standard fusion rockets were out of the question, of course—they would light up a radar screen like a Christmas tree. But there were other choices besides fusion rockets.

"She should start braking any time," said Gerald Mac-Dougal. "I pray to God this works."

Hijacker used cold gas rockets—nothing more or less than compressed-air jets. The jets were hideously inefficient and awkward. The engineers had had a devil of a time preventing the tanks of supercompressed air from throwing their own substantial radar shadows. It was a terrible solution. There had to be a better way. No one had found it, though. The best that could be said of the compressed-air rockets was that no one could think of anything less bad.

But, still, it ought to work. Radar of any sort was going to have trouble detecting rocket thrust that was literally nothing more than cold thin air.

The tracking officer spoke again, relentlessly calm. "We are showing change-of-rate on *Hijacker*. She has commenced her braking maneuver."

And now came the moment of truth. There had been no way to know until now. No way to be sure the CORE could not detect a compressed-air jet until they tried it.

"Any change in radar emissions?" Gerald asked again.

"Nothing, sir. *Hijacker* still braking."

"Come on, *Hijacker*," Dianne whispered, staring at the screen. Seconds turned to minutes, and the tiny brownish dot crept toward its target, a flea on its way to attack an elephant, moving more and more slowly as its braking maneuver continued. Time itself seemed to stretch out, expand.

Until it moved all too quickly.

"Change in backscatter pattern!" the tracking officer cried out. "Beam transmission seems unchanged, but we are reading a new interference pattern. I say again, a new backscatter pattern."

"What the hell sort of pattern?" Dianne demanded. Backscatter meant that whatever was causing the change was directly between the CORE and the *Terra Nova*, illuminated from behind as it was detected by the *TN*'s sensors.

"Searching archives for pattern match," the tracking officer said. "Oh my God." For the first time, the young officer betrayed emotion. Suddenly fear hung heavy in her words.

"Dust, ma'am. We . . . we have a pattern match on a radar beam reflecting off rock dust. And the cloud is expanding."

And Dianne's insides were suddenly nothing more than ice. She knew what was happening, what happened next. There was no way around it. *Hijacker*'s gas jets had struck the surface of the CORE, dislodged dust that had no business existing on that surface, kicked it up into open space. The CORE's radar beams were striking that dust—and if the *Terra Nova* could read the change in the beam, so could the CORE. *Hijacker*'s designers had considered the danger, and rejected it as minor. After all, this very CORE had been seen undergoing the most violent maneuvers. Surely the massive accelerations would have dislodged any dust layers long ago.

But no, they had been mistaken. And the Universe was about to extract its usual penalty for being wrong. The CORE would detect the dust cloud, refocus its radar beams to bear down on *Hijacker*, and that would be that. If the CORE focused its complete attention on the tiny volume of space that contained *Hijacker*, there could be no escape.

There was silence on the bridge. There was nothing to be said, nothing to be done. Perhaps the tracking officer should have kept up her reports, but silence said more than any words she could offer.

The CORE started to turn, coming about, bringing its nose to bear on *Hijacker*. The tiny brownish spot on the screen, the spot that was ten men and women, ten of their friends and lovers and colleagues, the spot that was months of planning and years of hope, hung helpless in the sky.

And then the CORE moved, crossed the distance between itself and *Hijacker* in the space of five heartbeats. The brown dot vanished, brushed aside as the CORE swept into the space it had occupied. Light flared in the display, and that was all. The display system's ArtInt faded out the target circle that had highlighted the ship's position, and the CORE resumed its previous heading.

Five hundred thousand kilometers away, there was a

cloud of debris, of smashed bodies in torn pressure suits, of crumpled machines and ruined engines. Perhaps not all of them were dead yet, perhaps the gods of luck had been cruel enough to catch one or two of them in their pressure suits, leaving them to survive for a time, beyond all hope, but still breathing, hearts still beating, helpless to do anything but watch the wreckage and the bodies disperse into the black and empty space of the Multisystem. Could there be a lonelier death?

Captain Dianne Steiger still stared in the direction of the viewscreen, but she saw nothing at all. "Nothing is changed," she said at last, in a voice that was cold and hard. "That CORE is still our best chance. Our only chance. It could be years before another one goes on a trajectory we can follow. We either solve this problem, board that CORE, or give up and die."

Gerald MacDougal looked over at her, and she looked back at him. After close to five years aboard ship together, she knew what he would say, how he would say it. She answered the words he did not need to speak.

"I know, Gerald. They are dead. We will mourn when there is time," she said. "But if we do not break out of this trap, find a way to get this ship to a planet, we might as well be as dead as *Hijacker*."

She slumped back in her command chair and stared at the terrifying emptiness in the screen, the emptiness where the *Hijacker* had been. "Find a way," she said. "Find a solution. We were nearly, nearly, there. Find the solution and give it to the second stealthship, the *Highwayman*."

Captain Dianne Steiger tried not to think about the next crew of ten she was sending out to likely death. But the *Terra Nova*'s survival, the mission, the people of Earth came first.

And so she spoke the words. "I want the *Highwayman* launched toward the CORE within a week."

"Dianne—Captain—we can't!" Gerald MacDougal protested. "We'd just be dooming another crew."

"Then *give me another choice,* Gerald," she snapped, turning to glare at him with desperate eyes.

Gerald stared right back at her. "At least let me break radio silence and contact Earth before we launch. It's a million-to-one shot, but maybe they've come up with something. There's no point in hiding out here anymore—that CORE is sure to have spotted us now. *Hijacker* was directly between us and the CORE. The CORE must have gotten a radar echo off us as well when it threw that beam onto *Hijacker*."

"Tracking?" Dianne asked, not breaking eye contact with Gerald.

"Dr. MacDougal is right, Captain," the tracking officer said. "There was a very strong direct pulse onto the hull. The CORE must have picked up the echo."

Dianne knew that there was no realistic hope that Earth had come up with anything. After five years of utter failure, the researchers had all given up or gotten bogged down in blind alleys. She knew that even a brief, tight-beam radio transmission might be enough to spook the CORE, send it to the attack. There was no sense in delay, no rational reason to agree.

But—but even she was horrified at the idea of trying again. The second stealthship could only have a lower chance of success than the first.

For the CORE would know to watch for them now.

To hell with sense and rational reason. "Very well," she said. "Go ahead and make your contact, Dr. MacDougal."

She sighed and stared at the main screen and the brooding bulk of the CORE. After all, what harm could there be in waiting a day or two before sending a second crew to its certain death?

Two

Leftovers

"Lucian Dreyfuss was my friend, and I was his. That's something not a whole lotta people can say.

"A lot of people will tell you he was a real angry person, and yeah, that's true. He always had a temper. But I bet no one else can tell you *why* he was so mad. Because he never thought he was good enough. He always thought he could do better. He was mad at himself. And then, when the Charonians came along, he *hated* them worse than anyone else. He wasn't like the rest of us. Back then, right at the beginning, everyone else was too confused by them, or couldn't believe in them, or couldn't see what they were. We were scared of them. They made us feel so little and weak that there wasn't any room left to feel anything more. Not Lucian. They didn't scare him. They just got him mad. . . .

". . . See, at first, most people wanted to think the Charonian disaster just *happened*, like an earthquake. An act of God, see? Not Lucian. He could get his mind *around* the Charonians, understand they were an *enemy*, not some weird force of nature, way before anyone else.

". . . The last job he did was to go down the Rabbit Hole. That's what we call the shaft from the Lunar surface down to where the Lunar Wheel is. He went down in a suit, and they sent down a TeleOperator rig with Larry Chao running it to go with him. They were gonna hang some sensors on the Wheel so we could listen in. That part worked out okay, and we got a lot of data. But the . . . the [expletive] Charonians caught them. Chopped the [expletive] VR suit to ribbons, and just *took* Lucian. We saw it back on the surface through the VR suit's video pickups. They grabbed him and ran down the [expletive] tunnel.

". . . I still hear him screaming, sometimes, when I go to bed. They *took* him, and we never found out what happened to him. That's the part that keeps my nightmares going. He just vanished off into the nowhere, off into fog and mystery. For my money, a guy who was that much alive deserves a better end than that."

—Extracts of transcribed recording, from *One Year After the Abduction: An Oral History of the Disaster*, Central City Archives, 2427

Central City
The Moon
THE SOLAR SYSTEM

Marcia MacDougal glanced at her wristaid for at least the dozenth time as the chancellor droned on. She knew that she really shouldn't do it. She knew it looked bad, that it was a disrespectful thing to do—especially for someone who was on the speaker's platform. The man was due some respect, after all. Chancellor Daltry had been running Armstrong University forever. But it seemed to Marcia that he had been speaking for about the same period of time.

Damn it, why couldn't the man finish? MacDougal wanted the ceremony to end so she could go—but she also knew she had to stay, and see the ceremony out.

Damnation! She should never have come back here. She should have stayed at the Pole, close to the action, ready to move. But yes, there was business to do back here, and yes, she had to be in the city for the Abduction Day ceremonies. She was, after all, a Conner, to use the slang term for a citizen of the Lunar Republic. Marcia was a refugee from Tycho Purple Penal, and thus an immigrant to the Lunar Republic. Like most immigrants, she took her citizenship seriously. She wanted to be here. It was an honor to be here.

But how could she have known that they would have picked now, *today*, to find something at the Pole? A breakthrough, Selby had said. At least a possible breakthrough. She hadn't been willing to say more than that.

"We mourn today," Chancellor Daltry said, "for that which is lost in the sense of misplaced, out of reach, and also for that which is lost in the sense of being hopelessly, utterly gone. We mourn for the Earth, but retain every hope and expectation that she lives. But we mourn also the lives lost, the destroyed worlds of the Solar System, the end of our previous way of life. In a sense, we are speaking not only for our dead, but to them, telling them all the things we desperately need for them to hear."

Nice old guy, Marcia thought, *but does he have to go on and on?* She went back to tuning out the words, and applauding when everyone else did. *Pretending* to listen was enough.

Marcia had said her own piece toward the beginning of the service. Surely that was all they could expect of her. Maybe not even that much.

There was no real need for her to remain. Maybe she

could sneak off the stage without anyone noticing. But Marcia was a rather striking woman, tall and slender, with smooth perfect skin the color of mahogany. Her eyes were bright and clear, dark brown in color, set in a round, expressive face. She had grown her luxuriant black hair out these last few years, and she wore it in a single thick braid down the middle of her back. Normally, she didn't mind being the sort of person people looked at, but right now it made it seem unlikely that she would able to thread her way across a stage full of chairs without causing a ruckus. She shifted in her seat, feeling restless—and even that movement was enough to prompt a loud squeak from her chair. No. Face it. She had to sit tight, and that was that.

At last the chancellor droned to a halt. Marcia applauded as briefly as she decently could, stood with the others, and then made her way off the platform. She slipped out through the edge of the departing crowd and hurried on her way.

But rush as she might, on this day, Abduction Day, it was impossible not to think on all that had been lost. Marcia looked about the dome as she walked. Central City had suffered tremendous damage in the post-Abduction pulse-quakes, and even now, much of it had yet to heal.

Central City had always been proud of its trees and its gardens, growing tall under the blue stone skies of the domes. Most of the decorative plant life had died during or after the quakes. Some plants were crushed or smashed or uprooted in the quake, but most died because the water-line systems that fed them were wrecked. Repair priority, quite rightly, was given to repairing the water system for the distinctly non-decorative hydroponic gardens that supplied the city with a large fraction of its food and air.

The city and the people had survived, but all too many of the trees and gardens died of thirst. Most of the gardens had come back and, here and there, a new sapling showed itself, green as life and fresh as hope; but even now, five years on, dead trees were everywhere. The city was cutting them down and replanting as best it could—but it had to move slowly. If it had cut down all the trees and sent them for recycling all at once, the city's biomass and carbon-cycle balance would have been thrown totally out of whack. The city could not afford the effort and materials needed to do a major biomass rebalance. So the dead trees stayed up, grey skeletons thrusting up toward the sky.

Everything in the city was like that. Everywhere there were scars that should have healed by now, except that Central City, and its people, were still working on the basic structural repairs. Nothing, absolutely nothing, could be imported. Earth wasn't there to ship anything, and the other worlds were far worse off than the Moon. The Moon had effectively been self-sufficient for years—but Earth had always been there as a backstop, as a source of sophisticated spare parts and luxury items. No more.

Sidewalks were out of true. Windows were cracked. Here and there, the paint on the dome had peeled or chipped, revealing spots of grey-black rock behind the sky blue facade. Buildings were repaired with braces and struts, rather than rebuilt. Everything strong and ugly, and nowhere a hint of grace. People were expected to make do.

Marcia hurried down a once-moving walkway that had stood still for five years, went down two levels to the nearest transport center. The daily hopper run to the North Pole was going to lift in twenty minutes, and she had to be on it. The survey teams searching through the unbelievably vast corpse of the Lunar Wheel had found something.

She checked her wristaid for the time again. She could still just make it if she hurried.

Marcia MacDougal was not much for false modesty. She knew she was one of the leading experts—no, *the* leading expert—in Charonian visual language and symbology. It was fascinating and useful work, but it did have its drawbacks—for instance, traveling via hopper. She was constantly shuttling back and forth between Central City and

Dreyfuss Station at the North Pole, and the trip never got any better.

Lunar travel used to mean leaving your comfortable surroundings, going aboard a cramped, uncomfortable roller to be jounced along on a bad road, or perhaps taking a sub-orbital hopper rocket, cramming yourself into the too-small seats and suffering through the roaring, rattling, crushing-heavy weight of the launch. It meant feeling a bit queasy as the roller hit a bad patch in the road or the hopper cut its engines and made that abrupt lurch into zero gee. It meant the thrill of fear when the roller seemed to come far too close to the edge of a precipice, or when the braking rockets appeared to be something more than a trifle late lighting up. It meant bad food, close quarters, and a distinct sense that time had stood still and you were going to be trapped in an over-sized tin can forever. But then you would arrive, and step through the pressure lock, and it would be over, and you would be back in civilization, with good air and proper food and enough space to stand up and turn around in.

Nowadays, lunar travel was exactly the same, but the comfortable surroundings at either end had deteriorated quite seriously. If Central City was a bit shabby these days, Dreyfuss Station was positively grim.

The hopper ride was miserable, made no less so by the fact that safety regulations required everyone to wear a pressure suit during the flight. Marcia had no real quarrel with that rule. She knew as well as anyone exactly what condition the hopper fleet was in, but it did not make the suits any more pleasant to wear. At least you didn't have to seal your suit, just be able to button up in a hurry. Wearing the thing unsealed was torture enough.

Having but little faith in the hull's integrity, Marcia breathed a half sigh of relief when the underpowered spacecraft made a safe—if slightly bumpy—landing at the North Pole spaceport.

At least the memorial services meant the hopper wasn't packed to the bulkheads the way it usually was. Marcia Mac-

Dougal waited with the two or three other passengers for the roller to dock up with the hopper. One obvious first-timer stood up and went over to wait by the hatch, but Marcia and the others waited it out in their seats. No sense standing on everybody else's toes in the low-ceilinged hatchway for the ten minutes it would take to get the two crotchety old vehicles docked. Marcia closed her eyes and tried to think of quiet, comfortable places. It wasn't easy.

At last the hatch opened with a weary creak. Marcia opened her eyes, pried herself out of her chair, grabbed her travel bag, and made her way to the hatch.

They filed into the roller and the hatch closed behind them. The first-timer made the mistake of sitting down for the ride, but Marcia and the others stood, holding onto one of the straps hanging from the overhead bulkhead. She slung the strap of her travel bag over her shoulder, and braced her feet as best she could. It was awkward, but it beat being thrown out of your seat on the first bounce. The roller's seatbelts had been "borrowed" for use on other vehicles years ago.

The motors whirred to life, and the elderly surface vehicle lurched into motion. The roller was in no better shape than it had been the last time she had ridden it, and it creaked and groaned most alarmingly as it jounced over the lunar surface. The newcomer bounced out of her chair three times before standing with the rest of them.

After a more than usually bone-rattling ride, the roller arrived at the station and entered the vehicular airlock. The hatch closed behind the roller, and Marcia listened as the air hissed into the airlock chamber. The roller's hull pinged and groaned as it adjusted to the change in pressure. The hatch opened, and she was there, even if "there" wasn't much of a place.

Travel bag still over her shoulder, she stepped out of the airlock chamber and into the main transport entrance of Dome One, Dreyfuss Station, to be welcomed by the rotting-sweatsock smell that summed up the whole of Dreyfuss Station so far as Marcia was concerned.

The transport section took up about half the hundred-meter diameter of Dome One. It had all the ambience of a third-rate loading and storage bay—which was, of course, all it really was.

Everything up here at the Pole had always been rather utilitarian, but the repeated cutbacks in maintenance had turned things positively grim in the last year or two. The air was a trifle too dry. There was just a hint of the ozone odor of overworked electrical system. A few of the light fixtures here and there were dark. A film of dust lay over everything, and a sad greyness seemed to have settled with the dust. The shabby feel of the place never failed to get to Marcia, every time she came back. The place was less than five years old, and yet it all seemed to be moldering away.

Someday they would get the budget and the resources to refurbish this place. Not for the first time, she considered the likely fact that the people who were around here all the time didn't even notice it anymore. Maybe that was the saddest thing of all.

Tunnels and chambers cut into the lunar rock, with a few surface domes. That was Dreyfuss Station. Yet there had been a time—and perhaps there would be a time once again—when those tunnels and domes were and would be something more than that. Once it had been a place with a purpose, a *mission,* the place where the people of the Moon would wrest the secrets of the Charonians from the ruined Lunar Wheel.

But no one had made any real progress toward that goal in a long, long time. The researchers had accumulated data, yes—huge masses of it. The people of the Moon now understood the biology and behavior of the Charonians far better than they ever had before. But none of that knowledge got them any closer to finding the Earth.

And, ultimately, what else mattered besides that?

Well, one thing did. At least it mattered to Marcia Mac-Dougal. It was why she had signed on to the Lunar Wheel survey in the first place. Her husband, Gerald MacDougal, serving aboard the *Terra Nova*. She had lost him when the Earth had been Abducted, and if there was one goal in her life, it was it getting him back. Mastering the Charonian symbol language was nothing to her but a way of moving toward that goal. Humanity might be able to undo what the Charonians had done—if humanity learned Charonian.

None of which did her any good at the moment. Where was Selby? She glanced around the arrival room, half-hoping that Selby wasn't going to be there. Yes, she had said she would meet her flight, and Marcia had agreed, but she couldn't help wishing she could slip off to her own quarters and have a little peace and quiet—

But no. There was Selby, on the far side of the room, waving her hand a bit frantically. Marcia sighed, gave her a token wave, and made her way over to her.

The theory had been offered more than once that England kept an even keel through the simple expedient of shipping a fair number of the dottier cases off to foreign parts. Selby Bogsworth-Stapleton lent credence to the theory. Marcia MacDougal had never met anyone quite like Selby. Normally, she rather enjoyed the other woman's company—in small doses. Selby never quite seemed to be on the same wavelength as everyone else. There she was, on a day of general public mourning, grinning from ear to ear and literally bouncing up and down with excitement.

Selby was about forty-five or fifty, something under average height. Her dark brown hair had a bit of grey in it, and was cut in a too-short sort of pageboy. She had pale skin, startling blue eyes, even white teeth, and a strange sort of nonchalant enthusiasm for practically everything. She was a just a trifle on the stocky side, though really still quite trim.

"Coo-ee! Marcia! Marcia MacDougal! Over here!" As if Marcia couldn't see her eight meters in front of her face. What was that coo-ee noise supposed to *mean*, anyway? Marcia stepped forward to greet her. "Hello, Selby," she said, reaching out to shake her hand.

"Hel*lo*, Dr. MacDougal," she said with exaggerated emphasis, a chirpy lilt in her voice. Instead of shaking hands, she sidestepped and gave Marcia a rather maternal peck on the cheek. "Always such a pleasure to see you. But you've been away so long this time I almost forgot you were gone."

"Well, I, ah . . . what? What did you say?"

She smiled and pulled Marcia along by the arm, eager to get moving. "Welcome back," she said, ignoring her question. "It's been nothing but dull going since you left—until the excitement started, of course. Non-stop, all-out, all-go ever since we got started," she went on, the sentences tumbling out of her, one after the other. "We've been down there doing the—well, you'll see. No matter. Working round the clock and then some. But I swear we've been at it so hard I didn't know the date until I realized what today was."

MacDougal never quite knew how to react to Selby's scrambled syntax. For her part, Selby never seemed to understand why people were constantly confused around her. It was as if she were speaking a private language of her own, one that made perfect sense to her, and that only resembled English by sheer chance. Marcia knew Tycho Purple Penal folk who were more understandable. "Sounds as if you've been busy," she said, for want of anything better to say.

"Oh, I suppose so. Maybe not all *that* much," she said, quite casually contradicting everything she had just said with an obviously spurious nonchalance. "Are you glad to be here?" she asked, quite out of the blue.

It was an absurd question, and Marcia was in no mood for nonsense, but at least it had the benefit of allowing a clear answer. "Not really," she said. "Today's not exactly a happy day. But you said you had something for me. Is it—"

Selby's voice turned serious, at least for the moment. She stopped and looked her straight in the eye. "Yes. I said it might be a breakthrough. Our Rosetta Stone, the key that might let us learn . . . learn everything. If we have the stomach for it. Don't bother getting back to your quarters. Just toss your gear in a locker and let's go right now," Selby said. "This will make better sense if you see for yourself. If it even makes sense *then.*"

It was not until that moment that Marcia realized Selby was still wearing her own pressure suit. She *hated* wearing that thing. She always stripped out of it the first chance she got. And she usually bent Marcia's ear for at least a good fifteen minutes no matter what the topic under discussion. If Selby stayed in her suit, and didn't stop to chat, then something was definitely up.

Selby seemed *too* excited. Marcia started to feel a nervous, queasy sensation in her stomach as she crossed to the single bank of luggage lockers and tossed her bag into one of the lockers that still worked. She came back, with more certainty in her stride than her heart. The sooner she found out what the hell they had found, the better. "All right, Selby," she said. "Let's see what you've got."

The entrance complex to the Rabbit Hole took up most of the rest of Dome One. They made their way through the redundant airlock sealing off the Vertical Transit Center from the rest of the dome. There was normal pressure on either side of the lock, and perhaps it would have been more convenient to leave both doors open and allow easier access—but this was a station on a shoestring, and lots of things could change air pressure on either side of that lock. Safety regs required full standard lock cycling and sealed airlocks at all times. They went through the lock. "All set to see what we shall see?" Selby asked, her tone more serious than her words.

"All set," Marcia said, trying hard to read Selby's expression through her helmet. She was always a bit strained and tense, but something about her cheeriness seemed even more forced than usual.

MacDougal followed Selby into the transit elevator and took a seat on the opposite side of the car from her, trying to get far enough away that it would be awkward for Selby to start a conversation. She buckled her seatbelt and waited.

The Rabbit Hole. At some time in the deep past, the

Charonians had dug the Lunar Wheel cavity, wrapping clear around the Moon forty kilometers beneath the surface. As part of that process, they had dug twin boreholes at the lunar North and South poles. They had dug these upward from the forty-kilometer level, almost but not quite to the surface, leaving the surface layers of rock undisturbed. As with most things regarding the Charonians, there were many theories as to why this might be so, but no real answer.

Five years before, search teams had used alternate-mode gravity detectors to locate the top of the North Pole borehole, which was promptly dubbed the Rabbit Hole. Back then, Lucian Dreyfuss and Chao's TeleOperator had ridden a jury-rigged sort of cable car down the forty-kilometer shaft.

Today, a sophisticated system of four vertical-shuttle cars, each with twenty seats, handled the traffic.

A clock display by the car door reported that the car would descend in five minutes. The car had been empty when Marcia and Selby arrived, but two or three other people came in and sat down in the middle of the car. Good. It made it that much easier to avoid talking to Selby. In practical terms, yes, they could have set their comm systems to a private frequency and had a lovely chat. Normally Selby would have done just that, no matter if they were two meters or ten kilometers away. But for whatever reason, just now it seemed she actually did not want to speak.

Selby Bogsworth-Stapleton, Ph.D., was a Leftover, that being the rather unfortunate and semi-derogatory term for anyone from Earth stranded in the Solar System by the Abduction. Most of the Leftovers on the Moon had come to the Moon as tourists, and thus represented a more or less random cross-section of terrestrial affluence; well-to-do travelers from all walks of life. Most had adapted to their new circumstances reasonably well in the past few years.

Still, even the most stable and best-readjusted of them had been wounded pretty badly. To Marcia, and to most people who lived on the Moon, the Earth had been a pretty thing in the sky, a distant place that people and things came from and went to. Marcia had been to Earth, but she was not *of* the Earth. It was important to her, she mourned its passing as deeply as anyone, but it was not her home. To her, and for most folk on the Moon, it was more of an abstraction than a location, with the whole planet, all its myriad places and endless variety, lumped together under the name "Earth."

But the Leftovers never spoke of themselves as being from Earth. They were from London, or Greenwich Village, or Cambridge or Fresno, from Kiev or Montevideo or Bangkok or Warsaw. Each of them had lost a different home, a different place, a different family. Everything they knew was gone, vanished. They had no way of knowing if their daughters or husbands or grandmothers lived. They knew that they themselves were lost to their loved ones. Their families might as well be dead, and, so far as their families were concerned, the Leftovers might as well be dead.

Marcia had only lost her husband, and she at least knew he had survived, where he had ended up. Her loss was trivial compared to Selby's. How could she bear up under a loss of her world, of her everything?

Some Leftovers had remarried, started new lives, new families. Some lived their lives as if Earth was just about to return at any moment.

But all of them, *all* of them, had that *look* in their eyes. No matter how they dealt with it, or refused to deal with it, that pain, that wound, bright and clear, was just beneath the surface. Perhaps the only thing different about Selby was that she wore her wounds a bit more obviously—and pretended harder than most they weren't there at all.

The departure clock counted down to zero, the door slid shut, and the car began its descent down the Rabbit Hole. It rolled downward, but only a few meters. Another airlock.

There was air pressure, if not air as such, on the other side of the lock. The Lunar Wheel was surrounded by a cloud of dismal green gas, a miasma of complex, foul-smelling compounds, residual gaseous waste products of the Wheel's biochemistry. It had been a lot worse five years ago, when they had first drilled the shaft and punched through into the environment the Wheel had built for itself. But no airlock was perfect. A lot of the muck had leaked away into Dreyfuss Station since then, necessitating extra-heavy-duty airscrubbers. Even they couldn't get all of it. Dreyfuss Station would never smell good. Some further fraction of it seemed to have been reabsorbed by the Wheel, or else some undetected vent was allowing it to escape. In any event, the gas pressure inside the Wheel cavity had been dropping steadily for years.

The lock doors cycled, and the car moved downward again.

There were windows in the car, but not much outside the car to look at. The walls of the shaft and the support cables for the transit elevators were illuminated by the car's running lights, turned a sickly green by the intervening gas. Usually you could spot a car headed toward the surface about halfway through the ride. A gleaming blob of light far below, moving upward at a most impressive speed, would rush past the downward car with a *swoosh* of noise and a noticeable jostling of the down car. It was disconcerting to a Conner like Marcia, quite unused to the effects of air pressure on vehicles. The other riders got up and went to the window to see the show.

But Marcia had seen it before. Right now, she was more interested in her traveling companion. Dr. Selby Bogsworth-Stapleton was an atypical Leftover. She had not come here as a tourist. She had come to the Moon to work. As an archaeologist. The only one on this world, though it might seem one more than was needed.

But archaeology was not as absurd as it sounded. Not quite, anyway. She was not, as some people assumed, some nut come to dig up the graves of imaginary ancient astronauts from Atlantis or from beyond the stars or something. People—regular, human people—had been on the Moon for centuries, and they had left more than a few interesting and important things behind. A good deal of her job was done just sitting at a comm panel, tooling through the historical data. She would dig through long-forgotten infobases, sift old records, go through long-forgotten datacubes and hardcopy records, finding the old details and key facts no one had seen in generations.

But she did fieldwork as well. Abandoned settlements, crashed vehicles, trash heaps and so on were scattered about the lunar surface. Selby had done some impressive digs under difficult circumstances, and had found enough evidence to rewrite a page or two of lunar history. Chancellor Daltry had talked about conversations with the dead at the memorial service. Selby had spent her working life talking with them.

From the archaeological point of view, the Lunar Wheel could be considered as one huge artifact—or one huge carcass, if you liked. Tyrone Vespasian, the director of Dreyfuss Station, had hired Selby his first day on the job—and, as he had told Marcia once or twice since, there had been few days since when he did not both congratulate himself on the choice and regret his decision. Selby was good at her job, there was no doubt about that. She had done any amount of first-class work. But she was also a royal pain in the neck.

The car began to slow as it came to the end of its journey. Smoothly, neatly, perfectly, it arrived at the base of the Rabbit Hole.

There was a slight pause as the car unsealed and matched air pressure with the outside. Marcia's suit whirred and hummed, adjusting to the increase in pressure. The elevator door opened and a few tendrils of greenish smog drifted into the car. Marcia undid her seatbelt, sealed her helmet, and followed the other passengers out the door. She stepped out to stand on the corpse of the Lunar Wheel. The greenish tinge was not quite as noticeable down here. The techs had fooled with the lights to mask it somewhat. But no one was going be tricked into thinking there was normal air down here.

Selby was leading the way forward, down to the tunnel

entrance, but Marcia hesitated for a moment. Beneath her feet was a continuous ribbon of material that wrapped clear around the Moon. She looked ahead, down a gaping tunnel that led off into the darkness. The surface she was standing on entered that tunnel like a road going though a mountain.

The tunnel itself was high and rounded, about twenty meters high at the center point, and about forty across. She turned around and looked the other way. There was the other end of the same damn tunnel, coming back to the same damn point, having wrapped clear around the Moon. She could set off down that tunnel and keep on walking until she was back where she started.

Incredible. And all of it built God knows how just to house the *thing*, the Wheel under her feet. The survey teams were just starting to explore the whole Wheel, but the drillings and sounding and excavations they had done so far suggested that most of it had the cross-section of a rounded-off oval about forty meters side to side and thirty top to bottom. In places it bulged out vertically or horizontally, the tunnel enlarging to accommodate it.

This one thing, this one object, went clear around the world. She had to look down at it, stare at it, marvel at it every time she came down here. Maybe that was why lately she came down so rarely. *Hell, we built the Ring of Charon, and that's practically the same size,* Marcia told herself. The difference was, of course, that the Ring had been built in open space. Digging a tunnel clear around a world was far beyond human capability—or, for that matter, human necessity. There had been no reason to hide the Ring of Charon. There was the question that nagged at the back of everything: what the devil had the Lunar Wheel been hiding from? It had taken tremendous effort to hide it. What could be so powerful that something as huge and mighty as the Wheel feared it, hid from it?

The surface of the Wheel was a dark, hard, flaky brown substance. It was, in effect, the thing's dead, dried-out skin. When the first teams had come down here, the area at the base of the Rabbit Hole had been covered in a layer of thin, flat, broken-up pieces of the stuff, with a consistency like that of dried leaves that crunched when you walked on them. The surface had been littered with bits of Charonian junk. Bits of dead carrier bug, carapaces from unknown Charonian forms, broken pieces that seemed a cross between the mechanical and the biological.

All of that had been cleared away, leaving the lower epidermal layers exposed. Bit by bit, those were drying up and flaking away as well. Bits of dead wheelskin were constantly drifting in from the tunnel. It was a struggle to keep the area clear.

One of the several well-worn paths in the epidermal layer led toward the east entrance to the tunnel. Marcia stood and stared at that entrance. Just over five years ago, a strange, wheeled Charonian had grabbed Lucian Dreyfuss off his feet and raced away with him in that direction. No one knew what had happened to him after that. Lucian Dreyfuss's personal abduction had become the stuff of legend, of folklore, a mystery that intrigued everyone—in part, no doubt, because it bore similarities to the real Abduction, but on a small enough scale that people could understand it. You could imagine one man being kidnapped, even if you couldn't imagine a whole world being snatched away. It had inspired all sorts of theories and search parties and explorations—but none of them had come to anything.

"Come on, now, Marcia," Selby said from up ahead. "Don't be a lollygagger. Off we go."

She nodded agreement and followed along behind. Work lights had been strung in the tunnel, affording a fairly bright illumination. A line of small white runcarts sat parked not far inside the entrance. Selby went to the first one in line and sat down at the controls, Marcia trailing a step or two behind, still more than a little reluctant to deal with all of this. Best to plunge on. "All right, Selby," she said. "Let's go get a look at this mystery of yours."

"Right," Selby said, her face set and determined. She

grabbed the car's steering wheel, jammed her foot on the accelerator, and took off.

The runcart lurched forward with a jolt before Marcia could attach her seatbelt. The cart took off at speed, Marcia hanging on for dear life. At least this time Selby was driving on the right-hand side of the road. When she forgot herself and reverted to driving on the left-hand side, as was the English habit, the ride was just that much more exciting.

Selby's driving settled down after a moment, and they moved down the tunnel at a steady clip. Marcia released her grip long enough to get her seatbelt fastened.

They drove out of the overhead lighting a minute or two after starting out, and plunged into the darkness with disconcerting abruptness. Selby flicked on the headlights and the car rushed into the tunnel, its wall looming up out of the darkness into the glare of the lights as they hurtled down the road.

The Wheel Tunnel moved ahead, seemingly straight as an arrow. So far as Marcia could tell, they were moving down a perfectly straight, infinitely long road.

But there were plenty of side caverns that were anything but straight. Here and there they passed lighted signs, each with a number on it. Each indicated a side cavern off the main Wheelway. The runcart rushed past them, past the entrances they marked, huge gaping holes to one side or the other of the tunnel, and one or two from its top. The glow of work lights was visible from some of the entrances. Some side caverns were little more than widenings in the main tunnel, or were simple, straight cul-de-sacs. Others led to absolute mazes of chambers and side tunnels wandering off in all directions—up, down, east, west, north, south—all at once.

The survey teams could easily be kept busy for the next several centuries exploring all the twisting labyrinthine turns of the side caverns. Some were mere empty holes in the rock. Some held nothing but a few bits of the ubiquitous flakes of the wheel's epidermal layers.

But others were filled with *things*. Bits of strange machines, dead Charonians of all sorts. Other chambers held God only knew what. One chamber was full of cubes of an unknown material somewhere between a metal and a plastic. There was a deep pit filled with some sort of tarry liquid. Another pit was half-filled with coils of some sort of rather flimsy rope or cable. Were the chambers maintenance depots? Kitchens? Medicine cabinets? Storehouses for art supplies?

But perhaps the most disturbing finds were the most recognizable and least mysterious—chambers full of bones and desiccated corpses. The remains of terrestrial animals.

Dinosaurs, to be exact.

It was more shocking, more disconcerting, than it was surprising. There had been direct evidence early on that the Charonians had visited Earth and taken some biological samples. There were strands of terrestrial DNA and RNA in the cell structure of a number of Charonian forms. But no one had expected the Charonians to do their lab work in a tunnel under the lunar surface.

The runcart rushed past a particularly bright-lit side cavern. Marcia spotted the number over the entrance. Chamber 281. In there, inside a huge, high-ceilinged cavern three kilometers across, the survey teams had found a half-dozen tyrannosaurs—some merely skeletal, the others desiccated whole remains. They had been tucked away since the end of the Cretaceous, along with dozens of what were either some kind of thescelosaurids, or perhaps orthinominids—ostrich-like dinosaurs—of some sort. There were twenty or thirty other, smaller types no one had been able to identify even that closely. No one on the Moon knew enough about dinosaurs to say more. If there had not been much need for archaeologists on the pre-Abduction Moon, there had been even less call for paleontologists.

But then Chamber 281 swept past, and they were off again into the darkness.

"Marcia?" Selby said, breaking the silence at last. "I

know you don't feel like talking just now, and neither do I, but I want to tell you something anyway. You won't be prepared for this unless you get ready first.''

Marcia smiled, her expression hidden behind her pressure suit helmet and the darkness. Say what else you might about the emotions of the moment, or about the woman herself, Selby brought incomprehensibility to a fine art. ''All right, Selby, what is it you have to tell me?''

''The dinosaurs, love. The dinosaurs. New information since the last time you paid a call. The chaps working on them think they died here instead of being killed on Earth. Found Lunar rocks in their gizzards, or some such. I didn't understand, exactly, but the point is they were alive here for quite a while. Like fifteen million years.''

''*What?*''

''They can do dating based on radioactive decay. Relative amounts of various forms of this or that atom—I don't know the precise details. And there might be some contamination muddling it all up, or something. But the chaps tell me some of the dinos died maybe fifteen million years after some of the others.''

''You're trying to tell me there were dinosaurs living in this tunnel for fifteen million years?''

''No, love, not a bit of it. Just that some of them *died* fifteen million years after the others.''

''I don't understand,'' Marcia said. What was Selby talking about?

''I know you don't,'' Selby said. ''That's for the best, just for now. But when you do understand, I think maybe it will make more sense to you after that.''

''Fine. Whatever,'' Marcia replied.

''We'll be there in a minute,'' Selby said.

In less time than that, Marcia spotted a new light far down the tunnel. It grew as they drew toward it, and Selby slowed the cart. It was another side cavern, a small one, off to the right. Worklights inside threw a warm glow into the greenish air of the tunnel.

"One of our survey workers found her about three days ago," Selby said. "Look, Marcia," she said in a softer voice, "punch over to comm circuit twelve, will you? The team doesn't use that one, and we'll be able to talk more private-like."

Marcia got the distinct impression that Selby was more concerned with her not hearing what the survey workers had to say. More than a bit mystified, Marcia did as she was told, but there was one question she needed to ask. "We're still very close to the Rabbit Hole. They've explored much further than this. Why did they just find the—the whatever it is—now?"

They got down off the runcart, and Selby led her to the cavern entrance. "You've got to understand there are hundreds, maybe thousands or tens of thousands of these side chambers," she said in apologetic tones. "We're still not a tenth of the way around in our initial survey of the tunnel. We're frightfully understaffed. No people at all, except for our workers. We're just starting in to map them all in, and there's nothing in a lot of them—the caverns I mean, not the workers. Sometimes it's all we can do to just poke our head in for a quick peek and then move on. Our records show this cavern was first mapped four years ago—but we didn't check it all the way. Three days ago, Peng Li was doing a follow-up and noticed the inner chambers. Come on inside."

Marcia followed her into the side chamber. The entrance was a circle cut out of the main tunnel, about a meter and a half across, about half a meter off the floor of the cavern. She climbed up into it and found herself in an oblong room about ten meters long, three high, and two wide. The chamber was empty.

"We're going to have to widen this out before very much longer," Selby said, half to herself. "Lots of gear we'll need to get in here. Anyway, there's the entrance Li found."

Marcia looked over and saw a hole in the floor of the room, at the far end, about the size and shape of a small maintenance accessway. A ladder was sticking up out of it.

Light was glowing up from it, and the exterior mikes on Marcia's suit were picking up the sounds of movement from inside. In the dark, on a quick check, it would be easy to miss.

"Right, now, in we go." Selby crossed the chamber and started down the ladder. She hesitated with her head just at ground level and looked back up at Marcia. "Now be careful here," she said. "No one has disturbed anything in this chamber yet. We want to make sure we have it photographed and scanned every way we possibly can before we move— ah, it." Her voice turned as stony as the cavern, and her face was expressionless, cold and firm through her suit helmet. "It is not as bad as I've made it out to be. But it's also much worse. Come."

She continued down the ladder. It took Marcia a moment or two before she could force herself to follow. She stepped onto the ladder and made her way down, moving very carefully, staring straight ahead. She stepped back from the ladder and found herself standing near the edge of a hemispherical chamber, a dome in the rock about ten meters high at the center. The room was dead empty except for a rack of too-bright lights shining almost exactly in her eyes—and one other thing, splayed out in the center of the floor. Good God, what *was* that? A human body?

"Lucian Dreyfuss," Selby said. "Or at least his pressure suit."

Marcia's eyes adjusted, and she could see more clearly. Fresh relief and fresh horror sprang to her heart at one and the same time.

It was indeed a pressure suit, lying flat on its back, arms and legs spread-eagled, sliced neatly open, straight down the centerline of the body, one continuous cut clean through the fabric of the suit, through the helmet, down the chest and abdomen packs, and finishing up at the crotch. The cut was surgically precise, slicing perfectly, flawlessly, through all the different materials, the two sides of the cut neatly peeled back. There were other, equally perfect cuts down the arms and legs of the suit, likewise peeled back.

Flecks and bits of Wheel epidermis had sifted down on the suit, and some sort of reaction with the Wheel's interior atmosphere had turned it from white to brown. It was an old shriveled thing that had been lying here in the darkness for five years, like the desiccated remains of some corpse mummified by chance. Marcia stared at the suit, her heart beating wildly, her breath suddenly short. Lucian Dreyfuss. He had vanished down that tunnel, and then had been laid out here in his suit, sliced out of it, picked like a pea from a pod and then taken—

"Where?" Marcia asked. Her voice was not steady, and she could not trust herself to say more.

Selby didn't need any other words to know what Marcia meant. "This way," she said. She led her around the edge of the chamber, careful not to come too close to the violated pressure suit.

She stepped behind the rack of worklights. Just behind it to one side was the entrance to yet another chamber. It had been hidden by the glare of the lights. It was a tall, broad passage, about fifteen meters long and three wide, leading downward at about a five-degree grade, the walls high, the ceiling vaulted.

Marcia followed Selby down the passage, moving slowly. Her mind pursued meaningless side questions. Why were the chambers built in this odd configuration? Why this large passage when the way to the exterior was so much smaller? None of that mattered in the slightest just now, but at least for a few seconds, it kept her mind off what she had just seen—and whatever she was about to see.

Light and movement filled the inner chamber, figures going back and forth, moving with the slightly awkward stiffness of people not completely used to working in pressure suits.

As they stepped into the chamber, all movement stopped. People stopped in their tracks and looked toward Marcia. The tableau held for a moment, and then, moving with one accord, everyone filed past Marcia, out of the chamber. Selby must have jumped to another comm channel and given the order to leave.

The third chamber was of precisely the same dimensions as the second one. But where the second room was empty but for the suit, this one was filled with all manner of artifacts, both human and Charonian. Marcia could not even identify most of the human gear. It was all on portable racks, and most of it looked vaguely medical, somehow. Lights gleamed, displays glowed, leads trailed off.

Three or four small dead Charonians of various sorts lay slumped over against the far wall of the chamber. Were they the ones who had cut Lucian from his suit and then—and then *what?*

Marcia stepped forward into the chamber, toward the cluster of human machines. Something lay on floor in the center of the chamber, hard to see with the machines in the way. A low hummock in the floor of the chamber, a discolored brownish lump that looked as if it had been melted and poured into place. It was translucent, and gleamed dimly. Someone had dusted it off, polished it up. Any number of wires led from the medical machines to various points on the lumpen shape.

"Oh, my God," Marcia whispered. She got closer, shoved past the surrounding monitoring gear, and looked down at the shape from above.

The shape of the thing was more complicated than she had thought. It was no simple blob in the floor. Instead it repeated exactly the same pose and orientation as the sliced-open pressure suits. It reminded Marcia irresistibly of the chalk outline policemen drew around a corpse in murder stories. There was the torso, and the head, and the arms and legs spread wide.

Every body part was in the same relative position as on the pressure suit, but everything was rounded, spread out, made large enough to surround that which was inside. It looked like some strange, misshapen, hideous caricature of a gingerbread man.

Marcia stepped forward, pulled her handlight out of the holster on her suit, and shone it down on the—the whatever it was.

Her throat went dry. There. Yes. She could *see* the body, ever so dimly, through the exterior shell, clearly enough to recognize the man she had known, slightly and briefly, five years before. Perfect, uncorrupted, intact, suspended in the brown substance a few inches off the floor. His eyes were shut, his expression calm. Only his hair was disordered, floating up around his head just a trifle.

Except—except—there were cables—no, not cables, not wires. Somehow, they had more of the look of living tissue than mechanical hardware. Marcia knelt down and looked closer. Elongated growths—call them tendrils—coming up from the floor of the cavern, and attached to Lucian's head and neck. Others were attached to his chest and his genitalia.

Sweet God. Sweet God. Of course. The dinosaurs. The damned dinosaurs Selby had been babbling about. Half of them died fifteen million years after the others because the Charonians had kept them alive, like this, for fifteen million years.

Alive. Sweet Jesus in Hell, Lucian Dreyfuss was in death alive, entombed inside that *thing*, with no way to get out. Marcia collapsed to her knees, and the tears fell from her eyes.

The Charonians had snatched him and put him, still living, in a specimen bottle. Good God, fifteen million years! Might he wait as long as the poor tyrannosaurs to be released from this nightmare *storage* into real, honest death?

And Selby was kneeling beside her, putting her arm around her, drawing her up to stand, leading her back the way they had come. "Come on, love. We found a small empty side cavern a few hundred meters down the way. We've set up a pressure bubble and a field office there. You and I need to talk."

Three

Penance and Remembrance

"There have been any number of attempts to portray Larry Chao as a maniac or a lunatic, as a destructive monster who went out of control. The truth is much simpler, and much less satisfying to those who need villains to blame for the ills of the world: the Larry Chao behind the myth was simply unlucky enough to be in the wrong place at the wrong time. The real Larry Chao is not a monster, but a man.

"A *good* man. That is the first thing that must be said about Larry Chao. He is a good man who accidentally committed the greatest crime in history, a good man who is guilty of nothing and responsible for everything. No one could possibly have dreamt that a gravity beam of the type he fired could do any more harm than shining a flashlight. Who could have imagined it would serve as an activation signal for a hidden alien black hole generator?

"The second thing to say is that he was a victim of forces he could not control. Fate, or history, or chance—whatever name you want to give it—saw to it *he* was the one who activated the experiment. I was in the room, I saw him do it, I approved of his action, and yet history has left no black mark on *me*. No matter how you divide up the guilt, or no matter what you do to demonstrate that it was wild, bizarre chance, the fact remains that it was Larry O'Shawnessy Chao who pushed that button.

"Sooner or later *someone* was going to discover how to shape the force of gravity as Larry did. But that inevitability is meaningless. There is no escaping the reality that it was *Larry who actually did it.* No escape for us—and certainly none for him."

> —Dr. Sondra Berghoff, statement for *Gravitics Research Station Oral History Project,* Charon DataPress, 2443

Armstrong Research Hangars
Central City Spaceport
THE MOON
Abduction Day

Larry O'Shawnessy Chao marked the dismal anniversary of Earth's disappearance by struggling to ignore it. Rather than commemorate the day, he had tried to do some tests on the *Graviton,* but he hadn't been able to concentrate on anything significant. So he had wasted his time doing a studious and careful job on an absurd and trivial task. No real purpose could be served by rerunning the standard electro-response testing regime yet again on yet another servo-claw from yet another long-dead Charonian scorpion robot. But the work had kept him focused, kept him absorbed.

Playing around with bits and pieces of the half-living, half-machine corpses of dead Charonians wasn't much, but it was all he was capable of at the moment.

He tried to concentrate on the claw, tracking out its bio-electronic circuits with painstaking care, for all the world as if he expected to find something meaningful there. *For all the world.* Now *there* was a poor choice of words.

Most days, recently, it had not been too bad. But today. Today, everything seemed to remind him of what had been. Today was different, no matter how hard he told himself it was not. Today, he could not keep the thoughts at bay.

Five years.

Five years since the Charonians awoke and swallowed Earth up, pulled the home world down a wormhole.

Damn it all, admit it to yourself, at least, he thought, savagely jabbing at the claw with a logic probe, pulsing far too much current through its contacts. The claw whirred and clacked in response, its razor-sharp teeth nearly snapping the probe in two.

Larry pulled the probe back and forced himself to calm down, to clear his mind. *All right then. Allow the thoughts inside your own mind. Even if you can't say the words, at least dare to think them. How long since you have even allowed yourself that much?* They all said it wasn't his fault, of course, but they could not know. They could not possibly understand.

Larry dropped his tools and kneaded his hands nervously. But just as it always did, the sight of his hands moving in that nervous gesture made him think of Pontius Pilate, washing his hands before the multitude. He pulled his hands apart, lay them down on the workbench, stared straight ahead at the blank wall. After a while, he found that, quite involuntarily, his hands were gripping the edge of the bench, holding on tightly, as if he feared that he would be ripped away from this time and place.

Dare to think it. The thought echoed insistently in his mind with a force that would not be denied, an intruder that would not depart until it was acknowledged.

All right, then. Accept it. *Today it is five years since I,*

Larry Chao, lost the Earth. There. He had thought the words. Five years ago, he had configured the Ring of Charon as a gravity laser and fired it. Five years ago he pressed a button and awoke the slumbering alien invaders, who in turn stole Earth and set to work tearing apart the surviving worlds of the Solar System. It was of microscopic consolation to Larry that he had then played a major part in stopping that destruction and preventing the Solar System's complete disassembly.

Five years of a loss immeasurable, to all people for the rest of time.

Never mind. Let it go. Do not let it engulf you. Larry picked up his tools and set to work again. The half-machine, half-animal alien claw was dead, its chiton-plastic skin drying up, turning brown, flaking off. The fierce pincers lay still and useless in front of him.

He was alone in the workshop. On this day, of all days, no one had the heart to do any work. Any number of remembrances and ceremonies were being held in or on every one of the half-wrecked worlds of the Solar System. Solemn figures were no doubt standing at attention on the Lunar surface right now, staring at Earthpoint, the blank spot in the sky where once the Earth had shone, where now there was nothing but an Earth-mass black hole, far too small to see.

But Larry knew he was not welcome at such events, not really. Few murderers, even those who killed unintentionally, were invited to memorial services for their victims.

Others might recall the mother world, speaking wistfully of the cool breezes, the tang of salt air, the wonder of walking unprotected under an open sky. Such could not be for him. To attend would be to rob the others of their chance to mourn undisturbed.

He picked up the probe and set back to work on the claw, for there was nothing else he could do, down here inside the corpse of the enemy. The Lunar Wheel had been a living thing, after all. Larry had helped to kill it, too. And Lucian Dreyfuss. His blood was on Larry's hands as well. They had never found his body. No doubt it was still down there, somewhere.

No. Do not think about that. Do not think of those days. Every human being tried at some time to forget those days. Forgetting was a vital survival skill.

Focus on the work. Try not to think. The claw. Finish the claw. Then go on to the sensory-cluster carapace. Study them well, seek out the hidden answers.

He had spent much of the last years in this place, sifting through the world-girdling wreckage of the Lunar Wheel, picking over the corpse of the half-creature half-machine.

It was dreary work, arduous, painstaking, endless, and Larry welcomed it. There were always tests to run, data to examine, debris to test. There was always a task at hand, a job that offered him escape from the churning knots in his heart. Work was his penance, his act of contrition.

Besides, somewhere inside the unimaginably huge Wheel, there had to be some sort of clue. There had to be. A scrap of data code, a bit of information that had not been scrambled in the final battle. The search teams would find something, sooner or later. And he would be on hand to help analyze it, decode it, take it apart, find *the* clue, *the* answer.

He longed for a whisper in his ear that could tell him how to find the Earth again.

Find the Earth. That was the only act of penance that would do any good whatsoever.

Assuming, of course, the Earth was still alive when they found her.

He applied the logic probe to the claw again, and this time it jerked spasmodically and threw itself off the table.

Sometime after midnight, when it was no longer Abduction Day, Larry started to feel a bit better. He was still too keyed up to sleep, to rest, but somehow his mind was clear again. He could see his way forward. He could look up from his meaningless tests and meticulous fiddlings and see more than his own failures. He could think on the things he had actually accomplished since then. He put his things away, tidied up the workbench, and walked out into the dark vastness of the main hangar. He paused by the entrance and slapped a wall switch, and light swelled up to fill the hangar, a cathedral of gleaming walls and shining equipment—with a small and rather scrappy-looking vehicle dead in the middle of it.

She didn't look like much, but then a lot of the great pioneering craft of the past hadn't either. The Wright *Flyer*, Armstrong's own *Eagle*, the *Demeter*, even the *Terra Nova*. None of them were ever beautiful, except to engineers. Larry Chao would be more than content if the *Graviton* were ranked with those names. She was the reason Larry had come back to the Moon.

But she *still* didn't look like much. She looked like something cobbled together out of spares and optimism, as well she might. Her hull and superstructure came from a surplus asteroid mining ship, her lift rockets were off an old cargo ship, and no one even knew what ship half her old flight hardware came from. Nor was it entirely comforting to know that no one knew exactly how she worked. But that was one of the drawbacks to blackbox engineering.

The *Graviton* was a short, squat cylinder sitting on four landing jacks. She was battleship grey, and as disreputable-looking a hulk as you could ask for.

But she was also the first gravitic-powered ship ever, riding a beam of gravity power controlled by the Ring of Charon. Her rocket engines were intended to do no more than get her well away from a planet before the gravitic system took over. Mission rules were very clear on that—the gravity-beam system was not to be activated until the ship was at least a million kilometers from any planet. It seemed highly doubtful that there were any other Charonians out there who might be roused by a gravity beam—but no one on the *Graviton* team, least of all Larry, wanted to take any chances.

The *Graviton*'s propulsion system used enough hardware

taken from dead Charonians that one or two wags had suggested that she be christened the *Graverobber*, but it might be years, if not decades, before humans could build their own g-beam hardware. The Charonians had used gravity-beam systems to propel asteroid-sized bodies around the Solar System at incredible velocities, and there were plenty of dead Charonians about from which to take equipment.

Even Larry, an expert on gravitics technology, was not certain how some of the Charonian hardware worked. It was enough, for now, that it did work, and had worked in the unpiloted test flights. The *Graviton* had taken the gravity beam from the Ring of Charon and accelerated up to fifty gravities—while retaining a standard Lunar gravity field inside the main cabin. They were nearly ready for test flights with humans aboard.

Larry looked up at the ugly little ship. It wasn't going to help get the Earth back. *But at least it was work, and valuable work.* Somehow, just looking at her made him feel better. He blinked, yawned and stretched. He didn't feel exactly *rested,* but he had the feel of being *sharp,* of being *ready.* Sleepless nights did that to him now and then. He had had plenty of chances to find that out in the past few years. He felt like working.

Larry stepped to the data display system and checked the work log. He was scheduled to do the modifications to the wave-coupler resonance chamber next. Might as well get on with it. Larry returned to his workshop, collected his tools, and went aboard the little ship. He set to work on the job, happy to be doing something worthwhile. He barely noticed as the rest of the work team came in.

His pocket phone rang at about eleven A.M. He set down his tools, pulled it out, and switched it on.

"Chao speaking," he said.

"Larry?"

That was all it took for Larry to recognize the voice, and his stomach turned to a block of ice. Marcia MacDougal. Not someone who would call just to chat. "Yes, this is Larry

Chao. Hello, Marcia.''

"Hello. Good to hear your voice. Listen, Larry, I'm calling from the North Pole.'' The North Pole. To anyone else
on the Moon, she would have said Dreyfuss Station. But not
to Larry. She couldn't say that to Larry. "Something has
come up and, well, you might say we want your opinion on
it. Is there any chance that you could get up here in a
hurry?''

"It's important?'' he asked, but it wasn't really a question. Marcia MacDougal wasn't the type to ask big favors
without explaining why. Unless it was important.

"Yes, it is. Very.''

Larry found he could do nothing but stare at the splitter
housing on the resonance chamber. It needed realignment.
He'd have to log that in.

He shut his eyes and let out a sigh. Maybe Marcia could
hear it, maybe she couldn't. He didn't care. He felt angry,
frustrated, hounded. He wanted to shout at the phone, throw
it against the wall, tell her to go to hell. But he knew he
would not, and that was part of what was making him angry.
He would agree to go, would do his duty, would do whatever
they asked, because he knew they would not ask for what
they did not need. Because they would not ask him if anyone
else would do.

"I can catch the 1600 hopper,'' he said. "No problem.''

"Thank you, Larry. Thank you very much. I'll be there to
meet you.''

"Good,'' Larry said. "See you then.''

"Until then,'' Marcia said, and the line went dead.

She hadn't said a damned thing about whatever it was.
And that only made Larry more certain of one thing.

He wasn't going to like it.

Lunar Wheel
Beneath Moon's Surface, North Pole Region

Eight hours after she called Larry Chao, Marcia MacDougal was wondering if calling him had been such a good idea. He had taken the sight of the un-corpse very well. A little *too* well. He had yet to show the slightest outward reaction, unless an impassive expression was his way to register shock. Now they were back in the improvised office Selby's team had set up in a chamber just down the Wheelway from where Lucian was.

She watched impassively as Selby poured Larry Chao a stiff three fingers of scotch and handed him the glass. Larry took a long hard gulp and winced at the taste. The distilleries here just hadn't gotten the hang of it yet. Scotland was sorely missed on the Moon, if any part of Earth was.

"Lucian Dreyfuss," Larry said, sitting in the operations bubble a hundred meters from where the undead man lay. "Lucian Dreyfuss. You brought me up here because you solved the Dreyfuss mystery."

"Yes, love, we did," Selby Bogsworth-Stapleton replied, her cheerful tones utterly unconvincing. Neither Selby nor Larry seemed to have much else to say, and Marcia couldn't think of anything herself.

Marcia stood, leaning one-shouldered against the wall of the field office, watching Larry closely. She knew Larry slightly, nowhere near well enough to guess how he would deal with this nightmare. Marcia was an expert in analyzing Charonian data and imagery, but she never had understood people that well.

And right now she wished, devoutly wished, that she were anyplace but here, down here in the Wheel, watching a neurotic Brit pour cheap bar scotch down a man who had earned his nervous breakdown. But maybe, just maybe, this was the first step on the long road that would get Earth—and her husband Gerald—home.

Selby poured herself a drink and then gestured with the

bottle, but Marcia just shook her head no. Larry took the bottle from Selby, though he hadn't finished his first drink yet. He held the bottle close to his body, as if it were some sort of shield. None of them seemed quite ready to speak.

Larry sat there, still in his suit, his helmet off, as Selby bustled about, getting her own suit off, trying to pretend everything was fine. Larry emptied his glass and then poured himself another. It was hard for Marcia to watch him. She found herself staring at a brownish splotch on the wall just over Selby's desk.

At last, Larry seemed to decide they were going to have to talk this thing through. "Is there any way to get him out of that thing?" he asked.

Selby sat down, stared at him for a minute, drummed her fingers on her desk, then knocked back the rest of her own scotch in one gulp. She stood again and started pacing the office. At last she spoke. "We don't know. But there's more to it than just getting him out."

"What do you mean?" Chao demanded. "He's in there. Can't you open that thing up?"

"Certainly," Marcia replied. "We've run tests on small samples of the material he's in. We can chip it away, or melt it off, or dissolve it. But then what?"

"We give him a decent burial, of course!" Larry replied.

"Except he's not dead, love," Selby said. "Not so far as we can tell." She reached across the desk, took the bottle back from Chao and poured herself another drink. She stared at her glass as she held it in both hands. "Not bloody much we do know for sure, really. But it could be us opening that thing up that kills him."

"Wait a second," Larry said, looking from one woman to the other. "I'm not clear. *Is* he dead, or isn't he?"

"We don't know," Marcia said. She pulled a chair up and sat down, close to Larry. "To be honest, I don't even know if that's a meaningful question. I've been studying Charonian symbol systems for five years, and I haven't spotted anything that suggests they make any distinction between living, unliving, and dead. The closest they come is 'on' and 'off.' "

"What are you saying?" Larry asked, fighting to stay calm.

Marcia shook her head and held her upturned palms in the air, a gesture of helplessness. "I can't answer your question. He could be either living or dead. Or it could be that he has been . . . been *taken* by the Charonians to such a degree that there is no such thing as Lucian Dreyfuss anymore, and asking if that object out there is his living or dead body would make as much sense as asking how deep is sunshine. That body is in as close to a state of perfect stasis as I have ever seen. I'd be willing to bet his last meal is still half-digested in his stomach, that his beard and fingernails haven't grown a millimeter. I bet that if we went down to the cell structure, we'd find there has been no decay, no change in energy state at all.

"I'm sure the Charonians could wake that body up, revive him, very easily. In that sense, yes, he is alive—but that's meaningless, because we don't know what that wakened body would contain. Lucian Dreyfuss? A mindwiped vegetable? A Charonian? Besides, even if that still is Lucian, and we *did* get him out alive, I doubt we could do it without inflicting severe damage. Even if he is still himself, but in stasis, would he be sane and functional, or a vegetable, after he was awakened?"

Marcia shook her head, and got to her feet again. She stood uncertainly over Larry, kneading her hands together nervously. "My best guess right now is that he isn't alive *or* dead. He's *off,* and we don't know how to turn him *on.* He has no heartbeat, no respiration, and we don't know how to give them to him. He has no spark of life."

"So what *does* he have?" Larry demanded. "Why have you got all those sensors hooked up to him if there's nothing there for them to sense?"

Marcia MacDougal hesitated a moment before she spoke. "There's not much you miss, is there?" she asked. "What he *has* are brainwaves and neural activity. Very slight, very faint, very slow. His brain is showing what looks like an REM dream state, greatly slowed down.''

''So he *isn't* dead. Why aren't you trying to wake him up?''

Selby swore under her breath, and turned in her chair, so she was facing half away from Larry and Marcia.

Marcia looked to Selby, and shook her head sadly. She stepped away from Larry and went to the access hatch window. She stood there, with her back to him, as she spoke, looking out into the endless caverns of the Lunar Wheel's domain. ''Because,'' she said, ''he's more use to us the way he is.''

''What?'' Larry jumped to his feet. ''What the hell gives you the right to—''

''Nothing gives me the right!'' Marcia spun around, looked him straight in the eye, her face set and determined. ''But this discovery gives *us* the *chance*. We are in a *war*, Larry. The last battle we fought ended five years ago, with our enemy's forces wiped out here in the Solar System and the Earth held hostage. Call that one a draw, because both sides lost a lot more than they won. God knows what battles Earth has fought on its own since then.

''But we here in the Solar System have been losing ground every day *since* that fight. You know that. The Moon is the strongest of all the surviving worlds, but things here just keep getting a little worse every day. We took too much damage, too many casualties, to be fully self-sufficient. Always more power cuts and shortages and rationing and making-do without. Perhaps some day we'll get down to a low enough level that things will stabilize—or perhaps we'll just keep going down and down without ever noticing when it's too late. I don't want things to end up that way. I want to fight back.''

''Against who?'' Larry asked. ''Lucian?''

''No, of course not,'' she said, lowering her voice, the moment of anger gone. Her hands were trembling, and she folded her arms tight against her body to hide it. "Against the Charonians. Against the Sphere and the bloody Multisystem that's got Earth. But what's left of Lucian Dreyfuss just might be the best weapon we've ever had against them."

Larry looked from one woman to the other. "What kind of weapon is a man who might as well be dead? What can he do for you?"

"Maybe, just maybe, he can get us information," Selby said in a very quiet voice. "Information straight from the dead horse's mouth."

"God damn it, stop babbling in riddles. Tell me what you're talking about!"

"The Wheel, that's what we're talking about," Selby said. "All the data that's locked up in the Wheel. Half my skills are in information retrieval. Marcia and I have both spent five *years* working on ways to get through to the Wheel's Heritage Memory. It *ought* to contain the accumulated memory of all the previous generations of Charonians."

"The Wheel is dead," Larry said. "How could its memory be intact?"

"It's not *dead,* it's *off.* Yes, what we would regard as the living portions of it are so badly damaged as to be irreparable, but the Wheel was almost entirely electronic and mechanical. The machine portion is only turned off, so to speak. The trouble is, we haven't been able to find the switch. Until now."

"Go on," Larry said, deeply suspicious. "What's different now?"

"Lucian is different," Marcia said. "I told you we were detecting brain activity in a body that hasn't had any metabolic activity in five years. His brain *should* have died, suffered irreversible harm, four minutes after his heart stopped pumping blood, five years ago. But it didn't. Somehow it is being sustained, and we are reasonably certain that reason has to do with the neural links attached to his head."

"The tendrils."

"Exactly, more or less," Selby said. She polished off the rest of her drink in one swig. "We can detect a lot of—activity—in the links. Of what sort, we don't know. Perhaps the Wheel was in the midst of taking down a copy of everything in Lucian's brain at the moment the Wheel died, and the connection stayed open. We just don't know, to echo the bloody chorus of the day. But the activity is repetitive, as if he is thinking the same thing over and over again, in extreme slow motion. The basic theory is that whatever was on his mind at the time they put him in there is *still* on his mind.

"But we *have* established that the connections through those—well, I suppose *tendrils* is as good a word as any—that those connections are two-way. Information going *both ways*, to and from Lucian, to and from the Wheel. Somehow, in some way, whatever part of Lucian's brain that is functional is in conversation with the Charonians."

"We've studied those tendrils very carefully," Marcia said, struggling to keep her voice steady, trying not to think about what they were asking this man to do. She forced herself to look Larry Chao straight in the eye. "We know exactly where the tendrils are positioned. One of them seems to be linked straight into Broca's area—one of the key speech centers in the brain. Another seems to connect into the optic nerve. We think we can hook into it. If Lucian Dreyfuss is still there, and sane, to at least some degree, we can take advantage of that, using off-the-shelf medical technology to reconnect sight and hearing. We should be able to tap into the tendrils, and pump sight and sound stimuli right to him. That part is standard virtual reality stuff. The technology is doable—but the psychology is tricky."

"What psychology?" Larry asked.

"Lucian Dreyfuss was kidnapped by monsters," Selby said. "He was then put into suspended animation, and is now exhibiting brain activity. It seems reasonable that he has had low-level brain activity for all that time. He has been in a place of darkness and terror, paralyzed, unable to move or breathe or speak, for five years. His time sense *should* have slowed with everything else, and that might have saved him, made that five years seem like a few hours or days or weeks. If he is in some analog of REM sleep, it might seem to be nothing more than a bad dream to him. Or it might not. He might have spent five years in a living nightmare.''

"We must assume that he is insane," Marcia said, "or at the very least in a very tenuous mental state.''

"But?" Larry asked. "It sounds like there is a but in all this.''

"But we think that we should be able to revive him to some degree, if we can reach him.'' She swallowed hard and forced herself to say the rest of it. "Our best shot would be contact with someone who knows him. We think someone who knew Lucian—someone Lucian knew—might be able to get through to him. That person could then guide him into the Wheel's Heritage Memory. Lucian would then be able to tell us . . . tell us any number of things. But it will have to be someone that Lucian knew, and trusted. Someone he won't be afraid of when he appears in a nightmare.''

Larry looked from one woman to the other, neither of them willing to return his gaze. "What the hell are you saying?" he demanded.

"Bloody hell," Selby said, emptying the dregs of the bottle into her glass. "It's perfectly simple, love. We were just wondering if you'd mind *terribly* much being hooked up to some ghoulish hardware, with all sorts of clever little wires coming out of it and stuck into those tendrils coming out of Lucian. We'd use a virtual reality system to insert you into his sight and hearing, and then *you* could have a lovely, lovely chat with him.''

She lifted her glass and emptied it in one swallow before looking at him, her face haggard and drawn. "We'd like you to help us violate your friend's corpse," she said, all the masks and playfulness gone, nothing left in her voice but loathing and disgust. "Doesn't *that* sound like fun?"

Four

The Autocrat Arrives

"Not so long ago, the Autocrat of Ceres, aside from his official position as the ruler of the minor planet Ceres, was the *de facto* head of state and sovereign leader of the entire Asteroid Belt, home to the smallest and most dispersed population in the Solar System. However, the Charonians killed so many people on the larger worlds, and forced so many refugees into the Belt, that the Asteroid Belt might now well have the largest aggregate population of any of the surviving geopolitical units in the Solar System.

"No one knows for sure. The Charonians left chaos in their wake, and the Belt was of course famous for being chaotic long *before* the Charonians awoke. Even before the Abduction, the population of the Belt was so dispersed—and cantankerous—that

it was hard to get even a rough idea of how many
people lived there.''
          —*Kings of Infinite Space—A History of the Cerean*
                    Autocracy, by Jerta Melsan,
                    Hera Dwellmod Press, 2468

Aboard the *Autarch*
In Transit from Ceres to Plutopoint
June 12, 2431

The Autocrat of Ceres prided himself on keeping an accurate
and complete journal. As with all other aspects of his life, he
kept his journal according to a rigid and careful schedule.
Each morning as he sat at his breakfast table, he dictated to
his private autoscribe, speaking in a clear, careful voice. He
found that writing about the day just past allowed him to
focus on the tasks for the day ahead.

"June twelfth, 2431," he began. "Nineteen days out
from Titan, the ship now almost completely decelerated. Assuming constant boost, we will arrive at Plutopoint and the
Ring of Charon this afternoon. I find that I have had much
time for quiet reflection on this long journey—perhaps too
much. I must admit that the rather austere circumstances of
my travel are in some ways a pleasure. I do not miss the
company of my usual retinue, for example, and the ceremonies of state dinners can become most tiresome.

"But it has been a long journey to Pluto—or rather, to
where Pluto once was. It is hard to escape one's own
thoughts in such quiet and tranquil surroundings. The crew
knows I wish privacy, and grants it to me.

"I find that I am paying less and less attention to my everyday work as it is radioed in to me from Ceres. I handle it
all, but not with the relentless attention demanded of me at
my court. Somehow the cases recede in importance as the
distance between myself and home grows greater. But it is
part of the task of the Autocrat to know when to step outside
the everyday. Should my people rely too much on my pres-

ence to adjudicate and execute the laws, they would fail to rely on themselves. It is part of my duty *not* to do my duty too well. The Autocracy is meant as a counterweight to the Belt's anarchy—not as a replacement for it. Neither must become too strong.

"It is not that I neglect my duties, but rather that I view them in a different way. The journals and diaries of my predecessors make it clear that the tradition of the Autocrat's Progress was established precisely to expand the Autocrat's horizons, alter the worldview of the Autocrat, and so it is with myself.

"Every artist should, now and again, step back from the day-to-day work on this detail or that, and examine the whole canvas. There is an art to governance, of that I have no doubt. More so under the Autocracy than other forms of government, I think. I govern by what I *might* do, or what I do *not* do, as much as by direct action.

"And so I step back and think over, not Xeg Mortoi's accusation of claim-jumping against his wife, but the circumstances of all humankind, and my place in them.

"I now understand more fully why I chose to take this trip at a time when I would be away from Ceres on the fifth terrestrial anniversary of Abduction Day. It is now time to stop mourning that catastrophe and to stop living with it as a part of the present. Now it must be accepted as part of the past. Now we must move forward, toward the future."

Pleased with the entry, the Autocrat closed the autoscribe and stepped to his compartment's single small porthole to look upon the unchanging stars. Plutopoint and the Ring of Charon were close now, very close, even if he could not see them from this port.

The Autocrat had a subtle and important agenda at Plutopoint. He had to prevent the Ring from coming under his control. Forces were combining to make it likely to happen, but Belt control of the Ring of Charon might well be the first step in producing far too great a concentration of power—political, technical, and economic—in the Solar System.

A Solar System dominated by Ceres would be unstable, ungovernable. Centralizing sufficient power to control the entire Solar System would require a tremendous investment in the tools of control. The Autocracy would be forced to become more powerful, *too* powerful, if it were to survive. It would have to deal in massive repression and control. The forces of anarchy would, quite inevitably, grow in power as well, forcing the Autocracy to respond. Terrorism, rebellion, and war could well be the final result. A classic case of the crisis of empire. No, the Autocracy—and the Autocrat—dared not become mightier than they were.

But how to force others to remain independent? How to use one's power to prevent the absorption of further power?

A pretty question. A very pretty question indeed.

But there were hopeful signs. The Ring was in the process of becoming a more powerful place. The Autocrat needed to find some way of using the enemy's strength against the Autocrat.

An interesting challenge.

The Ring of Charon Command Station
Plutopoint (Orbital Position of Destroyed
Pluto-Charon System)
THE SOLAR SYSTEM

Sondra Berghoff stood—or, more accurately, floated—at the entrance to the airlock, waiting, more than a bit nervously, for no less a personage than the Autocrat of Ceres himself. The Autocrat *was* a him, wasn't it? No, wait a second. A woman. She remembered seeing a picture in a news report. No, that had been some history article, about the last Autocrat but two. Well, the office was *supposed* to be depersonalized, to be held by someone willing to subsume all private concerns to the needs of justice and the good of the Belt. Or something. She had never followed Asteroid Belt politics or history that carefully.

Which was too bad, as a big dose of both was just about to be dumped in her lap. The Autocrat wanted to get a look at the Ring of Charon—and at Sondra.

Sondra didn't like that aspect of the situation, either. Five years ago she had gotten a lifetime supply of notoriety. The theft of the Earth was a defining moment in everyone's life. Fine, so be it—but Sondra had no desire for her role in those events to be *all* there was to her life, the one thing that summed her up.

She remembered her long-dead Great-uncle Sanchez. He had died at an advanced age when she was a child. A century before, Sanchez had been a teenager, working odd jobs at this station and that on the Moon.

Uncle Sanchez been one of the last ones to evacuate Farside Station, just before that mispiloted asteroid piled into it and turned lunar history upside down. But Sondra did not remember Uncle Sanchez as a witness to history, but as a boring old man who told the same stories over and over again, who spent his adult and elder years focused on the single day, the single moment of his youth, when he had happened to stumble, quite by accident, into the sweep of great events.

Uncle Sanchez had belonged to any number of clubs and organizations dedicated to researching and remembering the great impact. He had told his eyewitness account of that day so often Sondra could recite it from memory.

He had kept a fifty-kilo lump of rock in his living room, and told anyone who came within a kilometer of the place that it was the largest intact fragment of the asteroid.

A month after he died, his widow, Aunt Sally, lived up to her reputation for being unsentimental. Tired of having her front parlor cluttered up, she had the reputed asteroid fragment dumped out into the back yard, and good riddance. Somehow, Sondra had always thought of the big rock as being Uncle Sanchez, picked up and heaved out.

No thank you. Not for her. Okay, maybe she had been a

witness to history. Maybe she had even been a *part of* history. She had no desire to bore generations of relatives and strangers telling the same story over and over again.

And yet here she was, being trotted out as a curiosity, a historical artifact to be examined by an important visitor.

Besides which, she was not at all sure she *wanted* to meet the Autocrat of Ceres. If Simon Raphael were still alive, he would have gotten stuck with this duty—and done a better job of it as well. But he had died in his sleep two years before, and thanks to her damned notoriety Sondra had been appointed the new director of the Gravitics Research Station.

What sort of person had a title but not a name, anyway? It must be one hell of a job if you had to give up your name in order to take it. And why did they *do* that, anyway? Sondra knew she could get every boring detail of the boring tradition if she asked the right person, or if she trolled through the right datastore, but there wasn't any point. The Autocrat giving up his name was a bizarre and inexplicable tradition. Any purported explanation of it would merely serve to paper over the fact that it made no sense.

There was a clunk and a thud and a whir from the other side of the airlock and Sondra moved forward just a trifle. But no, there was always that moment when the lock *seemed* as if it were about to open, and then the inexplicable delay while everyone waited for something or other. It seemed likely to Sondra that such unexplained pauses had been going on long before there were airlocks, that there was always that gap of a few minutes between things *seeming* ready and really *being* ready.

What was he doing here, anyway? The common room had been buzzing with speculation for weeks. He was just here on a tour of inspection, someone would say, a traditional Autocrat's Progress. But then someone would point out that such progresses were normally confined to those places that recognized the Autocrat's authority. He was coming here to lay claim to the station in the name of the Asteroid Belt. He

wanted to take over the *Graviton* project. He was just here as
a tourist. He had a secret plan to use the Ring as some sort of
superweapon—against whom and on whose behalf was not
clear.

The airlock swung open, and the Great Man—he was
a man, after all—floated through the lock door, moving
himself along rather neatly on the guidebars set into the
bulkhead. He was short and pale-skinned, his face sharp-
featured, his sand-colored hair cut bottle-brush short. He had
a somewhat prominent nose and his mouth fell naturally into
a rather disapproving frown. And yet his eyes had some
glimmer of lightness and humor in their grey gaze. He was
dressed in a dark grey, loose-fitting tunic and baggy black
pants—comfortable and practical. He wore no insignia or
pendant or ring of office that Sondra could see. He had no
need to put his power, his authority, on display.

His eyes caught hers as he came out of the lock, and he
gave her a rather engaging smile.

For a split second, she allowed herself to believe that it
was going to be all right. This was someone she could deal
with. But then it struck her—she had no idea whatsoever
of the proper mode of address for an Autocrat. What
should she call him? Excellence? Sir? Your Autocracy?
How the hell did you talk to someone who didn't have a
damned *name*?

She decided to finesse the question of form of address by
avoiding it altogether. "Ah, um, welcome to the Ring of
Charon," she blurted out. "I am Dr. Sondra Berghoff, director of the facility." She stuck out her hand, not sure if that
was the thing to do or not. Apparently it was, because the
Autocrat accepted her hand. She pumped it, a bit too vigorously, and held onto it a moment or two longer than she
should have.

"I am pleased to meet you, Doctor," the Autocrat replied.
His voice was quiet, firm, and deep. "I have been looking
forward to this visit for some time."

"And we have been looking forward to having you here,

um, ah, ah . . .''

"Most people find it most convenient to treat 'Autocrat' as if it were my name and address me by it," her guest said, a hint of amusement at the corners of his mouth. "You may also simply address me as 'sir' without causing an interplanetary incident." Plainly, the man had come across this problem before.

"Ah, yes sir, very good sir," Sondra said, the words tumbling out. "I understand that you want an immediate tour of the facility?"

"Yes, indeed. I have been looking forward to it for some time."

"As we're nearly at peak view conditions, would you like to get a look at the Ring itself first?"

"Yes, by all means," the Autocrat said.

"Are you ready to go now, or is there anything you need to do about your ship?"

"My crew will see to all that," the Autocrat said, with a dismissive gesture. "They will remain aboard for some time yet, I am told."

"Very good, then. Won't you come this way?"

"Certainly."

She led him out of the airlock and docking complex and into a small, odd-looking elevator car. "Things are a little jury-rigged around here," she said as the doors pulled shut and sealed themselves. "We're going to be moving out of zero gee as the car descends," Sondra said. "Are you ready for it?"

"I've been moving in and out of varying gravity conditions my whole life," the Autocrat replied.

"Yes, yes, of course," Sondra said, embarrassed. "I wasn't thinking. In any event, here we go." Sondra pushed the button and the car started to move down.

"You were saying things were a bit jury-rigged," the Autocrat prompted.

"We used to control the Ring from the surface of Pluto," she said, "and of course we had to evacuate the surface in a hurry when the planet was destroyed and drawn into the black hole. We had to improvise the whole operation, rebuild from scratch. Pluto was destroyed, everyone got crammed onto the *Nenya*, the supply ship that serviced the research station.

"Once things were settled down, and we were getting supply ships coming in, again, we sent as many people back toward the Inner System as we could on the empty ships, so as to cut down on the number of mouths to feed." Sondra could feel weight returning as the car moved from the rotation axis down toward the living quarters.

"Some of the supply ships we didn't send back at all," she went on. "Instead we rebuilt them into additional crew quarters and working space. Finally we built a long rigid connection frame with the *Nenya* at one end and the rest of the quarters at the other, with the airlock axis you just came from right at the center of gravity, in zero gee. Sort of a dumbbell shape with the airlock in the middle of the long arm. Once we spun it up, we had artificial gravity at the two ends of the dumbbell. It's a little ironic, actually."

"What is?" the Autocrat asked.

"This is the foremost gravity research station there is, and we have a gravity generator of incredible power. But we're still using centrifugal force to make artificial gravity. Someday we'll know enough to develop a controlled gravity field. We're learning a lot with the *Graviton* project. Until we get it right, though, we spin away. In any event, the station is essentially complete. We're still adding bits and pieces, upgrading, that sort of thing. It's almost gotten to the point where it's comfortable. But it's still hard here," she said. "Sometimes it's very hard."

There was a moment's awkward silence as the car moved downward into the high-gee sections of the station. The doors opened and Sondra ushered the Autocrat out. "This way," she said, trying to sound bright, clipped, efficient.

She led him toward the rather cramped confines of the main wardroom. Ring-viewing conditions varied constantly.

They were almost at the peak of their six-day cycle, and she didn't want the Autocrat—or herself—to miss the sight. Everyone loved looking at the ring. It had taken some doing to chase everyone else out of the wardroom for the Autocrat's tour.

The lights in the wardroom were lowered to make it easier to see out into the sky. The room was quiet. In the gloom, it was a trifle hard to see the wardroom's oversized porthole—a mere spot of star-sprinkled greater darkness in the dark. But Sondra knew where it was, of course, from long practice. Even if she had not, her eye would have been caught by the movement of the heavens, slowly wheeling past the porthole.

"Ah," the Autocrat said. "There." He crossed the room, threading his way between the tables and chairs, and stood in front of the porthole, staring out. Sondra followed a step or two behind. Perhaps it would have been more respectful, more gracious, if she had allowed him to stand there alone, drink it all in by himself—but she could not resist. She had spent endless hours before that window, gazing on the ring, and would gladly have spent twice as many.

In the days of the dim, forgotten past, the first astronauts orbiting the Earth had stolen every moment they could from their tasks in order to gaze on the blue-white marvel sweeping past below. Ring-watching was like that—except that there had never been a sense of danger, or melancholy, in looking at the Earth.

For the Earth was gone—and it was, after all, the Ring that had sent it away. The Ring of Charon was, by any measure, the most powerful machine ever built by human hands. It had crushed Pluto and Charon down to quite literally nothing at all, down into a black hole. The Ring's beauty was a fearful thing.

The Ring was just that, a hollow toroid 1,600 kilometers in diameter, the Plutopoint Singularity at its centerpoint. The Ring was the direct descendant of the ever-larger particle accelerators built on Earth, and later in free space. When originally built, the Ring had circled the moon Charon, and had been designed to deal with its gravitational field alone. Now it circled the far more massive Plutopoint, and was stressed by far greater gravitic energies, energies that would have torn the Ring apart long ago if Sondra and the rest of her team had not found a way to mask and refocus some of the singularity's expressed mass.

The command center revolved around the Ring and the singularity at right angles to the Ring's plane, in a circular orbit roughly 20,000 kilometers out from the singularity. Twice an orbit the Ring was edge-on as seen from the station, and it was likewise face-on twice an orbit. The best time to see the ring was when it was face-on, with the Sun behind the station, lighting up the ring—albeit faintly.

The Ring hung in the sky, massive, perfect, gleaming, its running lights bright in the darkness. The cold stars floated, uncaring, behind it, in the silence of space. And at the Ring's center was the source of all its power.

The black hole, the singularity itself, was of course invisible. The event horizon was only a few meters across, and it was, after all, merely blackness in the black. Now and again, some bit of debris would be pulled into the horizon, and a bright spark would flare up as the bit of dust or misplaced screwdriver was torn apart by tidal forces, giving up some part of its mass as energy as it was sucked down into the singularity. But those flashes of light were rare, weak, tiny. The singularity pulled in nearly all the light and energy of the impact events.

Sondra stood next to the Autocrat in the gloom of the wardroom, staring out at the mighty Ring. "There it is," she said. "Our one weapon against the Charonians. Our one hope for finding the Earth. Though God knows what we could do if we ever *found* it."

"How long will it take, finding Earth?" the Autocrat asked.

Sondra shook her head. "We have no way of knowing. It's not as if we're actually going to open up a hole, look through it, and see the Earth. What we're doing is a tuning hunt, searching for the right gravity resonance pattern. If we can get our singularity resonating with a Charonian black hole, the resonance will induce a wormhole between the two. That's oversimplifying, of course, but that's the basic idea. The trouble is that there are millions, maybe billions, of combinations. We've hit on six that might be something, that make the meters twitch in ways that make us think we almost induced wormhole formation. We've worked the hell out of all the near-misses, run every conceivable variation on them—and gotten nowhere. Maybe one of them is this Multisystem place that stole Earth, and we just haven't got enough data. Maybe all of them were false positives. So how long until we find Earth? We don't know."

"Could you induce a wormhole if you got the pattern match?" the Autocrat asked. "Do you have the power, and the know-how?"

"Oh, yes," Sondra said. "God yes. Don't forget we've had a whole Solar System full of dead Charonians to take apart—and we've got this Plutopoint Singularity and the Earthpoint Singularity to play with. We've learned a tremendous amount about gravity—and manipulating gravity—in the last five years."

"That's one thing I've never understood. The Charonians placed a black hole—a singularity—there, and used it as one end of a wormhole link connecting back to their Multisystem. Why can't we do the same? Do a pattern match with the Earthpoint Singularity and establish a wormhole link between Plutopoint and Earthpoint? Or reactivate Earthpoint as a link to where Earth is?"

"Because that singularity was controlled by the Lunar Wheel, and the Lunar Wheel is dead. You need a functional ring accelerator—like the Ring of Charon—to modulate the gravitic energy and establish a resonance pattern in the first place. The Lunar Wheel's resonance match was lost, randomized, when the Wheel died, and we can't get it back—just as we lost the link to where Earth is. If *we* built a Ring about Earthpoint, we *could* set up a wormhole link between Plutopoint and Earthpoint, I suppose. But without the tuning data, it wouldn't let us link up with the Multisystem. Besides, building an Earthpoint Ring would bankrupt the Solar System. That one I know. We've run the numbers. If you want faster transport, the *Graviton* is the way to go.''

''Ah, yes,'' the Autocrat said, his eyes not moving off the Ring. ''The *Graviton*. You will be surprised to learn that I do not have much interest in her.''

Sondra *was* surprised—and then suspicious. ''No interest in a ship that should be able to make a run from the Moon to Plutopoint in no more than two or three days?''

''In a word, no. Not so long as such ships are based on technology we don't understand, and are built with parts stripped from dead aliens. How can we rely on Charonian machinery when Charonian machinery has been so full of unpleasant surprises in the past? If we humans could build gravity-beam ships that were entirely our own, then I would be *fascinated* by them.''

''But it will require a great deal of research before that is possible.''

''The Autocracy has always been eager to fund worthy research projects.''

''Our current sponsors on Mars and the Moon might not welcome that,'' Sondra said. ''They hope to develop such ships, and use our gravity beams to power them.

''*Your* gravity beams. They are yours, quite true. But we Belters are traders, and we fear monopoly. Your Ring is the only possible source of gravity beams, correct? No one else in the Solar System could produce them at present? Save the Earthpoint Ring we cannot now build?''

''You are right,'' Sondra said, choosing her words carefully. "It is a point which disturbs me as well," Sondra said. "A monopoly source of a vital commodity can very easily become a target, either for destruction or empire building—or both."

"All quite true. It would be in everyone's interests to forestall these problems before the first ships are built. We have a great deal to talk about, you and I." The Autocrat paused, and then spoke again in a more thoughtful tone. "It is possible that I will be forced to extend my stay."

Which will definitely drive the Moon and Mars crazy, Sondra thought. *But you know that. So why do you want to upset them? This is going to be more interesting than I thought.* "Feel free to stay as long as you wish," she said evenly. *As if I could stop you, with the* Autarch *and her crew armed to the teeth.*

"I thank you for your hospitality," he said.

"You are most welcome," Sondra said. "Is there more you wish to say regarding the *Graviton*?"

"Perhaps at another time. Just now, I wish to focus on the central issue. Earth," the Autocrat said. "Is there any hope at all of finding her?"

"There is more than hope," Sondra said, surprising herself with the vehemence of her tone. "We *will* get a tuning lock and find the Earth. Every other use of the Ring is secondary to our hunt for Earth, and nothing else will be allowed to interfere with it. If we get a tuning lock in the next five minutes, or if it takes a thousand years, until the Hunt for Earth is a religion, an act of faith, we will keep on until we find her. We have to believe that. We have to *know* that. We are the only hope the Solar System has for finding the Earth and undoing at least some of the damage."

"Then you see the Hunt for Earth as your mission, as your duty?" asked the Autocrat.

"Oh, no," Sondra said. "Not duty. Not mission. That's not it at all." She stared out the porthole at the massive ring and the tiny, invisible singularity that had once been Charon and Pluto. She saw, in her mind's eye, the lost Earth, the sundered families, the dead of all the disasters caused by the Charonians that the Ring had awakened. "Finding Earth is not our mission," she said. "Finding the Earth is our penance."

Five

Jam To-day

". . . No previous generation was ever forced to look on mortality in quite the way mine was. Ours was the first generation wherein the matter was no longer in human hands, and the first in a long time when universal mortality was a reasonable possibility.

"For the last five hundred years, humanity has had the ability to destroy itself—and has come horrifyingly close to using that ability more than once. But we were at least secure in the knowledge that humanity, and life, and Earth itself would survive so long as *we ourselves* did not destroy them. *We* were the only threat to our own survival, and to that of the planet.

"But then dawned the day of the Charonians, and all things changed. We survived on their sufferance.

We could die, at their whim, at any moment. In spite of all our learning, all our wisdom, all our power and technology, the people of Earth were suddenly as helpless as medieval peasants watching a cloud of locusts descend on their crops. There was nothing we could do. More galling still, there was not the slightest evidence the Charonians even knew we existed, any more than the locusts knew or cared who planted the crops they consumed.

"Since I was fourteen years old, I have been forced to face the possibility of my own imminent death, of Earth's destruction, of the extinction of virtually all terrestrial life, and of the subversion, the perversion, of whatever remnant of life survived in the service of the conqueror. I grew up knowing my species and my planet were completely at the mercy of beings ready and able to destroy our world if it suited their purposes.

"There is no end to the ways this knowledge has shaped—and warped—every aspect of life and thought for my generation."
—*Memoirs* by Dr. Sianna Colette, Columbia University Press, 2451

New York City
Earth
THE MULTISYSTEM
Abduction Day, June 7, 2431

After the ceremonies, after the memorial services, after the moment of silence, after the long day of mourning, Sianna Colette slept, and dreamed.

Sianna knew she was having her nightmare again, even as she slept. But she did not wish to awaken: this nightmare was a happy dream, until she awoke. Of course, that meant that being awake was the nightmare, but even in the midst of sleep, Sianna told herself she was too sensible to dwell on such thoughts.

In her dream, the Moon, the true and friendly Moon, shone outside Sianna's window by night. It was Earth's Moon, the true Moon, her cool light playing across Sianna's parents' yard, moonshadows wrapping the darkness in familiar mystery.

Sianna dreamt that the Sun, the real Sun, still rose in the east every day, and that his light was a shade subtly unlike the Sunstar's. In her dream, the real Sun cast his honest colors over the lands.

Sianna reveled in sunlight, the light of the *true* Sun, a warm shade of yellow-white from her childhood, a color that she could never quite recall and yet could never forget.

In her dream, at sunset, the fat, slow-moving stars of the space stations and the orbital habitats and spacecraft were still there, transiting the darkness, rivaling the real stars.

Stars. Yes, the stars were there, too. The sky was a velvet darkness spangled with stars and planets that shone as bright as hope. Proud ships still crossed the void. Earth rolled round the Sun on its comfortable and ancient orbit, and all was well.

But then she awoke, and it was all over.

Sianna opened her eyes, and the dream-smile faded from her lips. Over her head, even the once-blank ceiling served to remind her that her dream was dead. According to the landlord, the crack in the ceiling had popped open in the pulsequakes that jolted the world when the Moon's tidal influence suddenly wasn't there anymore.

Because now, of course, there was no Moon. Instead there was the hateful Moonpoint Ring, hanging neatly in the sky, precisely where the Moon was supposed to be, the Ring and the black hole in the center of the Ring providing exactly one Lunar mass, keeping the tides running in their ancient patterns.

Maybe that was enough to keep the fish happy. But who would want to look where the *Moon* was supposed to be and see an artificial Ring instead?

The whole sky was ruined. Sianna lay awake in bed, staring at the ceiling, determined that this one night she would not give the Charonians the satisfaction of looking on their sky.

Foolish thoughts. Why would beings capable of stealing all the worlds and suns of the Multisystem and gathering them in one place care in the slightest if Sianna Colette, nineteen-year-old Columbia University undergraduate and noted troublemaker, snubbed their sky?

Unless this, now, *was* the dream, truly was the nightmare. Perhaps this very night the survivors back in the Solar System had mastered gravitics, found the Earth, and pulled it home.

Sianna felt a stirring of hope. But then she snorted to herself, rolled over on her side and hugged at her pillow. In a pig's eye. Nonsense. Piffle.

But it *could* have happened. The sky that had vanished when she was a gawky fourteen-year-old *could* have returned. After all, it had vanished while she slept, five years ago.

What a horrible morning that had been, when she awoke. But no, don't think about it.

But it *could* have come back. The people in the Solar System could have rescued Earth, somehow.

Oh, hell and bother. She tossed the pillow across the tiny room. It struck the wall with a soft *whump* and slid to the floor. Might as well go take a look. Otherwise Sianna knew she would lie there half the night, torturing herself with the convincing delusions of her dreams.

She sat upright in bed, swung her feet around, slipped them precisely into her slippers, and stood up. Moving in the darkness, she went to the closet and pulled on her robe, moving carefully so as not to set the floor creaking. She did not wish to waken Rachel, her apartment mate, sleeping in the next room. She made sure she had her key and slipped out into the hallway. She moved confidently through the darkened hall to the stairwell door, her hand smoothly finding the handle in the darkness. She padded up the stairs, her slippers flip-flopping up the elderly treads.

She climbed the four flights to the roof and pushed open the door. She stepped out into a chilly spring evening and onto the little patch of roofgrass. Nearly every roof in New York sported some sort of greenery. Sometimes she wished that the super would go to the additional expense of planting trees instead of just grass, but then she would not be able to see the sky, and that would never do.

Sianna Colette *needed* to see the sky, needed to keep an eye on it, as she would watch a once-trusted friend who had turned on her once and might do so again. Now she looked upward, and felt the same numb, angry disappointment she always felt upon awaking from her dream of the skies of home. Anger at the Universe generally, and the Charonians especially, that the Earth was still in this place. Anger at herself for letting her muzzy-headed dreams trick her into believing, into hoping.

Sianna Colette looked upward into a firmament nothing like anything Nature had ever intended for the Earth.

The Moonpoint Ring hung low in the sky to the southwest, where the full Moon belonged. It was a hollow ring hanging edge-on in the grey-black sky, a circle in the sky, the same size as the Moon but much harder to see. At its center was the Moonpoint Singularity, a black hole. It was a most incongruous and alien object to be floating over the spires and skyscrapers and towers of Manhattan. The Naked Purple Habitat, the last surviving human habitation in space besides the *Terra Nova*, orbited the Moonpoint Singularity as well, actually inside the Moonpoint Ring, but it was too faint to be a naked-eye object in as murky a sky as this one.

Three Captive Suns were visible at the moment, each casting something like the same light as a full moon, each washing out a large swatch of the night sky. The brightest of the three was actually surrounded by a tiny ring of blue sky, fading out to dark grey at about twice the diameter of a full

Moon. Bright as they were, the Captive Suns would have been brighter still, if not for the dust shrouds that begloomed the Multisystem.

A good round dozen meteors flashed across the firmament in the first minute that Sianna looked at the sky, but she paid them no mind. In the Solar System, so many meteors would have been remarkable, but here they were a routine and distracting nuisance. In the Multisystem, space was chock-full of small debris.

Not counting the Captive Suns, there were no stars to be seen. Blame the dust for that, as well. Whether by design or by accident, thick clouds of dust and gas—thick by astronomical standards—filled and surrounded the Multisystem, blotting out the stars beyond and rendering the Multisystem invisible from the outside Universe. The astrophysicists down at the Multisystem Research Institute calculated that, from the outside, the Multisystem would be nothing more than a dull blob of infrared, undetectable from further off than a few tens of light-years.

Sianna also could see a dozen planets, two of them close enough to show disks. *So close and yet so far,* she thought. That so many other worlds were visible was perhaps the cruelest joke of the Earth's captivity. For no human could reach any of them. The COREs saw to that. COREs did not care if they pulverized a rogue asteroid or a spacecraft. They killed anything on an intercept course with a planet. Not that many of those planets would be pleasant places to be. They were life-bearing worlds, yes—but ruined ones. You could tell that from the telescope images and the spectroscopic data. The best estimate was that a mass landing of Charonians on a planet's surface would cause enough stress and damage to induce a mass extinction, like the one that wiped out the dinosaurs. A few revisionists believed it *was* the Charonians who wiped out the dinosaurs, though that seemed a bit far-fetched to Sianna.

Sianna glanced at her watch and noted the time. Past midnight. She had to get back to bed. Class tomorrow, and she had to study for her exams.

It all seemed so *normal*. That was the most infuriating thing. Earth kidnapped, all links with the rest of humanity severed, and yet life went relentlessly *on*. Earth had been snatched through a black hole, and yet Sianna still had to worry about studying and getting her laundry done. It didn't seem reasonable. Somehow, everyday life should have been hit harder by the disaster.

But here she was, worrying about exams. It *had* to be that way, if she was not to go mad.

The whole city, the whole world was like that, each person struggling to pull a thick blanket of normalcy down over the terror, the bewilderment, of everyday life. Whenever Sianna walked the streets of the city, she saw too many expressionless eyes, too many faces with that same blank stare. Indeed, numb denial had become the normal state of affairs.

Sianna felt a thin film of moisture in her eyes and blinked rapidly. Not now. Not tonight. She could cry some other time. Now she had to get back to bed.

She kept watching the sky. A dim dot of light, crawling slowly across the sky. And there was another one. COREs. Back in the old days, those dots of light would have been brighter, sharper—and they would have been spacecraft, space stations, orbital habitats.

Once Earth had a mighty empire of satellites, habitats and spacecraft back in the Solar System. Now nearly all of them were gone. Not much had survived the transit to the Multisystem, and most that did make it through had been smashed by the COREs.

Humanity had exactly two major space assets left, to wit, a habitat and a spacecraft. The *Terra Nova*, designed as a generational starship and pressed into service exploring the Multisystem as best it could. The habitat was the Naked Purple Habitat, or NaPurHab, and it almost didn't count. The Naked Purple, the movement that ran NaPurHab, was so far out on the edge that even the other lunatic fringe groups called them extreme. NaPurHab was valuable and important only because it was the only hab left. It was an asset that might someday prove useful, though the Purps hadn't been the most useful of partners in the struggle so far.

Everything else had been clobbered by the COREs. The *Terra Nova* survived because it had left Earth orbit before the COREs arrived. NaPurHab was still there because it had managed a stable orbit, not of the Earth, but of the Moon-point Ring's black hole.

Now Earth, NaPurHab and the *Terra Nova* were all held at bay by the same enemy: the COREs. A CORE was a self-propelled rock the size of an asteroid. And if one rock was not enough, why then the Charonians would send dozens, hundreds, thousands of rocks. They worked with brutal simplicity. They emitted massively powerful radar and used it to detect their targets. Then they aimed themselves at their targets and crashed into them.

If a shuttlecraft from NaPurHab tried to land on Earth, a CORE would smash the ship to smithereens. If the COREs decided that a craft launching from Earth to NaPurHab was a threat to Earth, then it too would be destroyed. About a third to a half of the resupply flights to NaPurHab made it through. The COREs had humanity quite thoroughly bottled up.

At least, Sianna thought, she was part of the organization, the Multisystem Research Institute, that was looking for a way out. She was just an undergraduate and part-time researcher, but she was contributing, in some tiny way. Any day now, MRI might find the COREs' weaknesses, actually solve the problem and let the people of Earth travel freely in space once again.

And if pigs were horses, then beggars would fly. Or however it goes. No, she had that all muddled. Sianna yawned and hugged her arms around her shoulders. She must be more tired than she thought. Time to go in and get back to bed.

But there was one more thing in the night sky of New York City, something she had to force herself to look at.

Where would it be? High in the east by this time of night.

She peered fiercely up at the gloomy half-dark sky. The Sphere. Sometimes it would glow a dull and sullen red. The prevailing school of thought was that the red glow meant the Sphere was expending some massive amount of power. Of course, the alternative theory was that the glow meant the Sphere was *absorbing* power, which just went to show how little anyone knew.

Ah. There it was. Hard to see it tonight. Just now, the Sphere was charcoal grey, a disk the size of a medium-large coin held at arm's length. It hung in the deep purple-blue of a patch of sky near one of the Captive Suns. When not indulging in its power surges—unless they were power absorptions—the Sphere was visible only by light reflected off the Sunstar and the other Captive Suns. Sometimes it was slightly backlit by light reflecting off the dust beyond it. In general, the sky inside the Multisystem was a dark charcoal-grey, illuminated by light reflecting off the dust clouds. In a fully dark sky, the Sphere would normally be more or less invisible—but then, there was no longer any such thing as a fully dark sky.

The Sphere. Calling it by such a simple name made it seem so normal, so *harmless*. It didn't look much bigger than the Moonpoint Ring, or some of the nearer planets on their unnervingly close approaches.

But the Sphere's circumference was just about the same as that of Earth's old orbit around the Sun. The Sunstar around which Earth now orbited, and all the other Captive Suns, and all the planets and meteors and dust clouds of the Multisystem, were chained to the Sphere by its artificially generated gravitic power.

The Sphere was many times farther from Earth than Pluto had been in the old days. At a distance where the Sun itself would be nothing but a bright point of light, the Sphere still showed a disk noticeably larger than a full Moon.

That harmless-looking Sphere had kidnapped the Earth. No one was exactly certain why the Sphere did it, though there were any number of entertaining theories. Earth had been collected as part of some long-term scientific experiment. Or the Sphere, with its god-like powers, wished to be treated as such, and had gathered Earth in to provide it with a fresh batch of worshipers. Sianna knew of at least three Sphere-worship sects in Manhattan alone. Or the Multisystem, with its many Captive Suns, each with large numbers of life-bearing worlds in attendance, was a wildlife refuge, a safe place to keep Earth while some of the Sphere's myriad underlings tore the Solar System apart and built a new Sphere around the Sun of the Solar System, thus producing an offspring to the present Sphere.

The consensus in scientific circles was that the last could well be reasonably close to the truth. The last word from the Solar System before all communication was lost was that the Sphere's minions had made a shambles of the place.

But there was no law requiring the consensus to be right. Sianna worked as an intern at Columbia's Multisystem Research Institute, and she heard things there. Saw papers she wasn't, strictly speaking, supposed to see.

Things that were not supposed to get out, ever, period. For if they got out, the sheer horror of the news would most emphatically change everyday life. Numb denial was preferable to mass panic.

The trouble was, of course, that sooner or later it *would* get out. The evidence was there to be seen, on the other worlds of the Multisystem.

Sianna turned her back on the Sphere. She went back inside and down the stairs. She slipped back into the apartment and back into bed, struggling mightily not to think about it all—and failing miserably.

She tried desperately to think about her upcoming exams, her laundry, the way her roommate slept till noon, about anything that did not matter. But none of that would come to mind, of course. Not with Fermi's Paradox scuttling about in her brain.

Hundreds of years before, a scientist named Enrico Fermi

had posited a famous question: *Where are they?* Where were the other intelligences in the Universe? Assume any sort of reasonable distribution of Earth-like planets, and assign any probability meaningfully higher than zero for intelligent life arising and surviving on such worlds. There were so many stars in the sky that even if only a microscopic fraction of them produced intelligent life, the skies should have been full of interstellar radio traffic at the very least, and perhaps starships as well. They should have been easy to detect. So why couldn't humanity find anything?

Earth's astronomers were now able to get a good close look at all the other Earth-like worlds in attendance on the Sphere. Explanatory evidence was plainly visible on those worlds. Now, at last, there was a simple, straightforward answer to Fermi's question. Now they knew.

Sianna stared again at the crack in her ceiling and swore silently. Now she had done it. She was going to lie awake half the night, worrying about it. But who could blame her, once she had seen the confidential reports?

Humankind could not detect any other intelligent races in the galaxy for a very simple reason:

The Charonians had, in effect, eaten them.

And soon, it would be humanity's turn.

What was left of the night passed in strange and uncomfortable dreams that skipped back and forth over Sianna's life, back to the comfortable certainties of her childhood, ignoring the fragile present, looking toward to her doubtful future. She saw visions of herself as a youth, as a hale and hearty old woman, as a shriveled young corpse being gobbled up by a Charonian worldeater. She saw the face of the first boy to kiss her, years before, and the faces of her children to be in years not yet come. Those futures and pasts, and many others besides, flickered through her mind, all seeming strangely cut off from her present, as if there were some barrier, some gap, between them. She found herself trying to reach the future, trying to walk toward it—but instead falling, falling into the gap that held her back from it.

Falling, falling, into deepness and darkness—

It seemed to Sianna that her eyes snapped open with an almost audible *click*, that her mind spontaneously uplinked into fully-awake turbo mode without her having any say in the matter. She shook her head bemusedly. She must be doing too much computer work if she was thinking of her own mind in programming terms.

The Sunstar gleamed in her window, the almost-right-colored light relentlessly cheerful. She popped up out of bed, her feet hitting the floor just as the invigorating odor of fresh, hot coffee wafted into her nose from the automatics in the kitchen. She blinked, stretched, and looked about herself eagerly, as if it were Easter morning and there were presents and painted eggs to be found.

Why on Earth did she feel so good? She should have felt like death warmed over after a night like that, not bright-eyed and bushy-tailed.

No, wait. It was not that she felt *good,* exactly. She considered for a moment. She felt stretched, taut, ready. She *was* tired and stiff. But the restless night had primed her somehow. She felt strangely pulled along by outside forces, as if someone or something else were full of energy and enthusiasm, were lifting her up, poking her to get her moving and alert.

Alert. That was the word for it. Ready for something that was going to come her way, something she could not pursue. Reaching for it would only make it recede into the grey distance.

A thought, an idea—no, a whole line of reasoning, was simmering there in the back of her head, biding its time, waiting for its moment.

Let it come. Let it alone. *Leave it alone and it will come home, wagging its tail behind it.* Sianna had learned the hard way, early on, that she could not force ideas. Thoughts and ideas were delicate things. Touch them and the bloom was gone.

She headed for the bathroom and a good hot shower, moving carefully, trying to keep her mind from pouncing on whatever-it-was in the back of her head. She tried to think quietly, thinking of the little, the light, the unimportant, so as not to disturb her subconscious. She found herself moving quietly, like a host tiptoeing about when a guest is sleeping.

Think of other things. Enjoy the shower. Tell yourself you can find something nice to wear, even if the laundry should have been done a week ago. Go to the kitchen, get your coffee, make toast and think about putting jam on it. But don't do it. *The rule is, jam to-morrow and jam yesterday—but never jam to-day,* she told herself with mock seriousness.

Wait a second. Sianna looked up from her plate of buttered, jamless toast and stared unseeing at the wall. The ancient, whimsical paradox was part of it, part of the whatever-it-was in the back of her mind that she was trying to tempt out into the open.

Time. Something about time. Her dreams had been about time, about gaps in time.

There. She had it. She knew. The *Saint Anthony*. There. There it was. Sianna crunched down on a biteful of toast, a feeling of triumph washing over her. She had known it would come to her. The *Saint Anthony*, the probe the people back in the Solar System had managed to drop through the wormhole just before contact was lost, five years before. The literature mentioned its onboard clock being wrong. Everyone had always assumed it was a malfunction, though one or two rather fringy theorists insisted that the time shift had been a real effect, a distortion in space-time caused by transit through a wormhole. The unmanned probe's onboard clock had been thirty-seven minutes fast, or some such number.

Conventional wisdom had it that the clock circuitry had been scrambled a bit during the probe's admittedly rough ride. That didn't make a great deal of sense, of course. Any malf that could scramble the clock circuit should have fouled up all sorts of other things. Okay, suppose it *hadn't* been a malfunction? What had happened to those missing minutes? No, wait up. Think it through. Not missing minutes. *Extra* minutes. If the *Saint Anthony* chronometers were right, it had come from thirty-seven minutes in the future. It had experienced thirty-seven more minutes of time than Earth.

That was what reminded her of the White Queen's rules concerning jam, except it was the thirty-seven minutes, and not the jam, that were always somewhen else, out of reach. One slice of time was forever missing, a gap between the *Saint Anthony*'s experience of the Universe and Earth's. Suppose the clock error was a real effect. Suppose the *Saint Anthony*'s clock was an accurate report of what time it was back in the Solar System. That, in turn, meant that the Solar System had somehow jumped thirty-seven minutes into the future as seen from Earth and the Multisystem.

In the yesterdays before the Charonians took Earth, Earth and the Solar System had kept the same time. The far-off dream of MRI was that maybe, somehow, the Earth could be taken home to the Solar System. Then Earth and Solar System could be to-gether in some far off time to-morrow. Sianna put the archaic hyphen in the words as she thought it out. So why did the two places not have the same time to-day?

Nice question, all right. But how to find the answer? Why thirty-seven minutes? Why not forty-two minutes, or three days, or 123 years? What if that duration, thirty-seven minutes, held the answers, or at least some guide to the questions?

Where had those minutes been lost—or gained? Which of the two—Earth or the Solar System—had gone forward or backward in time, and how, and why?

Had the *Saint Anthony* been thrown forward in time during its transit through the wormhole? Or had the Earth been thrown *backward* in time?

But no, she was getting muddled. The *Saint Anthony* had been sent through the same wormhole that had taken the

Earth. All sorts of mathematical models allowed for a wormhole to induce time distortions—but none of them would cause the wormhole to be *selective* about it.

That was why no one believed the *SA* time data. Any time distortion should have hit the probe and the planet equally. Unless, of course, everyone had it wrong and Earth had not fallen through the same hole. If the Earth had arrived in the Multisystem through some other mechanism, instead of through the wormhole that linked Moonpoint here in the Multisystem and Earth point back in the Solar System, then all bets about how the Multisystem worked were off, and the Charonians had some completely unknown mechanisms up their sleeves. It was bad enough that they were the masters of gravity power. If they could control time as well, humanity might as well just quit now.

Alternatively, something had happened to Earth since its arrival. But what, and how? And how was it no one had noticed it happening? Sianna shut her eyes and shook her head to clear it. It was all too damned confusing. No wonder everyone had decided the on-board clock data had to be erroneous. If its clock was right, then it might mean that everything else of the precious little they knew about the Multisystem was wrong.

So what the devil *had* happened? Was the whole Earth missing thirty-seven minutes of its own existence? How could that be? And what alternative explanations might there be? Thoughtful, Sianna took a bite of toast and tried to keep from getting too excited. She had the very definite feeling that she was on to something.

Slowly, carefully, methodically, she told herself. She set to work making a proper breakfast, oatmeal with milk, an orange, two sausages. It was the sort of day when she would forget to eat. Best to fill up now so she'd be able to work longer before she collapsed. Getting the automatics to make breakfast required only the tiniest fraction of her attention. She put the rest of her mind to work on the question at hand. By the time she had demolished her meal without tasting a bit of it, she had a good half-dozen ideas. She had to get down to the institute and start digging. She left the dishes for the kitchen to take care of.

She popped the crusts of her toast into her mouth and hurried on her way, the crunching in her mouth almost drowning out the thoughts in her head.

Naked Purple Habitat (NaPurHab)
In Orbit of the Moonpoint Singularity

''Round and round she goes, and where she stops, no-bo-dy knows,'' Eyeball whispered to herself.

Eyeballer Maximus Lock-on, big cheeze of the astronomy section, stared out the observation port of the Naked Purple Habitat, out onto the cold black of space, and whispered the old patter to herself.

''Nobody knows,'' she whispered again. More and more often, she found herself wishing for the old daze, for her old job, for the times back when that statement had made sense, even if it had not been strictly *true*.

Rare was the roulette wheel in Nevada Free State where *someone* didn't capiche where she stopped. But the marks had dug that—the license fees for an honest house were way higher than those for a shady one. In the long run, the marks knew, you got a better deal in one of the clip joints. Folks were more pleasant, too. The only geeks who gambled in the honest houses were the flamers so raging they had been bounced out of all the dives.

But that was the past, and Nevada Free State was not likely to figure large in Eyeball's plans for the future. Nev-Free was back in the old daze, back when they was all in the Solar Area. ''Solar System'' was the straight name, but ''system'' implied a logic and order, and MomNature was not big on too much order. Still, it was hard to devote your life to the battle against order and reason in a Universe that seemed intent on killing you for nogood reason. Didn't used to be that way. Used to be e-z-r to be anti-reason back when the Universe seemed more reasonable.

Eyeball sighed as she thought of backhome Nevada. She glanced toward the number four monitor, showing a pic of Earth. So near and yet so far. Nothing was going to get from NaPurHab to Nevada no how, or to any other part of Earth, not when there was a fleet of big damn paranoid skymountains whirling around the planet, keeping anything from getting too close. Damned COREs.

No way no how no one would ever get back to the simple pleasures of running a dishonest gambling house. Still, the present circs had compensation for a gambler. At present, Eyeball was concerned with a roulette wheel of somewhat larger proportions, and a game with more serious stakes. She was more worried by orbital mechanics than gambling laws.

Five years ago, during the Big Drop, what the straights back on Earth called the Abduction, the Naked Purple Habitat had been dragged along with Earth when Earth was stolen. NaPurHab was sent wheeling across the sky in an unstable, decaying orbit.

In a desperation throwdice move, the Maximum Windbag had dropped the habitat into the only stable orbit the hab could reach. From then till now, the hab had ridden an orbit around the Moonpoint Singularity, an orbit so tight it was actually inside Moonpoint Ring.

NaPurHab had spent the last five years in a fast, tight orbit of the black hole, the singularity, that sat at the center of the Moonpoint Ring.

That was how the hab had gotten *into* the game. Eyeball had just wrapped the calcs that old time and manner of its getting thrown out. ''Round and round she goes,'' Eyeball whispered to herself again. But she did not complete the little couplet this time. She knew exactly where this one would stop.

She glanced at the ticktock. Assuming the situation did not change, and the hab did not correct its orbit, NaPurHab would impact on the Moonpoint Singularity in 123 days, 47 minutes, and 19 seconds. That assumption, however, was a helluva big one. The situation had been doing nothing *but* change.

Moonpoint Ring's swing around the hole was flopping up down all ways always, and that was bad. To put it another way, the orbit of the Moonpoint Ring around the wormhole was becoming more and more unstable, and that in turn was destabilizing NaPurHab's orbital track.

As to howcum Moonpoint Ring's swing around was failing, Eyeball couldn't say. It was almost as if the big Windbag Charonians didn't give no more of a damn. Moonpoint Ring's orbit had never been more than metastable since the Big Drop, but used to be it had always gotten a noodge back toward equilibrium when things were looking bad. Not now, not no way. Charonians weren't lifting a finger, or a tentacle, or whatever was they had.

And doing all the correct it burns was getting tough. The tanks were getting low. Ever time, it took a bigger and bigger swig of propellant to hold the hab swingaround together. Meantime, it was getting more and more difficult for Earth to top the tank, send refills. God or whoever or whatever bless the straights back on Earth for doing what they could, but weren't much they *could* do.

Eyeball could see lines on a chart move good as anyone. Sooner or later, they would not be able to hold it together and the hab would pile it in. And the way things were falling apart, Eyeball had a deep hunch NaPurHab was going to go down soonerthanlater.

Sucked up by a black hole. Not a good way to check out.

Notcool notcool notcool.

"Where she stops, no one *wanna* know," Eyeball whispered to herself.

Six

Grail of the Sphere

"Denial is a remarkable thing. With it, all things impossible are made possible, and vice versa. In the years following the Abduction, denial—the refusal to accept the facts of reality—came to be a major survival mechanism not only for individuals, but for society as a whole. Coupled with the refusal to see the Universe as it existed was the determination to see it as it was *not,* a will to build castles in the air out of what *ought* to have been.

"After a time, of course, the question became whether the cure was worse than the disease, whether it would indeed be possible for individuals—or society—to survive the survival mechanism."

—Dr. Wolf Bernhardt, Director-General, U.N. Directorate of Spatial Research, address on the

occasion of dedicating the *Hijacker* Memorial,
June 4, 2436

Multisystem Research Institute
New York City

The Multisystem Research Institute at Columbia University in the city of New York was a goddamned big hole in the ground, but that was not much of a novelty in mid-twenty-fifth-century New York. Belowground construction had been popular even before the Abduction. Automated Lunar excavating technology had proved to be quite practical on Earth, environmental control was easy underground, and there weren't many prime abovegrounds available.

After the Abduction, of course, the fad had really taken hold. Post-Abduction New York was even moodier and more paranoid than the city had been in times past. People wanted to hide.

Some people had—or pretended to have—reasons for going underground that had nothing to do with the Charonians. Many people felt safer underground. Well, maybe they were safer from street crime and bad weather and that sort of thing. But no one was really thinking about *those* dangers, even when they talked about them. They simply served as a nice series of plausible reasons for going underground.

Even if there was no real safety underground, people who lived and worked below street level did not have to see the sky. That was the major attraction. Underground living was downright fashionable.

However, there was such a thing as overdoing it—and that's what MRI had done. Such was Sianna's first thought every morning as she stepped into the high-speed elevator. She was early this morning, and all alone in the elevator car. Somehow that made it worse. She stood with her back to the rear wall of the car and reached out to either side. She wrapped both her hands tightly around the waist-high guardrail, and let her breath out slowly.

"Main Level," she said to the elevator, and braced herself as best she could against the stomach-knotting drop. MRI main level was three hundred meters below ground level, and the speed with which the elevators could make the run was an inexplicable point of pride among the staff. Sianna would just as soon have gone twice as slowly and gotten half as queasy.

The motors whirred, the car started its descent, and Sianna was suddenly strongly aware of just what size—and flavor—breakfast she had had. She shut her eyes, determined not to listen to the air whistling past the car, the humming of the motors, the deeper vibration of the car's drop down into the depths, a deep thrumming noise that seemed to be making the unconvincing promise that it would be *over soon, over soon, over soon.* The imaginary voices were never much comfort. After all, Sianna was afraid the ride would end *too* soon—and too suddenly.

Then came that blissful moment when her knees half-buckled and her weight suddenly spiked high and then slowly reduced itself to normal. The elevator car decelerated to a smooth and perfect stop, once again not dropping like a stone and smashing into the bottom of the shaft, once again not reducing Sianna to a shapeless, hideous blob the consistency of strawberry jam.

That was the rule. Sianna smiled weakly to herself as the doors opened and her ears popped with the change in pressure. *Jam tomorrow and jam yesterday—but never jam today.*

Well, maybe not—but she never would trust that damned elevator.

With a distinct sense of relief, Sianna stepped out of the car and onto the observation platform. The elevator banks opened up onto a raised stonework observation platform ten meters above the main level. Two long, wide stairways in front and two long swooping ramps at the sides led down to "ground" level. The MRI designers had been deeply concerned no one be reminded of the endless megatons of rock overhead, of the fact that this grand, well-lit place was in reality an artificial cave deep in the Earth.

But for Sianna, who had no illusions about MRI's location, something was still tickling the back of her head, telling her that this was it, today was the day. Today things were going to *happen*. She felt obliged to approach the day with a certain sense of occasion. Sianna forced herself to savor the moment, the view. Somehow, she knew that she would want to remember this day hereafter. She would want to remember what this place looked like *now, today*.

The MRI Main Level was not in and of itself a building. It was only a shell, a container to hold the actual labs and offices, a dome 150 meters wide and 300 meters long.

The ceiling of the chamber was done up in an absurd and deeply comforting imitation of a blue sky dotted with puffy white clouds. A combination of active-matrix paint and hidden projectors allowed the clouds to move across the sky. A brilliant yellow-white dazzle of light, too bright to look upon, tracked across the ceiling in place of the Sun. Now it hung in the eastern end of the ceiling, a bit redder than it would be when closer to the middle.

At night, the dome was lit up with the night sky of the Solar System, with the Moon and stars and planets all precisely as they would be as seen from New York City—if New York were back in the Solar System, and if New York City produced no light pollution. Illusions within illusions. No one had seen that many stars in New York's night sky since the invention of the light bulb.

Endless effort and design had gone into making the stone sky seem to lift away toward infinity. None of it fooled Sianna, however.

She did not, did not, did not like enclosed places. Maybe that was why she hated the Charonians so much—they had put the Earth in a box, closed it off from the Universe, sealed the whole world off from the outside.

Sianna had been to Cambridge in England and wandered the ancient quadrangles of King's College, Queens' College,

Jesus College and all the rest, and been fascinated by how they all conformed to the same basic design, the same layout of student rooms, dining hall, library, office and chapel laid out around a quadrangle. She had loved the feel of age and centuries hanging off the colleges, the sense that they had stayed the same here while all else had changed. She had loved the worn stones of the walkway, the way the present had been set down in whatever odd corners the past was not taking up. MRI had been laid out to the same pattern, a new and strange change rung on the same pattern twelve hundred years later. But was it conscious praise of the past, or self-deceptive denial of present reality? No centuries had molded this place. It was artificial.

Sianna had heard someone describe MRI as a campus-under-glass, and that was pretty close. The buildings themselves ranged from the ivy-covered brick of the Simulation Center to the mushroom-shaped biocrete of the Main Operations Building. Sianna could almost imagine Alice's Caterpillar sitting on top of the Ops Building, gravely smoking his hookah. She smiled to herself. She had Carroll on the brain this morning, she did.

One side of the campus was given over to a fair-sized lawn, and most incongruous of all, a duck pond. A mama duck and her ducklings were moving across the water. The two swans were still snoozing in the shade of one of the pondside trees.

Sianna turned and made her way down the stairs and onto the pathway that led past the pond to the Main Ops building.

The unreality of the place suddenly seemed the most palpable thing about it. Piped-in air treated to smell like fresh air, the errant breeze created by computer-controlled ductwork, the springiness of the thick-growing, robot-tended lawn beneath her feet all suddenly seemed too real, like the over-vivid hallucinations of a fever-dream.

Somehow the real things suddenly felt false. The quacking and fussing of the ducks as they splashed about in the water, the slight residual queasiness in her stomach, even the distant echo of a human voice from some unseen conversation elsewhere in the dome—all seemed part of some grand illusion.

Everything is fine, the dome of the main level told all who came there. *Everything is under control. You are safe here, and all is as it should be.*

Except the only reason the place existed was that the Earth had been stolen by aliens and *nothing* was as it should be.

Sianna frowned as she made her way toward the Main Ops building. She entered the place through one of the glass doors in the base of the mushroom stem, and got into one of the elevators that led up to the main body of the building. If the main center for the study of the enemy was so deeply immersed in denial of the situation, if the people researching the problem insisted on seeing the night sky as it *ought* to be, not as it *was*—then what hope could there truly be?

Ten minutes later, a mug of good, strong, steaming-hot tea in her hand, her face directed toward the largest and blankest of the windowless walls that made up her cubicle, Sianna felt better. She was alone, her mind was clear, the problem was in front of her.

Quiet and alone, she allowed her mind the pleasure of wrapping itself up in the mystery of those missing thirty-seven minutes. *Let's see,* she told herself. *Assume there was nothing at all wrong with the* Saint Anthony's *clock. If so, then those thirty-seven minutes were real. So what could cause the probe to jump around in time when*—

"Hello, Sianna. Good morning," a quiet voice said from behind her.

Sianna jumped, splashing tea on the desk. It was Wally, of course.

Damnation, couldn't he ever make some noise? Or knock? She cursed under her breath and set the mug down. No, he never would change. If she wanted to quit jumping out of her skin, she would have to rearrange the furniture in here so her back wasn't to the door, or, worse, shut the door.

Sianna did not relish being in an enclosed space *that* small. Besides, she was damned if she would change *her* space and the way she did things in it to suit someone else.

"Hello, Wally," she said, her back still to the doorway as she calmed herself, trying to compose her face as she blotted up the spilled tea with a piece of tissue from the dispenser. She felt a strong impulse to bite his head off, but there was no point in scaring the poor guy to death. Wally did not deal well with anger.

Throwing the tissue into the recycle bin, she swiveled her chair around to face the doorway, her expression blandly polite.

Wally Sturgis was standing nervously just outside her door. God only knew how he managed to look shy and nervous without moving a muscle, but he managed it. "Hello Sianna. What brings you, ah—*in*—so early this morning?" he asked, still not quite daring to make eye contact with her.

Wally was a forty-two-year-old doctoral candidate on loan to the Multisystem Research Institute from the Simulations and Modeling Lab in Columbia's math department. He was the absolute archetype of the eternal student—locked into one niche in life that he could never escape, and completely unaware that he was locked into anything.

Sianna sighed inwardly, and spoke in a fair imitation of a cheerful voice. "Just had an idea or two I wanted to work on before the rest of the crowd came in," she said. "I wanted a little peace and quiet, that's all." There was some hope, however faint, that he might take the hint.

No such luck. "Uh-huh, uh-huh," Wally said, nodding vigorously as he sidled through the door and sat down in the visitor's chair, keeping himself as far from her as possible. He sat down, folded his hands tightly in his lap and stared intently at a spot on the floor just to the left of her feet.

"I know how that is," he said. "You can get a lot more done when nobody is around. I hate it when people just barge in and— Ah. Oh." Suddenly the light went on in his head. He looked up, startled, making eye contact for the first time. Sianna repressed a smile as she watched an expression of dismay slowly appear on Wally's face. Only he could wander in and disrupt someone and then sympathize about the perils of being disrupted.

Sianna knew she ought to say something, ought to smooth over the awkward moment with a word or two that would make Wally feel better. But half out of mischief, and half because it wouldn't kill Wally to be embarrassed enough not to barge in the next time, she said nothing.

The first time she had met Wally, back when she was an underage freshman four years ago, Sianna had asked him some polite question about whether he liked doing simulations. Wally had started his reply in a low, quiet, shy voice Sianna could barely hear—but as he started warming to his topic, he spoke louder, faster, his face becoming animated and excited as he described the virtues and perils of pseudo-fractal regressions and high n-dimensional projection arrays. He had gone on for twenty minutes before Sianna could find a way to escape.

Not long after that, Sianna had made it her mission in life to reform Wally, to show him the big wide grown-up world. Why, precisely, a gawky fifteen-year-old should want to do such a thing was not entirely clear to her, even at the time.

Whatever drew him to her, made her feel for him, it certainly wasn't his looks. He was short and spindly-looking. What there was of his shaggy brown hair hung straggling down about his shoulders, uncombed and unkempt.

A large and prominent bald spot on the top of his head spoke to the fact that this was not a man much given to vanity or appearances. After all, a man could slap a dab of cream on his head twice a day and clear up baldness in a month—but that presupposed that the man cared that he was balding, and could remember to apply the medication every day. Wally didn't qualify on either score.

His clothes told much the same story, from the slept-in look of his rumpled dark-blue shirt and wrinkled, musty dark grey work pants to the battered look of his ped-slippers. Still, even these clothes suggested some sort of progress. For Wally, wearing any other color but black was a real fashion statement.

He had bushy eyebrows, deep-set eyes of indeterminate color, a rather beakish nose, and an unfashionably large and unkempt beard that didn't somehow seem to match his handlebar mustache. His rumpled face held that pallor peculiar to people who never see the Sun at all, and never expose themselves to the weather. It looked as if he had not slept in a while.

None of that meant anything, of course. He always looked that way. Wally could have been in those clothes for three days, nursing a computer run nonstop—or he could have just rolled out of bed, taken a bracing hot shower, and stepped into clean fresh clothes. Sianna had concluded that Wally's unchanging appearance was a result of years of effort, the cumulative effect of decades in the student lifestyle. He had been pulling all-nighters at random intervals all his adult life, each one etching the lines of exhaustion and rumpledness a little deeper.

The consensus around the Institute was that Wally would develop normal social skills—and complete his doctorate— just about the time he was due to retire.

Clearly he didn't have the skills yet. He *still* hadn't apologized for barging in. He sat there, with that damned hangdog look on his face. She could never read that look. Was he embarrassed? Was he trying to think of something to say? Did he think that he had already said enough? Was he waiting for her to speak?

Sianna gave in. She would have to break the ice, as usual.

"Oh, it's all right, Wally. Life goes on. But how about you?"

"What do you mean?" he asked, in a daydreamy voice. At a guess, he had already forgotten asking her why she was here.

What went *on* in that head? Sianna spoke in her calmest voice, for all the world like a patient grade-school teacher dealing with a slow student. "Why are you here, Wally?" she asked.

"Huh? What? Well, uh, I was transferred over from Columbia because—"

"No, Wally," Sianna said, struggling to keep her voice from rising. "Why are you here this *morning?* You look a little punchy. Have you been here all night?"

Wally looked surprised and glanced down at himself, clearly wondering what about his appearance would make someone think he was short of sleep. "Me? Nope. Got to bed about nine last night. I'm just coming in for the day. Dr. Sakalov wants me to set up his Sphere-interior simulation. He thinks he's finally figured out where Charon Central is."

"Not Charon Central again. Don't they ever quit?"

Wally smiled, and his eyes crinkled up with pleasure. "I guess not. Dr. Sakalov really thinks he has it this time. But—ah—ah—I *almost* hope he's wrong again. Every time he is, he gets me higher-priority access to sim time so I can prove his next theory." Wally grinned broadly, very much amused.

Sianna frowned. "Maybe it's a joke to you, but not to me, Wally. It's all guesses and theory and philosophy and logic-chopping. Sakalov's trying to prove the Multisystem is controlled from the Sphere core because he *wants* to believe it, not because there's any proof. Because it fits his theories—hell, his *theology*—about how the Charonians work." Maybe that was a bit overstated, but Sianna wasn't the only one who thought Sakalov got a bit mystical at times. "It's about as scientific as the quest for the Holy Grail, or creating the Philosopher's Stone, or squaring the circle. You look for something so hard you end up trying to invent it when it turns out not to exist."

"But . . . well . . . I don't know," Wally said. Wally didn't like arguing, or any sort of confrontation, and he wasn't very good at it.

"Look," Sianna said, "someday, yes, maybe if we're lucky, we'll find Charon Central—if it even exists—and maybe that will be vital information. But for the time being, the Charonians have us penned up pretty damned tight. What use is proving Charon Central is in the Sphere when we can't get to the Sphere? No one can even get off-planet!''

''Sure they can,'' Wally objected, clearly unconscious that he was using ''they'' to refer to the human race. ''They send supplies to NaPurHab and the *Terra Nova.*''

''Come on, Wally, where have you been? Yes, we can send supplies, but we can't send *people.* The COREs in Earth orbit smash one outbound cargo ship out of two during boost phase. And *nothing* can come inbound to Earth *from* NaPurHab or the *Terra Nova.* The COREs smash up anything that even gets close to an intercept course with Earth.''

''Well, okay, it isn't easy,'' Wally said. ''Maybe we can't get to Charon Central yet, but what's wrong with trying to figure out where it is?''

''Nothing, except that all the time and effort they put into chasing the Center is lost to doing research that might get us out of this mess. Like getting past the COREs so we can land ships, maybe.''

''I *like* doing the Charon Central sims!'' Wally said, a bit petulantly. ''I've done COREs a million times. They're boring.''

Only Wally would see relative degrees of fun as a reason to do one simulation over another. ''It isn't a question of what you like, Wally,'' Sianna said. ''It's a question of which is going to help the most. The COREs are—''

''COREs, COREs, COREs,'' Wally said, losing his temper. ''That's all you ever talk about. It seems to me that you're as obsessed with them as Sakalov is with Charon Central. *You* don't ever seem to get anywhere, either.''

Sianna opened her mouth to protest, and then shut it again. There was too much justice in what he said for her to say anything. Maybe the COREs represented a more immediate problem, but if so, the problem didn't show any more sign of being solved than the Charon Central mystery. He had a point. Dammit, now she was the one who had to apologize.

But Wally was already out of the visitor's chair, stomping

off down the hall to his own cubicle. Hell. Sianna wanted to get up and go after him, but she knew Wally wouldn't listen to an apology—or anything else—until he calmed down. On the plus side, at least he had left her cubicle.

The trouble was, Wally had a point, one that she had not quite faced for herself—and when Wally Sturgis could see something you could not, then you were pretty damned self-absorbed.

Here she was, completely distracted from her own area of research, off on an ill-defined wild goose chase, listening to whispered hints from her subconscious, looking for messages in dreams, working on hunches and instinct. What the devil kind of science would that sort of nonsense produce?

Maybe it all *was* hopeless. Maybe nothing was left to any of them but the need to keep busy, keep the mind and body occupied. Maybe all of MRI was nothing but a huge distraction from a cruel and unchangeable reality. Maybe humankind was utterly, totally helpless in the face of the Charonians, and humanity would be wiped out in the exact moment that best suited the Charonian whim.

But Sianna was not quite ready to descend into gloom. Maybe they *were* all doomed. Well, even if that was the case, it could do no harm to solve the puzzle. The hell with it. She turned back to the question at hand.

Seven

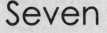

Rules and Exceptions

The Mind of the Sphere was afraid. It was obvious by now that the tremors, the vibrations, in the wormhole net were no flaw, no illusion, no mistake. The Adversary was awake and on the move. But there was still time, if not much of it. The Sphere had been preparing its battle forces, its plan of attack for some time now. Already, great forces were on the move, not only to fight, but to serve as diversions, to shore up weak points in defenses, to serve as scouts and sensors. But now. Now there could be no doubt. What had been a possibility was now a certainty. The Adversary would attack.

It had been the trouble with that new world that had done it. There was no doubt of that. The capture of that world had been a more awkward bit of business than nearly anything the Sphere could find in the whole of its Heritage Memory. It was a wonder that the awkward, unshielded—and, in some cases, unexplained—bursts of gravitic radiation hadn't at-

tracted the Adversary sooner.

But perhaps the scales were soon to be balanced. Since it was the new world's wormhole link that had attracted the Adversary, it would be the new world's link that the Adversary would most likely attack.

And if there was one thing clear from all the data in the Sphere's Heritage Memory, it was that the world closest to the Adversary's arrival point was always the first casualty of the attack.

Multisystem Research Institute
New York City

Three hours of staring at the wall had Sianna no further ahead than before. What the hell did that thirty-seven minutes mean? What was the source on that number, anyway? She had never seen the actual raw data for herself.

Maybe some systematic error no one had ever noticed, some glitch in the datastream, accounted for some or all of the discrepancy.

Clearly, it was time to examine the primary source material. Sianna reached for her notepack and started a search of MRI's databanks. There were a lot of references, of course. It would take a while to go through all of them.

There was certainly enough material to examine. She had seen clips and snippets of the *Anthony* data before, of course, but she had never looked at it in any organized way. A strange thought, that. This entire Institute had been founded to study information from just two sources: observations made here in the Multisystem, and the data transmitted from the Solar System after the Abduction. The *Saint Anthony,* named for the patron saint of lost objects, was the sole and only source of post-Abduction Solar System information.

Sianna checked the reference-use codes on the main index to the *Anthony* data. The data did get used—but not much. According to the use log, whole weeks often passed without a single researcher accessing the primary data.

Even though Sianna knew the hard-edged facts of what had happened back in the Solar System, the words and numbers and pictures from the *Anthony* were shocking, devastating. The Charonians had left the Solar System half-wrecked.

Once it had been awakened by that infamous gravity-beam test, the Lunar Wheel sent out a wake-up call to the thousands of Charonians that had lain dormant in the Solar System for millions of years. The Landers, massive Charonians that had been hidden in the Asteroid Belt and the Oort Cloud, set to work tearing the worlds of the Solar System apart. The planets were to serve as the raw material out of which the Charonians would build a new Dyson Sphere, the center of a new Multisystem.

The Landers used a sort of reactionless gravitic propulsion that allowed them to travel *fast,* and they had made a good start of their work before the people of the Solar System sent the *Saint Anthony* through the wormhole. The *Anthony,* using a tight comm beam aimed straight through the wormhole, had transmitted a tremendous amount of information back and forth between Earth and the Solar System before a CORE smashed into the *Anthony,* cutting the link with the home system.

Then the wormhole link itself shut down, the Moonpoint Ring on the Multisystem side of the wormhole stopped functioning as well—and all hope of further contact with Earth was lost.

The best guess for what that meant—and the most hopeful explanation—was that the people of the Solar System had managed to send a self-destruct command through the Charonian communications system, killing all the Solar System Charonians. In any event, *something* had killed the Moonpoint Ring here in the Multisphere and cut the wormhole link.

But suppose the Charonians had cut the link for their own, unknowable purposes, and then proceeded to disassemble the Solar System at their leisure? No one on Earth had any way of knowing. It was an article of faith, and nothing more, that the Solar System survived.

No sense in being gloomy, though. Sianna sat up a little straighter, blinked, and shifted in her seat to get a bit more comfortable. The Solar System was still there. It *had* to be.

The images told a horrible story. The dust clouds around Mars, the horrible damage done to Saturn's rings, the chaotic disruption of Jupiter's weather patterns.

Either there were different breeds of Lander for each planet, or else every Lander had the ability to adapt to any kind of world. Mercury, Venus, and Mars all had suffered Landers on their surfaces. The Landers had proceeded to tear up the planetary surfaces and propel them into free space.

The Martian satellites had been completely destroyed. The Asteroid Belt was in chaos—many of the asteroids had been disguised, dormant Landers all along. Once the disguised Landers awakened, they launched themselves to the attack. Most headed straight for the major worlds, but some set to work attacking other asteroids, everything from nameless, numberless hunks of rock forty meters across right on up to Ceres itself.

Jupiter's Red Spot wasn't there anymore, nor was much of the planet's banding system. The Landers had disrupted the planet's weather system, setting up artificial spin storms that accelerated Jupiter's atmospheric gases past escape velocity. The Jovian moons were savaged as well. Saturn and its satellites were in as bad a shape or worse, with the added tragedy of the ring system's destruction. At the time *Anthony* had died, Landers were reported moving for Uranus, Neptune, and Pluto. All the worlds were under attack.

Except one, said a tiny voice inside Sianna's head.

Well, yes. There *was* an exception. One world went untouched. But that was so obvious that no one ever gave it any thought.

The Moon.

What was that old saw about exceptions proving the rule? Sianna had never really understood that one. But maybe at least the exception could tell her something about the rules.

No Lander had ever moved on the Moon. Even when the Multisystem Sphere had started sending its own Landers through the wormhole to support the attack on the Solar System, they had all headed for the other worlds. None had made the mere 300,000-kilometer trip to the Moon.

The standard explanation for that was that the Moon had been pretty well infested with a Charonian presence as it was—after all, the Lunar Wheel was there, forty or so kilometers down below the surface, circling right around the Moon from pole to pole.

Why would the Charonians attack one of their own, as it were? The explanation was close to self-evident. But that was not enough for Sianna. Not this morning. Something about it jangled in her head, teased at her. It was part of the puzzle, another hint coming at her from her own subconscious. Let it come. Let it come.

One thing she was able to establish as she slogged through the *Saint Anthony* data: the thirty-seven minutes were real— or at least the *SA* thought they were. Every time-stamp on the data from every source aboard the probe showed exactly the same time discrepancy—37 minutes, 23.43 seconds to be precise.

With that settled, she needed to see one other thing. She had seen it many times before, of course. But that whisper inside herself told her to look at it again, look at it now, for it was part of the whole.

The Shattered Sphere.

The *Saint Anthony* had transmitted one image, along with all the others, of an event no human had ever witnessed. It was a moving three-dee image, a holographic movie, transmitted by the Multisystem Sphere through the wormhole into the Solar System and then intercepted by comm workers on the Moon. Indeed, it was the first Charonian imagery ever decoded. She punched it up and watched it run.

A massive Sphere, the color of old dried blood, hung in the sky, spinning slowly. Faint lines were etched into its surface. They looked like lines of latitude and longitude.

Suddenly, the Sphere's rotation began to wobble, skewing about more and more erratically. Two spots on its upper surface began to glow in a warmer red, and suddenly flared up and flashed over into glare-bright white. The flare was over as soon as it began. Two blinding-bright points of light swept out of the Sphere's interior and vanished out into space. The Sphere itself was left behind, tumbling wildly, with a pair of massive, blackened holes torn through its surface.

The ruined thing vanished and was replaced by the original image of a whole Sphere, rotating steadily and smoothly on its axis. The wobble set in again, the flashover happened, and the two glowing dots rushed away. The original intercepted message had looped over and over again, repetition perhaps being the standard Charonian way of emphasizing something.

Back when they had first intercepted and decoded the image, no one in the Solar System had the faintest idea what the image could be. Now everyone knew. The Sphere in the image was a Dyson Sphere, identical to the one that ruled the Multisystem. There could be no doubt of that.

Equally certain, the data transmitted by the *Saint Anthony* showed that all the Charonians in the Solar System had plunged into frantic, hasty activity the moment the image arrived, as if it were a warning of coming danger. That interpretation was clearly anthropomorphic. Humans might read the image that way, but would Charonians? What *did* the image mean? Was it a prediction of what was to happen to this Dyson Sphere? Was it a warning of what *might* happen? Was it an image of some other Dyson Sphere?

Or was the smashing of a Sphere *good* news, somehow—the cosmic equivalent of a huge egg hatching? That seemed damned implausible, but no one knew. And what were the two things that flew out of the Sphere?

Likewise puzzling was the apparent rotation period in the image. The Sphere in the image spun at about three rotations per minute. The Multisystem Sphere had a rotation period of about 1.3 standard years. If you assumed the Sphere in the image loop rotated at the same speed and worked the time scale out, then the events displayed in the thirty seconds of imagery had taken something like six months in real life. That made sense at the scale of the Multisystem Sphere. Scale the image loop up to the physical size of the real Sphere, run it at the same speed as the image loop, and the Sphere would be rotating at something over light speed. Most analysts believed the rotation could best be explained as evidence that the image was stylized in some way. That seemed plausible, if a trifle pat.

But the image itself fit. Fit into *what*, Sianna did not yet know, but it fit. The more Sianna stared at the endlessly repeating destruction of the Shattered Sphere, the more sure she was that the imagery held a clue to whatever it was she felt herself on the verge of finding.

But what the hell *was* she looking for? She was beginning to think that her subconscious already knew the answer, whereas she barely knew the question.

Sianna did not feel herself to be on the best of terms with her subconscious: it seemed to her that it often made her work to get what it already had. It was going to make her stumble her own way toward the inspiration that would set it all free. The clues, the knowledge, were inside her head, but her subconscious was going to make her find the stimuli, the images, the words, that would bring it all to the fore. So, how best to give her subconscious a poke?

Wait a second.

Wally. Sianna blinked at the screen and the images in it. She had been staring at the loop of imagery, the Sphere smashing, the two objects flying out of it, over and over again for ten minutes without seeing it. She shut her eyes and afterimages of the dying Sphere danced behind her eyelids. Sianna leaned back in her chair, opened her eyes, and looked up at a blank spot in the ceiling. Wally.

Something Wally had been talking about, something that whispered at the bottom of her skull. A hint, a guide toward an idea. Something that prodded her toward whatever it was she was looking for. His Charon Central and her thirty-seven minutes. Could the two be linked, somehow? Or was she just grasping at straws?

She turned toward where he had been, half-expecting him to be in the chair, staring into space. Then she remembered him leaving. She was getting as bad as he was.

She got up out of her chair, stretched, and rubbed her eyes. Something Wally said. All right, go find him, and get him to say it again. Wally's cubicle was just six doors down. She stepped out into the hallway and walked over. He had the door to his cubicle shut. Wally, it seemed, didn't have much problem with enclosed spaces. Sianna knocked, but got no response. She tried again, but still nothing. Either he wasn't in there or else . . .

She opened the door and sighed to herself. He was there all right—more or less. Wally sat slumped over in a blown-out old recliner he had unearthed somewhere, his body settled down in the chair so that his knees were higher than his head. Wally was completely unaware of where he was—and that was just as well, considering the shape the room was in. It was as messy as Sianna's cubicle was clean. Empty food containers overflowed the recycle bin. Papers were stacked everywhere, in no apparent order. The light seemed dimmer in here, somehow. It smelled a bit moldy.

Wally was oblivious to all, clearly off in his own world, thinking about who knew what. He stared off into space, eyes locked on some unseen image. Hell and damnation. Now if she said anything, *she* would be interrupting *him*, breaking *his* train of thought—and his thoughts were valuable things.

But she had to break in. She was close to something. She could feel it. Wally did not have the knowledge, but she knew there was something he could say, something he could tell her, that would make it all clear to her. Maybe it didn't even matter what he said. Her subconscious was telling her his words would hold the answer, and therefore they would.

"Wally," she said. "Wally. Come on." She reached out a careful, gentle hand and gave him a nudge.

Wally jumped a bit, startled, and looked about in bewilderment for a moment. "What? What?"

"Okay, Wally, you win. Show me what you have. Let's see what Sakalov's dreamed up this time."

Eight

Wheels Within Wheels

The Adversary ventured, somewhat reluctantly, fully out into fast-time space. There were certainly benefits to be had, gains to be made, here in the cold, flat Universe outside the wormhole web. But it was, nonetheless, a most unpleasant place to be.

But no matter. It would not have to stay here long. There was no need to lose precious time and energy searching for its prey.

It had a good, solid lock on the wormhole link that had betrayed itself with those bursts of sympathetic vibration. Something, somewhere, had gone through a wormhole in such a way as to set off remarkably powerful vibrations.

An easy transit back toward the dead system it had left behind, the dead system where last it had fed. The trivial challenge of forcing the wormhole open, the brushing back of whatever pathetic defenses its prey could muster—and then the Adversary would kill and feed on the energy so obligingly stored up by its prey. Stored up by the Sphere.

Simulation Center
Multisystem Research Institute
New York City

The Sphere hung perfect in the night, glowing brick red in the darkness, strong and solid. The fine cross-hatching etched in its surface like tidy lines of latitude and longitude added to the sense of serenity and order. All was as it should be, all was under control.

Sianna walked a bit closer, brushing past the lightfleck of a Captive Sun, walking straight through holographic projections of several planets, all but microscopic at this scale, until the Sphere was right in front of her, a meter from her face. She had to admit it was impressive. Wally did indeed do good work.

"We have the whole Multisystem mapped into the simulation now," Wally said with obvious pride. "All the Captive Suns and the known planets, of course. But also every known Charonian installation and object, all the way down to the COREs."

Sianna had seen other sims of the Multisystem, of course, but she had never seen a full run of a full three-dee animated sim—and this was one of the best.

"What sort of detail can you get?" she asked.

"Well, it varies, of course," Wally replied. "Some things we know to twelve decimal places, and others we're just guessing at. The *Terra Nova* has done good long-range mapping surveys of the closer planets and good spectroscopic and mass studies of pretty much all the Captive Suns. The most distant Captive Worlds and a few of the Captive Suns that are behind dust clouds we don't know so well. And of course we don't have completely reliable masses for a lot of the objects in the Multisystem—just apparent masses. Our only way to measure the mass of a body is by measuring the movement of bodies near it. From that we get a measure of gravity, and from there to mass. Back in the Solar System, it was a straight conversion, cut and dried. Here, we have to guess what is a straight, ordinary gravity field and what is an artificial field imposed by the Charonians.''

Sianna nodded. ''But what about the Sphere and its behavior? How good is your detail on that?''

''Not so good,'' Wally admitted. ''We, ah, have to fudge a lot on that.''

No surprise there, either. The Sphere was a completely artificial object. How the hell could you determine which motions were the result of natural forces and which were deliberate action? You could not derive information about either mass or density from, say, the orbits of the Captive Suns, for the Suns' orbits made no sense whatever. The Sunstar, about which the Earth revolved, orbited the Sphere at the same radial rate, and thus with the same orbital period, as Captive Sun Fifteen—even though CS-15 was a billion kilometers closer to the Sphere, and exactly 180 degrees ahead of the Sunstar.

Sianna found the Sunstar, and then CS-15, in the simulation. CS-15 was always invisible from Earth, of course, hidden behind the bulk of the Sphere. The *Terra Nova* had spotted it and reported back.

She found her way around other parts of the simulation. Captive Suns Seven to Eleven were at varying distances from the Sphere, but they were spaced exactly ninety degrees apart from each other, and shared an orbital plane forty-five degrees away from the Sunstar's.

And there, CS-4, -5, and -6. The three stars shared their orbit, spaced a perfect 120 degrees apart from each other. Other sets of suns were likewise lined up like beads on a string, orbiting in impossibly perfect alignment.

Some of the arrangements of stars seemed sensible enough, in that they kept the Captive Suns out of each other's way. Others were completely inexplicable. Maybe the stellar orbital arrangements simply appealed to the

Charonian sense of aesthetics.

The worlds that orbited the Captive Suns were arranged by equally mysterious criteria, but they were not Sianna's concern right now. She had asked Wally to show her the Sphere. And he wanted to show off his latest handiwork.

Wally knew everything—more than everything—there was to know about simulation modeling, and absolutely nothing about anything else. He almost never left the campus, and didn't even go aboveground that much. He supposedly had an apartment topside somewhere, in Morningside Heights, but his cubicle was his real home; that and a series of cots scattered around the labs.

All he cared about, or paid any attention to, was his work, the problem he was called upon to solve, the simulation someone asked him to create. To Wally, nothing but his simulations were real.

Wally had showed off some of his previous triumphs to her now and again. She had stood where she was right now, and watched real-time, highly detailed re-creations of dinosaur mating dances, seen the Moon born in the impact of a Mars-sized object on the proto-Earth, seen imaginary "fast-life" creatures in invented environments evolve at the rate of a generation a minute. Sianna could almost understand why the real world wasn't of much interest to Wally. If his simulations were that intense, if life in this tank had the hallucinatory, fever-dream, hard-edged sense of being more real than reality, how could anyone expect him to deal with—or be much interested in—the ordinary world?

Math department legend had it that Wally did not find out that the Earth had been abducted by the Charonians until six months after the fact, and only then because he was asked to design a simulation of the Multisystem's gravity-control system. He went from a steadfast belief that the rest of the faculty were pulling yet another elaborate practical joke on him directly to a steadfast acceptance and an utter lack of interest in the new situation. It did not affect him personally, therefore it did not exist.

Until now, of course. He had to simulate it now, and therefore reality affected him. A rather inside-out way of looking at the world.

Sianna stood there a moment longer, allowing herself a grudging admiration of the Multisystem's might and grandeur. The glowering Sphere, the Captive Suns gleaming bright and perfect against the inky blackness of the dust clouds, wheeling about the sky in their forced, artificial orbits, shining yellow jewels imprisoned in a setting of terrible beauty and ponderous strength. The Captive Worlds, gleaming dots of blue-green life and light in the darkness, the ruination of their surfaces invisible at this scale. It was beautiful, in its own horrible way. She felt a deep pang of guilt in her gut for admitting even that much.

A sadness, a feeling of loss and tragedy, hung over the sullen domain of the Sphere. She glanced behind herself and saw the Earth hanging there, a tiny dot over her left shoulder. She felt a tear in her eye, and blinked to clear her vision.

"All right, Wally," she said, her voice not quite steady. She looked back toward the center of the tank, where the Sphere glowed its angry red. "Show me Sakalov's latest." She felt relieved to see the Multisystem imagery vanish, and the simulated Sphere swell up into a ball three meters across.

Sianna watched it grow, some part of her still thinking, still hoping, that maybe Sakalov might have found the key, the answer.

If he had, it was a neat trick. There was damn all little to go on. The Sphere was perfectly round, rotated slowly about its axis, was 2.15 astronomical units, or just under three hundred million kilometers, in diameter. It was 232 astronomical units from Earth, and its color shifted from one shade of red to another, perhaps in relation to energy input or output. A pattern of lines resembling lines of longitude and latitude were visible on its surface. Its mass was impossible to estimate. It radiated little more than perfectly ordinary visible light, a bit of ultraviolet, a lot of radio frequency energy, and a fair amount of short and long infrared.

That was all that was truly known. Any ideas about the rest—what it was made of, how or why the Charonians had built it, how old it was, what it was for—were merest guesswork. For the last five years, Professor Yuri Sakalov had been working over that pathetic supply of information, struggling to divine the true nature of the Sphere, to pinpoint the location and nature of Charon Central, the control center for the entire Multisystem. Sianna had lost count of the theories Sakalov had presented.

Against all sense and logic, Sianna found herself standing there in the darkness, watching Wally's light show, hoping against hope that Sakalov had finally found Charon Central.

For even with all her railing against it and objections to it, Sianna had to admit that the whole idea of the Charon Central was a wonderfully seductive, dazzling notion.

One thing was clear from everything transmitted back from the disaster in the Solar System: the Charonians worked to a very clear hierarchical pattern. There had to be a top to the pyramid.

Many of each lower-function type served a single, higher-function type, which in turn served a still higher function master. Study of video from the attack on Mars as transmitted back by the *Saint Anthony* made that clear: a gang of mindless carrier bugs worked under a somewhat more sophisticated scorpion-form, and all the hundreds of scorps were controlled by a single Lander. All the thousands of Landers were controlled by the Lunar Wheel, buried deep under the Moon's surface.

Mind, that was a greatly simplified example, leaving out a number of intermediate forms. And there were many other subsidiary forms in other sub-hierarchies, and any number of ideas of how exactly all the hierarchies nested into one another. The whole Sphere system was a rigid hierarchal command structure—but where and what was the ultimate commander?

Maybe, just maybe, Wally was about to show her. "All

right, that's the Sphere exterior as we know it,'' Wally said from behind her.

Sianna stepped closer and examined the image. ''Hold it a second, Wal. Something real small is orbiting the Sphere around its equator. That some part of your theory?''

''No, that's real, not hypothetical,'' Wally answered, clearly pleased that Sianna had asked. The answer gave him a chance to show off his thoroughness. ''Dr. Sakalov detected that body a few weeks ago. Very dark, very faint, real small, not more than a few thousand kilometers across. Just some piece of skyjunk, but it shows how detailed our model of the Multisystem is.''

''I guess so,'' Sianna said, a bit doubtfully.

''Anyway, that's what we *know* about the Sphere,'' Wally said. ''Now let me show you what Sakalov thinks is inside.''

Sianna watched the image of the Sphere shift and change, and found herself thinking back on all the old theories she had heard before.

The Sphere is hollow, with a standard G-type star inside. Charon Central is located on a planet orbiting that star within the Sphere. Except every calculation showed that the infrared waste heat plus the energy needed to keep the stars and planets in their courses required somewhat more energy than a G star could supply. Neither could a G star provide the instantaneous energy to transit the Earth into the system. Assuming that the Sphere had been built around a star in order to collect and store its energy, either that star was of a type more energetic than a G class—unlikely, as the Dyson Sphere seemed to want only G-class stars and standard habitable worlds—or else whatever was in there was no longer a star: the Sphere had rebuilt the original star into something different. A matter-antimatter system, a spatial interstitial generator, or something else, something quite beyond human understanding.

The image of the Sphere transformed itself into a cutaway, showing a featureless interior with an indeterminate bright light at its center.

The Sphere is a foamed-up solid mass of extremely low density, made up of processing nodes linked by synapse-like filaments, with an unknown power source or sources embedded within it. It is itself the control center, the brain of the Multisystem. Except the Sphere was larger around than Earth's old orbit, and speed-of-light delays alone would make such a system hopelessly impractical. A thought would take over half an hour to travel from one side of the Sphere and back again. The human brain had a signal delay on the order of one-thirtieth of a second. If that was taken as a rough upper limit for processor delay in a practical thinking machine, and one assumed thoughts moving at the speed of light, that would dictate a "brain" not much larger than the Moon. Besides, even with a hopelessly inefficient architecture and very low capacity processing nodes and synapses, what could there possibly be to think about, what problem could be complex enough, to require a "brain" the size of the Sphere?

Now the interior of the image began to resolve itself. The brightness at the center resolved itself into a churning roil of energy. Sianna recognized a fairly standard representation of a "white hole," the point where the mass and energy that vanished down a black hole re-emerged into the outside Universe.

The Sphere is actually a series of concentric Spheres, nested one inside the other, and the master race, the true Charonians, are ordinary beings, not so different from human beings. They live inside the Sphere and run the Multisystem for their own, unknown purposes. It was a reassuring idea, in that it made the Charonians a bit less god-like. But no evidence of such "ordinary" Charonians had ever been spotted anywhere in the Multisystem. Besides, what point in creating and operating something as huge and complex as the Multisystem if you never ventured out into it? And what need of the planets and the Captive Suns if you lived inside a Sphere that provided limitless living space, millions of times more surface area than Earth?

The image resolved itself still further. The latitude and longitude lines were visible on the inner surface of the Sphere, and Sianna saw filaments of some sort reaching down toward the power source at the center, drawing energy in, directing it along the longitudinal lines. The lines began to glow, shining brighter and brighter, the power coursing upward toward the north and south poles of the Sphere. Sianna recognized the pulse pattern as a standardized visual notation for gravity generation.

Suddenly the pattern made sense. Each line of longitude made a complete ring around the planet, going pole to pole. Sakalov was suggesting that each ring was a gravitic wave generator, like the Moonpoint Ring or the Lunar Wheel or the Ring of Charon writ large, with dozens of generators banded together, the better to focus and direct the power stream.

Now the Sphere tipped over, displaying the north polar region to Sianna. The image flickered and pulsed with power. Wally zoomed in closer and closer, until Sianna took an involuntary step backwards. Now she could see a tiny, detailed cluster of pyramidical structures at the pole, and recognized them as scaled-up versions of the so-called Amalgam Creatures, the devices—or animals—the Charonians had built on the terrestrial planets and the larger satellites of the Solar System. In the Solar System, the Amalgams had focused and directed the gravity beams used to tear up the planetary surfaces and launch them into free space.

Here, presumably, they were to transmit the gravity beams outward. That part did not ring true somehow. After the buildup Wally had given Sakalov's new idea, it came down to some pyramids around the north pole? "Wally," she asked, stepping back toward where Wally stood at the control panel, "have you guys gotten some new imagery that shows those structures at the poles?"

Wally cleared his throat in obvious embarrassment. "Ah, no, not exactly," he admitted. "They are, ah, conjectural. Dr. Sakalov says the control structures are really big, but way below the limits of resolution we can get on images of the Sphere. But they *make sense,*" he said, with just a little too much emphasis to be convincing.

"Hold it, Wally. Never mind the pretty pictures. Give it to me in words."

Belittling his simulations was not the best way to get on Wally's good side. However, he did manage to hold his temper and stick to the subject. "Well, we did a lot of analysis of how much energy would be required to do the work the Sphere does, and a lot of horizon-position relationship analysis."

"Huh?"

"Sorry. We worked through where the stars and planets and so forth were when their orbits and courses were adjusted, and what points on the Sphere they were visible from at that moment. Almost all of the course adjustments came when the star or planet was in direct line-of-sight with one of the poles."

Sianna worked that through in her head for a moment. "Wally, that would be equally true for any two points on opposite sides of the Sphere!"

"Yes, but we detected a slight skew toward—"

"Oh, come on."

"It's the first theory that explains what the longitude lines are," Wally said, beating a bit of a retreat.

"Okay, I'll give you that," Sianna conceded. "But what about the latitude lines, the ones parallel to the Sphere's equator. What are *they?*"

"Well, I—"

"Okay, never mind that. Just walk me through the whole idea. You've got a white hole in the center. Why is that?"

"The Charonians use black holes all the time. Stands to reason they'd use the same technology to create power."

"But you have no evidence? No new particle detection or anything that might support the idea?"

"Well, no," Wally admitted. "But the simulated energy profiles match up pretty well. Anyway, the white hole

dumps power into the Sphere. The power shunt beams you
see there transfer that energy to the Longitudinal Generators.
The LGs focus that energy at the north and south poles of the
Sphere, and the gravity-control systems direct it outward to
control the Multisystem. You said yourself that it makes
sense for the lines of longitude to be gravity generators. If
they are, the poles are natural focus points. It only makes
sense that Charon Central would be there on the scene to
control the gravity power transmission.''

''But you have no imagery, no evidence, to support that
theory, do you?'' said Sianna. It was a statement, not a question.

''We have logic,'' Wally responded, now openly defensive. ''We have the behavioral evidence. The Sphere puts
out gravitic energy—it has to be produced somewhere, and
be transmitted from somewhere. Dr. Sakalov is extrapolat-
ing from known Charonian structures. We know they tend to
stay close to the same designs a lot. COREs are a lot like the
Landers they saw in the Solar System. He's taken the Amalgams and scaled them up to match what we know of the
Sphere.''

''First off,'' Sianna said, ''the Solar System Amalgams
received gravity power transmitted by the Lunar Wheel.
You have super-Amalgams *transmitting* power. Second, the
Solar System Amalgams were a few tens of kilometers high
at most. You've got *these* things at least, what, a thousand
klicks high? But even past that, I don't like your logic.
Amalgam Creatures exist elsewhere, therefore giant Amalgams exist here? We feel they must exist, therefore they do?
Come on, Wally. Do you really think that any of this makes
sense? It's right up there with epicycles.''

''What are epicycles?''

''A good lesson in why facts can't follow from theory.
The philosophers and astronomers before Copernicus had
this whole crazy system worked out with the planets and the
Sun and the stars orbiting Earth in perfectly circular orbits,
because the circle is the perfect form.''

"But the planets don't—"

"Of course they don't. They move in ellipses. But when the theory first got trotted out, no one really knew that. As the instruments got better, people started to notice the orbits weren't perfect circles. So they decided that the planets orbited in small circles that were centered on the big circle of their main orbit, like the Moon going around and around the Earth without the Earth being there."

Sianna stopped herself for a moment. Something about the Moon going around an Earth that wasn't there, something she could not quite put her finger on. It resonated with something. She blinked, came back to the moment, and went on with what she had been saying.

"Even that didn't match the observed movement perfectly," she continued, "so they decided the planets moved around the circle that was moving around their orbital path in *another* set of perfect circles, like a satellite going around the Moon while the Moon goes around the Earth—except with Earth *and* Moon not being there. I think they got up to four or five sets of epicycles."

"So what's your point?" Wally asked.

"My point is Sakalov's doing the same thing. The facts and his theories don't fit, so he changes the facts to fit the theories, adjusting reality to match his preconceived notions of how reality *should* be. Then when that doesn't fit, he changes the facts a little bit more, and a bit more. Everything here is one conjecture built on other."

Wally pointed at the image of the Sphere as it hung in mid-air. "Nothing in there contradicts anything we know," he said.

"That's not good enough," Sianna snapped back. "You can't present a theory on the basis of there being no evidence *against* it. Where's the evidence *for* it?"

"My dear, you are quite right," a new voice said. The voice was gentle and low, with just a hint of a cultured Russian accent. "We have not one bit of evidence."

Sianna gasped and spun around. Wally, standing by the

control panel, brought the house lights up a bit to reveal that two visitors had arrived. Two men. One of them Sianna did not recognize, but the other was none other than Dr. Yuri Sakalov. *Oh great,* Sianna thought. *There goes my career. How long has he been standing there?*

Dr. Sakalov and his companion stepped further into the room. "I must confess that I had thought of the parallels with epicycle theory myself," Sakalov said. "However, I am not lost and confused on account of theology, or a need to be proven right. We desperately need an answer—*any* answer we can find. It almost doesn't matter what question it answers. *Anything* would be a starting place. One right idea might be the key in the lock that sets us all free."

Sakalov looked thoughtfully at Sianna for a moment, and then turned his gaze toward the model of the Sphere. He was an elderly man, dressed in a rumpled worksuit, his hair silver-grey and pulled back in a rather old-fashioned-looking ponytail. His face was deeply lined, with sad, quiet eyes, a slightly bulbous nose, and an expressive mouth. He wore a small, neatly trimmed beard. There was a rather distracted air about him.

"I chose to focus on Charon Central," he went on, "because I believe that when we know where and what it is, and how it works, we will have that key in the lock. We will understand our enemies, and have some hope of defeating them. I believe that my new model has some real merit. It sounds as if you hold my previous ideas in low regard. Tell me, with the new idea—do you think I am grasping at straws?"

Sianna looked at the old man, her heart pounding with fear. *Sakalov.* Why did it have to be Sakalov? And who was that with him in the dark? His silent companion was standing in shadow, and it was hard to see much of him in the dim light. He was a younger man, blond-headed, his expression guarded. There was something rather severe about his whole demeanor. Suddenly she placed him, and she broke out into a cold sweat. Unless she was very much mistaken, he was

Wolf Bernhardt himself, head of the DSI, the man who wrote most of the checks that kept the Multisystem Research Institute going. One wrong word in front of *him* and—

"Miss Colette?" Dr. Sakalov asked.

"Um, ah . . . ah. I don't know what to say, doctor," she said, stalling for time.

"Surely you have some opinion. You were speaking most forcefully a moment ago."

Sianna swallowed hard and looked the old man in the eye. She battled back her fear, made herself look at the man and not the caricature of the doddering old eccentric she carried in her head. Maybe his ideas were wrong, even mad, maybe he was building castles in the air, but at least he was *trying* to make sense of it all. How many people his age—mercy, he must be at least a hundred—even tried that much, instead of sticking their heads in the sand and pretending everything was all right?

Sianna was used to the world as it was. For all the short years of her adolescence and young adulthood, humanity had been a hunted, threatened species, knowing itself to be hopelessly outmatched by an invincible opponent. But Dr. Sakalov had lived his whole life, up until his twilight years, in a Universe where humankind was unchallenged and alone. What must it have been like to see all that destroyed and brought low at the end of his days? What would it be like for an astronomer to have the night sky stolen from him?

Dr. Sakalov was asking for the truth, for her honest opinion. She had to give it to him. "Well, all right, yes sir," she said, struggling to keep her voice steady. "With all due respect, as best I can see, your only concrete reason for thinking Charon Central is at one of the poles seems to be that the longitudinal features meet up there." She hesitated a moment more, marshaling her thoughts, trying to find the proper words. "You, ah, ah, offer the theory that longitudinal lines are actually huge gravity generators. That's a reasonable assumption, and makes a lot of sense—but you have no *proof*. Building on that assumption, you make a series of completely unwarranted further assumptions about what it would mean *if* the longitudinal lines *were* gravitic generators, and based on *those*, you conclude Charon Central is at one of the poles. Your conclusion is based on pure conjecture, not proof."

Sakalov looked at Sianna, his expression dour and unreadable. "Go on," he said quietly.

Sianna wanted to shut up, but some part of her insisted on going on—and unfortunately, that part seemed to be controlling her mouth at the moment. "Well, ah, sir, you are working from extremely thin and highly circumstantial evidence," she said, "and I'm afraid you are stretching it well past its limits. I don't even see how this theory aids you in your goal. Even if Charon Central were where you say it was, how could we ever reach it? What could we do about it? How does this help us?"

Sakalov brought himself up to his full height and cleared his throat, a bit self-importantly. "The truth is not always convenient, young lady. I cannot decide *where* it would be convenient to place Charon Central, and then work backwards to the proof of the theory."

"But—" Sianna began, and then bit her tongue. Enough was enough.

"But what?" Bernhardt asked from the shadows, speaking for the first time.

Great. All she needed was to draw *him* into the argument. "Nothing," Sianna said, looking down at the floor.

"I am thinking you are having something more than nothing on your mind, dear miss, and I am thinking you had best tell me what it is," Bernhardt said, in a tone of voice that made it clear he expected an answer, not an evasion.

MRI folklore had it that Dr. Bernhardt's English took on a slightly German syntax when he was agitated, but Sianna would have been just as happy if she had never had the chance to confirm the story. Sianna tried to say something. Anything. "Ah . . . ah, well," she began, not quite sure where she was going.

"What more do you have to say, please?" Bernhardt asked, the courtesy of his words completely missing from his tone of voice.

Sianna realized her arms were wrapped around her chest, as if ready to shield her body from a blow. She put her arms at her sides, and then behind her back. She clamped her hands together so she wouldn't knot herself up in a pretzel again. She shut her eyes for a second, took a deep breath, and spoke, being careful to direct her words not at Bernhardt, but at the slightly less intimidating Dr. Sakalov. "Well, sir, before this, all your theories have been based on the idea that Charon Central was the absolute apex of the Charonian command hierarchy.

"You have worked from the assumption that you could derive a unique physical location that was ideally and uniquely suited to be Charon Central. Your theory was that the Charonians were utterly rational, and therefore the location of Charon Central could be established by entirely rational means. Each site would offer advantages and disadvantages, and the Charonians would balance all the pluses and minuses until they derived the optimal site."

Sakalov cocked his head to one side and nodded. "I am impressed that you have studied my work so well, but what of it? How does that invalidate my new approach?"

"Because—because—by the criterion of unique qualification, your new location for Charon Central cannot be right. A polar control center does not offer a single ideal location, but two equally valid ones. Where would it be? North pole, south pole, or both? And if one and not the other, what is your criterion for choosing?"

That brought a low chuckle, but not from Sakalov. Dr. Bernhardt stepped forward and patted the older man on the shoulder. "I think she has you there, Yuri," his voice far gentler than it had been. Bernhardt turned toward Sianna, and smiled, but the expression did not look as if it really belonged on his face. "I made exactly the same objection in my office not half an hour ago."

"And I make exactly the same answer to you both," Sakalov said. "There *is* a deciding variable that renders one more optimal. Charon Central is located on the south pole of the Sphere. More of the planets and Captive Suns are visible from that point than from any other on the Sphere."

"And that just happens to be the pole we won't see until the Earth and Sunstar complete another half-orbit around the Sphere, a small matter of a hundred years or so from now," Bernhardt said, still with that most artificial smile in place. It wasn't insincerity, Sianna decided. Bernhardt was just unused to smiling. Not that it mattered, but maybe if she focused on what sort of smile the man had, then she wouldn't be thinking about how this nice chat was destroying her career.

"That is inconsequential!" Sakalov protested. "All that is needed to prove my theory is to send the *Terra Nova* on a course that will bring the south pole into view and—"

"Yuri, Yuri. Do you know how many requests I get a *week* asking—or demanding—that I send the *Terra Nova* to this location or that?"

"But this is—"

"Most urgent and important," Bernhardt said, finishing Sakalov's sentence. "They all say that. Sometimes I think that if someone sent in a request and described it as minor and trivial, that would have a better chance of getting my attention."

"But you *must* listen—"

"Yes, yes, I know I must," Bernhardt said. "That is, after all, why I am here. For you to convince me. Convince me, and I will try and convince Captain Steiger to set such a course, though after today's news I warn you she will not be in much of a mood to listen."

"Today's news?" Sianna blurted out, instantly wishing she had kept her mouth shut. *Shut up, shut up, shut UP!* she told herself.

Bernhardt looked surprised, as if he had forgotten she and Wally were there—and perhaps he had. He looked from

Sianna to Wally and back again, and shrugged. "Well, you both have the standard clearances, no doubt, and the news will be all over MRI soon enough. The *Terra Nova* sent a small stealthy ship out in an attempt to board a CORE. All hands aboard the stealthship were lost and the ship destroyed. Captain Steiger broke radio silence to ask if we had any ideas that might aid their next attempt."

Sianna's blood ran cold. Never mind for the moment that she had no clearances at all—technically, she was not even supposed to be in the sim center. That was of no consequence. Those words *"next attempt."* Here they were, safely deep in the bowels of the Earth, fiddling around with meaningless questions of the whichness of what, asking each other where the enemy's imaginary fortresses might be—and people, real people, were dying out there, in battle against the real enemy.

MRI was nothing but a bunch of dreamy time-markers far below Manhattan, but the crew of the *Terra Nova* was asking *their* advice before sacrificing themselves anew.

If *that* didn't chastise a person, bring on a feeling of humility and unworthiness, then nothing would. "Do—do we have any advice to give them?" she asked.

"No," Bernhardt said, his voice quiet and sad. He let his answer hang there for a moment, and the brief silence spoke volumes to Sianna. *People are dying out there and we're letting them down.* She herself had gone in early, not to grub away at her proper work on CORE research, but to go glory-chasing after some completely meaningless thirty-seven-minute hiccup in a long-destroyed space probe's chronometer. And to compound the crime, she had been distracted from *that* nonsense by the even more foolish nonsense of Sakalov's pursuit of Charon Central.

At last Bernhardt spoke again. "But perhaps there is no need to say more about the *Terra Nova.* In any event, it's quite possible that they are safer in that ship than we are here. I think, Yuri, that perhaps it's time I showed you what I brought you here to see. I think you will see that the arrival of the SCOREs makes any discussion of what goes on at the Sphere a bit academic. We are going to have other worries.''

"SCOREs?" Sianna asked. She had heard the term go past once or twice, in the lab, but no one seemed ready or willing to explain what the acronym meant.

"Small Close-Orbiting Radar Emitters," Bernhardt said, a bit absently. "Hmmph. Wally, I was going to operate the equipment myself, but as long as you're here, if you could run that simulation of the SCOREs you did last week—''

"Yes, sir," Wally said. He bent over his control panel for a moment." Good God, Wally had been working with Dr. Bernhardt himself? Why hadn't he ever said anything about it? But Sianna knew the answer even before she was done asking herself the question. What Bernhardt said next confirmed it, even if it didn't make her feel any better.

"Needless to say, this is all top secret data," Bernhardt said. "If it gets out prematurely—''

"Ah, sir, excuse me," Sianna said. Better fess up now before she got in even deeper. "Sir, I don't have top secret clearance. I don't have *any* clearances."

Dr. Wolf Bernhardt swiveled his head about and regarded her for a full five seconds. "You don't," he said at last. "Most unfortunate, considering what you have heard already. What is your name, young lady?"

"Ah . . . Sianna Colette," she said, her heart pounding with fear. Oh God, what was he going to do with her?

"Wally—Mr. Sturgis. Can you vouch for this person?"

"Ah, yessir. I know her. She's okay," Wally said as he made his adjustments. From his tone of voice, Sianna knew that he wasn't paying all that much attention. He could have been talking about the weather—and Wally hadn't been outside for weeks.

"Very well, Miss Colette. You have top secret clearance *now*. I would suggest you read and obey the regulations, or else you might find yourself in some difficulty." That done, he cocked his head back towards Wally and the control panel. "Are you ready?"

''Yes, Dr. Bernhardt.''

''Then you may begin.''

—And the Universe of the Multisphere *shifted,* changed.

The Sphere itself vanished, and suddenly it was the Earth hanging in the blackness. The background stars and planets shifted their positions, and the perspective veered about until they were looking at Earth in half-phase, with the Sunstar out of view to the left. They were looking at the planet from a point a few thousand kilometers back along the planet's orbital path. Sianna could see tiny dots hanging in space all around the Earth, the COREs, guarding the planet against the deluge of skyjunk that filled the Multisphere.

The view pulled back, getting further and further from the planet. The Moonpoint Ring came into view to the right.

There was something odd about the background of the scene. Then Sianna realized what it was—there were stars visible. Not the Captive Suns and planets, though they were there too, but points of light hanging in the firmament. ''What are—''

''Those are the SCORES. Wally's enhanced them to make them visible, of course,'' Bernhardt said, his attention on the sim and not on Sianna. ''In reality, they are about as dark as lumps of coal, under one hundred meters across. Fairly bright in radar frequencies, once you know where to look. We had a hell of a time detecting them with our ground-based gear. *Terra Nova* hasn't been doing sky survey work, and she's missed them so far. NaPurHab just started watching for them. But once they get this data, you can bet they'll be looking for them. Wally, can you lose the Captives and the other objects we're not interested in?''

Suddenly the suns and planets vanished, and only the dots of light were left. Sianna noticed they seemed to be concentrated in one quadrant of the sky.

''How long ago is this image?'' Bernhardt asked.

''Ah, this is a real-time image,'' Wally said. ''Or close enough, really. Latest data from the automatic tracking systems. Enhanced and enlarged, of course, or we wouldn't be able to see anything at this scale.''

''Hmmph. Backtrack thirty days, speed up the time display by factor ten thousand, and move forward to the present time,'' Bernhardt said.

After a moment's pause, the image jumped and skewed as Wally set in the new commands. Then the three-dimensional ghosts of reality settled down. The Earth's rotation was obvious now, one day taking just over eight and half seconds. Sianna looked past the planet to the sky beyond.

Now the dots of light were smaller, dimmer, and spread out in a rough toroid of space that spanned half the sky.

But the images were moving, coming closer, converging, moving toward one point in the sky in front of Earth. The inner edges of the toroidal area converged on each other until the dots of light were moving in a loose, flattened spherical volume of space, following behind the ring. The tiny dots grew closer, brighter, and the ring moved in, still somewhat ahead of the smaller points of light.

Sianna stepped around to the Sunstar side of the simulation and watched it from there. Dozens, perhaps hundreds, of the things were moving in toward Earth. It took just under five minutes for the imagery to run up to the present moment and then stop dead at the real-time position. One thing was clear from watching the displays: the objects were moving, not toward Earth, but toward the Moonpoint Ring. What the devil did they want with the Ring?

''What are they?'' Sianna asked. ''Where do they come from?''

''As to the first, we don't know, though we have some unpleasant guesses,'' Bernhardt said. ''The detection teams that spotted them called them Small COREs, because that's what they look like and act like. That got shortened to SCOREs very quickly. As for why they come from where they do, I have an idea, but no proof. The SCOREs are too small to track easily much past the distance we have displayed here, but if you backtrack their course, they seem to come from a rough halo of space around the Sphere.

Roughly speaking, Earth is looking down at the north pole of the Sphere, and the rough halo suggests—''

''These were launched from facilities around the Sphere's equator,'' Sakalov said.

''Precisely. What that means, I don't know. Maybe they were launched from some sort of portals around the equator of the Sphere. Maybe they were launched from your south pole Charon Central site and moved Sphere-north from every point along the Sphere's circumference. We don't know. I might add that we have several indications that there are similar streams of SCOREs moving toward most of the Captive Worlds. We can't tell for sure, precisely because these objects are so hard to track and detect. But we have spotted some small objects that resemble these SCOREs moving toward some of the other Captives. In any event, there is tremendous new activity in the Multisystem. We have no idea why it should happen at this moment, but I doubt it is good news for Earth.''

Sianna noticed something. There was a different class of objects coming in ahead of the others. Wally had them color-coded red. She counted sixteen of them. ''What are those?'' she asked, pointing at them.

''They are different,'' Bernhardt said. ''Faster, larger, moving in a more direct path than the other ones. And they are rather complex in shape. We can't tell much more than that yet, but they are certainly not the simple oblong typical of most spacegoing Charonians.''

The director stepped around to the other side of the sim from Sianna and pointed at the larger objects. ''Note that these larger units seem to be leading the SCOREs in, moving a trifle faster,'' Bernhardt said. ''It would seem they must be in place first before, ah, other events.''

''Maybe they are a repair kit for the Moonpoint Ring,'' Sianna suggested.

The director frowned. ''An interesting thought. Better than anything else we've come up with. In any event, the SCOREs are likewise making for the Moonpoint Ring. We assume they are heading there for some sort of preparation or processing before they . . . well, before other events. Wally, run the images forward in time at the same rate, showing our best-guess projection.''

The ring and the SCOREs moved closer and closer to Earth. The larger objects arrived and merged, rather vaguely, with the image of the Moonpoint Ring. From that, Sianna gathered that the research teams were sure the big objects were headed for the Ring, but had no idea what they were going to do upon arrival.

''Ah, sir, NaPurHab orbits the black hole at the center of the Moonpoint Ring,'' Sianna said. ''What happens to it in all this?''

''We *think* its orbit should remain stable. But we don't know. We have of course notified the Purple leadership, and they will be watching, I assure you. There is still some time left before there is any possibility of danger.'' Bernhardt didn't seem much interested in the problem, as if he were more interested in something else than the thousands of people aboard the habitat. ''It's just about here that the first of the SCOREs will be visible to the amateur telescopes,'' he said. ''No hope of keeping the lid on it past then. We have between now and then to prepare for their—ah—arrival.''

Suddenly it dawned on Sianna. Calling them SCOREs had misled her—as perhaps it was meant to mislead the public. She had envisioned them merely as little brothers to the big COREs, taking up positions around the Earth.

But no, these were not COREs. Bernhardt thought they were invaders, attackers. This was the beginning of a Breeding Binge.

Breeding Binges had just been theory up to now, though there was a lot of evidence supporting the theory, much of it plainly visible on some of the closer Captive Worlds. Binges were the whole reason for the Multisystem. The Charonians needed planetary surfaces for breeding during one part of their life cycle.

The night before, she had stared at the ceiling, wondering

when the Breeders would come and make use of the Earth. Now she knew.

Her mind was racing, her body bathed in fear sweat. Time started up again in the simulation, and the SCOREs and the large objects moved in toward Earth and the Moonpoint Ring. The SCOREs—the invaders, the Binge Breeders— came in, did a close pass around the Moonpoint Ring, and then turned toward Earth. They came closer and closer, reached the planet—and disappeared. For one crazy moment, Sianna felt a wave of relief. She gasped, and realized she had been holding her breath. They would vanish. Everything would be all right. She had imagined the Binge Breeders landing, crashing, tearing into the landscape, but no, it was going to be all right.

"We can't show the damage or the ground action in a space-based simulation, of course," Bernhardt said. "But it will be severe. Wally, you're still working on the ground sims?"

"Yes, sir," Wally said. "Course, the infosets are pretty vague. I won't be able to give you much detail, and some of it's going to be speculative."

"I am sure it will be up to your usual high standards," the director said.

Sianna shut her eyes and cursed herself for an idiot. Of course. At this scale, with Earth the size of a basketball, what would there be to see? But of course the disaster would still come.

"So it's finally going to happen," Sakalov said. "I had been hoping I wouldn't live to see it."

"We'll all live to see the *start* of it," said Bernhardt. "You've seen the images from the Solar System, what just a handful of Charonians were able to do to Mars. These SCOREs are a different type of Charonian, of course, and they will probably behave quite differently.

"But I have no doubt they will do quite a bit of damage. The Charonians hunted our world down, and brought it back here, to the Multisphere, to their larder. Now they are ready to dine. They will land on Earth, and breed, and breed and breed and breed. They could wreck the planetary ecosphere completely. We can see other Captive Worlds where that has happened. Even if things don't go that badly, they could still do some very serious damage.''

"So what do we do?" Sianna asked.

Wolf Bernhardt looked at her, then at Wally and at Dr. Sakalov. "First, we do all we can to resupply NaPurHab and the *Terra Nova*. We launch as many loads of spares and equipment at them as we can. If Earth is severely enough damaged, it is possible that *they* will be all there is left of us. We must do all we can to make sure they are in as good condition as possible. Then we use the interceptor missiles and the ground attack forces and all the other weapons we have built against this day," he said. "We shoot down as many of them as we can, and kill as many of them as we can on the ground. Maybe we can drive back the first wave, and maybe the Charonians will conclude Earth is not a good place for a Breeding Binge. But I have no doubt that, if it chooses to do so, Charon Central can keep sending SCOREs—Breeders— long after our defenses are overwhelmed. And then the Breeders will land, and go about their business.

"And as to what we do then—I haven't the faintest idea, except for one thing." Wolf Bernhardt put his hands in his pockets, looked toward the simulation, and let out a deep sigh. "I expect," he said, "that a lot of us will die."

Nine

Death of the Past

"There are times when I don't much mind being called a Leftover—but other times when I find it bloody infuriating. Why mark *me* out because I was one of the ones left behind? Haven't we all lost someone? Is there anyone in the Solar System who didn't lose someone, or some part of their past, when Earth vanished? And is there a single one of you lot who wasn't lost *by* someone back on Earth?

"And if you *weren't* lost to someone, if there is no one on the other side who cares a sausage for you, then dearie, I feel sorry for you."

> —Dr. Selby Bogsworth-Stapleton, letter to the editor, *Lunar Times,* May 3, 2431

Aboard the *Terra Nova*
Deep Space
THE MULTISYSTEM

Gerald MacDougal, second-in-command of the *Terra Nova,*
lay awake in his bunk, staring at the overhead bulkhead. He
knew he should be trying to sleep, but this was one night
when sleep would not come.

Gerald missed his wife.

Marcia. He could turn over on his side and look at her picture, taped on the bulkhead next to his bed, but there was no
need. He had spent endless hours in the last five years staring at that photo. It was the only one of her that he had, and it
was his most prized possession.

It was a quite ordinary flat photo, no three-dee, no animation. She smiled out at the camera, her two elbows resting on
the picnic table, with her chin balanced on the palms of her
hands, her long fingers hidden under her frizzy black hair,
though the tip of her left index finger peeked through, just by
her ear.

Her dark brown eyes were half-hidden by her bangs, but
they shone with love and happiness. She was grinning, ear to
ear, gleaming white teeth showing, with one tooth just a little
crooked, and a tiny little scar on one cheek where she had
caught a chip of flying rock in some childhood accident,
before she had escaped Tycho Purple Penal.

No, he didn't have to look at the picture.

She had been off-planet when the Abduction struck,
working at the VISOR station orbiting Venus, while he
worked on his own projects back on Earth. Even then, they
had been forced to settle for video messages sent from so far
away the speed-of-light delay made conversation impossible. Back then, that distance seemed impossibly wide. Now,
it seemed trivial. What were a few tens or hundreds of millions of kilometers, compared to the unknown number of
light-years between them now?

At last he did turn his gaze toward the picture, but he was

seeing through it, rather than looking at it. How had five-plus years changed her? Had her hair gone grey? Were there a few more laugh lines around her eyes?

He didn't even want to contemplate the other disasters that might have befallen her. One of the last messages relayed by the *Saint Anthony* had confirmed that Marcia had survived at least *that* long, and to know that much was a great blessing. Gerald offered a silent prayer of thanks for that. Many aboard ship, and back on Earth, had no way of knowing if their loved ones in the Solar System had survived the disaster. All they knew was that the much smaller population of the Solar System had suffered more casualties than all of Earth.

But what of the five years since? He believed firmly, because he had to, that she still lived—but suppose she did not? Suppose she had died five minutes after sending that last message? Suppose she was dying *now*, this moment, while he lay here, safe and warm, and he did not know?

He calmed himself. No. She lived. He *knew* that. He had always felt that he would *know* if she died. He would be able to feel it, and never mind the distance and the logical impossibility of the idea. He could *feel* her being alive, the way he could feel his own heart beating. He would know if she died, the way he would know if his right arm were cut off.

But what of himself? Dear God, how had five years changed *him?* How much had *he* aged? Five years cooped up in this oversized tin can—he had gained weight, lost muscle tone. That happened in space, no matter how much one exercised. And what about his soul, his spirit? Had five years of fruitless effort and failure soured him, embittered him? He did not believe so, but there was no way to tell.

He swung his feet around to the floor and sat up in bed. Enough. It was foolish to think that he was so changed that she would no longer love him, no longer be attracted to him. He had more faith in her—and confidence in himself—than that. But, still, he did not want to be a *disappointment* to her.

And she would be disappointed indeed to see him moping

around in his quarters. There was work to be done. Even if the launch had been delayed for the time being, the second stealthship, the *Highwayman*, still needed to be prepared for its flight, prepared for the next attempt on a CORE. He got up, left his cabin, and made his way down toward the flight deck. There were stores to check, systems to test, hardware to inspect.

Gerald, of course, took a special interest in preparing the *Highwayman*.

He was going to command her. No matter how much Dianne Steiger protested, he was going to be aboard the little ship.

Gerald MacDougal had had his fill of sending others out to die. He would go himself, next time.

And would hope that Marcia would understand, and forgive him.

Multisystem Research Institute
New York City
EARTH

Sianna made her way back to the Main Ops building and her cubicle, sat down in her chair, leaned back and sighed. What a bloody disaster of a morning! The news from Bernhardt was bad by itself, but that was only part of it. She had wasted the morning and made a fool of herself in front of the big boss. The fate of the planet, the idea of universal doom, was a bit too much to deal with. The excellent odds that she would get fired seemed a little closer to home, a bit more tangible, plenty all by itself to bring on the storm clouds.

She might as well give up on the day before depression, guilt, and frustration had their chance to feed on each other.

With a supreme effort of will, she stood up, shoved her chair in behind her desk, and left.

Sianna made her way aboveground without even being aware of the elevator's terrors. She stepped out into the bright June sunshine, blinking miserably at the perfect robin's-egg blue sky. She trudged home, unaware of the fresh, clean smell in the air and the playful little breezes that chased each other around the city streets. She dragged herself home to her apartment building, aware of little more than being miserable.

How much worse a morning could it possibly have been? she asked herself as she waited for the elevator. The elevator arrived. She got in and rode to her floor. She stepped out of it to clomp down the hallway to her apartment.

Incredible that she had started the day with her subconscious hinting that she was on the verge of a discovery, a breakthrough! She had actually thought that Wally—Wally—was going to inspire her. So much for the subconscious. *Wally* telling her something that would unlock the doors to the knowledge hidden inside her? The only real piece of new, solid, information *he* offered up was that a silly little worldlet orbited the Sphere all by itself. She might as well wait for her toaster to reveal the secrets of the Universe.

To hell with it. She reached the door to her apartment, and waited the infuriating ten seconds it took for the door to recognize her, unbolt, and open up. Damned-fool old-fashioned door. When was the landlord going to install something that didn't take all day to let her in?

At last the door came open, and she flounced her way into the apartment. She marched straight to her room, hurled her handbag down onto the floor, and flung herself at the bed, landing with a satisfyingly loud if muffled thud.

If only she could learn to grow up. Or maybe the trouble was that she already *had* grown up, and was forever doomed to retain all the foolishness of childhood. Sometimes it seemed to her that the foolishness was all that remained of her—as if she were the Cheshire Cat, and her foolish smile was lasting quite a while after the rest of her—career hopes, academic standing, maturity—had faded away.

She frowned, shook her head, and hugged her arms

around her pillow, burying her face in it.

Suddenly, two other images popped into her head, quite unbidden. Epicycles, as she herself has described them—*like a satellite going around the Moon while the Moon goes around the Earth—except the Earth* and *Moon aren't there.* And the Sphere, the Sphere as she had first seen it in Wally's simulation, glowing red, a huge thing with stars and worlds in orbit about it; the Sphere's circumference bigger around than Earth's old orbit—

Sianna spun around until she was lying on her back, staring at the pulsequake cracks in the ceiling. Her lips moved silently. Her heart started to pound. Suddenly she sat bolt upright in bed.

She had it. She had it. *She knew.* In half a minute she was out the door, headed back toward the lab. She had to find Wally and get to work on this.

Sianna paced eagerly up and down the sim room, rubbing her hands together. She had it. She *knew* she had it. If there were ever a moment in her life where she knew the right answer, this was it.

Wally fed the last of Sianna's instructions into the simulator system and stared at his setup screens. "Well, it's all in there," he said. "Now what?"

Sianna stopped in her pacing at the far side of the room from Wally, then turned and faced him. "Throw it up on the main display system," she said. "Show it to me. Give me a minute-a-year time rate, starting ten years ago."

The room darkened, and the Solar System appeared. Not the Multisystem, but Earth's own *home* system, the way it had been before the Charonians. Sianna stepped out into the midst of the worlds, marveling at their tiny perfection. Wally had set the system to run in enhanced imagery mode, the planets and other bodies scaled up, made larger and brighter so they were easy to see. Even so, the worlds were little things, delicate jewels set in a vast, velvet darkness.

All was as it should be, all was as it had been and was no

longer. The nine worlds orbited the gleaming Sun, the dust motes of the asteroids moved in their myriad paths in the emptiness between Mars and Jupiter. Comets hovered in the outer depths of the Oort Cloud. Pluto hung in the outer reaches of the system, with his moon Charon still in attendance.

The Ring of Charon, the only human-made object large enough to be visible in this scale, was there, a wheel in space wrapped around the circumference of Charon. It looked like an oversized wedding band with a black ball floating at its center. There was Jupiter with all his moons, and his Red Spot, and his modest rings. There was Saturn, with that grand and gaudy ring system, and Mars with both moons.

All the planets still had the satellites and ring systems they were supposed to have. All was well.

Except that it wasn't, of course. The Lunar Wheel slumbered in the depths of the Moon, and soon it was to awaken. Sianna had not realized how hard it was going to be to watch it all happen again. Even in a simulator, even in pursuit of a breakthrough, there was nothing pleasurable in watching the disaster all over again.

One year a minute, starting ten years back. Sianna turned and found the Earth, close in by the Sun, the Moon wheeling steadily about the blue-white marble that floated in the darkness. There, on that world, ten years ago, she had been growing up, perhaps just a little too fast. She imagined a submicroscopic nine-year-old version of her self back in a miniature France on the simulated world in front of her. She remembered being teased by the other children over her funny name and its funnier spelling, desperately hoping her mother's job in America would come through and Sianna could move away from the cruel taunts.

A year a minute, and the tiny Earth swung once around the Sun. A ten-year-old with frizzy hair, skinned knees, and easily hurt feelings learned that children in New York, children everywhere, could be cruel—but also learned that she was brave enough to endure it, and that in enduring the taunts came acceptance.

Another minute, and a second year went past, and a third, and Sianna remembered kissing a boy for the first time. A tall, gawky boy with a forgotten name and a half-remembered, sharp-featured face. It shocked her that she could not bring his name to mind. Her whole world had revolved about him! Now all she could remember about him was the kiss itself, out on the hill behind the school, and the clumsy, tingly, exciting feel of it all. For some reason, she associated a distinct smell of butterscotch with the event, though she couldn't imagine why.

She smiled to recall that gentle moment in her confused adolescence, the mad crush she had had on the boy, the silly romance they had shared for an eyeblink-short span of spring days. It was all over in real life nearly as fast as she imagined the time rushing past on the simulated miniature Earth.

Four minutes, four years gone by, and the Sianna-that-was on the miniature Earth was discovering a larger world than boys and giggling, was looking up at the busy night sky and wondering if perhaps there was a place in it for her.

She was starting to plan, to think, to map out what she imagined was a sensible route through life. Left too much on her own by her always-working parents, never quite sure where she stood with them, thirteen-year-old Sianna had set out to put *everything* in its proper place. Her room was always neat, her homework always perfect, her world always in order. She had worked out her future as well, in relentless detail. She would go to this school, get that degree, work at this job, meet and marry that sort of man, have this number of children by that age.

Sianna shook her head, remembering, marveling at the sensible, orderly, rigid future she had worked out for herself. Looking back from here, from just a few years on, it all seemed so silly. Even if the Charonians had not come, if everything hadn't changed, *no* life could be mapped out that tidily. You couldn't always do what was sensible. More often you just worked with what you had, dealt with the situation in front of you. Even if you were a Charonian.

The mini-Earth swung round the imaginary Sun in its comfortable orbit, making something like its four billion, seven hundred and fifty millionth revolution about the Sun. Its last revolution. Sianna stood there in the dark, watching, remembering, knowing what was about to happen, crying in the darkness for the loss she was about to watch.

Four and a half, five minutes, four and a half years gone by, and her parents were happy and well, though perhaps not as attentive as other kids' parents. Both of them had always been more intent on their work than their child. Always friendly, always there with a smile, and maybe even a brief hug or a pat on the arm, but somehow never very approachable. They never had time *now,* but they would make it up to her later. Except the Charonians came, and they could never, ever, make it up to her.

Five minutes. Five years. She glanced at the time-date display, and knew it was about to start. "Slow up here, Wally," she said. "A minute a day here."

The planets slowed abruptly, and time seemed to freeze for a moment before Sianna could detect the motion in the slowed-down rhythms. *Now,* she told herself. *Just about now.*

Wally had programmed the gravity beams to appear as bright red lines, even though they were as invisible as gravity in real life. A slash of red light stretched out across the darkness, reaching from Pluto, from the Ring of Charon. The first test beams, sent to all of the major test facilities on the inner planets and moons.

At the time and distance scales Wally was using, a light beam took long minutes to cross the long reaches of space from Pluto and Charon to the inner worlds. The Ring of Charon had fired ten-minute pulses at each of the inner worlds.

"Slow down again," Sianna whispered. She had to see

this, understand it perfectly. "Give me a minute per hour."

Again the display slowed, and again time seemed to stop before moving on more slowly. Now blood-red spears of light, each ten light-minutes long, were moving down into the Solar System from the Ring of Charon. One to Saturn's moon Titan, then to Jupiter's Ganymede, then Mars and Venus. The spears of light touched each world in turn, harmlessly, undetectable save by the most sophisticated of gravity-wave detectors. Now all the beams, all but the last, had struck. "Normal rate time now, Wally," Sianna whispered.

Sianna looked down on the shining blue-white globe of Earth, clouds and sea and sky shining, glitter-bright. Somewhere down on that perfect miniature she could imagine that it was just past noon on a perfect June day. She knew where she had been when it happened. Everyone did. Down there, Sianna and her friends were just going outside to have lunch in the school quadrangle, chattering away about how many days of school were left until vacation, what to wear to school next day, how to get the calculus homework done. They were just reaching the crest of the hill when it happened. It was not until much later that she learned where her parents had been, but now she could visualize it all so perfectly that it was almost as if she had been with them, as well. There, down on that tiny jewel of a world, her parents were just about to meet for lunch at one of their favorite spots. A restaurant in a four-hundred-year-old brownstone, probably constructed long before anyone had even thought about building codes.

Time seemed to slow again, but this time it had nothing to do with Wally adjusting the controls. *This* was the moment that changed it all, the instant that made Sianna what she was, that changed the life of every human being.

The last spear of light reached for Earth, touched it, brushed past it and hit the Moon. And inside the Moon the Lunar Wheel awoke. A disk of blue-white something/nothing appeared between Earth and Moon, swept toward the planet—and Earth was gone. The blue-white disk vanished.

That was that. Earth was gone.

"That's all we have from direct observation for what happened back in the Solar System, Sianna," Wally said, his voice quiet and reserved. "From here on in, it's all conjectures and best guesses, and a little bit of hard information from the *Saint Anthony* data."

"Right, Wally."

That was the end of what they *knew* happened in the Solar System, because that was the last moment when Earth was *in* the Solar System. Earth was gone from the simulation now, just as she had vanished from the Solar System in reality. *The Solar System.* Think about what happened there, not about what happened to Earth.

Don't think about the way the restaurant building collapsed in the pulsequakes, or how no one found them for days. Don't think that the sight of that blue-white wall of *something* falling down out of the sky again and again, or about the mad things that happened to the sky afterward— the sky turning to blood, then night turning to day and back again, or the chaotic reports flooding in from all over of spacecraft and habitats gone missing and crashing, of panic and death, fear and disaster everywhere—

No. Stop. Do not think about it. Do not think at all. Observe. Absorb. She shut her eyes and settled herself down before she faced the next step. *Focus on the Solar System. We've always thought about* our *situation—but what about* their *situation?* "Go to a ten-seconds-a-day time scale and give me the best-guess display of what happened next," she said, keeping her voice steady as she could. The rubble of that restaurant—No. Don't think about it.

"Okay," Wally said. "From here on in we're guessing."

Time flashed back into high gear. The Moon, bereft of the Earth's gravitational anchoring, wobbled for a time, and then restabilized as the Multisystem sent the Earthpoint Singularity, to anchor the Moon in its old orbit a black hole of almost precisely the Earth's mass, and to provide a transit point for the invaders that were on the way. In Wally's sim, the Earthpoint Singularity, invisible in real life, showed as a ruby-red pinpoint of light.

Meanwhile, even before their allies came through Earthpoint, the Charonians in the Solar System gave up more of their secrets. Landers that had slept for thousands or millions of years, camouflaged as asteroids, started moving out from the Asteroid Belt and the distant Kuiper Belt and Oort Cloud, shown in the display as dimmer points of red.

The Charonian Landers swarmed out across the Solar System, heading toward all the major worlds and attacking them. Landers from the Multisystem starting coming through Earthpoint, streaming to the attack everywhere—everywhere except the Moon.

She needed to see better. "Okay, Wally. Magnify planet and satellite images by a factor of five hundred." Mars, Jupiter, Venus, all the worlds were suddenly huge, with vivid detail plain to see. Chaos boiled everywhere. A dust cloud started to form around Mars. Jupiter's Red Spot started to churn. Saturn's rings disintegrated. Then, out at the edge of the Solar System, something strange started to happen. Charon shrank away to nothing, and then Pluto started to collapse in on itself. The Ring of Charon crushed one world, then the other, swallowing them up to form a human-controlled black hole with the power to strike back—at least once—at the invaders. Planet and satellite vanished, their place taken by a ruby-red spot of light at the centerpoint of the Ring.

"How sure are we on this?" Sianna asked, gesturing toward the image of the new Plutopoint black hole. Even just looking at it made her feel a little bit queasy, a little bit soiled. There was something fundamentally *wrong,* indecent, about destroying a world, no matter how great the necessity.

"The computers put the probability at over ninety-five percent, but I'd say that's on the low side. *Something* back in the Solar System developed enough power to kick a massive jolt of gravity power through the Lunar Wheel and on through it to the Moonpoint Ring here in the Multisystem.''

Wally worked the controls and expanded the image of the Ring until it was five meters top to bottom, spinning smoothly around the angry red eye at its center. His voice was deep and thoughtful, as if this were one of the few realities he had faced—perhaps because the way he could face was it in a simulator. "Over the years I've run, a—a *million* sims of what must have happened back there," he said.

"And it had to be this way?" Sianna asked. "No other choice?"

Wally shut his eyes and nodded—his way of emphasizing a point. He opened them again and pointed at the blood-red image of the black hole. "Unless they learned how to spin a massless black hole somehow—and I don't think they could have—then, well, the *only* way to punch that much power through would be by drawing on at *least* a Pluto's worth of mass in a black hole. Dr. Sakalov says that might be conservative. *He* thinks they might have been forced to pull in some of the Neptunian moons as well. But I don't think they would have had time to do that. Things were moving fast—and the—the System was in pretty bad shape by then. Hard to do *anything.*''

"But God Almighty," Sianna protested, "what a thing to do! They smashed a *world,* a four-billion-year old *world,* just to save a bunch of over-brainy apes from being eaten."

"No," Wally said, a bit sharply. Clearly he had thought about this for a while. The hesitation was gone from his voice. "Saving themselves—saving the only species with our kind of intelligence that we know of—that was reason enough to do it. But they had better reasons than that." He walked over to the simulator controls and brought the imagery back to its previous state, with enlarged images of the worlds hanging in their correct relative positions. "They did it to save all of this. If the people in the Solar System hadn't stopped them, the Charonians would have taken Pluto apart anyway. They had to sacrifice one planet, and one satellite, to save all the rest."

"If they *did* manage to save them," Sianna said.

Wally nodded sadly. "We're just guessing at that. For all we know, the Solar System Charonians didn't die, and there's nothing left back there at all. We *think* they fought them off, but there's—there's no way to be sure," Wally replied. He seemed about to say something more, but then he stopped himself. Sianna nodded sadly. What more was there to say?

"I know," she said. Strange to hear Wally saying such things. But he was, after all, a human being. How could any living person *not* brood about such things now and again? Even Wally had to look outside himself once in a while. "No one ever likes to think about that—but it's exactly that possibility that I want to look at. That's why we're here right now. To look at . . . at that. At the Solar System dying."

"Huh? Why?"

"Because I think there are some answers there, in the way it would have died. The way it might have died," Sianna said. "I *know* there are."

Ten

Do It Yourself

"In the most cold-blooded analysis, and speaking on a purely logical level, without reference to theology or philosophy, life is not reasonable. Life does not make any sense. It has no purpose other than its own perpetuation.

"The only purpose of life is more life, a fact which does not seem to bother us—though one would think it might. We mock organizations whose only purpose seems to be their own survival. We are offended by makework projects which seem to accomplish nothing beyond keeping workers working. We are scandalized when some opportunistic person shoves a fellow creature aside in order the reach for the main chance.

"How is it then, in the grander scheme of things, that we are not bothered that the only reason for making babies is to make more babies as a way of making more babies after that? Why are we not upset to see a mother determined to protect her family at any and all costs to others, as well as to herself? How many otherwise immoral acts are excused because they are for the sake of a child?

"The answer, of course, is that we know life must perpetuate itself, at all cost, for if it fails to do so, all is lost. This is our most basic instinct. No living thing could survive without this knowledge embedded in its every gene. . . .

". . . Life must live off life, which is to say it must live off death. Even the most gentle of vegetarian species lives by killing and eating plants. Life's perpetuation, its renewal, and acts of creation, are of necessity exactly balanced by acts of destruction."

—Gerald MacDougal, *Aspects of Life,* MRI Press, 2429

Multisystem Research Institute
New York City

"All right, then," Sianna said. "You're in charge, Wally. Start from where we left off and assume the Charonians won. Take apart the whole damn Solar System and build me a Dyson Sphere, a Multisystem. I want to see how it's done."

"But, um, ah . . . I don't know if I have the simulation routines to—"

"Then we'll write new routines," Sianna said, cutting him off. "I'm near the *answers*, Wally. Damned near. If things break the way I think they will, then"—she paused to choose her words—"then all sorts of things might be possible."

Wally blinked at her, a bit owlishly, and then nodded. "Okay," he said. "What do you want the sim results to be?"

There! *That* was the question that had crippled them for so long. Not *what are the results,* but *what do you want the results to be?* That mindset, and a distinct reluctance to consider the possibility of ultimate, final disaster in the Solar System, were the two reasons no one had seen the answer.

"I want the sim to do whatever *it* wants to do," she said. "Reset to the moment the Lunar Wheel woke up. Factor out all human interference, and let's see what the Charonians would do with the cards they were dealt."

In that sense, at least, the Charonians were like everyone else. They had to work with what they had; not deal with what was logical, but with the available Universe.

That was the point that everyone missed. Sakalov viewed them as supremely logical beings, and maybe they were. But the Charonians did not live in a logical or rational Universe—and they did not spring from nowhere. Like every other life-form—if you considered them a life-form—they had evolved. There seemed little doubt that they had directed their own evolution, but all the same, the current form had to keep itself alive while it was on its way to creating the new one. Whales still had toe bones. Birds still had lizard feet. You used the structures you had and modified them.

And if one thing was certain about the Charonians, it was that they had not always been what they were now. Sometime, somehow in the past, creatures had built starships, filled them with the lifecode, the DNA equivalent, of the life from the home world and sent the starships out into space. But the starships had the ability to modify their cargo of living beings, and they had taken over. Life served machinery instead of machinery serving life, until the two merged into one. The end result of that was the strange complex webs of interdependent beings that humans called Charonians.

Coming into the Universe tends to leave some scars. Humans had belly buttons. Sianna was very close to certain she knew what Charonians had.

"Think like a Charonian," Sianna said, going over to where Wally was working. "You've got the whole Solar

System for raw materials, and you want to build a Dyson Sphere. How would you go about doing it?''

Wally looked thoughtful. ''What sort of assumptions do I make?''

''No assumptions. Just aim for the end result of a Sphere like the one here. Just do your best guess,'' Sianna said.

''But what about—''

''Just make it up as you go along,'' Sianna said. She didn't want to say as much to Wally, but she was relying more on his hunches and guesses and instincts than the results of deliberate thought. Sometimes, when he tried too hard, Wally thought like a regular person. Sianna was half-hoping that the way he looked at the world when he worked at his own level would be closer to the Charonian viewpoint. Not that she could say any of *that,* of course. ''You've been doing these sims right along. Do it by feel. Take the tools that make the most sense to you.''

''Okay, then,'' Wally said, leaning back in his chair. ''I have a lot of stuff in the data library, and a bunch of ideas I never had a chance to try out. You understand I'll have to do a lot of guessing. We don't know how the Charonians do a lot of things.''

''Like what?''

''Ah, well, for starters, they must have some way to do easy, efficient, straightforward matter transmutation. That's the big thing,'' he said. ''Hydrogen and helium make up something like ninety percent of the Solar System. They'd *have* to be able to turn hydrogen and helium into other elements. We'll just have to do a black box on that. Let's see. We'll need some Charonian forms we haven't seen yet. Sphere constructors, transporters, energy collectors. Probably some sort of interim structures along the way. . . .''

Wally kept talking, but his voice got lower and less distinct until he was just muttering to himself, and Sianna could not follow it. But he was caught up in the spirit of the thing, and that was all that mattered. Once Wally got his teeth into a problem, he did not let it go.

Suddenly the interior of the Sim Center chamber began to shift and change, slowly at first, but then with greater and greater violence. The darkened room flared into glaring light. The images of the planets turned ghostly pale, then transformed into ghostly white wire balls, mere schematics rather than true images. Wally was conserving processing power, doing bare-bones imaging while he set up. Then the wire balls began to shift position, zipping and flashing across the darkened sky as Wally brought the setup to where he wanted it. Sianna found herself ducking, a bit too late, as the wireframe image of Jupiter skimmed across the room—and right through her.

"Okay," Wally said, clearly talking to himself, "we'll need places to store and process raw materials, and, ah, transmuters, and transporters, and oh, let's see . . ." His voice started to take on a strange enthusiasm, and an odd little gleam came into his eye. Sianna had asked him to play God, and it was obvious he liked the idea.

Strange shapes, changing and evolving, appeared in the air around Sianna, and then vanished before they completed themselves. Wally was trying out ideas, scenarios, procedures half in his head and half in the sim chamber. It was all most disconcerting.

But then quite suddenly, it all stopped, and the room dropped into total darkness. "Okay," Wally's voice announced from the midst of the utter blackness. "I think I have it. At least a first-draft idea, anyway. Here we go."

The room remained in darkness for a moment. Then the planets reappeared, moving fast enough that even Saturn's motion was visible. Sianna checked the time display—Wally had gone back to the moment the Lunar Wheel had awakened, and was running the system at a year every thirty seconds. At that speed, the individual Charonians were barely visible, little more than a hazy cloud about each of the planets. But Sianna could see the results of their handiwork quite plainly.

The planets were coming apart at the seams, dissolving

before her eyes as the Charonians tore up the worlds and hurled their component matter out into free space. The Lunar Wheel, hidden deep inside the Moon, commanded the operation, sending out stabbing bolts of gravity power for the other Charonian forms to absorb. The time display rolled forward at a frantic pace, quickly sweeping past the time when the Solar System had managed to stop the Charonians—or at least the moment where everyone *hoped* they had been stopped.

The pace of destruction accelerated as more and more Charonians poured through the wormhole links. The smaller and then the larger satellites of the gas giants evaporated. Mars was the first planet to go, shredded away until its component mass was nothing but a cloud of dust and rubble. One by one, the rest of the worlds of the Solar System followed suit, ground down to nothing. At last, even Jupiter wasn't there anymore, the king of the planets reduced to a cloud of gas and dust. All the worlds were gone. All but the Moon. *All but the Moon—the Moon, where the Lunar Wheel lived.*

"Okay," Wally said. "From here on in it's all totally hypothetical. We know that once the Landers were on the ground, they came together, kinda merged into larger Amalgam Creatures. I figure the Charonians would just keep going with that idea. Once the worlds are torn up, the Amalgams would merge together and form black box monsters."

"Black box monsters?"

"Huh? Oh, you haven't hung out in the theory bull sessions, I guess. Well, the things would be huge—maybe a hundred, two, three hundred kilometers across. That's what I call a monster. And a black box—you know, a machine where you know *what* it does but not *how* it does it. If the Charonians want to use the debris fields that used to be the planets, they have to be able to collect that matter, transmute it into whatever elements and materials they will need, and then form those up into, ah, well, call 'em Sphere modules. Sections of the Sphere's skin, structural support, that sort of thing. Anyway, I've just sorta guessed at what the BBMs for a given job would look like. Here, I'll do an enlargement on a cluster of them. Lemme slow down the time rate and zoom in a bit so you can see what's going on.''

A cluster of tiny dots near Mars' old orbit suddenly started to grow, swelling up until they filled half the sim chamber. The BBMs were huge, complex, malevolent-looking things. They looked like clusters of pyramidical Amalgam Creatures stuck together into various shapes.

One of them was sucking in matter from the surrounding debris field—debris that had once been Mars—and extruding it in the form of long, flattened sheets. No doubt, at least in this simulation, those sheets would one day be the outer skin of the Solar System Dyson Sphere.

Sianna felt that knot in her stomach again. Suppose they had all talked themselves into the notion that their kith and kin back home were still alive? Suppose what she was seeing here was what was really happening back there?

Don't think about it. Don't think. As the sheets of Sphere skin came out of the thing that was making them, another breed of Charonian was grappling the sheets and hauling them away.

"It's all guesswork," Wally said. "We've never seen these forms. But they'd have to have *some* sort of creatures to do these things. Maybe they have more than one type. One to transmute, and one to take the transmuted matter and form it up as needed. Or maybe—God knows how—they've found some way to sidestep transmutation and do it all on the, ah, *chemical* level rather than the atomic one. So they could build superstrong molecules out of hydrogen and helium and trace amounts of the other elements. But somehow or another, they have to take the raw material of the planets and rework it into the components of the Sphere."

"Fine, Wally, fine. Now, keep it going, Wally," Sianna said. "What happens next?"

"Well, once you have the transmuters—or whatever—up and running, it's a question of getting the material to where the Sphere is going to be. And you'd need a hole spinner."

"A what?"

"Well, the Lunar Wheel provided all the gravity power to the other Charonians in the system—but it didn't *generate* any of that power, as best we can tell. It was a conduit for gee power being transmitted by its parent sphere, here in the Multisystem. And we know the Charonians use a lot of black holes—for wormhole transport, to keep tidal stresses balanced, to generate power, all that kind of stuff. Sooner or later, the Lunar Wheel is going to need to make its own power, and build its own holes."

"But there isn't enough mass in the Solar System to create a new Sphere and make black holes of any size."

"Right. But do you really need mass? In theory, with enough energy to throw around, you can create a massless black hole—a virtual black hole—basically by shoving enough power down into a singularity. *We* have no idea how to do it—but we aren't the Charonians. Either they are stealing mass from other star systems, or else they are spinning massless holes by tapping into huge amounts of energy from the Sun." Wally worked the controls again.

The image zoomed out again, making most of the inner Solar System visible. The planets were all gone—and something new was coming into being. A huge object, shaped like a wide flat bowl, was under construction well inside the old orbit of Mercury. Even as Sianna watched, tiny, midge-like transports were hauling sections of material into position and attaching them to the huge object. "That's your hole spinner?" Sianna asked.

"Yeah, but, ah, hold on a second. Why make 'em do the work twice?" The image froze and jumbled for a second. When it cleared, the huge bowl was now a long, wide arc, shaped like a slice of melon skin. "There. That's more like it," Wally said. "With that shape they can pull it out away from the Sun later and use it as a section of the final Sphere." The simulation started up again, this time with an arc-shaped power collector driving the hole spinner.

The two of them stood watching the simulation running

for a few minutes of speeded-up time. The hole spinner did its work, generating massless black holes that appeared as tiny dots of fiery red in the simulator. The holes mated themselves to ring-shaped accelerators that could draw on and control the gravity power the holes produced. Wally adjusted the controls and sent several Ring-and-Hole units out toward the huge machines that were building sections of shell material. "Now we have wormhole pairs to move things through," Wally said. "That'll speed things up."

As soon as the Ring-and-Hole units were on station, the transports stopped carrying the shell sections across space and started short-cutting through the wormhole links.

"Hmmmm, wait a second. Another thing," Wally said. "Rovers. Gotta make me some Rovers." He stopped the simulator for a moment and started keying in some adjustments.

"Rovers?" Sianna asked.

"Yeah, Rovers. I dunno what they'd look like, but some kind of really *big* things that could go out and snatch stars. Like really big Ring-and-Hole units, I guess. Ones that could use gravitic acceleration to send themselves toward the nearest stars at some sort of reasonable speed. Don't forget, the whole point of the Multisystem is to be a planet farm. You need stars to anchor the planets and give them light and heat. And you need planets, of course."

"Good God. I forgot about that," Sianna said. It was a sobering thought. She had thought she had the whole thing figured out, but how could that be if she had forgotten something that basic? It could throw off her whole idea. "But do you need to start building them so soon?" she asked. "Why not wait until after the Sphere is built?"

"Because it takes so damn long to travel from one star system to the next," Wally explained. "The Rovers have to travel in normal space. Once they are on station, they can just shift the star through. But it's going to take fifty or a hundred years to get to the closest G-class stars. Longer for some of the ones further off. If we're going to make the

Solar System into something like the Multisystem, we're talking a good dozen stars. Course, I can multiplex the system. Send Rover One to Alpha Centauri, say, and then have it set up a wormhole, and send Rover Two through it. Rover Two could then press on to the next closest star in that direction. The other reason to build Rovers early is so I can snatch extra raw materials for the Dyson Sphere and other constructs from other star systems.''

Sianna nodded agreement, though she understood that explanation a lot more poorly than she let on. She stood there and watched as Wally worked his controls, diverting resources toward a new construction site in the farther reaches of what had once been the Solar System. He started time moving at a minute-a-year and then sat back to watch the show. Constructor teams fabricated huge new Ring-and-Hole systems and sent them on their ways, out beyond the limits of the Solar System. Once the Rovers were on their way, the new construction site set to work manufacturing Sphere shell material.

''Okay,'' Wally said. ''I think we're on course here now.'' He lifted his hands from the controls, folded his arms, and watched the Sphere sections grow, huge bowl-shaped forms taking shape just inside Earth's old orbit. Then the linkups began. First the equatorial regions were joined into one. The arc-shaped form of the hole spinner was pulled back from its interior orbit to form a large fraction of the circumference.

From there, huge arcs of Sphere shell began to reach for the poles. But the polar arcs didn't hold. They began to buck and sway.

''Hell!'' Wally said, reaching out to freeze the program. ''Dynamic loads are too high.''

''How so?''

''Simple. The equatorial areas are orbiting the Sun with just about Earth's old orbital speed, but as you get away from the equator, the surface moves more and more slowly. Basic rule of a rotating sphere. If the entire surface rotates as a rigid unit, speed of rotation goes from zero at the pole to maximum at the equator.''

"Then why not cut the rotation and get rid of the stress?'' Sianna asked.

"Hmmm. The *real* Sphere here in the Multisystem rotates at about a normal orbital velocity, but I suppose the Charonians could have spun the Sphere back up *after* it was complete. Once the whole Sphere is built, it's more rigid and a lot stronger. We'll do it that way, and be more conservative in our assembly strategy.'' Wally ran the simulation backwards, with bits of Sphere shell vanishing, melting away.

He stopped at the moment just before the final equatorial section was dropped into position. He ran it forward from there, making the final linkup and then pausing further construction for a full year while he attached gravitic thrusters to the equatorial ring and used them to slow to a halt. "Of course, now every part of the equatorial ring is going to want to fall in toward the Sun, but all the inward stresses will cancel each other out—unless some outside perturbation throws it out of whack. If you view it as a static system, it's stable, but without a spin, it's an *unstable dynamic* system. Doesn't matter, though, because we can use the gravitic thrusters to keep it in trim.''

The sections of Sphere shell material started to go again, but this time in a different pattern. This time, instead of building great arcs up toward the poles, the shell sections were added evenly all around the edge of the equatorial ring, adding equally to its northern and southern edges, working to make sure the whole system stayed in trim and balance. Sianna blinked and rubbed her eyes. There was something quite dizzying about the way Wally was running things.

The simulation seemed so intensely *real* when it was running at a steady clip and seen from one viewpoint. The degree of detail, the sharpness, the clarity of the images all gave the simulation a tremendous degree of verisimilitude. It was easy to imagine a real Dyson Sphere abuilding out there, and that she, Sianna, was watching it from the observation port of a nearby spacecraft. It took an act of will to remember that the images she saw were wholly imaginary. It was all brighter, more solid, more logical, more *authentic* than reality ever was.

But then Wally would slow time, speed it up, freeze it, run it backwards, pan and shift and zoom and flip the viewing angles, project this diagnostic screen or that status display over part of the sim, and the whole thing would be shown up for the dream, the hallucination it was.

God help them all if it was real, if this was what was happening to the Solar System in real life, instead of in a simulator nightmare.

Sianna took a deep breath and forced herself to concentrate on the matter at hand. She had already missed some key details. Did that mean her central idea was wrong as well? One way to find out. Watch the sim and see what happens.

Once Wally had the assembly-pattern problem worked out, things proceeded smoothly for a while, the Sphere growing steadily from the equator toward the two poles.

Quite abruptly, two fiery-bright points of light appeared in the outer edge of the system, spaced well away from each other. "Alpha Centauri A and B," Wally said. "The first Captive Suns for the new system. Going to be tough to stabilize them this early on. Take some doing." Sianna glanced at the display that showed elapsed time for the simulation. She was startled to see that more than a hundred years had already gone by since the initial Charonian attack, five years in her own past. She was seeing a century into a future that might have been.

But then something started to go wrong. The Moon, the last natural object of any size in the simulated Solar System, started to wobble in its orbit. "Hold it a second," Wally said. "The Moon's orbit is going unstable. Gravity from the Captive Suns is throwing it off."

Another knot tied itself in Sianna's stomach. She hadn't foreseen this, either. It might be enough to blow off her whole theory, but if it *did* ruin things, then her theory was too flimsy for the real world anyway. She was tempted to nudge Wally toward her idea, but no. She was trying to get him to think like a Charonian. If anything, she should encourage him away from her idea. "So who cares about the Moon's orbit, or the Moon, for that matter?" she asked in a level voice. "Why not just get rid of it altogether?"

"No, no I can't," Wally said. "Hold it a second." His hands flew over the controls. "Stabilize it," he muttered to himself. "Maybe a six-sided rosette pattern. That give us a dynamic load balance? Yeah, that ought to do it." Five Ring-and-Hole sets moved out from the various construction sites and positioned themselves at equidistant points along the Moon's orbit, so that the five anchor rings and the Moon were sixty degrees apart from each other in orbit.

"That seems like a lot of trouble just to hold the Moon in place," Sianna said again, quite perversely pushing in the direction opposite to the one she wanted Wally to go. "Why *not* just get rid of it?" Sianna asked.

"Can't," Wally said. "It *is* a lot of trouble, I agree, but I'm stuck with the Moon. Remember the Lunar Wheel, inside the Moon, started this whole thing off by grabbing the Earth. The Wheel was the central conduit for power for the first twenty years or so, receiving gravity energy transmitted through the wormhole link by our Sphere. Once the Solar System started being a net gravitic energy producer, most of that power still had to move through the Lunar Wheel. In fact, the Lunar Wheel's power transmission capacity had to go way up—and the Wheel had to handle a *lot* of new processing power."

Wally pulled up a large image of the Moon, guiding the picture through the air until it hung a few feet in front of his head. "Here's a cutaway," Wally said, and a quarter-section slice of the Moon vanished, revealing the interior. Instead of just the Lunar Wheel wrapping once around the Moon's core, there were dozens, perhaps hundreds, of ring-shaped objects wrapped around the world. "This is all guesswork, of course," Wally said. "I don't know *how* they would add capacity, or what it would look like, but I do˙know the Wheel would have to add capacity as the building project went along. The sim was programmed to add it as needed. And this doesn't even show the processing systems, the artificial intelligence centers that are managing construction and keeping the system stable.

"So yeah, it would be *logical* to cut the Moon out of the loop at this point. The Sphere is big enough to handle all the power control, but there are so many power and logic and comm interconnects through there that removing them all would be like the Sphere performing brain surgery on itself. The connections and control links to all the operations in the system are so complex, so keyed to synchronizations with the Moon's orbit, that I wouldn't even want to adjust the Moon's orbit, because of all the other things you'd have to adjust as a result.

"See, at this point, the Moon is not just the only survivor of the Solar System's worlds, it's pretty much the de facto command center for the whole—" Wally stopped his work and looked up sharply as the light came on in his head. *"Command center,"* he whispered to himself.

He blanked the simulation, saved it back to the central data library, and brought up the simulation of the Multisystem that he had showed to Sianna in the long-ago morning of this endless day.

That had just been today? A wave of exhaustion swept over Sianna. How long ago had that morning been? Was it still the same day? What time was it now? Sianna knew she could find out the current, correct time, down to the nanosecond if she liked, by checking with any of a dozen instruments, starting with the clock on Wally's control panel. But she did not *want* to look. She felt as if she were outside of time itself, and that being out of time was part of how she was getting the answer. Somehow the moment, the magic, the way things were falling into place would end if she knew what time it was in the outside world. And now the answers were so close.

Wally had the sim of the real-life Multisystem up and running now. He brought up a close-in image of the Sphere, of the huge, brooding globe—and the tiny, barely visible dot that orbited so close to it.

Sianna stared at it, knowing that Wally was seeing what she did, was understanding what the simulated destruction of the Solar System had told them. There it was. The only planet-sized body to orbit the Sphere directly. The lone, lifeless, uninhabitable world in a Multisystem built to store and preserve living worlds.

Charon Central, the control station for the whole system, a system built by a species that had remade itself again and again over the eons. But the Charonians had remade themselves not through logic, but through history, through growth and death and evolution and residual effects, by improvising and working with what they had, by using one problem to solve another.

"The Lone World," Sianna said.

"Yeah," Wally said, staring at it in amazement. "Charon Central." Sianna grinned, nodded, and grabbed him by the shoulder. However that sideways mind of his worked, Wally had followed the same logic she had, and then gotten the same answer. She was *right*. Oh, there would be all sorts of battles and struggles ahead to convince the others, but that was trivial, a mere detail. She knew she was *right*. She had spent this day and this night underground, cut out from the sky and the stars, here in this place where time seemed so plastic that she felt cut out of time herself. But it had been worth it. Worth it to find this truth that would—

Out of time. Wait a second. Wait just a second. *Out of time.*

She turned and grabbed Wally by the arm. "Wally! Those Ring-and-Hole sets you made co-orbital with the Moon in the simulation. That was the best way to stabilize the orbit?"

Wally shrugged. "Best I could see."

"And those were standard R-H sets, right? They could do anything that other R-H sets could do?"

"Sure. They're big, heavy-duty units, but yeah, they could do the normal stuff. Why not?"

Sianna did not answer, but instead nodded to herself, thinking it through. The last link was there, just coming into reach. Yes. Yes.

"Wally. What's the orbital circumference for the Lone World? For the real one, not the Moon in the simulation."

"The circumference? Well, um, let's see. Circumference of an ellipse is um, ah . . ." Wally picked up a pencil and starting working it out on a scratch pad. Sianna was treated to the rare sight of a master of computer math struggling over a simple problem on paper. "Ah . . . that's ah . . . no, wait. Carry the . . . right. Right. Okay. Rough number would be about 665,000,000 kilometers. But why—"

"Good. Fine. What does that come to in light-minutes? How long would it take for a beam of light to travel that far?"

"Huh? What? Easy enough. Just divide out by the speed of light—um, just under thirty-seven minutes. But why—"

Thirty-seven minutes. God knows how, but it all fit! The same number that had been nudging at her subconscious all morning. *Thirty-seven minutes.* The time period that it would take a beam of light to travel the circumference of the Lone World's orbit. *Thirty-seven minutes.* The time discrepancy between the *Saint Anthony*'s clocks and all the clocks of Earth. Somehow, Earth had been accelerated to light speed, sent once around the orbit, and then decanted back into normal space. Sianna looked out toward the tiny dot of the Lone World, imagining the R-H sets that must be strung out along its orbit. Why, she did not know, but it had to be. She didn't know *how* they did it, either, but that number, thirty-seven minutes, told her they *had* done it. For some reason Earth had been pulled out of time, suspended, dropped into stasis, and moved once around the Lone World's orbit at the speed of light.

Sianna felt her heart pounding, her weary soul alive with excitement and enthusiasm. She had it. She knew she had it.

But even in her moment of victory, Sianna's subconscious found something to throw up in her face. A cloud popped up to cover the sunlight, and Sianna felt the all-too-familiar knot in her stomach, her guilty conscience reminding her of the consequences of wasted time.

Damnation. There was always *something* to ruin the fun.

Her finals started tomorrow and she hadn't even *thought* of studying.

Eleven

What Cats Won't See

". . . There can be no doubt that his role in the Abduction caused Larry Chao to become somewhat unbalanced. All witnesses agree that he suffered tremendous guilt and shame, along with and on top of the shock and survivor guilt that everyone suffered. There has been much discussion of how this might have shaped his later actions. However, another, less well-known incident has not received anywhere near as much study, though it no doubt had as much to do with his disordered state of mind when he destroyed Pluto and Charon not long after.

"Soon after the discovery of the Rabbit Hole and the entryway to the Lunar Wheel, Lucian Dreyfuss was sent down to attach a new form of gravity-wave detector on the then-still-functioning Lunar Wheel. Dreyfuss was accompanied by a TeleOperator, and the TeleOperator was controlled by Chao. The TeleOperator was capable of providing extremely detailed sensory feedback to the controller—too detailed, as it turned out.

"Almost immediately upon arrival at the bottom of the Rabbit Hole, Dreyfuss and Chao were attacked by two mobile Charonians of a previously unknown form. Dreyfuss was abducted, and later officially presumed dead. Chao's TeleOperator was decapitated and suffered various other serious injuries, even as highly realistic sensory feedback was still being fed back to Chao. The result was a classic case of TeleOperator Trauma Psychosis. In effect, Chao experienced—and survived—his own violent and grisly death. He was actually under heavy sedation for much of the journey to Pluto—and the catastrophe he would quite deliberately cause there."

—Farnsworth Johnson, *Decision at the Ring of Charon: A Revisionist View of Larry Chao's Role in the Destruction of Pluto,* Mariner Valley Academic Press, Mars, 2428

Lucian Dreyfuss looked past the TeleOperator, the human-form machine Larry Chao was controlling from the Moon's surface. Lucian peered through the visor of his pressure suit at the two monstrous robotic creatures, and felt his heart freeze solid with fear. "Behind you!" he cried out to Larry. The TeleOperator turned to look.

"Oh my God," Lucian said. The Charonian robots were brutal, aggressive-looking things. They had long cylindrical bodies and rode on two sets of wheels. Each of them had four long, sharp, vicious-looking manipulator arms ending with cruel, sharp-looking grip clamps where their hands should have been. They were plainly aware of the intruders.

"They know we're here," the TeleOperator said in Larry's voice. Lucian was about to say something, anything, in reply—and then the Charonians moved. Fast. Before Lu-

cian was even in motion, one of them was right in front of him. Its grabber arms swung down and snatched at him, lifted him up off his feet. Lucian tried to scream, but the sound stuck in his throat. He reached out toward Larry's TeleOperator, but then he was in motion, the alien thing taking him away.

Away.

Away.

Down the tunnel, down the endless tunnel, down into the dark and the blackness, bouncing and jouncing along, held upside down in the pitch darkness as the Charonian moved in a headlong rush down the tunnel. Now Lucian did find his voice, and he did scream, and scream again, and again, until there was nothing left of his voice.

They snatched at him, grappled him, peeled him out of his suit, forced his body into some sort of strange hibernation, and sealed him away in whatever it was that held him—

And so he slept.

And so he dreamed.

For a long time he had been still, truly asleep, truly inert. But now something had roused him, bestirred him just enough for him to dream, to remember it, to relive his own capture, his own nightmare undeath once again.

Again.

And again.

Lucian Dreyfuss looked past the TeleOperator, the human-form machine Larry Chao was controlling from the Moon's surface. Lucian peered through the visor . . .

The Wheelway
The Moon
THE SOLAR SYSTEM

"Lucian!" Larry shouted, waving his arms, desperately trying to get his attention. "Lucian! Over here! Look at *me*! Not at the damned TeleOperator. Look at *me*—"

But Lucian heard nothing. He stepped right through

Larry's image as he turned to look at the Charonians behind the TeleOperator. "Behind you!" Lucian called out.

Larry turned around and followed—or at least used the joystick to move his image, to try once again to make Lucian see the image of him, make him see Larry in street clothes, Larry dressed normally, a bit of everyday life. But no. It was useless. Worse than useless. Lucian didn't see Larry at all. Just the TeleOperator Larry had controlled that day, the image of the robotic body playing its part in the drama that was playing itself out over and over. Lucian could see the ghost of the machine Larry had been working that day, but not Larry himself.

If anything, Lucian was less aware of Larry with each repetition, not more. Lucian was getting canalized, caught more and more deeply in those last few minutes of life as he was forced to relive them over and over. The events were burned into Lucian's mind, and his mind absolutely refused to see anything else. And seeing them over and over again was not much of a pleasure for Larry, either.

Larry Chao let go of the joystick and pulled the viewhelmet off. He peeled the electrodes off the sides of his head. His face was drenched in sweat. Dear God, what Lucian had been through. And now to be locked inside his last moments, to relive the terror of his own capture over and over and over again.

Somehow, some subunit of the dead Lunar Wheel had kept feeding the same input to Lucian, over and over again, for the last five years. The images of Lucian's own last minutes. Maybe the Charonians thought they could make sense of it all by running it over and over again. Maybe that fragment of the Wheel had been dealing with that incident at the moment the Wheel had died and just gotten locked into it.

The medical-studies team said the Charonians had run two sets of neuro taps into Lucian—one that ran visual and aural input into his nervous system, and another that monitored what his brain actually saw and heard. It was not mind reading, not telepathy, but it was damned close. The Charonians could make whatever they wanted go into Lucian's eyes and ears—and then monitor what his brain actually saw, what Lucian made of it all.

No human surgeon could hope to place those kinds of sensory input and output links, but human techs could tap into the links. They had done so—and added a computer-generated image of the present-day Larry Chao to the inputs.

"I can't do it," Larry said at last, not looking up, not looking at anyone or anything. "I can't do it."

Larry stepped down from his chair and turned to face the two women at the control panel. "I can't do it," he said again, shaking his head, sitting down on the rest chair. His legs didn't seem too steady. He forced himself to settle down, take it easy.

It had all seemed so logical, somehow. Inject a sim, a computer-generated image of Larry Chao's body, into Lucian's sight and sound links. Hook up the sim to a mike so it would mouth Chao's speech in real time, and mimic his facial expressions, at least a little bit.

Meanwhile, tap into the outputs of Lucian's sight and sound links to interpret what Lucian was seeing and hearing in his dream, moment by moment, then merge that imagery with other data sources to back-angle the scene and feed images to Larry's viewhelmet, so that *Larry* in the VR control unit would see *Lucian* from where the Larry Chao sim was standing.

In short, the computer trickery was supposed to inject Larry's image into the scene Lucian was seeing, and let Lucian see Larry standing in the middle of Lucian's dream. Let Larry wander around inside a dead man's dreams.

Except it wasn't working.

Larry thought of Lucian, lying in the chamber a bit down the Wheelway, still entombed, with human probes and wires and inductive optic-nerve readers and cables snaking around the Charonian tendril net that led from his body.

Damnation. Why the *hell* was Lucian stuck in those last moments? Why couldn't they break him out?

Marcia MacDougal stepped from behind the control panel, snagged another chair, and sat down in front of him. "You're tired," she said. "We'll try it again in the morning. You need to rest."

Selby Bogsworth-Stapleton brought him a glass of water and squatted down in front of him. She handed him the water and gave him an encouraging pat on the knee. "Have a rest," she said. "We can have another go at it later."

"No," he said. "Neither of you understand. I can *try* again, right now, if you want. That's not what I mean. What I'm saying is I can't *do* it. You're projecting my image into his dream, or nightmare, or whatever, but *he's not seeing me*. He's not aware of me. He is not consciously refusing to react. He can't see me at all. The visual inputs are getting fed to his brain, but his brain isn't accepting. All he's seeing is his own memory. He just keeps looping through the last few minutes of his life, over and over again."

"No change at all?" Selby asked.

"Oh, yeah, it changes," Larry growled. "It gets more vivid every time. You saw the repeater screens on the console. That last run was solid, sharp as a tack. First time we barely got anything at all but static. The run time's getting faster too, I think. Hard to tell from inside the VR and the viewhelmet, but it seems like it."

"It is," Selby said. "By about a factor of ten since the first time."

"That's the computer getting better at its job," Marcia said. "We've fed it more angles of the playback from the real event, the real first trip down the Rabbit Hole. It's processing faster, doing better data-smoothing and integration of—"

"That's some of it, yes," Larry said, cutting her off. "But there's more. We're feeding Lucian direct stimulus, and it's—well, it's *stimulating* him. There's more power behind his thoughts. *He's* seeing more clearly each time, feeling it all more powerfully, running through it faster."

"We *are* getting an uptick in his brain-wave amplitude,"

Marcia admitted, "and it is speeding up. But he *has* to be able to see you. We're pumping your image straight to his optic center."

"*You've* never owned a cat. I can see that," Selby said.

Larry and Marcia both looked at her in confusion.

"Cats!" Selby said. "They refuse to see what they don't believe in. Put some strange object that they don't want to deal with in front of them and they'll act as if it's not there. To them, it *isn't* there."

"So what you're saying is that Lucian doesn't see Larry because he doesn't *believe* in Larry," Marcia said.

"I suppose that's one way to say it," Selby said. "The thing of it is that we can manipulate what goes into his optic nerve and into his auditory receptors, but that's not the same as changing what he *thinks*. It's what he *thinks* he's hearing and seeing that matters."

"And what *I'm* saying is that we have to look at the, ah, other way of doing this," Larry said, forcing himself to be firm, determined. He did not want to do this. "It's not enough for me to be there, shouting to get his attention. We have to break him out of the rote pattern of his memory. We can't just tell him what he is seeing isn't happening. We have to change what he's seeing."

Selby and Marcia exchanged glances at each other, and Selby cleared her throat, a bit awkwardly. "We were both rather hoping that it wouldn't come to that," she said. "We were a bit worried that might not be the most *pleasant* sort of thing for you to do. It would be rather—stressful."

"You think it might make me go nuts," Larry said bluntly. "I don't think it will. And if it does, well, I'll get better after a while. If we don't try it, Lucian is stuck in his own death forever, and I can't wish that on him."

Neither of the women said anything.

"Look, I don't like it either," Larry said. "But I wasn't there. Larry Chao wasn't *there*. The TeleOperator was. And floating an image of the T.O. around with a joystick won't work, either. We'd have to hook a full-movement, full-action VR system up, let it drive the imagery of the TeleOperator, have me speak *through* the T.O. to Lucian, and find ways to shift the imagery. *And* be ready for it to take five or ten or twenty times before we can break Lucian out.''

''We'd have to be ready to disrupt the Charonian inputs to his optic nerve,'' Marcia said thoughtfully. ''Be ready to substitute our own inputs. Work up a whole script, a whole plan, to snap Lucian out of it. We'd have to have the techs back in here,'' she said, thinking it over. ''It'd have to be a much more invasive setup. All we've been doing is trying to overlay your image onto Lucian's existing memories. You're talking about revising the images he already has.''

''So be more invasive,'' Larry said, his voice clipped and hard.

''It might disrupt Lucian's brain-wave patterns,'' Marcia said. ''It could kill him if we do it wrong.''

''You think being dead isn't better than the way he is *now?*'' Larry demanded. ''He's been reliving the same moments of terror over and over again for the last five years, experiencing what amounts to his own death again and again, all that time—except *he never gets to die.* I know the information we might get is important, but I almost don't care about it just now. I just can't leave him like *that.* Either we kill him and let him be dead, stay dead, in peace, or else—or else do *something* so he doesn't have to watch his own *death* anymore.''

Twelve

Signal and Noise

"Straight/Strait science *rotz* when it leans *twoheavy* on mind games, and the *simmy-shimmies* we do these *daze iz* just *mindgames bigtime*. They *query*, most *bleary*, what if ?, *not* what's happening? Every suit inna lab jacket has lost it now/ then *frum* knot/not knowing *bee/tween* sim-sham and *coldhardhere*.

"*Lotsatime* the jacket runs the *muddle-model* and *seez reallife* ain't dancing with the dream. The *punch-*

"Conventional science becomes decadent when it relies too much on thought experiments—and the present-day multimode simulations are really nothing more than hugely elaborate thought experiments. They ask *what would happen if*, rather than *what is really happening*.

"Every working scientist has experienced at least occasional difficulty in distinguishing between simulation and reality. It is far from rare *line is a jacket doping out a new gag to show why the dream-up is cool, reallife the fool. We go downhill from thar, tweaking to peak a waycool muddle-model, not whoa-stopping to pull the jokers from the deck and deal a new game.*

"We take sim one and fake anew sim two from one, butt one was de-based on sim zero wayback. Our/are thinking goes too deep into keen dream perfectland, all hot mat and cool pics, farout from realword and we dig that more, get pulled in more than by our/are sights of realworld. Waymuch we hand the lab jackets one taste of cleanandtidy perfectland, and a core sample of the crap coming out of Momnature's dirty old real-life kitchen. Which they gonna want for dinner, maybe without even knowing/no-ing they lose cuz they dunno they choose?

"Science/seance liketime takes a dive when it bites into tha tumor of rumor, whennit scoops up pocket-fulla oldtimes know/no/ledge and duzzent check that change for itself. We know

for a researcher to discover that reality does not behave as predicted in the model—and then proceed with a new experiment to show why reality was in error. We start to worry about building the perfect model, the perfect simulation, rather than dealing with the imperfections of the theories that produce the model.

"We base new experiments on results from a simulation that was itself developed based on the results of a previous sim. Our studies too often deal with an idealized universe of formulae and advanced displays, a place that is far removed from the real world, and yet is sometimes more compelling, more interesting, than our perceptions of reality. Too often, the modern researcher is given the choice between an ideal world and reality. Is it any wonder that they often choose the ideal dream, sometimes without even being aware of it?

"Science also fails when it merely relies on received knowledge, takes on faith what the past teaches, rather we *screw the pooch plenty times. How cum we figure alltha houndz inna past wuz safe? Rule one: ya don't believe what you don't add up yerself. Say-another-way: It ain't stitched right for the labjack if you can't show it ain't so/sew. If it be real science and no seance, ya gotta cookit yerself and show it's right with every bite.*

"Science supposed to be knowing growing by showing, and count thoz cards. Nowdaze straight/ strait/ jacket/ suit science looks like we're/whir suits and labjacks getting close/ clothes to being handed a marked and burning deck— and willing 2 take Monte Monty's word 4=(how many cards)*R/innit."

than going out to look for itself. When we acknowledge our own failings, our own limitations, is it not the height of presumption to assume that our predecessors got everything right? No data should be accepted as correct unless it is testable and confirmable. That which is not subject to proof is not science; that which *is* subject to proof must be tested again and again if it is to remain science.

"Science is meant to be a means of increasing knowledge by taking a skeptical look at the real world. The contemporary conventional approach to science is becoming little more than a credulous glance at a simulation."

—Eyeballer Maximus Lock-on *NaPurno/Knowway (The Naked Purple Way of Knowing)*, Datastreemdream Prezz, NaPurHab, published 100101111110 (A.D. 2430) (translation by the author)

Multisystem Research Institute
New York City
Earth
THE MULTISYSTEM

The simulation came toward its ending, again. The images froze in front of a gaggle of excited scientists and researchers, again. Half of them promptly began arguing every possible point raised by the sim with the other half. Again.

Sianna Colette was close to asleep on her feet. She had long ago lost all track of time. But now, down in this subterranean hole, in the dark, with the same depiction of imaginary times to come being shown backwards and forwards at various rates of passage, over and over again—each time with minor improvements and refinements, courtesy the relentlessly eager and energetic Wally—she had lost all *connection* with time as well.

Yesterday, they had gotten to the top people by blundering into them. No such luck today. Sakalov was nowhere to be found, and none of Bernhardt's people would think of disturbing him on the say-so of an undergrad and an overage sim hack. Seeing Bernhardt, as she had the day before—if it had been the day before, and not merely some far-off frontier of the same endless day—was no more an everyday occurrence than getting a good hard look at the Easter Bunny. In the normal course of events, Sianna would have as much chance of seeing Wolf Bernhardt as she would of getting the Autocrat of Ceres to come to lunch.

The only way to get this thing to anyone's attention was to move it up the food chain, one step at a time. They had to show it to each person's superior, convince *that* superior of the idea's logic, and then get that person to get his or her superiors to come down and have a look for *them*selves.

This was the third showing of the sim, each time to a slightly larger and more prestigious audience. None of the lower ranks seemed interested in clearing out, once they had dragged their bosses down, with the result that it was getting more than a little crowded in the sim tank. The air conditioning was not quite able to hold its own. That in and of itself tended to degrade the authenticity of the presentation. Outer space was not supposed to smell like a locker room.

The lights came up a bit so that everyone could see each other and talk more easily. It worked; the decibel level went up almost as fast as the lights. Sianna looked toward Wally at the controls. Nice touch, knowing that people don't like to talk in the dark. But then, it made sense that the only insight Wally would have on the human psyche would involve how they reacted to a sim.

Look at him over there. Wally should have been as exhausted as Sianna, but instead he was glorying in it all. Very probably more people were paying attention to him right now, taking him seriously, than at any other time in his life. He was surrounded by a whole mob of researchers who usually paid him just enough mind to make jokes about him, all of them asking questions, making suggestions, in short treating him like a colleague rather than as some lower form of life.

Sianna blinked awake as her head sagged forward. Dammit! Had she dozed off? For how long? A minute? An hour? She peered through the darkness and the clamor of the crowd. Something was happening. A knot of people was standing about the latest arrival on the scene, Dr. Ursula Gruber, director of Observational Research, and one of the most dignified-looking women Sianna had ever seen. Her iron-grey hair was done up in a bun, and pulled back tight. She was in a stiff white lab suit, and her grey eyes had a firm and steady gaze.

Gruber was surrounded by her own subordinates, and seemed to be in the midst of a spirited conversation with them, judging by the expression on her face. Sianna could not hear much of the discussion, but at last Gruber raised her hands and spoke in a louder tone. ''All right. Settle down so I can make the call.'' Gruber pulled her phone from her pocket and punched in a code.

Gruber was far enough up the food chain that it might be Bernhardt's office she was calling, and that Bernhardt would take the call. Gruber was gesturing toward the simulation, clearly talking about it.

At last Sianna couldn't take it any longer. She ventured close enough to hear what Gruber was saying.

''Yes, yes, we are all here in the Simulation Center. In the tank. I have just seen it. It has some real internal logic. It might well be significant. What? I am sorry, they are all talking here. Oh. That Wally Sturgis fellow is running it. Yes, Sturgis. No, I don't think he—I'm sorry, please say again. What was that?'' She waved her hand, gesturing for silence, and then covered her free ear up with her hand and listened for a moment. ''One moment. I will ask.'' Gruber hit the mute button on her phone and looked around the room, a rather sharp expression on her face. ''Which one is Colette?'' she called out. ''Sianna Colette?''

Sianna felt a sudden cold lump in the pit of her stomach. She stepped forward, and was all too aware that the people around her were stepping aside, making way. Suddenly she was alone in the middle of a circle of eyes. Behind her, the simulated Dyson Sphere went on building itself out of the rubble of a ruined imaginary Solar System.

''I'm Sianna Colette,'' she said, her voice sounding a bit high and squeaky, even to herself.

''Dr. Bernhardt wants to know if this is your idea?'' Gruber asked. She gestured at the simulation, at the highlighted image of what everyone was already calling the Lone World. ''Did *you* think of this?''

There was no use denying it. Not when she knew half this crowd of people, and she and Wally had called them all in to see her clever new theory. ''Yes ma'am. I did,'' Sianna admitted, feeling very much the way she had back in school when she was caught red-handed doing whatever it was she wasn't supposed to be doing. Having you dead to rights was never enough. They always wanted you to *admit* it as well.

Gruber nodded, raised her phone, and spoke into it again. ''Yes, it was Colette,'' Gruber said, and then listened for a moment longer before nodding to the voice on the other end of the line. ''Very well,'' she said. ''I will tell her.'' She shut off the phone and dropped it in her pocket. ''Dr. Bernhardt wishes me to tell you he will be down right away.''

And the cold lump in Sianna's stomach turned into a solid block of ice.

*   *   *

The waiting seemed an eternity to Sianna. Would Bernhardt fire her from MRI? Order her public expulsion from Columbia for misuse of institute facilities and wasting people's time? Or would he merely humiliate her, give her a public dressing-down in front of everyone and leave her to draw her own conclusions about her future prospects?

The crowd stood around her, a mass of irresolute faces. All the talking had died out, and the excitement seemed to have drained out of the room.

Sianna looked toward Wally, still sitting at his precious control board. She caught his eye, but he just looked at her in bafflement and shook his head.

At last the main doors of the sim chamber swung open, and in walked Wolf Bernhardt, Yuri Sakalov once again in tow. Sianna stood, alone, in the center of the semi-darkened room. She braced herself for what was to come, even as a wave of exhaustion swept over her.

Bernhardt was coming closer. She felt sure that she was going to faint. Her knees turned weak, and the room got a bit wobbly. He was almost to her—but then he marched right past her without breaking stride. Maybe his eyes weren't adapted to the dim illumination and he hadn't seen her. Maybe he didn't recognize her. Or maybe she was utterly beneath his notice.

Sakalov saw her, though, and gave her a completely unreadable look as he walked past.

The two of them walked right over to Gruber, who was standing over Wally at the control center. "Now then," Bernhardt said. "Dr. Gruber tells me there is a new theory that might provide certain insights. I wish to know more."

"Shall I, ah, run it, ah, the ah, simulation, for you, Dr. Bernhardt?" Wally sounded even more hesitant and nervous than usual.

Bernhardt looked down at him in cold annoyance. "I do not, Mr. Sturgis, need to look at pretty pictures in order to follow an argument." He looked up at Dr. Gruber. "*Frau Doktor* Gruber. Please summarize for me, if you would."

"Certainly." Gruber, Bernhardt and Sakalov went off to one side of the room. The three of them spoke in low tones for five long minutes, Bernhardt mostly listening, nodding now and then, Sakalov asking an occasional question in a voice too low for Sianna to hear. Bernhardt had no reaction at all to what Gruber said, but Sakalov seemed to grow more and more agitated.

At last Bernhardt had heard enough. He nodded one last time, gave Gruber a pat on the shoulder, and turned toward Wally. "Perhaps I will have a look at the simulation after all. You will transmit a recording of the finalized run to my office within one hour. In the meantime, I will speak to you, Miss Colette, and Dr. Sakalov out in the corridor. Miss Colette? Come, if you please."

He turned, rather abruptly, and walked out into the hall without looking to see if any of them were following.

Sakalov followed dutifully behind. Wally saved the current settings on the simulation and stood up to follow, a bit slowly. Sianna trailed behind the others, once again struggling to ignore the forest of eyes that surrounded her.

She reached the open door and stepped from dark into light, from the gloom of the sim tank to the over-bright glare of the white-on-white hallway.

She closed the door behind her and paused, squinting, peering about to see where the others had gone. There they were, just up the hall to the right. All three waiting, stern-faced, for her to catch them up.

She forced herself to walk toward them, stiff-legged, her arms folded protectively in front of her chest. Her eyes locked with Bernhardt's grim-faced gaze.

But then, as she got to them, Bernhardt's face lost its fixed expression. He grabbed her by the arm, looked over her shoulder to see if anyone was behind her, and pulled her around the corner, Wally and Sakalov following behind.

Sianna glanced over her shoulder, but saw for herself there was nothing there worth looking at. But then she looked back toward Bernhardt, and saw something most remarkable indeed.

He was grinning. *Grinning*. Sianna had never even thought German face muscles could ` ove that way. "You've got it!" he said to an astonished ⌣ianna. "We need to be careful, and collect the proof, but there isn't the slightest doubt in my mind that you're right. Wouldn't you agree, Dr. Sakalov?"

"Yes, yes," Sakalov said, taking her right hand and shaking it vigorously. "At the cost of admitting I was wrong, I have to admit your theory holds together far better than anything I've ever done."

"But . . . I . . . I . . ." Sianna's voice trailed off for a moment before she managed to say anything more. "But, the way you came in just now, and the way you acte⌐—"

Bernhardt laughed out loud. "Psychology," he said. "There's very little of my job left that has to do with being a scientist. Always it is politics and psychology. Five years ago, I was instructed to find a captain for the *Terra Nova* and send the ship off to explore the Dyson Sphere—straight to the Sphere itself with no precautions. That would have been a suicide mission. So I chose Captain Steiger and gave her orders I *knew* she would disobey the moment she could. You have to know your people. After the way you argued with Dr. Sakalov yesterday, I didn't think that *you* would put forward a theory that you had not thought out carefully, so I came down ready to listen.

"But it is not just a question of knowing you are right. It is a question of being heard, of the signal not being lost in the noise. I know that I am not the most popular man down here. They know I am careful and efficient, but that I refuse to write the checks they want; I say no to their projects. So sometimes the people at MRI are *for* whatever I am *against*. Besides that, Dr. Sakalov is well thought of. If I charged down here and endorsed a theory that refuted much of his work—well, for some, that would be enough to turn them against your ideas for good. By being standoffish, I make them determined to prove me wrong." Bernhardt reached out and patted Sianna on the arm. "You have done superb work. Now you must go home and get some rest."

Sianna could do nothing more than stand there, blinking in astonishment. She had always thought being a scientist just meant working to find out the truth.

A lot she knew.

Sianna's feet were dragging as she left the Sim Center. She got herself across the underground campus fairyland of the MRI Main Level and made her way up to the elevator banks. She was tired enough, and emotionally flattened enough, that getting into the steel coffin of the elevator and watching the doors close her in didn't bother her at all. She was too numb to react to anything.

It seemed as if life had broken every promise it had ever made to her. Life had pulled her away from her childhood home, plopped her down in a foreign land, killed her parents, delivered her into an age of crisis and emergency that had no time to deal with teenage orphans.

Anything good and hopeful had always been snatched away. In the general scheme of things, it was high time that Columbia and MRI rejected her as well. And yet, somehow, they had failed to do so, even when given a prize opportunity to do so. They were *congratulating* her.

The elevator slowed to a halt at ground level and the doors opened. Sianna stepped blinking into the sunlight, disoriented by the bright light and open spaces, the sharpness and clarity of it all. She walked out onto the broad expanses of the central plaza, feeling more than a bit muzzy and lost.

It was like the feeling she got coming out of a matinee, stepping from a darkened theater into the sunlit street after her eyes had spent two or three hours telling her body that it was after dark. Sianna felt like that, only a dozen times more so. She felt like she had indeed been out of time for a while, and now was being thrust, most unwillingly, back into it.

In any event, it *was* still daytime. She looked toward the

Sunstar, and gauged its position in the sky. *About three in the afternoon,* she decided. Or had they been down there more than a whole day? No, that couldn't be. Or maybe it could. Bother to all of it.

She looked up at the late-afternoon sky, gleaming perfect robin's-egg blue. The air was sweet, with just a hint of new-mown grass in the air, wafting down from the roof gardens and Central Park. The air was alive with sound as well—laughter and conversation, the whirring hum of traffic, the busy background bustle of the city, awake and alive. Even in the midst of her exhaustion, it gave her a lift, put a bounce back in her step. She still wanted to go home and get to bed, but home and bed were suddenly a destination, a reward, rather than a place to go hide.

It was amazing what the simple sight of the *real* open sky, even the Multisystem sky, could do for her spirits.

She got back to her apartment, freshened up, and got ready for bed, grateful that her roommate was still out. She set the phone to take messages without disturbing her and went to bed. It was over now. She had done her bit, found the idea that everyone had been looking for. Now the *really* smart people could work on it. She could get some rest, get up early, and get cracking on those books.

She snuggled down into her pillow and went to sleep.

Next morning Sianna woke up at five A.M., and was out of bed in an instant, feeling quite virtuous, and perhaps a little bit smug. One exam today, and she had never felt readier for work in her life.

She breezed through breakfast and set to work on studying for her finals, happily working through a series of transformational analyses just for practice. She got to her exam at noon and plowed through the problems in no time. She was the third one to finish—even with having triple-checked all her work.

She treated herself to a browse through a bookshop on the

way home, and got back to her apartment about three. She made herself a late lunch and indulged herself by reading half a novel instead of studying for her history exam.

It wasn't until nearly eight-thirty that, looking up from her book, she thought to check her message system. She had forgotten that she had left the comm switched to message-taking. Dozens of people could have called and she never would have known it.

But there was only one text, the time tag showing that it had come in some time at about five A.M.

Be in my office at 0900 hours tomorrow. W. Bernhardt.

No request, no please. Just the flat order. There was a sudden knot in her throat, and her hands turned sweaty. She had thought she had done her part, that she could let everyone else worry about it.

A lot she knew. Again.

Thirteen

Carrot and Stick

"Is the Multisystem all one creature? A complex ecology of interdependent forms? Something in between, like a huge coral reef of tiny beings making up a greater whole? Or is the question utterly meaningless? Is there no analog or pattern available to the human mind that would provide a useful understanding of what a Charonian is?

"All we can know for certain is that the Charonians had once been very different, and then came to be what they are. Coming into the Universe leaves a scar or two, and change is never complete. The same is true of humanity: our navels are the scars of umbilicals we lost, and the white blood cells that swim in our veins are the descendants of parasitic amoebae that survived by turning from foe to friend. In the process of remaking themselves, the Charonians surely kept some mark of their old selves—and their old weaknesses—behind.

"No matter how well we think we know them, those residuals, those bits of heritage from their unknown past, will at time cause wholly unexpected behavior."

Larry Chao, *An Essay on the Charonians*
(unpublished), 2427

DSI Headquarters
New York City
EARTH

Night had fallen long before, but Wolf Bernhardt was still at work, preparing his cables, carefully composing the messages. He had to get the phrasing right, exactly right, if he was to be sure of NaPurHab and the *Terra Nova* cooperating in their own salvation.

Well, actually, NaPurHab shouldn't be any great challenge. *We're sending you lots of free supplies. Please take them.* It wouldn't take much more than that. The *Terra Nova* would be the real challenge.

But NaPurHab had already been a fight, here on the ground. It had been tremendously hard to get the backing he needed to provide those supplies, to do a full-scale resupply operation. Thank God he had won through.

It was frustrating to be the only one who understood that the Naked Purple Habitat was itself important, above and beyond the lives of the people on board. It was a vital, irreplaceable observation post. And if the Breeding Binge went as badly it might, NaPurHab might well be the largest surviving human population. It might well be that the survivors on Earth would be begging NaPurHab to rescue them in the none-too-distant future. Earth *needed* NaPurHab. In the grand scheme of things, who cared who operated it, or if the occupants were a nuisance at times?

But now, events were suddenly moving. He would use the

latest data about the SCOREs, and this new information from that Colette girl, to throw a scare *and* a bit of excitement at the finance committee. It would cement the commitment for a massive and immediate resupply mission to NaPurHab, enough gear and supplies to maintain them for years longer, maybe decades if need be.

But the *Terra Nova*. Would the Colette girl's ideas be enough to tempt Steiger away from the suicidal *Highwayman* mission? Or was Steiger bound and determined to attempt boarding a CORE again?

Supplies. Supplies were the answer. Lift cargo earmarked for the *Terra Nova* to NaPurHab. Give them another reason to break off.

But how to phrase it? What sort of message would tempt Steiger into coming in? Don't forget she was not the only one on board that ship. Get MacDougal interested in resupply, and in the Lone World, and Steiger could be goaded into action.

If he played this thing right, there were all sorts of possibilities. It was all cold-blooded, yes. It was using crisis and fear and hope to manipulate people and events. Parts of Wolf could see that, and did not like what they saw.

But those parts were in the minority. The rest of him, the larger part of him, saw his complicated, manipulative schemes and saw they might be the catalyst for all sorts of progress against the enemy. Unless, of course, his urge to do something, *anything*, now that it seemed he finally had the tools in hand, was the catalyst for getting them all killed.

Wolf forced that thought from his mind. No. Forward. The only way out was forward. For the one thing he was absolutely sure of was what the evidence of the other Captive Worlds told them: doing nothing was a *sure* way to get them all killed.

He got back to work.

Terra Nova
Deep Space

Captain Dianne Steiger stared at the message printout, trying to think it through. Even the simplest communication from Earth was likely to have four or five layers of hidden meaning. This one was chock full of news, that was for certain. Enough news that she could, with no little relief, cancel the flight of the *Highwayman*.

But Wolf Bernhardt was a wily old campaigner. It never paid to take him strictly at face value. She could do with some advice. "ArtInt. Locate the first officer, give him the captain's compliments, and ask if he could come to my quarters."

"One moment," an artificial voice said. "Message relayed. The first officer is on his way."

Good. Good. She was eager to see what Gerald would make of all this. She went back to the top of the message and started reading again.

She had just finished it when the doortone sounded. Dianne stood up from behind her desk, crossed and opened the door, still holding the message printout.

"Hi, boss," Gerald said. "What's up?"

"You tell me." She gestured for him to come in and handed the message page to him as she shut the door. "Read it," she told him, handing him the printout.

He stood there, reading, as she went over to flop down on the couch. She was tired. She was very, very tired. The job was wearing her down. She shut her eyes and rubbed her face with both hands.

Flying the ship was simple. But it was damned hard to keep morale high on a ship wherein the crew had realized long ago that most of them were likely to spend the rest of their lives on board, were likely to *die* on board, likely never to get off this ship, even after death.

No poetic burials in space on the *Terra Nova*. No. The ship's ecosystem could not afford to waste that much organic material. Not counting the *Hijacker* disaster, there had been three suicides and two accidental deaths since the *TN* departed Earth, and all of them had been ''buried'' in the tertiary nutrient development facility, a rather polite way of saying they had been recycled.

That was what they had to look forward to, in lieu of hope. And the death of the *Hijacker* hadn't helped matters.

Was that all that was left to them? To wander in space, waiting for death to take them all, one by one? Maybe not. Maybe the message from Earth actually meant something. If they had really found Charon Central . . . She folded her hands on her stomach and stared at the overhead bulkhead. ''What do you think, Gerald?'' she asked, trying hard to sound blasé about it.

''If it's true, it's wonderful,'' Gerald said. ''If this Lone World place is Charon Central, we finally have something to work for, a goal.''

Dianne looked up at him, and saw the excited expression on his face. She felt something like a touch of envy to see his enthusiasm. Why couldn't she feel that way? When had she turned into such a jaded cynic that even a breakthrough like this left her cold? Or was it just her sense of caution, her determination to keep the ship safe?

''What do you mean, a goal?'' she asked. ''You're not suggesting we head for this Lone World, are you? It's got to be the most heavily protected point in the whole system. It's the damned Sphere's brain, after all. Must be swarming with COREs. We'd never get within a million klicks of the place.''

''No, we don't go for it now—but eventually, yes. It says here they expect to start reading message traffic off it soon. They hope to be able to decode them against their existing Charonian language sets. If we could find the command for 'don't smash incoming ships,' we *could* go there.'' Gerald shrugged. ''Maybe we can't do it now, but it is a goal we can set our sights on.''

''You're ahead of Bernhardt on that one,'' Dianne said,

sitting up on the couch. "Even he doesn't make that suggestion. In fact, there's not *any* of the usual 'suggestions' in that message."

The *Terra Nova* was, of course, nominally under Bernhardt's personal control, in his capacity as head of the DSI. But Dianne had made it clear from the outset that her ship was too precious an asset to be trifled with. It was the only ship in deep space that Earth had or was likely to have. The *TN* was the only means Earth had of operating outside the cordon set up by the COREs. Dianne had made it clear quite some time ago that the *TN* would not be exposed to needless risk. Dianne was determined to refuse any order she regarded as too dangerous.

What with the harebrained ideas that Bernhardt had been forced to pass along over the years, pretty much *all* of the orders from Earth involved undue risk. Bernhardt knew that as well as Dianne did, and so he almost always sent "requests" or "advisories" instead of commands, thus keeping the Earthside powers-that-be happy while providing Dianne with an out. That was one good thing about commanding a ship in deep space—no committees of second-guessers looking over your shoulder.

But no vague requests on the resupply signal. No code words to keep Bernhardt's "advisers" happy. Dianne suddenly realized what that meant. "Give me that message again for a second," she said, standing up. Gerald handed over the printout, and she checked it again. Yes, she had it right. He had sent it just a few hours after first hearing of this Colette person's theory—and after working hours in New York. And there was something a bit Teutonic about the phrasing, come to think of it.

"You know," Dianne said, "I think old Wolf Bernhardt drafted this himself, and sent it after hours. On the rush. Plus there's nothing about 'acting upon the advice of experts in the field' or anything like that. He didn't consult with the usual advisory teams."

"Maybe he wanted to get it to us fast," Gerald said.

"And I can guess his reason for it. This," she said, waving the printout, "is all the excuse I need to cancel the *Highwayman*."

"I won't pretend to be disappointed," Gerald said.

"But you were bound and determined to go," Dianne said, perching on one corner of her desk.

"If anyone was going to go. The *Highwayman* would have been destroyed the same way as *Hijacker*. I couldn't have asked anyone else to go."

"So in spite of all your brave words to the contrary, you thought it was a suicide mission."

"We both know it was a desperation mission," he said. "It was the only hope we had of accomplishing anything. But suddenly we're not desperate anymore."

"The voice of optimism," Dianne said. "But there's bad news too." She took a second printout off her desk and handed it to Gerald. "That's a somewhat more official message. It more or less confirms all those SCORE things are headed for Earth space. MRI definitely thinks what we think: it's a Breeding Binge."

"My God," Gerald said. He took the second printout, and looked at it without reading it.

"Yeah," Dianne said. She crossed the room and lay back down on her couch. "Not good. Bernhardt isn't sure they'll be able to fight them off. He's sending supplies to NaPurHab, for us and for them. Another temptation to break off our next attempt on the CORE."

"Hmmmm. Beat us with the stick and tempt us with the carrot. Not too subtle. And neither are the orders." Gerald read out loud from the second printout. " 'In light of this new and important information, you are ordered to break off contact with the CORE, return to near-Earth space and prepare to rendezvous with NaPurHab.' "

"Well, what do you think?" Dianne asked.

"I think it's been a long time since Bernhardt gave us a direct order," Gerald replied.

"That's because it's been a longer time since we *obeyed* a

direct order. Maybe that's a hint that he really wants us to do it this time.''

''Sounds like you think we ought to comply,'' Gerald said.

Dianne propped herself up on her elbows and looked to Gerald, nodding thoughtfully. ''Sounds like I do,'' she agreed.

''There's one other thing,'' Gerald said. ''One I don't like much. Maybe we should send back a request that they send us some people.''

''People?'' Dianne asked.

''Experts,'' Gerald said. ''We've got some good techs on board here—but if we ever do go for the Lone World, I'd like some of the real experts with us.''

''How would they get here?''

''On the cargo flights to NaPurHab. We'd collect them the same time as the cargo.''

''Do you have any idea how risky a flight that is?''

Gerald nodded, his eyes on the floor. ''Yes I do,'' he said. ''But if there is a Breeding Binge on the way, the risks in staying home aren't much lower. We may never get another chance for new personnel again. And a few of the people who tracked down this Lone World might make all the difference later on.''

''What's your latest estimate on how bad a Breeding Binge could be?'' Dianne asked.

''If Earth manages to kill off the first wave and the Charonians give up after that, maybe about as bad as a small nuclear war. If the Charonians don't give up, maybe the collapse of civilization,'' Gerald said. ''Maybe a mass extinction.''

Dianne did not speak for a moment. There was nothing that could be said to that. But Gerald might be right about having some of those experts on board. If Earth fell, and the *Terra Nova* had to fight on alone, Dianne would want all the expertise she could get.

''All right,'' she said. ''Send in that request, and sign both

our names to it. Then start passing boost orders. Start to secure for main-engine firing, and compute the standard spread
of possible course options. Calculate minimum time, minimum fuel, and intermediates, and bring me the results in six
hours. Eight hours until boost.''

Gerald nodded. He stood there a moment, as if he were
trying to think of something to say himself. But he left it to a
simple ''Yes ma'am.''

He turned and left, closing the hatch behind him.

Captain Dianne Steiger shut her eyes and rolled over on
her side. Sleep. If the ship was going to get under way in a
few hours, she needed to get some sleep. She really ought to
get off the couch and get into bed.

But underneath her calm, underneath her exhaustion,
there was something more.

There in the fear, mixed in with the horror of the news,
with the terrible thought of a Breeding Binge, there was a
thrill of excitement as well.

At last, she thought. *At last.*

The call to arms had come.

Fourteen

Garbage In

"If you look into the background of how the Abduction happened, it is at least possible it could have been avoided altogether, if a senior scientist had been willing to listen to a subordinate."
—Dr. Wolf Bernhardt, address on the occasion of dedicating the *Hijacker* Memorial, June 4, 2436

DSI Headquarters
New York City
EARTH

The Sunstar was high in the east as Sianna stepped into Bernhardt's office. Normally, Sianna was not that aware of the sun's position when she was in an office, but then most offices had opaque walls.

Wolf Bernhardt's New York office was not anywhere

near as far aboveground as the MRI main level was below, but it seemed that way. It was in a twenty-third-century monstrosity of a NeoGoth tower on Columbus Avenue, about twenty-five blocks south of Columbia. The office itself was huge, a big, sparsely furnished space. The floor was gleaming hardwood, and the walls plain white. Bernhardt's desk, easily the size of Sianna's whole office, was an immaculate slab of polished white wood.

There were no pictures on the wall, no shelves, no decoration. It was a room perfect for a man given over to neatness. But insofar as Sianna was interested, the key fact was that the door into the room was on the north side of the room, and the south wall, behind Bernhardt's desk, was a single huge pane of non-reflective glass, affording a completely unobstructed view that took in the whole Manhattan skyline from a hundred meters up. The spires and towers of the city gleamed in the morning light, framed by a perfect blue sky beyond.

Every fear Sianna had ever had of enclosed spaces vanished, at least for the moment, to be replaced instantly by acute agoraphobia, before she settled down. It was all right. It was all right. Just a spectacular view. Nothing to be afraid of. After a moment's hesitation, she stepped through the door into the room. At first her eyes were fixed on the emptiness, and the glorious city beyond, where a wall was supposed to be. But then she tore her eyes away and looked around the room.

Wally and Sakalov were already there, sitting in two of the visitor's chairs. Wally had a pocket computer out, and seemed ready to read something off the screen. But of course, it would have been more remarkable if he *didn't* have some sort of hardware with him. Sakalov had a notepack as well, the sort that was mostly used to show flat images.

A tray full of coffee things, pastries and fruit and breads, sat on Bernhardt's desk, and all three men had been helping themselves. That in and of itself was incredible.

For a man like that to be in this celebratory a mood was amazing. For Wolf Bernhardt to put out coffee and danish, exposing his immaculate office to the risk of crumbs and coffee spills, was right up there with the Pope leading a conga line. But be that as it may, all three men were quite plainly happy and relaxed, leaning back in their chairs.

She realized that she had her arms folded up tight in front of her chest. She forced her arms to her sides.

"Ah, Miss Colette," Bernhardt said, his voice buoyant and expansive. He did not take his feet down off the desk, let alone stand up to greet her. Instead, he kept his comfortable position and waved her toward the chair closest to the window. "You're just in time. Mr. Sturgis and Dr. Sakalov were just expounding a bit on your idea about the Earth being held in a sort of stasis orbit for those missing thirty-seven minutes. Sit, sit. Have some coffee."

Sianna forced herself to move toward the desk and the coffee things, certain that everyone in the room was watching her every move and could tell just how self-conscious she was. Moving with what she hoped was studied casualness, she took a cup and poured for herself. She took her cup and saucer, crossed to her chair, and sat down, swiveling around in the chair to partially hide her face from Bernhardt without being rude. She hoped.

She looked toward Wally and tried to look as if she were paying attention to what he was saying, instead of being scared to death of Bernhardt and a trifle over-aware of the invisible glass wall and the sheer drop-off behind it, a mere two meters behind her back.

"—of course, most wormhole links are instantaneous," Wally was saying. "That only makes sense if you were trying for fast transportation. But you don't *have* to make wormholes that way. Suppose you, ah, were after something else, like a holding tank, say. Some way to hold something—say, a planet.

"Everyone's always assumed the Sphere was ready and waiting for Earth. They figured that since the Sphere managed to get Earth into an orbit and get the Moonpoint Ring set up for Earth in just a few seconds—the few seconds it took for Earth to come through the hole. The trouble with that theory is that Earth's new orbit isn't very *stable*. It's a major anomaly.''

"What do you mean?" Bernhardt asked.

"Well, most of the Captive Worlds around the other Captive Suns in the Multisystem move in orbits that should be good for at least several million years. But Earth was dropped too close to the orbits of a lot of other planets that orbit the Sunstar. Dr. Sakalov showed that the Sunstar system was stable *before* Earth was dropped into it."

Dr. Sakalov nodded and spoke, looking at Bernhardt. "Those same simulations show that the Sunstar's system of planets was rendered highly *un*stable by Earth's arrival. The interaction of all the gravitational forces throws things off. Earth's orbit, and the orbits of the neighboring planets, will start deteriorating within about three hundred years at the outside—maybe a lot less. The Sphere will have to do constant active maintenance on the orbits to keep them under control.

"At first we assumed that was the norm for the Multisystem. We've proved it's the exception. All the other Captive Worlds are in far more stable orbits. But why? Why did the Sphere put *us* in an unstable, unsuitable orbit, without waiting until such time as it could arrange a more stable pattern?

"Miss Colette's theory answers that problem," Sakalov went on, answering his own question. "It allows the Sphere enough time to do *some* preparation—but not enough to do a perfect job. If she is right, then the Sphere put Earth in this stasis orbit while it rushed to prepare a place for it. Thirty-seven minutes is not much time, of course, but it is more than the forty or fifty seconds of elapsed time recorded on Earth between the moment of Abduction and arrival in our present orbit. I suspect that holding Earth in a stasis orbit put great demands on the Sphere, or else it would have maintained the stasis longer and prepared a more stable orbit.''

"But what the devil is a stasis orbit?" Bernhardt demanded.

"You catch the Earth in a wormhole, and then use the Mtabe modal transformation sequence model," Wally said, in a tone of voice that made it clear how obvious it was. Sianna almost expected him to add *of course*. "The modal transformation causes the wormhole itself to move through space as a standing wave front."

"Huh?" Sianna said, making her first contribution to the discussion.

"It's simple," Wally said, without a trace of irony in his voice. "Drop the Earth into the wormhole, pinch the endpoints of the wormhole, seal the ends to form a closed volume, and you've got the Earth inside a singularity that can be manipulated. Viewed from the outside, you have a supermassive charged particle that can be guided electromagnetically. If you then create magnetic lines of force between Ring-and-Hole sets co-orbiting with the Lone World, you have what amounts to a huge storage ring, one large and powerful enough to hold an Earth-mass pinched wormhole particle." Wally shrugged. "Trouble is, the pinched wormhole particle will tend to evaporate spontaneously. It won't last long. Of course, if you accelerate the hole to near light velocity, then relativistic time dilation kicks in and the hole lasts longer."

"Of course," Bernhardt said, with amused sarcasm.

But that sort of thing went right past Wally. He went on with his explanation, completely unaware that even Sakalov's eyes were showing signs of glazing over. "The main thing is, the pinched hole won't last long. You have to drop Earth out of the hole *before* it evaporates, get Earth back into normal space, and then drop the planet down into a *new* hole, pinch *that* one off, and send it back along the next leg of the storage ring. Keep repeating the procedure as long as you want."

"But why didn't it hold us longer, if this is what happened?" Bernhardt asked. "I can see that the Sphere might need to have the Earth complete an orbit for some mechanical reason we don't know about, but surely the Sphere could have held us in stasis longer and prepared a more stable orbit somehow.''

Sakalov shrugged. ''My guess is that the Sphere simply did not have the energy reserves to hold the planet in stasis more than one orbit. It would require tremendous power to do all the things Wally is describing so casually. And even the Sphere has a limit on its energy output.''

''Just out of curiosity, what would happen if the Sphere was unable to provide enough power?'' Bernhardt asked. ''Would the Earth have dropped out of the stasis orbit?''

''Well, yes, that would be the problem. You'd get an uncontrolled spontaneous evaporation of the pinched wormhole,'' Wally said, as if evaporating wormholes were some sort of annoying household nuisance, like dustballs under the bed.

''And what would that mean?'' Bernhardt asked.

Wally shifted awkwardly in his seat and grinned, a bit embarrassed. ''$E = MC^2$. Earth's mass would be expressed as energy.''

''Which would of course be a great inconvenience to us all,'' Sakalov observed, rather dryly. ''The explosion would almost certainly be enough to destroy the Sphere, and probably vaporize most of the planets of the closer-in Captive Suns as well.''

Bernhardt raised his eyebrows. ''Just as well the Sphere knows what it is doing, then.'' He bent his head back and stared at the ceiling for a moment. ''Leaving the destruction of the Earth to one side, if I'm following you, what you're describing would jibe with what people saw at the time Earth was abducted: the sky quite abruptly turning from dark to night and back again, with repeated drops through the blue-white zones that seem to be what the throat of a wormhole looks like. Many witnesses in the Northern Hemisphere saw what must have been the Sphere, but so close up that it resembled a flat plane stretching across the sky.''

"So the idea fits?" Sianna asked, feeling rather tentative about speaking up, even if it was *her* idea they were discussing. They were going into an awful lot of detail, considering that the discussion of stasis orbits and co-orbiting R-H sets was wholly hypothetical.

"So it would seem," Bernhardt said in a voice that was quite alarmingly cheerful. "And it is not the only thing that fits. That is the splendid thing about your theory, you know. It explains everything we know to date. But it's a good theory for two other equally important reasons. Do you know what they are?"

"Because it makes testable predictions and is subject to disproof," Sianna blurted out, her competitive classroom instincts kicking in. It was the right answer, of course, but she instantly regretted giving it. Bernhardt had obviously wanted her to *ask* for the answer, not give it. Wally gave her a funny look, as if to say even *he* could tell that was a rhetorical question.

"Ah, yes, exactly," Bernhardt said, thrown off his stride just a trifle. "You have given us a theory we can *test*. We can study this Lone World and see if it behaves as your theory requires. We must see if we can detect commands coming from it, for example. The study should be made far easier because we can focus our attention on this one small body, rather than searching the whole vast expanse of the Sphere for Charon Central."

Sianna nodded, not quite knowing what to say—and having no desire to speak out of turn again.

"Our friend Dr. Gruber has started already, in fact," Sakalov said. He lifted the notepack he had been holding and gave it to Sianna. She set her cup down on the desk and took the pack. "Images and data pulled down yesterday, last night, and this morning," Sakalov said. "Gruber wangled time on instruments all over the world, and on the *Terra Nova*. Have a look for yourself."

Sometimes Sianna worried that people assumed she was much smarter than she really was. How in the world did

Sakalov come to assume she was smart enough to interpret raw images and data without guidance or explanation?

But then she switched on the notepack, and all doubts faded away. It was all so *obvious*.

"Gruber searched the entire circumference of the Lone World's orbit—or at least the fraction of it currently visible from Earth," Sakalov said. "Since we are nearly over the Sphere's northern pole, and the Lone World orbits along the Sphere's equator, we can see about nine-tenths of its orbit from here. Those are all visible-light images you have there, but we are hoping for infrared and ultraviolet from the *Terra Nova.*"

Sianna nodded, not really hearing what he was saying. There they were. Five, six, seven of them, all of them showing the signs of heavy magnification and intense image-enhancement. There were fuzzy, faint, murky images of ring shapes, some seen nearly from the edge, others somewhat foreshortened, and one perfectly face-on. The black holes at their center would be completely invisible, of course, but Sianna found herself straining to see them all the same.

"The only thing I got wrong is the number of them," Wally said proudly. "We only have images on seven R-H sets so far, but the spacing of those tells us there must be eighteen of them altogether, and including at least one R-H set orbiting the Lone World."

"A prediction tested and proved correct right there," Bernhardt said.

Sianna nodded absently and worked the display controls. As Bernhardt himself had pointed out, pretty pictures were all very well, but there was more to analysis than that.

Ursula Gruber had directed whatever detectors she could find, of whatever kind they might be, at the Lone World.

The trouble was that the Lone World was a dim, tiny target at a great distance. It was smaller than the Moon, eight times farther from Earth than Pluto had been from the Sun, and separated by only a few million kilometers from a larger object, an object known to throw off a bit of radiation itself—the Sphere. In fact, to make things even trickier, the Lone World was transiting the Sphere at the moment. "Transiting" was nothing more than a fancy way of saying the Lone World was in front of the Sphere as seen from Earth; the positioning made it that much harder to observe the smaller body.

"Obviously, you're looking for something that could be a communications signal, a command system, right?" Sianna asked.

"That's right," Dr. Bernhardt said. "Gruber's already pulled in more data than one analysis team could handle in a week. Once we find the correct command channel, there will be less to analyze, but for now we must examine every wavelength we can detect."

"Why do you assume the Charonians will only use one data channel?" Sianna asked. "We use more than one frequency, and we know they do, too."

Bernhardt looked confused for a moment. He took his feet down off the desk and turned to face Sianna directly. "I beg your pardon?" he asked.

"The first signal they intercepted back in the Solar System. The Shattered Sphere signal and reply," Sianna said, paying more attention to the data discrimination reports in the notepack than to her own words. Gruber had picked up a lot of data already, in IR, UV, and lots of radio bands, and rejected them all as "natural" or "static." How could she be so sure?

"Ah, Miss Colette, you were discussing the first Charonian signal received?" Sakalov said, rather gently.

"Huh? Oh. Right. The first signal was at a frequency of twenty-one centimeters, with the reply at forty-two centimeters. So we know they use more than one bandwidth for signaling. That only makes sense—some frequencies are better for a given purpose than others. One might allow you to transmit more data more quickly, but another might punch through a dust cloud more easily."

"And, ah, don't forget the Solar System reported the

Charonians were using modulated gravity waves to send signals," Wally said. "We assume the Multisystem Charonians use MG waves as well, but all our active-process gravity-wave detectors blew up as soon as Earth got here."

"Yes, I well remember that," Bernhardt said, with a slight smile. "I was in the next building over from one of the detectors that blew. Every active detector built since then has blown as soon as it was powered up. Too much gravity energy for an active-process detector to handle, and we never had much luck with the alternate-mode detectors based on Charonian technology. But we can still use the old-fashioned passive detectors, and they tell us enough to know Charon Central does not send commands over gravity waves."

"How so?" Wally asked, in slightly suspicious tones.

"The passive detectors aren't sensitive to high-frequency gravity modulation," Bernhardt replied, "but they do detect harmonics, reverberations in the lower frequencies induced by the higher frequencies, and we can usually correlate the harmonics with some sort of activity. If the Lone World were putting out high-end MG waves, we would have spotted that long ago."

"Right," Sianna agreed, a bit vague about what, exactly, she was agreeing with. Her mind was working on something else. "Besides, I don't think MG waves could be all that efficient as a pure signal system. Yes, anything that can be modulated can be used to send a signal—but there are lots of much easier, more efficient things to modulate than gravity waves. Like radio bands."

"That's the problem," Sakalov said. "Gruber's people did checks all through the EM bands—especially radio. They compared the data we've gotten from the Lone World against all the data types we've received over the last five years. The Lone World puts out a lot of radio energy, but most of it is natural. Gruber suggests that there's a lot of interaction between the Lone World's magnetic fields and the Sphere's surface. In fact, that sort of interaction accounts for one family of very annoying transient bursts of static we've seen for years. Anyway, once Gruber's team eliminated natural radio sources and the GIGO data, there wasn't much left.''

Sianna looked up at Sakalov without really seeing him. *GIGO.* Garbage In, Garbage Out. One of the oldest and most arcane bits of computer slang. It used to mean that if the data that went in was no go, your results wouldn't be of much use. But meanings change over time. These days, *GIGO* referred to data that had already been classified as garbage—static, transient spikes or dips caused by power fluctuation, image degradation cause by flaws in the equipment.

Already classified as garbage. Hold it a moment. Who looks for anything in the places they've already looked? Sianna worked the notepack controls.

''Miss Colette?'' Dr. Sakalov was still waiting for her to say something.

''Ah, um, just a second, sir.'' Okay then. They were saying that all of these emissions were GIGO data, pure noise. Someone had *decided* data *like* them were noise long before anyone even knew the Lone World existed. Knowing full well they were all waiting for her, Sianna rushed through a series of sorts and checks and groupings on the data, not quite knowing what she was looking for.

She looked up suddenly, staring with unseeing eyes past Bernhardt's shoulder at the magnificent vista beyond. Wait a minute. That was it. She knew *exactly* what she was looking for. Vagueness. Yes. Yes.

''I have an idea,'' she said at last. ''We have a signal source with no meaningful signals. What if we've spent the last five years detecting signals without a source and discarding them as meaningless static? After all, the Sphere puts out a lot of noise.''

''We all know *that*,'' Bernhardt said, with just a trace of impatience.

''Yes, but we know it too well,'' Sianna said. ''I've been working on data for the CORE project, and every time there's anything in the radio bands that we don't understand, it gets charted as an 'EM anomaly' or a 'transient event' like the ones Dr. Sakalov mentioned. Once we name something, we assume we understand it, and we ignore it.''

''So you're saying Gruber's people have eliminated a lot of real signals, called them noise or static instead?'' Bernhardt asked.

Sianna shook her head. ''No, not her people—her *computers*. All the initial data processing is automated. If the computer is told that datapoints with thus-and-such characteristics are garbage, it discards every subsequent datapoint with the same profile. The humans running the data-processing system never even get to see that stuff unless they wade through all the raw data manually.''

''And we just got through saying that going through even the non-rejected data we have after twelve hours could take a week,'' Bernhardt said.

''Yes sir. But if you'll pardon the expression, it's possible that searching that non-rejected data makes about as much sense as what the drunk did when he dropped his keys on a dark street.''

''I beg your pardon?'' Bernhardt said.

Sakalov let out a dry chuckle. ''The young lady has indeed attended my lectures, Wolf. It is an example I often use. The drunk drops his keys in the dark, but searches for them under a street lamp, where the light is better.''

''So you are suggesting that the Lone World is transmitting its orders at frequencies we don't even *know* we aren't looking at?'' Bernhardt said.

Sianna nodded. ''It's possible,'' she said. ''After all, we don't know for sure what a command signal from Charon Central looks like.''

''Quite so,'' Sakalov said. ''We assume it will in large part resemble the signals intercepted in the Solar System and the signals we have intercepted as they are sent between lower-function Charonians—except it's obvious the command signals don't resemble those signals completely, or else we would have spotted them by now.''

''So what could they be?'' Bernhardt asked.

Sakalov nodded toward the notepack that Sianna was holding. ''Anything in there, or maybe a dozen other things that *aren't* there. Or maybe the command signals are expressed as some complex phase relationship between two seemingly unrelated signals.'' Sakalov shrugged. ''Maybe they're meant to be read backwards. Or maybe they are modulated or digitalized at such a high—or low—rate of speed we didn't recognize them as signals.''

''Too fast I can understand,'' Bernhardt said. ''But too *slow*?''

''It would be damned tough to recognize a Morse code message if the dots were two weeks long and the dashes were a month.''

''Hmmph.'' Bernhardt turned toward Sianna. ''So, now that you have said we must comb through all the parts of the haystack that we thought we could ignore, where do you suggest we start?''

''With the vague stuff,'' Sianna said. ''There's lots of well-explained natural sources, but the rejected-data log is full of things labeled 'General Static' and 'Unspecified Transient EM event.' If we have a look at all that—''

''And *then* compare *that* against any old rejected data,'' Wally said, cutting in eagerly. ''We could look at stuff from what we now know to be the Lone World's orbital track,'' he went on, leaning forward eagerly. ''I bet we've got a big old stack of old data labeled 'static' that came from the Lone World—even though we didn't know the Lone World was there until just a little while ago.''

''Yes! Right!'' Sianna said,

Sianna stood up and started pacing excitedly. ''For five years we've been observing the Sphere, and for all that time there's been this tiny, hard-to-see dot going around it, sometimes at the edge of the Sphere as seen from Earth, sometimes in front of it, sometimes behind. We're bound to have picked up all sorts of stuff from the Lone World without knowing what it was.'' She paused for a second and thought. ''Hey, data coming from the now-known coordinates of the co-orbital R-H sets too! They'd make a perfectly good signal-relay network.'' She paused in her pacing and turned toward Dr. Sakalov. ''The data archives will still have all that, won't they?''

''They never erase *anything* down there,'' Dr. Sakalov said, quite cheerfully. ''Tell me, Wally: do you think that you could set up a search that would find what we're looking for?''

''Sure I could,'' Wally said. ''All it would take is a good ArtInt searching for vague source coding in the old data, correlating the backtracked orbital coordinates in question. Next we run that against Gruber's new data, and then . . .'' His voice trailed off as he caught the boss's eye.

Bernhardt glared at Wally and then at Sianna with something of the irritation and impatience he was famous for. ''None of this has very much to do with why I wanted to see you all.''

''It doesn't?'' Sianna asked, suddenly feeling quite deflated. She sat back down in her chair.

''No, it doesn't,'' Bernhardt said. ''Oh, I suppose there is a tangential connection, but it is merely—'' Bernhardt stopped dead and shook his head. ''Dear God, now you have me doing it. No. We will stay on the subject this time. In my job, sometimes I have to act like a scientist with a theory, and sometimes like a general fighting a war. A scientist would wait until there was proof that the Lone World was Charon Central. A general has to take more chances than that, gamble that the proof will be forthcoming. I have to take a chance like that now.

''As you know, the SCOREs are on their way—and we all know the probable aftermath of their arrival. We must assume that, once they get here, it will be impossible to launch anything off Earth. As you know, we have a massive effort under way to resupply our off-Earth assets before that time. We are launching everything we can toward NaPurHab.

Food, equipment, fuel, what have you. I have already ordered *Terra Nova* to break off her attempt to land a prize crew on a CORE. She has confirmed that she intends to return to Earth space and dock with NaPurHab.

"From there, she intends to proceed, however her captain sees fit, toward precisely one goal. If Captain Steiger decides to pursue the immediate goal at once, so be it. However, I would expect that she will instead invest in months, perhaps years, of research, study, rehearsal and simulation. However, sooner or later, she is to proceed toward the Lone World, land on that planet, and attempt to seize control of the Multisystem."

"Good God," Sakalov said. "But how has there been time to plan this, work out procedures?"

"There hasn't," Bernhardt said. He stood up and turned to face the window wall, a mere thickness of glass between him and the deep canyons of Manhattan. "We have been setting up the resupply mission for weeks, based on standing contingency plans, ever since we spotted the incoming SCOREs.

"But that is almost incidental. *If* the Lone World is Charon Central, and *if* we can somehow get to it and make it ours, even if we merely find a way to kill it, cripple it—then we will have won. The risks are great, and there are any number of guesses piled on guesses. But if I wait until I am sure of my facts, then we will have lost the moment. The SCOREs will have reached Earth, and God only knows what happens then.

"But there is something else. The *Terra Nova* has asked for more than supplies. She has asked that we send her . . . send her some expertise. I have reached that conclusion that to do so would be very risky—but potentially, most valuable.

"But there is little time, and little cargo space available. If I had my way, the *Terra Nova* would rendezvous with a full complement of our greatest experts on the Charonians. But that cannot be. I have no time to examine all the personnel reports, interview candidates, request volunteers, all of that. So I am left with my own instincts, my hunches, my feelings.

"So I am going to send them you three."

There was dead silence in the room. Sianna could not believe what she was hearing.

"I will send you three," Bernhardt said again. "A wise old man who still knows how to learn, a genius who does not know all that she is, and a dreamer of visions that lead to truth. I will not make any pretense that you have any choice in the matter, or that I am looking for volunteers. *There is no time.* The charter establishing my office gave me the power to draft whomever I wish for whatever task I wish in order to protect the people of Earth."

Sianna stood up, feeling a bit dizzy, and opened her mouth to protest. But no words came. Bernhardt just kept right on talking.

"So. There is only one question I have for each of you," he said. "How soon can you leave?"

Fifteen

Puppet on a String

"We forget what our lives were like back then, before it all happened, back when Earth and Moon shared a sky, and the Solar System was whole and complete. We thought we were alone in the Universe. We thought we were safe. No one had ever heard of the Charonians. No one even knew the Wheel was buried under the Lunar surface until Larry woke it up and it dropped Earth through a black hole.

"We will never regain that innocence—but we can only judge Larry Chao by the standards of the Universe that existed up until the moment he pressed that button.

"In that lost world of the innocent past, he must be found not guilty of committing any intentional wrong. But Larry Chao has never stopped trying to atone for what he did—at a cost to himself that few of us would be willing to face."

—Dr. Sondra Berghoff, statement for *Gravitics Research Station Oral History Project,* Charon DataPress, 2443

Wheelway
The Moon
THE SOLAR SYSTEM

Three days after the first attempt to contact Lucian Dreyfuss, they were almost ready to try again.

Larry Chao was doing his best to sit still as the techs hooked him in to the virtual reality system, trying not to think about what came next. They were going to fire this thing up and run him through the moments leading up to his own death. All right, not *his* death, but as close to it as Larry wished to come. When the Charonians had attacked in the tunnel five years ago, the T.O. had been destroyed while Larry was controlling it, and it had been realistic enough to convince Larry he *had* died, at least for a while. The nightmares had taken a long time to go away—and they had come back last night.

But no, don't think about it. The one bright side was that Larry had been "killed" a few seconds *after* the Charonians grabbed Lucian and made off with him. Lucian, therefore, had not witnessed Larry's death and, therefore, was not reliving it, over and over again. Larry would not have to re-enact his own decapitation.

The down side was that, for whatever reason, the slice of time Lucian was looping through over and over started just a few seconds before the Charonians attacked. The idea was to break the loop before the Charonians hit, force Lucian to perceive a sequence of events fed to his optical and audio centers, not by the Charonians, but by the human virtual reality teams. In effect, they would feed Lucian a hallucination to break him out of psychosis. Of course, Larry had been dropped *into* psychosis by experiencing the real events through the TeleOperator five years ago, but that was beside the point. Even Larry had to admit the possible reward was worth the risk.

They had used a limited-mobility setup the first time they had tried to break through to Lucian, but this time they were using a full TeleOperator control rig, identical to the one Larry had used five years ago in the Rabbit Hole. This time, the T.O.'s inputs and outputs were not hooked up to an actual robot body, but to a computer simulation of a robot body.

Larry's entire body still had to be completely encased in the T.O. control unit, which was, in effect, an exoskeleton with the operator inside. Later, when they had the thing powered up, the machinery would respond to his slightest motion, and he would be able to move his arms and legs and head freely. But until the power-amp circuits were on, the T.O. was so much inert metal and his body was completely immobilized by the weight of the machinery. Even when the thing was powered up, Larry would not actually walk when he moved his legs—the rig had him suspended in mid-air. His body would stay still while his simulated self moved about. He was, and would be, in the center of it all, but absolutely unable to move. That summed up the last five years of Larry's life pretty well.

"How's that feel?" the VR tech asked.

"Hmm? Oh, ah, fine, I guess," Larry said. Actually, the straps were rather tight, but minor things like that didn't seem to matter just now. They wanted him to die again, and no one seemed to think that was asking a lot.

But even if they *had* understood his terror, they would have strapped him into the TeleOperator control system all the same. Even a chance of cracking open the Lunar Wheel's Heritage Memory could easily be worth a life or two—even if the lives in question were his and Lucian's.

"So was he a friend of yours?" the tech asked.

"Hmm? What?" Larry said.

"Lucian Dreyfuss."

"Oh, I knew him all right."

"So you were friends."

"No," Larry said, looking straight ahead, determined not to look at the tech. "We weren't friends. I never much liked him. And he blamed me for . . . for well, what happened."

"Oh," the tech said. "Sorry. I didn't—"

"It's okay," Larry said. Now he turned to look at the man, and forced himself to smile. "It was a while ago. I've gotten over it." Now *there* was a lie. The Abduction, the disaster in the Rabbit Hole, pushing the button that killed Pluto and saved the rest of the Solar System. He was nowhere near over those things. There were days he had hopes of getting *past* those memories—but this was no such day.

"Oh. Well, um . . . ah, hold still now while I attach the electrodes," the tech said, clearly embarrassed.

But Larry was only vaguely aware that the tech was still there. Memories. This whole thing revolved around memories. His, Lucian's, and the Wheel's. The Wheel's Heritage Memory, with the sum total not only of its own experience, but that of all its ancestors as well. Find that, and they could read the history of the Charonians.

There was no end to the information, the answers, the discoveries that might be found there—if the Heritage memory had not been destroyed when the Lunar Wheel died, if it were still accessible, if Lucian's dead mind could show them the way in.

"Okay, VR viewhelmet coming down," the tech said. "You're going to be in the dark for a second until we get this thing hooked up."

The tech placed the helmet on Larry's head and swung the visor down, and Larry's world went black.

He sat there, waiting in the dark, wishing it wouldn't happen at all, wishing it would hurry up and be over with.

Dream on. If Larry was sure of one thing, it was that this was going to be a long haul.

Finally, after some space of time that might have been a

minute or an hour, it began. The exoskeleton came alive, a tiny thrill of motion quivering through it as the power came on. The viewhelmet visors lit up, a miniaturized video screen in front of each eye, their views just slightly offset from each other so as to provide realistic binocular vision and depth perception. Larry found himself—or his simulated robot body—in a featureless room, with various rather generic objects and obstacles scattered about. A warm-up room.

Marcia MacDougal's voice came over the helmet's earphones. "All right, Larry. We're all set here in control. Try out the suit for a few minutes, and then let's see if you can get Lucian's attention."

"Okay," Larry said, "but bear with me for a few minutes. It's, ah, been a while since I did this. I'm probably very rusty."

"That's all right, love," Selby said in some sort of attempt at an encouraging tone of voice. "Once you learn, you never forget. Just like riding a bicycle."

"That's good to know," Larry said. "But I've never ridden a bicycle."

Larry stood up, and the exoskeleton moved with him, smoothly, all but silently. He lifted his left foot, moved it forward, set it down. The feedback system provided him with a slight jolt as his foot came down. He moved his right foot, set it down a bit more gently, and he was walking. His field of view lurched from side to side a bit as he moved. He came to a set of steps in the imaginary warm-up room. He paused at the foot of the stairs, then walked up them as carefully as he could, tottering a bit here and there. There was a wide platform at the top. He turned around and made his way back down the stairs, having a bit more trouble keeping his balance. He got back to ground level without incident, though, then walked over to a pair of pyramid-shaped objects, each with a handle at its apex. The red one was marked "100 KILOGRAMS" while the blue one said "300 KILO-GRAMS." Larry bent down and moved "his" arm to pick up the red one. The exoskeleton was far stronger than a human being, and Larry was able to pick the weight up easily. The weight might be wholly imaginary, but the computer simulator did a very credible job of giving it a realistic heft. Larry straight-armed the weight, held it out to his side, and let it go. It fell to the ground with a heavy thud, and Larry felt the non-existent floor vibrate beneath his feet. "Very realistic," he said to the team in the control room.

He turned toward the heavier weight and tried lifting it. At first, he couldn't budge it. He pulled harder and managed to get it off the ground, though it felt as if he was about to pull his arm out of its socket. "Maybe too realistic," he said, and set it down.

Larry worked the warm-ups for a minute or two longer, getting the feel of the suit, finding that his old training was coming back to him after all. Someday he would have to learn to ride a bike.

"All right," he said. "I think I'm ready for it. Link me into Lucian whenever you're ready."

"Ah, you don't want to do a few dry runs first?" Selby asked. "We can put you in the virtual reality sim of the Rabbit Hole without Lucian in it for a while. Let you get used to it first. Beat up on some simulated Charonians for a while?"

"No," Larry said, his voice a bit sharper than he had intended. "Maybe that makes sense, but to be perfectly honest, I'm more worried about losing my nerve than not being well-rehearsed. This isn't easy for me."

"That I can believe," Selby said. "Stand by. We have to jam the optical and audio signals coming from the Wheel and substitute our own. Might take a minute to get it working."

"Just give me a heads-up when you're ready," Larry said.

"Will do. Selby out." The line went dead as Selby cut her mike, and Larry moved around the warm-up room a bit more as he waited. He tried a few jumping-jacks and push-ups, just to see what the hardware could do. Very smooth. Very nice work indeed. Intellectually, he knew that he was still right where he had started, in the exoskeleton, not in the imaginary warm-up room he saw through the video screens. He had lifted nothing at all when he had picked up the hundred-kilo weight, and exactly the same amount of nothing when he had strained over the three-hundred-kilo one. The exoskeleton had simply put the appropriate strain on his arm and body to mimic the weights. But there was no point in reminding him that it was not real. Not when the whole point was to make the illusion as believable as possible.

What was taking them so long? You'd think they'd have had the whole thing set up before getting him into the suit. *Take it easy,* he told himself. *This is a complicated lash-up.* Any number of things might go wrong or need a last-minute adjustment. Larry knew he was being unreasonable, but he didn't care. He was scared.

He realized he was pacing nervously, back and forth, up and down around the warm-up room. He drew himself up short, forced himself—or at least his projected self inside the VR simulation—to stand still.

"Larry?" It was Marcia MacDougal's voice. "Ready when you are."

Larry suddenly realized he was sweating profusely. "Go—go ahead," he said, his voice tight and dry.

The warm-up room faded away, and Larry Chao stood in uncharted darkness.

"All right," MacDougal said. "Here we go." The darkness faded, and the base of the Rabbit Hole—the base of the Hole as it had been five years before—bloomed up out of blackness. "This is our feed now," MacDougal whispered in his ear. "We're feeding the same scene to both you and Lucian."

Larry felt his heart pounding, and his vision blurred for a moment. But then it cleared, and nothing had changed. This was the place, the horrible place where he had died. And there was Lucian, directly ahead of him, standing there in his pressure suit, looking past Larry's shoulder at whatever was behind him. Lucian, alive, exactly as he had been.

It seemed as if time stopped in that one moment—and maybe it did. Maybe it was not some trick of his mind, but a glitch in the computer program, that had frozen time.

Where am I? Larry asked himself. *Am I inside the computer, inside Lucian's mind, just here to feed a figment to his imagination? Am I inside the TeleOperator the computer is simulating? Who is the puppet, and who is pulling the string?*

Yes, I know I'm in the VR exoskeleton, but what does that matter? The VR video is not what I see, or hear. I see the past, the real past, the moment just before I died.

And suddenly he realized that it was not just Lucian who needed to break out of this moment. *He* had died here too, and had lived to tell the tale. *But I never* did *tell the tale to anyone, not really. Never talked about it. Never dealt with it. Never faced it. Now I can. I can make it go away, make it never happen.*

"Behind you!" Lucian called, the dead man speaking the dead man's words in the dead man's voice.

Larry turned around, and saw the two wheeled Charonians, just as they had been. For a moment, fear flared anew in his heart. But this time he would not let them kill him. This time the computers were controlling the sims, and the Charonians were programmed to lose.

With a strange sense of exaltation, Larry lunged for the closer Charonian, grabbed at one of its manipulator arms, yanked it from its socket and hurled it away. Larry smashed the TeleOperator's fist through the thing's carapace, and the machinery inside sparked and flared. He spun about, kicked the other one in the midsection, flipped it over so that its wheels spun helplessly in mid-air. He grabbed at the left rear wheel and pulled it off.

"Oh my God," Lucian said. Larry spun around and looked at—what? at Lucian? at Lucian's computer projection as directed by the simulator? At a projection of Lucian's body as controlled by his mind?

"He's still in it," MacDougal's voice, whispering. "We're getting his visual output here, and he still sees it the old way. It's a bit muddled here and there, but he's seeing what he's always seen—"

"They know we're here," Larry's voice said through the headphones, though he had not spoken. It was Lucian's memory of his voice, of what he had said five years before. Larry was hearing his own ghost, and the idea terrified him.

Then Lucian's body flew up in the air, lifted by invisible arms, and he was carried away, down the tunnel, by enemies unseen.

"Good God," MacDougal said. "I'm watching Lucian's optic nerve output, and *he* saw the Charonian you just killed pick him up and run out of the tunnel with him. He didn't see your actions at all. The computer sim matched what Lucian thought was happening to him and carried him out, even if the simulated Charonians weren't there to move him. Incredible."

"Yeah," Larry agreed, panting. He realized he was still holding the Charonian's left rear wheel, and he flung it away.

"We're going to have to reset, try again to snap him out of it," MacDougal said. "Do you think you can do it again?"

Larry looked down at the computer-generated phantoms of the *things* that attacked him, killed him five years before. He was whole, and they were bits of mangled metal. "Oh, yeah," he said, "I can do that as often as you like."

Two more times, three, four, a dozen more times, until Larry lost track of how long ago he had lost track, until even the idea of revenge had lost its savor. The simulated Charonians would always lose.

Killing them the first few times had been good for Larry's soul, but by the twentieth time—if this *was* the twentieth time—his strongest reaction to killing the wheeled Charonians was that his arms were getting tired. He grabbed at the second one and kicked a hole clean through this time, just to give his arms a rest.

Larry turned around and watched Lucian being borne away by invisible hands once again—but there was definitely something jerky, uncertain, about the motion. Lucian was still heading down that damned tunnel, but it was less smooth every time.

"Okay," MacDougal said. "One more time, from the top."

"Right," Larry said, his voice weary. The base of the Rabbit Hole faded to darkness, then reappeared once again. Lucian—or at least the computer image of Lucian in his pressure suit—was back where he had started.

But Lucian's image—Lucian—didn't stay there. He stepped forward toward Larry, did not cry out a warning. He had changed.

Changed. Larry turned and saw the wheeled Charonians there. Should he attack again? No. Nothing brutal, nothing violent this time. Enough of destruction. Show Lucian something else. Make it different. Larry raised his hand, palm out, to the simulated Charonians, praying that whoever was operating their images would have the wit to follow his lead. "Stop," Larry said. "Go away. Don't bother us anymore. We don't want you here."

The two alien machines regarded him for a moment—and then wheeled backwards, turned around, and rolled away. Larry watched them going, knowing that at least some of his own nightmares were leaving with them. He had exorcised his own demons.

But what of Lucian?

Larry turned back, toward Lucian's image as it came toward him, moving slowly, awkwardly, the image a bit jerky, Lucian's mind moving his body in ways it had not used in a long time.

"Lar-ree?" Lucian asked. "Lar-ree . . . tha you?"

Sixteen

The Only Way to Travel

"It is almost impossible, and certainly pointless, to explain the Naked Purple Movement. Even the term 'Movement' is misleading, as it implies a large group moving purposefully toward a goal. While the number of the Purple has at times been large, no one would say they have ever moved toward any clear goal. They are not known as the Pointless Cause for nothing.

"At least the term 'Naked Purple' is meaningful. Paint yourself purple, and wander around naked in public, and you will achieve what at least passes for the basic Naked Purple goal: you will be annoying, disconcerting, and confusing to outsiders. In their strange dress, in their often belligerent—and yet whimsical—rejection of the norms and ideas of society, in their deliberately incomprehensible speeches and writings, the Naked Purple work to shake things up, turn things upside down, force us to look at things in a new way. While it is true that this is often a good thing to do, few would deny that the Purple tend to overdo it. . . .

". . . The catastrophe of the Abduction wiped out every other orbital facility. Only NaPurHab, the Naked Purple Habitat, survived. While that can be ascribed mostly to luck, I for one would like to suggest that it was destiny as well. Who else better suited to spend their lives in close orbit of a black hole?"

—_Memoirs,_ Dr. Simon Raphael, First Director of
the Gravitics Research Institute, Pluto.
Published posthumously, 2429

NaPurHab
Orbiting the Moonpoint Singularity
THE MULTISYSTEM

"And here be coming numero uno," Mudflap Shooflyer announced as the first of the Charonian _things_ arrived.

"Thanks, Mud, but they didn't name me for my hearing," Eyeball growled as she stared out the porthole. "I can see it."

"No harm in saying it," Mud replied.

"But what the foggy blue that thing gone _do_?" asked Ohio Template Windbag. "Weirdest looking thing seen in _some_ time. 'Cepting you, 'course, Mudflap."

"Thanks for nod, hefe," Mudflap said, clearly pleased with the compliment.

"Pipe down anytime you like, boys," Eyeball said, struggling to concentrate on her instruments. Bad enough that Mudball smelled the way you'd expect a chap with that label would. Chatter made it worse. "Else clear out and watch from elsewheres."

"Sorry. Will zip it," Ohio said. At least Ohio had a reason for being here. He did, after all, run the hab. But why did he have to bring a schnorrer like Mud along? Maybe it was Be Nice to Losers Day. Eyeball knew it was sometime this week, but she'd been too busy to check her calendar.

Her hardware was all ticking along fine, recording everything. What *was* the thing going to do? She punched up the long-range scope and set it to auto-track the thing.

The massive Charonian sure as hell wasn't like any SCORE or CORE Eyeball had ever heard tell of. Most of them were shaped like short, fat cigars. This thing was more or less rectilinear, and about twenty times the size of the biggest CORE on record. It had what appeared to be cantilevered swivel capture latches running along the edges of one long face. It was also dazzle-brite white in color, a definite departure for the Charonians, who usually favored a dirty grey for most of their gear. Sum up, a big white shoebox shape with legs. There were fifteen more just like it on the way.

Now it was hanging in space, inside the Moonpoint Ring, and exactly abeam of the Ring's interior surface, lining up with it perfectly. And then, suddenly the thing was *moving*, straight for the Ring, fast, like maybe it was going to ram it or some such. Oh, God damn, don't let it be. Were those things here to smash up dead Moonpoint Ring, clear the way for something else? The hab would get caught in debris for sure, beat to rubble.

But the big white box stopped moving as sudden as it had started, less than a hundred meters from the Ring's inner surface. Its legs unfolded and it moved gently in, settling itself neatly into place before the legs wrapped themselves around the ring.

It sat there, quiet and peaceful, and that was that.

"Now what the hell was that 'bout?" Mudflap demanded.

"Won't know for sure till rest of them arrive," Eyeball said. "But my guess is the Charonian docs is paying a housecall."

Kourou Spaceport
Guiana, South America
EARTH

The briefing room was a dreary, windowless grey box. It was aseptic rather than antiseptic, too grey and too drenched with disinfectants for anything to grow, but a grimy, cold little spot for all that. Even without the disinfectants, it was too dispirited a place for any but the most determined of germs, and nothing around here seemed all that determined.

The air conditioning was winning out over the ferocious heat of the launch base. Maybe winning by a little too much. The spaceport was only a few hundred kilometers north of the equator, and every time Sianna stepped outside, she felt as if she were walking into a sodden wall of heat.

Sianna, Wally, and Sakalov sat on one side of a rickety, stained old table, the debris of some previous meeting still in evidence here and there—crumbled bits of paper, a dried-up spot of spilled tea. A far cry from the luxurious appointments in Bernhardt's office only two weeks before.

Bailey, the briefing officer, sat on the other side of the table. His coveralls were rumpled, and he hadn't shaved in quite a while. He was a slouchy, sallow-faced, rubbery-skinned little man, with what appeared to be the stub of a cigarette hanging out of the edge of his mouth. He looked as if he had not been to bed in ten years, and did not care.

"Aw right," Bailey said, taking a noisy slurp from his coffee mug, "let's get this thing started. You folks mind if I don't throw ninety-four different sims up on the screen? I'd rather just use plain English."

Wally seemed as if he were about to say something, but then he thought better of it. Bailey nodded, scratched himself, and went on.

"Good. Then here's the short form: we've started the massive cargo lift to NaPurHab. We're lifting at least fifteen major cargo craft a day, every day for the next three weeks, plus all the smaller stuff we can manage. We want to send everything we can, with lots of spares, because a lot of it won't get there.''

''The loss rate is still close to thirty percent, isn't it?'' Sakalov asked, as if he were asking about the price of onions, rather than his own odds of survival.

''Worse than that,'' Bailey said, a bit reluctantly. ''The CORES have been getting more and more aggressive. We *expect* the loss rate to get a hell of a lot worse real soon. We have to assume that once the main body of SCORES hits town, we will lose whatever remaining access to space we still have. The odds on a given cargo getting through will go way down. Say, to one in a hundred. We *might* be able to launch in radar-transparent stealthships, but that is very tough engineering.

''The good news is that we have gotten better and better at analyzing what the COREs do. Over the years, we have thrown a lot of cargoes at NaPurHab—and seen which ones get taken out. We know what sort of craft, moving in what sort of trajectories, the COREs are most likely to attack. We can send our cargoes in the lower-risk trajectories—and send you people in the lowest-risk ones of all. But there *is* a better-than-zero chance that the COREs will attack any given object more than two meters long within about three hundred thousand kilometers of Earth. If the COREs decide that you might impact on Earth, they will attack you.''

''Wonderful,'' Sianna said. ''How about if we bend over and you send us in one-meter-long ships?''

''Don't think we haven't thought about it,'' Bailey said, ''but we'd have to launch you rolled in a ball. You wouldn't survive the boost phase. We've also learned that the odds don't change much for smaller-size craft. Once you're over that two-meter threshold, it doesn't much matter if you're two and a half meters or two hundred fifty.''

''Great,'' Sianna said.

''I know,'' Bailey said. ''But the best we can do is get you up and out of here at the lowest-risk trajectories during the launch windows we've calculated to be lowest risk. And we want to get you up there sooner rather than later. The SCOREs are headed this way. We don't know what they will do when they get here, but we have to assume they will join the COREs in attacking our ships.''

"So when *do* the SCOREs arrive?" Wally asked.

"We don't know that, either," Bailey admitted sourly. "One cluster of them will boost and then coast, and then another, and another, while the first drifts off course until there's a course correction."

"Sounds like limits on the ability of the Sphere to transmit gravity power," Sakalov said. "It must be directing a single gravity-power beam from one cluster of SCOREs to the next, nudging each group when it can spare the power from some other need. The Sphere is spreading itself pretty thin."

Bailey looked annoyed. "You know so much, you want to give out the info?"

"Ah, no, no. Please, forgive me."

"Okay, we *think* their arrival has something to do with the Ghoul Modules—"

"The *what?*" Sianna interrupted.

"Oh, right, you weren't around for that one," Bailey said. "That's what the Purps are calling the large Charonian devices that are docking themselves to the Moonpoint Ring. The last of them docked to the ring this morning, and they seem to be pumping power into the ring. It looks very much to us as if they are there to bring the dead ring back to life, reactivate it. Ghouls."

"But why?" Sianna asked.

"To proceed with the Sphere's original purpose in setting up the Moonpoint Ring," Sakalov said. "To get through to the Solar System and start building a new Multisystem there."

"Hey, real smart," Bailey said, his voice dripping with sarcasm. "But *our* team has been thinking on this for more than five seconds, and if you can prepare yourself for a shock, they see another possibility. We think it's meant to be used as a bolt-hole. We've known for years the Sphere was afraid of something. Maybe that something is getting close and the Sphere wants a back door. Some hole it can open up, go through, and pull the hole in after itself.''

''The Dyson Sphere is way too big to get through the Moonpoint wormhole,'' Wally objected.

''But the Lone World is the *real* Sphere,'' Sianna reminded him. ''It's the brains of the outfit. The Lone World could go through the hole with a whole slew of smaller Charonians and set up shop someplace new, build a new Sphere.''

''What would it use for power once it was cut off from the gravity generators in the Dyson Sphere?'' Wally asked.

''Who knows?'' Sianna replied. ''Maybe it can store power. Maybe it could absorb solar power in a pinch. If the Lone World drops itself through a wormhole, it'll have done its homework so it can survive on the other side.

''The bigger question is—why is it setting up *our* Moonpoint Ring for its bolt-hole? It must have links to a zillion wormholes. Why does it want to go through ours?''

Bailey nodded, as if he were actually conceding that someone else besides himself might be capable of having an idea. ''Good question. The answer is it *isn't* going to go through the Moonpoint Hole. Best we can tell, the Sphere is getting *dozens* of old wormholes ready. At least we see a lot of things that look like Ghoul Modules headed toward a lot of other inactive rings in the Multisystem.''

''Misdirection,'' Sakalov said thoughtfully. ''Another little bit of evidence that the Sphere—or the Lone World—is in a war, a battle, a fight, with *somebody*. You don't set up deception plans unless there is someone who needs deceiving.''

''Or if you want someone to think you've run when you haven't,'' Sianna cut in. ''The Lone World creates a hundred places it *might* run, and then it hides in-system, leaving its enemy thinking it's gone through one of the holes.''

''So where would it hide?'' Bailey asked. ''You're talking about a world the size of Earth's *Moon* here.''

Sianna shrugged. "Hide in plain sight. Disguise itself as a normal planet. Hide inside the Dyson Sphere. For all we know, its interior is a whole maze, designed specifically to conceal the Lone World in time of danger. Who knows?''

"Hmmph. Maybe so. You people are supposed to be the *ex*perts on all that stuff. But maybe we should get back to what you three will be doing.''

"And what will we be doing?'' Sakalov asked. "How will we be getting to the *Terra Nova?*''

"That part I don't know,'' Bailey said with an evil grin. "We're just getting you as far as the hab. The *Nova* will come and get you herself, I guess.''

"Yes, yes, we know that,'' Sakalov said. "But how are we to get to NaPurHab?''

Bailey laughed unpleasantly, and Sianna disliked him even more.

"Permods,'' Bailey said.

"Oh, dear me,'' Sakalov said. "I was afraid you were going to say that.''

"What are permods?'' Wally asked.

"There's no way a regular passenger ship would make it past the COREs,'' Bailey said, ignoring Wally's question. "Not the way they're behaving recently. Too big, too good a target. We're going to stuff you in personnel modules and put your mods in with a bunch of cargo containers on three different ships on three different days.

"And we're going to have our own little deception plan, by the way. We're going to throw all sorts of decoys and chaff and electronic countermeasures into the mix. Saturate the COREs' patrol zones with so many targets they won't be able to handle them all.''

"What do you estimate as the loss rate for cargo while your countermeasures are running?'' Sianna asked.

"Twenty percent,'' Bailey said. "But we think *your* odds are going to be a lot better than that in the permods. Tougher targets.''

"How *much* better?"

Bailey put the cigarette up to his mouth and took a good hard pull on it. He shifted his gaze away from Sianna and looked down at his coffee cup. "We figure the odds on any one of you getting hit by a CORE are eighty-five percent against. You'll be sent during the period of maximum countermeasures. Besides that, your permods will be carried in small, fast cargo carriers. You ought to make it."

Dr. Sakalov sighed and shook his head. "The odds are about what I expected them to be. But I have been dreading the idea of traveling by permod."

Wally frowned and looked at Sakalov. "Permod? Personnel modules? What's wrong with them?"

Bailey smiled unhappily, pulled the butt of his cigarette out of his mouth and dropped it in his coffee cup, where it went out with a *phut* and a hiss. "Oh, you'll find out," he said. "You'll find out soon enough."

Sianna Colette, dressed only in the flimsiest of hospital gowns, having had the last proper shower she was going to have for a long time, steeled herself to enter the suiting room. Come on. She could do this. Wally had done this. Sakalov had done this.

Suiting room. There was a laugh. A nice, non-threatening name borrowed from other facilities where they really *did* put you in pressure suits.

Sianna stepped out into the suiting room, wearing nothing but the paper-thin robe she was going to have to lose in a minute, feeling far colder than could be explained by the slight chill in the room. The suit technician, a rather grim-faced middle-aged woman in a rumpled blue jumper, was waiting for her.

Sianna wanted to look anywhere but at the suit tech, but she forced herself to stare the rather bored, surly-looking woman in the eye. No, she was only imagining all that. There was nothing at all unpleasant about the woman's expression. Sianna just could not shake the idea that she was being punished, and therefore the suit tech *ought* to look angry with her. Try as she might, though, she could only keep eye contact for a few seconds or so. The tech scared her.

Something about the woman's face put Sianna in mind of Madame Bermley, the chief warder at the first boarding school Sianna had been sent to after her parents died.

That school, as a consequence, had also been the first school Sianna had been kicked *out* of—and Bermley had been the one to do the kicking. Bermley had always had it in for Sianna, always seemed to be able to brush past her young girl's brashness and bring all the frailties and fears underneath to the surface.

Sianna looked away, pretending to be deeply interested in the blank wall behind the tech, but she could see, out of the corner of her eye, that the tech was looking her up and down, just the way Bermley had, and Sianna's skin came out in blushes and goose bumps all at once.

No, *not* the way Bermley had. Bermley had been searching for weaknesses. The tech was sizing her up the way a butcher might examine a side of beef, or a mortician might cast a professional eye over the corpse of a stranger.

The tech had no interest in her, other than as a payload that was rather awkward to load, and a tricky one to maintain once in place. No doubt the tech bore no meaningful resemblance at all to Bermley, and the whole thing was in Sianna's mind. But none of that mattered: Sianna could not help what she felt. Still, she *had* more than half expected to be kicked out of MRI for causing trouble—and if launching her clear off the Earth wasn't kicking her out, then what was?

"All right, dearie. Ready to get on in?" the tech asked, her voice far gentler than Sianna had expected.

"Ah, um, almost," Sianna said. "Just—just a second." Sianna looked down at the personnel module, a box for transporting a person to space at absolutely minimum cost in the smallest space possible. The permod was lightweight, and could be loaded and boosted in any number of launch systems. This one was to be stacked in with a hold full of cargo modules and boosted direct to NaPurHab.

The personnel module was completely self-contained, and could keep a human being alive for perhaps weeks at a time in a pinch—if the human didn't mind losing all semblance of dignity, and, perhaps, any shred of sanity. The permod treated a human being like a slab of meat that had to be kept at a certain temperature, in a certain atmosphere, with nutrient going in one end and waste products coming out the other. It was, in effect, a storage locker designed to hold a person.

Sianna did not like it, to put it mildly. The fact that the permod was almost precisely the size and shape of a coffin did not do much to make her feel better.

The permod was a banged-up rectangular slab of a box, formerly a gleaming jet-black but now scuffed up and banged around to a gunmetal grey.

The suit tech stepped down on a treadle switch set into one corner of the module, and the safety catches released with a disconcertingly loud clunk. The tech pulled open a small access panel and yanked on the lever inside it. The top of the module swung open in exactly the manner of a coffin. Whoever had designed this thing had not given much thought to the psychology of the occupant.

Sianna stepped forward and peered inside. She had gotten a quick training session the day before, but reality was rarely in conformity with training or expectations. The interior was an off-white rubber sort of material, all smooth, rounded contours. The outlines of a human body were molded into the bottom to create a form-fitting shape that was dished-out a bit wider than it ought to be at the base of the torso. Naturally. There was the issue of sanitation, after all.

"All right, time for the plumbing," the tech said. "Off with the robe now."

Sianna swallowed hard and undid the knot. She *hated* getting naked in front of other people. That had been part of what had done her in at Bermley's school. They were very big on physical education there, with the concomitant communal showers. Sianna had earned plenty of demerits in her sometimes devious battles to avoid those.

The robe dropped to the floor, and Sianna stared straight ahead at the tiled wall, determined that the suit tech be utterly invisible. A hand Sianna was determined not to see presented her with the waste control unit, an ungainly white object shaped roughly like an oversized, rigidized diaper that opened up with a hinge between the legs. Tube couplings whose purposes she did not wish to consider came out of it here and there.

Sianna took the thing in her two hands with as much enthusiasm as she would have felt in accepting a dead rat. She opened the clamshell hinge and looked inside. The interior was coated with a clear lubricant gel intended to keep the parts of it that touched her skin from chafing. The parts of the interior that wouldn't touch her were all odd-shaped recesses and discreet bits of valving and tubing.

It didn't do to examine certain things too closely. Best to get on with it. She got ready to step into the thing.

"All right, now," the tech said. "Could you spread your legs just a bit there?" Sianna forced herself to think of the cool, impersonal training session the day before, and the fact that she had had no trouble at all getting the waste control unit onto the mannequin.

All right, then, *she* would be a mannequin. It wouldn't be her she was putting it on, but an inanimate object. Spread the legs. Swing the unit around and hold it between the legs. Use her right hand to push the rear half up against the buttocks— good, clinical, impersonal word, *buttocks*—stoop down just a bit to open up her—no, *the*—legs, reach down with the left hand and pull the front half up and closed. Snap the six latches shut, and the mannequin had the unit on.

It hung loosely on Sianna's body. She switched on the inflator, and felt the unit snug up to her body in a most disturbing way. It felt cold, and stiff, and sterile. The lubricant was unpleasantly cool and slick again her skin.

All right, she had it on. The suit tech could now be allowed to exist, at least somewhat. The tech nodded her approval. "Good. Fine. Nice fit. But wait until we get you launched and you're in zero gee before you try the thing out. The suction system will pull off the waste products while you're in zero gee, but you'll get one hell of a mess if you try using it on the ground. Okay?"

"Okay, yes, sure, fine," Sianna said, her mind an utter blank.

"Good. All right." The tech stepped around in front of her and started to point out the controls. Sianna forced herself to look down. "Suction is that green switch on the left front. Post-use sanitizer is the red switch on the right front. And make sure the suction system is on and running *before* you try anything unless you want big problems. But once it's powered up, you can urinate and defecate normally."

Normally? How the hell was she supposed to do anything *normally* when she was wearing a fiberglass diaper and stuffed into a coffin?

Coffin. Damnation. She had been trying to avoid thinking about that part of it. *Coffins. Death. Sealed in. Closed spaces. Tiny space, no space, lost in deep space, out of control sealed in a black death box blasted into the sky—*

No. Stop. Calm. Calm.

But there *was* no calm. There was only raging fear and the pounding of her heart, and the thought of the fast-coming moment when the tech would close the lid on her and—

God, no. Not that. She wanted to grab the suit tech by the collar and shake her and scream that this was all madness, that she was far too sane and sensible to stuff herself into that box and be blasted into space. But she said nothing, did nothing. "That's it," the suit tech said, completely oblivious to Sianna's rising sense of panic—or perhaps determinedly ignoring it. "All set." The tech seemed to have a limitless supply of meaningless little phrases of encouragement. "We need to spray you down next."

Sianna nodded, not quite willing to speak. The spray was

a combination of a skin moisturizer, to combat chafing, and an antiseptic-antifungal agent, to keep her from molding over in the confines of the module as she became increasingly ripe over the next few days.

"Okay, dear. Stand with your arms and legs apart."

Sianna stood there with her eyes closed, legs spread, arms out straight, feeling naked and skinny and foolish and young and scared. There was a sort of gurgling hiss, and she cringed as the cool mist struck her back. She felt the spray working over her back, her legs, her sides, her stomach, her breasts, her neck. A bit of it spattered onto her face.

"Oops. Okay, keep your eyes shut. This stuff can't hurt you, but you don't want an eyeful of it, either. Hold on just a second." There was the bump of the sprayer being set down, and the sound of footsteps, then the tech's voice again, gentle and close, right in front of her face. "Easy now. Coming in with a towel."

Sianna felt the tech cradling the back of her head in one hand, and the soft terry cloth of the towel against her face. For a fraction of a moment, she was back in the safety of her childhood, in the bathtub, her mother using a towel to get the soap out of her eyes.

"Good. Open up now."

Sianna did so, reluctantly, and found herself back in the relentless present, the harsh lights of the suiting room—and the waiting personnel module.

"All set now, dearie. Now let's get the shirt and leggings on and we'll be all squared away."

Maybe you'll *be squared away,* Sianna thought. *I'll be climbing into that box.*

The tech stepped back to her workbench and came back with what looked like long limp boots. "All right, left leg up first."

Sianna did as she was told. She stood on one leg, then the other, as the tech slipped the leggings on and did up the fabric-clasps that held them on. The shirt went on in something more like the normal manner, buttoning up the front. Both leggings and shirt were made of a very warm, soft, absorbent flannel cotton—the one concession to comfort in the whole operation. They felt good next to her skin.

"How . . . how long?" Sianna asked.

"How long until launch, or how long a ride it's going to be?" the tech asked.

"Both," Sianna said. She was having a little trouble speaking.

"Two hours until boost, and it's going to be just about a three-day ride. Long time to be in a box, but you won't be anywhere near the record. And you should be asleep most of that time, anyway."

"Suppose I, ah, *can't* sleep?"

"Then you take a pill, and sleep until it wears off and then take another pill. Keeping you zonked out saves on life support—and boredom. All right then, let's get you in there." *And, maybe, if we keep you asleep enough of the time, you won't go insane quite so fast.* Even if the tech didn't say the words, Sianna knew they were there. Thrown off balance by the bulk of the waste control unit, Sianna tottered most unwillingly toward the module.

After all the briefing and preparation, getting in seemed almost too simple. Sianna simply sat down on the edge of the module, and then put first one leg and then the other over the edge, bracing herself with a hand on either side of the box as she eased herself down into the module, as if she were getting into a bathtub full of slightly over-hot water. Except getting into a tub didn't put her on the ragged edge of terror. She sat up in the module, and found that her waste control unit wasn't quite fitting into the recess intended for it. She wiggled herself down a bit, and it dropped into place rather neatly and a bit abruptly, like one of those puzzle games where you roll a ball into a hole.

"Lie down, dear," the tech said. Sianna did as she was told. She found herself lying very still, staring at the ceiling. The tech leaned over her for a minute, checking this and that, attaching hoses to the waste control unit and to the interior of the module.

"All set there. Now, I want you to try the sanitation system. Red switch on the left first, then the green on the right."

What point in color-coding the switches if she has to lie on her back and can't see them? But Sianna reached down and found them after some fumbling. She flipped the left switch. There was a sudden, high whirring noise, and the feel of cold air blowing past her skin. She threw the right switch, and jumped a bit as warm water jetted through the unit. She shut down the water jet and let the suction system run a bit longer to help dry her off. She shut off the left switch and listened as the purifier kicked in, reclaiming the water for its next use in cleaning—or as drinking water. Even the lunatic optimist who had run yesterday's training session and had told her how great the system was allowed as how the water wasn't likely to taste real good after the fourth or fifth time.

"Real good. That's working fine," the tech said.

Wonderful. Just first-rate. What could be better. All set. Here we go. Couldn't the woman say anything else?

"Okay, now," the tech said. "I'm going to close up now, and this hatch isn't going to open until you're safe at NaPur-Hab. You'll have the use of your arms and hands for an hour or so, but once you get loaded into the launcher, the restraint system is going to come on. The airbags will inflate and hold you in place. You have *got* to get your arms down into the recesses molded into the padding before that happens.

"You're going to be boosted at about ten gees. More if they change the flight plan. If your arm is lying against your stomach or something when the restraints inflate, it will be pinned in place. If *that* happens, you'll be lucky to get away with a broken arm and crushed ribs. Internal injuries and bleeding, more likely." The tech pointed to a small panel light that read "PREPARE FOR RESTRAINT" set into the inner lid of the module. "When that light goes off, arms and legs in the restraint recesses, and no excuses. You *ought* to have three minutes warning, but people who count on 'ought' get dead. If your nose itches after that light goes on, don't scratch. Do you understand?''

''Ah, yes ma'am.''

The tech smiled, reached down and patted her on the shoulder. ''Good. Have a good trip, and say hi to the Purps for me.''

''Okay,'' Sianna said, and waved good-bye.

The tech stood up, reached up for the lid, and pushed it down on top of Sianna. The lid slammed shut with a resounding boom, and Sianna could hear the capture latches snapping shut.

She was in this box, sealed in it, with absolutely no way out, almost before she even knew she was in it. Probably the tech had done that on purpose. No sense giving a silly, panicky girl a chance to start screaming or scrambling out.

And no way out. No way out. No way out. Sianna calmed herself. No sense pounding on the lid, or screaming. The permod's interior was well-padded, and quite soundproof. If the engineers who had designed these things showed little interest in the psychology of the passengers, at least they had seen to it that panicked passengers weren't going to be any bother.

There was, quite sensibly, no way to open a personnel module from the inside. The danger of a panicky transportee popping the thing open at the wrong time was far greater than the danger of a transportee not being able to get out someplace it was safe.

She lay there, staring at the module lid, determined not to panic. The permod was really just a spacesuit shaped like a box, after all, she tried to tell herself, in the most reassuring inner voice she could. Being in a pressure suit had never bothered her. She had worn one on that trip to the Moon with her parents, a million years ago. She had worn one of those tourist suits to take a walk on the surface, and you couldn't open up one of *those* without help. Yes. That hadn't bothered her. And this shouldn't bother her. No. It shouldn't. It was reasonable reasonable reasonable that she could NOT GET OUT.

Sianna found that her fists were balled up and she was about to start pounding on the lid of her coffin—no, her *permod*. Yes. Use the ghastly, artificial word. Far better than calling the thing by its real name. But it *was* her coffin, or might well be, if things went wrong, and she might as well be in here, locked in here. The SCOREs were going to get her and she was going to be dead. Dead, dead, dead.

Wait a second. There was an external view control, right? She could look out. Yes. That would help a lot. She stared intently at the control panel directly over her face. Which one was it? She stabbed a nervous finger at one button, then another. There. That turned the monitor on, anyway. The flat screen came to life, about thirty centimeters in front of her face. Good. Nothing on it but a status display. Air good, temp good, clock showing the time. But what about the external view? External. There! An old-fashioned selector knob. She twisted it hard to the right and—

There! Her breath came out in gasps of relief. The outside world was still there, just outside. Granted, it was nothing but a view of the suiting room ceiling, but it was *there*, and it was outside this tiny box she was trapped in. Trapped. No. Don't think about being trapped. Trapped in this box for three long, long days with no way—

Hold it. Hold it. Three deep breaths. She was going to have to spend three days in this box. No sense panicking just yet. Plenty of time for that later. The permod was all toughened padding inside, the comm and display and dispenser controls carefully recessed so you couldn't switch them on by accident. Damn thing was a miniaturized spacegoing padded cell.

Well, that made sense. A padded cell was going to be all she was good for by the end of this.

There was a clunk and a thump and a bump on the outside of the permod, and Sianna could feel it moving. She looked up at the exterior view, and could see the ceiling moving around.

This was it, she realized. She was being moved, about to be loaded into the cargo hold of the booster that would lift her toward God only knew what.

Out into space, out toward a visit with the lunatics of the Naked Purple, there to wait for the *Terra Nova* and a journey toward the Lone World, and whatever awaited them all there.

Suddenly spending a few days in a nice, quiet tin can seemed like the least of her problems.

Come on, she told herself. Wally was doing this. An old man like Sakalov was doing this. *She* could do it.

Couldn't she?

Seventeen

Conversations with the Dead

Q: Clearly everything was put together in a rush, and the team had to be ready to improvise. What was the most surprising part of the encounter?

A: The most unexpected thing about the effort to contact Lucian Dreyfuss, the thing we had done the least to prepare for, was success. We had gone to all sorts of extremes finding a way to communicate with him, but there was absolutely no way to know what to expect if we did get through. And when we did make contact, conditions were less than ideal.

Q: In what way?

A: By the time Lucian Dreyfuss finally responded, we—that is, the contact team—had been at it for eight hours. That doesn't seem like such a long time, but anyone who's ever run a TeleOperator unit can tell you just how tiring it can be. The systems monitors didn't have an easy time of it, either. Everything was new, untried, and it was damned difficult to keep it all going. We all knew that if the illusion was broken, even for a moment, it could all be over.

When we *did* break through to Lucian, at the end of that eight hours, all of a sudden, the workday wasn't over—it had just begun. I was there in the Tele-Operator exoskeleton, drenched with sweat, ready to quit, just wanting to go home and go to sleep—and all of a sudden, there he was. Also, bear in mind that Lucian Dreyfuss had been in a very different place, existing in a very different way, for the previous five years. His perception of time was very different from ours. I couldn't explain to him it had already been a long day and I was going to knock off. We had no idea whether he was aware any time had passed, or if he would experience a rest period as five minutes or ten years. I had to go to work and stay at it, then and there.

Q: So what thought went through your mind at that moment?

A: The same one as everyone else on the team: *Now what?*

—Larry Chao, interview with *The Rabbit Hole*, house magazine of the Dreyfuss Memorial Research Station. Volume IV, Number 6 (August 2431)

I am who? Who? Lu-cian Drey-fuss, yes or was, and am dead. Cannot see, cannot hear, cannot move—and yet do those things, and more. They find me. I remember them. I was one them. Am one them. Body mine lies inert, mind lost and broken—but awake, rise I do, and walk, yet do not. They wake me, come for me. Robot Larry come. I before dream long time. Dream truth, dream in enemy's mind, enemy's fear. Must tell them. But words lost, or near. Mind lost. Life lost. But must try. Try help, tell. Am one them. Yes or was.

Dreyfuss Memorial Research Center
The North Pole
The Moon
THE SOLAR SYSTEM

The world was a mist, the universe was a fog, and two bizarre figures—a ghost in a pressure suit, and an angular robotic machine—strode through the nonexistent cosmos together. It was the landscape of Lucian's mind, a ghost's mind, his visual outputs picked up by the computers and reprocessed to present the same image from Larry's perspective.

And they were walking through it. But why walk? They were walking through Lucian's imagination. Why couldn't Lucian just *will* them to be wherever it was they were going? The fogs and mists shifted again, rather abruptly, and Larry braced himself for the change. Now, suddenly, they were walking through a tunnel—not quite the Wheelway, but not quite the homier, human tunnels of a Lunar settlement, either. Something in between. The scale was that of the Charonian tunnel, but this passage had the walkways and lighting and direction signs of Central City or Tycho Under. Larry tried to read a few of the signs, but they seemed to be nonsense words, random characters that weren't quite the alphabet.

Why the hell is he still in the suit? Larry wondered, not for the first time. Lucian was projecting his own image of himself into the system now. He could have visualized himself in street clothes, or stark naked, or as a giant chicken, and the sim computers would have presented him to Larry that way. Perhaps he had seen himself inside that suit for so long he could not imagine any other way of being. How much time *had* passed for him since the Charonians had taken him? Had the five years seemed like five years to him, or five minutes, or five centuries?

Larry stumbled again, and almost fell. An imaginary landscape created in a ghost's mind and processed through a computer—and he was tripping over it. He was tired, dead tired, barely able to stay on his feet.

"Lucian. Stop," he called out. "Please, wait. Where are we going?

Lucian's image turned around and walked back toward him, clearly unhappy at the delay, his movement agitated and a bit jerky and awkward. "Place. Place near," he said, plainly struggling for the words. "Moving close. Getting here near. Hurry please." The words seemed pulled out of him, as if each syllable was a struggle.

"No, Lucian," Larry said, squatting down. It was time to try and talk this out. "We *aren't* getting near. We aren't moving. We're in the same place as when we started."

"Come," Lucian said. "Come. Hurry."

But Larry did not move. "Lucian—do you know what has happened? Do you know how it is you are seeing me?"

"Yes no hard." That was about as ambiguous as an answer got. Lucian had spoken very little since his awakening, and then only in those awkward, cryptic phrases.

Instead of speaking, he walked, leading Larry along, clearly intent on bringing him to see something. What that something might be, Larry could not imagine.

"Come," Lucian said, gesturing vigorously, urging him on.

"No. Not yet," Larry said. "Soon. But I must rest. This is very hard for me. I am very tired."

"Hard *me,*" Lucian said. "But you rest okay. But fast."

"Okay," Larry said. "I'll rest fast." He sat down on the tunnel floor and leaned back against the wall. Not that the wall was there, of course. Just the computers putting some pressure and resistance against the exoskeleton where the wall was supposed to be, the visual system shifting his perspective to produce a view of the tunnel from a seated position. Hard to remember it was all illusion. Larry used the chin switch and keyed over to the control room intercom channel. "How long now?" he asked.

"Six hours since he woke up," Marcia said. "Fourteen

since we started. How are you holding up?''

"Not so good," Larry said, "I'll keep going as long as I can, but I'm about to fall on my face here.''

"We know, Larry, we know. I'm dead beat too, and I'm not driving the TeleOperator. We just don't want to lose him again. We're afraid if you take a long enough break to get out of the suit and sleep, he'll think you've abandoned him. Maybe he won't want to talk anymore.''

"Can't you bring someone else? Bring Tyrone Vespasian in, throw his image in here for a while?'' Lucian had known Tyrone well, and the two of them had been friends. Surely Lucian—or whatever Lucian was now—would be able to relate to Tyrone.

"Vespasian's here, and he's eager to try it. Believe me, we've almost had to tie him down. We'll use Tyrone soon enough, once we're settled in. Once we're sure Lucian isn't going to jump back in his hole and pull it in after him.''

"Look, I can't do this forever," Larry said. "Doesn't Lucian understand that? That people need rest?''

"We can't know what he understands," Marcia said. "We don't even know if that really *is* Lucian, in any normal sense of the word.''

"The longer this goes on, the more I think it *isn't* him," Larry agreed, looking toward Lucian's pressure-suited figure as it stood anxiously watching Larry. "I can't quite put my finger on it, but somehow he's not really there. It's like he's a recording, an image of himself.''

"I don't follow you.''

"People change, minute to minute. They show you different sides, different aspects. You and I are treating each other differently now than we did at the beginning of the day. Reactions vary. Moods vary. Not Lucian. He's exactly the same as he was at the start. It's like he's locked into one mood, one moment, one idea. We only get to see one aspect, because that's all there is.''

"Hmmmm. Could be the rest of it is there, and he just needs to figure how to let it out?''

"Not likely we'll understand him if he does," Larry said darkly. "He's not exactly easy to follow. In more ways than one."

"Ah, something new on that," Marcia said. "We've been pulling in every expert we can, and they believe he's got some sort of damage to his speech centers—or else the Charonians didn't do such a good job connecting to them."

"In other words, he can't talk very well," Larry said. "That much I could have told you."

"He may not be very good at it, but he's *trying,*" Marcia said. "Trying very hard. Our tame experts tell me he probably can't *understand* speech very well, either, that's he's having trouble with words in any form. Massive dyslexia. The signs in that imaginary tunnel you're in aren't intelligible, for example."

"So?"

"So if he can't talk, and he can't write, all he's got left is visual signaling, and he's having trouble with that, too."

"Wait a minute. So he's walking me through this imaginary maze to show me something he can't talk about? Showing me is the only language he's got left?"

"Right."

"Then why doesn't he take me straight to what I need to see? Bring up the image I need to see?"

Marcia did not answer at first. "Marcia? Did you hear me?"

"I heard you. I was just trying to work up the nerve to answer you. Look, this next is just my idea, all right? I haven't talked it through, and there's no data to back it up."

"All right. You've got me good and nervous," Larry said.

"Okay. I was thinking. Yes, he's walking through *a* mind. But why are we assuming it's *his* mind?"

"My God. The Wheel." Larry looked around the tunnel in sudden alarm, half-expecting to see a horde of Charonians materialize.

"Why not? The Wheel's dead, but most of it was electronics and circuits and memory blocks. They're not going to rot. The circuits, the pathways, are still there, if you know how to read and interpret them."

"But wait," Larry protested. "This tunnel looks halfway like humans made it. Charonians don't make signs or light fixtures."

"You're seeing some element of the Wheel's dead, frozen memory as perceived and interpreted by Lucian. *His* mind is making analogs and interpretations of what's really there. That's why he can't lead you directly to what it is he wants to show you. He's in the Wheel's memory system, and the Wheel's dead, with half the circuits destroyed. He's trying to find his way through, trying to find a way forward and lead you there."

"Sweet God. That almost makes sense." Larry stood up, and winced as the exoskeleton chafed against his shoulder. Walking through an alien mind . . . The back of his neck tingled, and he felt the overwhelming urge to look behind himself—as if there could be something there. Suddenly he wasn't tired anymore. He toggled back to the comm circuit. "Come on," he said to Lucian. "Let's get this over with."

"Come," Lucian said. "Times goes. Not long."

Marcia MacDougal watched the repeater video through eyes numbed with weariness. The central display on her terminal was repeating the imagery being fed to the VR system's right-eye display. It jerked and wobbled and swayed with every movement of Larry's head. It was important for her to see what he saw, but it was not easy to watch. Selby, sitting at the console next to Marcia's, wasn't having a much easier time of it. She looked like death warmed over, and Tyrone Vespasian was not in much better shape.

Larry was standing up, turning, facing forward, following Lucian as they moved through the world that Lucian was imagining for them. The tunnel shimmered, shook, dissolved, and suddenly the two of them were walking along the lunar surface, the now-vanished Earth riding in the sky. Larry must have been having a hell of a time dealing with the abrupt changes of scenery. It seemed as if they were moving through random images dredged from Lucian's past.

"Bloody mess, isn't it?" Selby asked.

Marcia sighed, nodded, and rubbed her eyes. She wasn't quite sure which mess Selby was referring to. There were so many to chose from. She leaned back in her chair and looked up at the confusion of the control center. That was a laugh. If there was one thing completely absent here, it was control. It was a jumble of hardware in a bubble tent inside a side tunnel of the Wheelway. No one even understood exactly what was going on. They had used Lucian Dreyfuss's preserved body as their lab rat—but now the lab rat had taken over the experiment, and sent the research staff scuttling in all directions. There was nothing here but too many bodies and too much computer gear crammed into too small a space, all the consoles and computers and simulators jammed in every which way, all the experts they had pulled in from everywhere hovering about, trying to watch and understand and be helpful. The most help most of them could offer would be to go home, but Marcia couldn't think of any polite—or effective—way of telling them that.

They had pulled in experts in brain structure, in abnormal psychology, in virtual reality simulation systems and Tele-Operator operations and Charonian artifacts and medical imaging and vision systems and a half-dozen other disciplines besides. There *were* no experts in putting them all together. Yet. Maybe there would be when this was over.

For the moment, Marcia would have traded the whole roomful of brainpower for one person who could give her solid, definitive answers to a pair of questions: What in the world was Lucian Dreyfuss *doing*? *Was* there any purpose to his actions, or was Lucian just wandering some hallucinatory interior landscape at random, his mind unhinged, with Larry forced to follow behind?

Sooner or later—almost certainly sooner—they were going to have to get Larry out of that suit and give him some rest. Then would be the moment to bring out Vespasian, let him try and keep Lucian company for a while.

But Marcia knew, better than anyone, just how fragile their link to Lucian was, how many variables were tangled up together. No one completely understood the hookup they were using. If Marcia was right, somewhere on the other side of the circuit the human VR system was indirectly linked into the Lunar Wheel's memory system, with Lucian Dreyfuss serving as the link between them. They were *that* close to breaking into the enemy's Heritage Memory. She wasn't about to make any changes that might break that link before she had to. If that meant driving Larry to and beyond the point of exhaustion, then so be it.

She looked back to the display terminal and saw the image change again—no, not change. Take flight. She watched as Lucian Dreyfuss looked up into the stars as seen from the Moon—and then stepped up into the sky.

She blinked and looked again. Yes. Lucian was walking on nothing, striding upward and forward.

"Marcia—he just started flying!" Larry said over her headphones.

"Follow him," she said. "This is the first impossible thing he's done since he woke up. It could be important. He's been in fog, tunnels, and enclosed, covered spaces. Maybe he's been looking for the sky all this time. He wanted to show us something in the sky."

"But he's not walking on anything!"

"Neither have you been," she said. "You've been in illusion the whole time. You think that's the *real* lunar surface under your feet? Just walk like you're climbing stairs, the way he is. He's controlling the illusion. If he thinks you're moving upward, you'll move upward. Follow him!"

"Um, ah, okay." The image lurched from side to side as Larry moved in exaggerated upward steps. "I'm, ah, climbing," he said. "My God, it's working. I'm following him up. My God!"

The view tilted upward as Larry looked toward Lucian, several meters above him. "Can you see?" he asked. "He's stopped moving his legs. He's just flying along. I'm going to try it, see if it makes him think I should fall.''

Marcia watched anxiously and the picture stopped bucking and swaying. Larry had stopped moving his feet. No, he wasn't falling. How could Larry fall when he was still in the T.O. rig in the chamber just down the passage? Illusion was befuddling stuff.

Never mind. For whatever reason, Lucian no longer needed Larry to pretend to move in order for Lucian to take him along. Perhaps Lucian was getting better at controlling his environment—if you could call a self-induced delusion an environment.

But then she noticed what Larry was seeing, and forgot about such trivia.

The stars were changing.

They were shifting position, rearranging themselves, coalescing, some growing brighter, and others fading away. Something was coming closer, growing bigger.

A Sphere. A Dyson Sphere. The twin of the one they had seen in the images from the Multisystem.

"Oh my God," she said. "We're in. Lucian's showing images from the Heritage Memory."

"Images of bloody what?" Selby asked.

"I haven't the faintest idea," Marcia said.

The Dyson Sphere was suddenly huge, and close, surrounded by a cloud of Captive Suns and Captive Worlds. An ordered, stately dominion, all its stars and planets dancing attendance on the Sphere.

Then, from out of the darkness, something came, flashing out of a hole in space. There was a flurry of action, too fast to see. The screen filled with a jumble of images and symbols that came too fast to see or understand. "Let's hope the recorders got that," Vespasian said. "Could you make sense of it?"

"Not me," Marcia said. Selby shook her head *no*, but did not speak. Instead she watched the screen.

Something was moving in from the outer Multisystem, a

bright orange spark of throbbing light.

"What the devil is *that*?" Vespasian demanded.

"No idea," Selby said. "But either it's bloody huge or this is some sort of schematic symbolized display, things scaled up." Now there was movement on the screen as a swarm of objects converged on the orange dot of light. "If those are Charonians, this *must* be scaled up. They don't have anything that can move like that much above asteroid-size. At least so far as we know."

One after another, and then in great swarms, the Charonians moved toward the intruder, smashed into it—and were destroyed, smashed down to nothing. The intruder moved inward, toward the Sphere, unstoppable. More and more defenders moved in, each wave more frantic than the last, as the intruder came closer to the Sphere. Then the screen blanked for a moment, and there was another flurry of incomprehensible symbols and schematics before the image of the intruder and the Sphere reappeared.

"What in blazes the devil are we looking at?" Vespasian asked.

Marcia shook her head without taking her eyes from the display screen. "I don't know exactly," she said, "but it looks familiar. I've seen something like this before."

"What are you talking about? How could you have—"

"Ssssh. Quiet. Let me watch."

Now the intruder was dodging and weaving, ducking the cloud of Charonian defenders. It broke through the last of them and moved toward the Sphere, closer and closer.

With one last lunging thrust, it smashed into the Sphere, punching a hole in it, diving inward. For a brief moment, nothing seemed to happen—and then the intruder, the dot of light, erupted from another place on the Sphere and moved outward, dragging along a second bright point of light with it.

"That's the Shattered Sphere sequence!" Marcia said. "Frame by frame, exactly the same images that the Sphere in Earth's Multisystem sent to the Lunar Wheel. The transmission we intercepted.''

But this image did not stop the way the Shattered Sphere imagery had. The two bright sparks of light did not pass out of the field of view. This time the view stayed with them. They moved out, away from the Sphere, toward a Ring-and-Hole pair in the farthest reaches of the system. They dove toward the hole—and disappeared.

But even then the imagery did not end. Instead it swung back toward the Sphere, showed it pitching and wobbling, its stately, ordered spin decaying into a chaotic tumble. Clearly, the Sphere was dead. Without the Sphere to regulate and control the orbits of the suns and worlds, the whole system of stars and planets careened out of control. The image pulled back to show the Captive Suns beginning to drift away, toward the depths of interstellar space.

Stars made close passes to each other, and their gravity fields stripped planets away, ejecting worlds into the darkness, or pulling planets down into collisions with Captive Suns or into direct impacts with other worlds.

The system was a ruin.

The image faded to black, and then Lucian's voice spoke to the darkness, to Larry, to the team in the control room. "There is it," he said. "Sleep now tired. Very tired." And that was all. Darkness and silence.

Marcia punched up the intercom key. "Larry," she said. "Did you get that? Larry?"

But there was no answer. She tried it again. "Larry? Larry, come in." Suddenly worried, Marcia got up from her console and rushed down the cable-snaked corridor, Selby at her heels. They rushed past the glaring worklights, to the chamber where the techs had assembled the TeleOperator's exoskeleton.

By the time they got there, the techs already had the exoskeleton open. They were taking him down. His skin was pasty-white, his body limp as a rag in the arms of the techs. For a half-second, Marcia thought he was dead, but then his face twitched, his arm raised up. The techs moved him over to a cot on the other side of the room and lay him down there.

"I don't know," the head tech said before Marcia could ask anything. "Looks like it might be some sort of sensory overload reaction. Too much comes in at once and your brain just shuts down. You pass out cold. If that's all it is, then he'll be okay after he comes to."

But then Larry made a low grunting noise, rolled over on his side—and started to snore.

"He's not unconscious," Marcia said. "He's asleep. Dead asleep."

"Well, wake him up!" Selby said. "Ask him what all of that meant!"

"No," Marcia said. "Let him sleep. The poor man certainly deserves it." She looked down at him, and shook her head. Dear God, what he had been through. Today, and in his life. If ever a man deserved a little peace, it was Larry Chao. "Let him sleep," she said again. She turned and looked at Selby. "If he has any answers, they'll just have to wait until he wakes up. God knows we have enough to work on until then."

Eighteen

In the Can

"In all our attempts to understand the behavior of the Charonians, our most common failing is in neglecting to remember they are partly living. There is an *animal* side to these creatures, living beings that are part and parcel of the cybernetic synergisms called Charonians. We think of Charonians as machines, as computers, as robots, as self-propelled spaceships and automated terraforming construction systems. The Charonians are all of these things—but only half their heritage is mechanistic.

"The machine side of the Charonians responds to logic, to orders, to programming. But consider the living side. The living side responds to the same primordial urges that drive all animals, all living things. Fear, excitement, the urge to procreate, the herd mentality, whatever warped and distorted shreds of instinct that still whisper through the lifecode of a hundred worlds. We imagine the overmind, the controlling consciousness of the Charonians, as making its will known through logical, rational, cold, hard orders issued to other machines.

"That all might well be the case. But it might well be just as accurate to think of a nervous shepherd trying to cajole a herd of frightened sheep back toward safety—or a ruthless hunter shouting commands to a pack of half-trained wolfhounds."

—Dr. Ursula Gruber, *Speculations on the Enemy*, MRI Press, 2430

The Guardian was one of many. Hundreds of its kind orbited this world, and thousands more patrolled the skies over the other planets of the Multisystem. The Guardian was far down in the Charonian hierarchy, and its freedom of action was severely limited. It had no significant capacity for free will. All it could really do was whatever it was told to do, and it had been told to detect and destroy any large body that threatened the world it guarded—a protection this world was much in need of.

For reasons unknown, this world seemed to suffer from far more than its share of space debris—much of which erupted from the planet itself. How that could be, the Guardian neither knew nor cared. Perhaps the objects rising off the planet were the spawn of some sort of aberrant rogue Breeders, though they did not match any of the profile points for rogues. But such complexities were beyond its comprehension and well outside its area of concern. All it knew was that it must destroy whatever threatened the world that it guarded.

But the Guardian was not pure machine. The organic part of its being was a tiny, but vital, fraction that gave the Guardian some small shred of what might be termed imagination, some minute capacity for abstract thought.

These abilities allowed the Guardian to conceive of its

*own capacity for error, let it look forward to the conse-
quences of those mistakes. Normally these were of no great
consequence. But just at present the Multisystem was on
edge. Through all the myriad communications links and nets
ran the murmur of danger, the rumor of fear. The emotional
underlay built on itself, reinforced itself. The Guardian was
growing more wary, more fearful, and therefore more zeal-
ous. It watched for error, and struggled to prevent it, or
foresee it.*

*It might have misread the orbit of this object, failed to ac-
count for the variable that would cause that body to shift its
orbits, failed to realize those seemingly inert objects were
actually rogue Breeders that might awaken at any time and
savage a fallow world.*

*Far better to attack a hundred truly harmless lumps of
skyrock, reduce them to unthreatening rubble, than to let a
single truly threatening target get through.*

*And yet, there were always limits to capacity, varying
degrees of threat, the need to conserve today's resources so
as to be prepared for tomorrow's dangers. There was even,
as a secondary consideration, the safety of the Guardian itself. Guardians had no particular need or desire for self-
preservation—but were acutely aware that the Multisystem
as a whole needed to conserve resources. The Guardian
would be happy to sacrifice itself—if the gain to the Multisystem outweighed the loss of an asset.*

*The Guardian could not meet all potential threats to the
world it shielded. Especially not now. Not when there was so
much activity, and when soon, very soon, things would get
even busier. And yet . . . and yet . . . its superiors were forcing the Guardian, all the Guardians, into higher and higher
states of alert. The Guardian, of course, obeyed its orders,
but it also responded to the tone, the mood, the emotion behind an order. Fear, real, deep fear, lay behind the commands from on high, and that fear was seeping into the
Guardian, even as it was instructed to conserve its energy,*

choose its targets carefully, stand ready for the greater battles to come.

Go forward/hold back; be vigilant now/prepare for future battle; kill all possible enemies/make no wasteful mistakes. *The dissonance was most disturbing.*

The Guardian longed for better, clearer guidance—but preparation for battle was going on at every level of the hierarchy, and every being was swamped as the entire Multisystem girded itself for the coming crisis.

It had a job to do. It could focus on that, find solidity and sureness there.

A target headed out from the planet on a long, looping trajectory that would lead it out toward the singularity and back toward the planet, coming dangerously near it. It might well be perturbed into a planetary impact course. The target was a significant potential threat that the Guardian could deal with easily. The Guardian swung itself about and calculated an intercept course. It came about broadside to the target, and moved toward it at maximum acceleration.

Within seconds, the Guardian was moving at sufficiently high velocity to pulverize the object. It ceased acceleration, made a tiny course correction, and prepared for impact.

The Guardian smashed into the target, sending debris spinning off into space in all directions, leaving a new crater in the Guardian's exterior, bits of twisted metal and plastic fused into its surface. The impact left the Guardian a trifle shaken for a moment or two, but that was to be expected.

The Guardian slowed itself and settled into a new patrol orbit.

Watching.

Waiting.

Afraid.

Kourou Spaceport
Earth
THE MULTISYSTEM

Wolf Bernhardt paced the floor of the control center. He was exhausted, barely able to keep his eyes open, but too wound up even to imagine rest. Halfway there. Halfway. Half the cargo carriers on their way. Loss rates were high—not as high as feared, but not as low as hoped.

But so far, so good.

"Confirming CORE P322 impact with *Cargo Craft 47*," Joanne Beadle announced. "*CC47* destroyed."

"Manifest?" Wolf asked, not even looking toward her. Was it something irreplaceable? Would they have to rush a new cargo craft to replace it, send a new craft up against higher odds than the one that had been destroyed?

"Just a moment. Ah, medical supplies, sir. But it's a duplicate. Redundant to *CC15*, which NaPurHab has already taken aboard. No need for relaunch."

"That's something, anyway." But what about the cargoes—and lives—he could *not* afford to lose?

Launch Bay Eight
Kourou Spaceport

"We have a green board," the bland, artificial voice announced over the comm speaker. "Launch in one minute." It was just as well that the restraint system had activated, and that Sianna was completely immobilized, with the airbags inflated down from above to hold her body in place. Otherwise she would have been severely tempted to reach up and claw the damned speaker right out of the console. That damned robot voice was getting on her nerves. Repeating the same bloody message every half minute, nothing changing but the time. The display screen had switched to a countdown clock, the numbers flicking downward in over-big, over-bright letters. She wanted to turn her head away, but the restraint pads had inflated around her head as well, holding it quite gently but quite firmly in place. You could snap your neck by having your head turned when a high-gee boost kicked in, and the permod designers had taken no chances.

"We have a green board," the voice said again. "Launch in thirty seconds."

Sianna could feel the sweat on her body, the airbags pinning her in place. She was hot. She concentrated on that, trying not to worry about other things. After all, being in a box, and being restrained, utterly immobilized into the bargain, could be enough to drive a claustrophobic person completely around the bend, if that claustrophobic person thought about it.

At least it was almost over. In another thirty seconds, she would be on her way. Wait a second. Over? Nowhere near. She would have three days in this thing.

If she had three days. No one wanted to tell her what the loss rate really was, what her odds of survival *really* were. How many cargo vehicles were making it through? Ninety-nine out of a hundred? One out of a hundred? Half? None? And even if the odds were good *now*, the very reason for making the lift now was the knowledge that the odds were about to get much, much worse. Suppose they were too late, and the SCOREs and COREs had shifted from passive defense to aggressive attack right *now*?

Still, the sooner they lit the candle on this thing and got moving, the sooner she would get out of this machine. Out. Dear God, *out*. It wasn't just a word, it was a prayer for deliverance. She had only been in here two hours, and she was already half out of her *mind*. How the hell was she going to say sane for three *days*?

"We have a green board. Launch in twenty seconds." There was a pause, and then—"We have a green board. Launch in ten seconds. Nine. Eight. Seven. Six. Five. Four. Three. Two. One. Zero."

With a shuddering, towering roar, the booster leaped into the sky. Sianna was shoved down into the padding beneath her, and a brutal fist slammed down into her gut. The crushing load shocked her, amazed her. How could anything be so heavy? How could *she* be so heavy? The air was squeezing its way out of her lungs, she could feel her heart straining to move her blood. And then—and then—

And then she could feel unconsciousness coming near, offering her a release from all the terrors and fears. She reached for it, and took it, and knew no more.

Joanne Beadle stared at the ops screen and tried to remember what sleep, real sleep, felt like. She had grabbed a catnap here and there over the last few days, but not *real* sleep, head on a pillow, body on a bed and no one to bother you for eight solid hours.

She blinked, rubbed her eyes, and yawned. Watch the screens. Watch the screens. Ignore Wolf Bernhardt hovering behind her. He had been there ever since that Colette person had boosted away, long hours ago. But pretend he's not there. Watch the screens and pray, and wonder when to do the very little she could do. For the most part the COREs moved far too fast, maneuvered far too violently, for there to be any hope of a human-built spacecraft avoiding them. But for this all-out effort, at least *some* countermeasures were available. Ground-based radars were ready to throw powerful jamming signals into the sky, and cargo carriers full of decoy targets were ready to send the enemy chasing after dozens or hundreds of targets—but no one was ready to use those just yet. Not when that might give the enemy time to react.

Which left Joanne with just two questions. When *would* they use their countermeasures? And, would any of them work?

The Mind of the Sphere—or at least that fraction of itself not presently dedicated to other tasks—looked out over its domain, and knew that all was not well. True, its Captive Suns still plied their steady orbits, and the Captive Worlds remained green and fertile, ready to serve as fit nurseries for the Great Breeding that was soon to come.

But what good were healthy Captive Worlds to a Sphere robbed of all its energy sources and cut off from its communications? What breeding could happen on a cold, dead world, sundered from its sun when the stabilizing beams of gravitic potential could no longer hold the system together?

The Sphere had received warning enough to know how grave was the danger, not only to itself, but to all the systems of its clan, all those to whom it was root or branch. If the Adversary succeeded in conquering this system, it would regain entry into all the myriad ways of the Consortium of Spheres. It knew that it must be prepared to die—must be willing to accept death from others—rather than let that happen. Its own root system, its own parent, had died in just that way, and all had thought that was an end to it. But now—now the Adversary was reawakened, back on the trail, hunting again, and all the death and sacrifice and subterfuge that had gone before were useless.

The Sphere knew it must prepare—but even in the midst of those preparations, it knew that all might well be for nothing. Nor could it oversee all the preparations directly. There was too much to do, and the Sphere could not form itself into too many units. There were limits beyond which it was dangerous to subdivide. It was forced to leave its underlings to fend for themselves, under minimal supervision.

The Adversary could strike from any or all of a dozen or more directions, and might well slip past even the most relentless defenses. The Adversary had no qualms about sacrificing many, or even most, of its forces, for even if one of its number won through, then the battle would be over.

Therefore the Sphere had to prepare everywhere for every possible Adversary tactic—but knew, too, that such was an impossibility. It simply did not have the power, the resources, the forces, to make secure all the possible battlegrounds.

But it had to try. All other issues had to give way before the question of survival.

The Sphere refocused itself on the question of defensive strategy. It might have years until the onslaught. It might have milliseconds. Whenever it came, the Multisystem would be as ready as the Sphere could make it.

Permod Three
Aboard *Cargo Craft 108*
Deep Space, En Route to NaPurHab
THE MULTISYSTEM

Out. Out. OUT! Sianna realized that she was pounding on the lid of the permod, shouting at the top of her lungs. Hold it. Stop. How long had she been doing that? She couldn't remember waking up, couldn't remember the restraint system releasing her. When had she started screaming? How long had she been at it? How long had she been out?

A fresh wave of dizziness overcame her, and she shut her eyes, but that only made it worse, made it feel as if her head were spinning.

She opened her eyes and stared straight up at the blank, black video screen. Calmly now. Take a deep breath. Another. Easy. Easy. She unclenched her fists and lowered her hands, folded them on her stomach. Easy. Easy. Her face was sweaty, and she wiped it with the back of her hand. She ran her hand through her hair. She could tell it was a mass of sweaty tangles, but there was not much she could do about that just now.

Calmly. Calmly. Nothing could hurt her in here. That was the whole idea of the permod, after all. A box for keeping a person alive and well.

She was all right. Everything was fine.

A pill. A knockout pill. She could take it, and sleep, and not be afraid. She reached for the tiny padded door marked with a red cross—but then she stopped herself. No. Not yet. Maybe not at all. She was off on a journey into the unknown, after all. She was bound to face a lot of things more terrifying than brief and safe confinement in a box.

She would have to *face* those dangers, not sleep through them. No. No pills.

The Guardian watched over its patch of space, straining to extend its radar senses just a bit more, see just a little farther into the darkness of space. The task was made no easier by the fact that all its fellow Guardians were doing the same, or by the fact that space seemed filled with the strange debris being flung out by the planet it protected. There seemed to be more and more and more of it.

Where was it all coming from? What did it all mean? Was it perhaps some strange new danger? Perhaps some scheme of the Adversary's? The spawn of some malfunctioning rogue Breeder that had landed on the planet and begun breeding on its own, without the Sphere's wishing it? The Guardian struggled against its own rising fear, knowing full well that its judgment could be impaired by such panicky emotion.

But no counterweight, no calm and soothing word of command came from on high to reassure the Guardian. No one told it what to do. How could it serve properly without instruction?

Surely action, any action, was better than inaction at such a time. There! There was a target. It was not a threat at present, but space was full of targets that maneuvered, shifted their orbits, re-aimed themselves. This one could do that! It might be a covert infiltration ship, filled with the agents of the Adversary.

Attack. The Guardian realized it must attack. It reoriented its radars, focusing its main beam down on the target. It shifted its course, made ready for the kill.

Kourou Spaceport
Earth

Joanne Beadle got up from her console and stretched. At some unnoticed moment of the night, the ops center had turned quiet, shifting from a mood of taut urgency to something more akin to quiet expectancy. Joanne looked about the large, semi-darkened room. There were empty consoles now, people slipping off for naps, operators getting friends to cover while they made a stop at the head or grabbed a hurried bite to eat.

Joanne Beadle had wide-set grey eyes and dark brown hair that set off her pale skin. She was a careful, owlish sort of person, slow and thoughtful, but ready to move fast once she was sure she was ready. She prided herself on being able to learn fast and remember it all—and she had needed to be able to do both things for this job. The spaceport director had chosen her as Bernhardt's on-site technical adviser during his visit, and stuck her with that job the moment Bernhardt arrived at the spaceport. She was supposed to be able to answer all his questions about the operation, the Charonians, the Moonpoint Ring, and the SCOREs. It was a lot of studying on short notice. She had been holding her own so far, but it was nice to get a moment's peace.

Joanne looked behind her. Dr. Wolf Bernhardt slept on a dumpy couch in the corner, his body twisted into a posture that could not be comfortable, his face looking drawn and exhausted, even in sleep. There was some ancient quote from somewhere about this sort of moment—something about the last moment of night, just before morning, where everything seemed to have stopped for good and all. It all felt changeless, as if this was going to be forever. A little dark, a little quiet, a never-ending stream of cargo ships lifting off Earth—some getting to NaPurHab, some being destroyed.

The business of getting the cargo convoys to NaPurHab had settled down from panicky improvisation to a steady, grinding battle of endurance. The Charonians had nearly all the advantages, of course, and once the cargo ships were launched, there was not a great deal the control operators could do.

But here and there were holes in the patrol patterns, craft that could be shifted to other courses and so moved out of

danger. There were chances to fool the Charonian radar.
More often of course, they could only mark down another
ship as destroyed and determine if it was necessary—or possible—to launch a replacement cargo.

Joanne stretched again, took a few steps back and forth to
get the kinks out, and sat back down. Nothing changing, everything the same. . . .

—The alarm went off and Joanne jerked to attention. She
reached out and shut off the audio alert out of sheer reflex
with one hand while she called up display details with the
other.

She stared at the display for fully a half a minute before
she understood it—and then wished she didn't. Something
cold gripped at her insides. Sakalov. The old man, the nice
old man who had never hurt anyone. He was in that carrier.

Bernhardt. She had to wake Bernhardt. For a tiny, fleeting
moment, she toyed with the idea of leaving him alone. There
was no *logical* reason to wake him. There was nothing he
could do, and the knowledge would bring him no benefit.
Would he really want to witness the death of his old friend,
the man *he* had sent out—the man he had killed? Yes, he
would be angry at her for not alerting him—but he would not
live the rest of his life with the memory of watching his
friend die.

Then it dawned on her that Wolf Bernhardt had remained
here for the sole *purpose* of watching his friends die, if need
be. He was here to face the consequences of his actions.

She went over to him, reached out with a hesitant arm and
shook his shoulder. "Sir. Sir. CORE 326 is targeting *Cargo
Craft 43*—Sakalov's permod is—"

Bernhardt's eyes snapped open, and he was on his feet, at
the display controls, punching at the touchpads to display
full data on CORE 326. He stared at the screen, his face expressionless, so calm and thoughtful that he might as well be
reading over the budget projections for the next quarter. He
stabbed down a finger and switched the commlink over to
another setting.

"Countermeasures," a man's voice answered from somewhere.

"Countermeasures, this is Bernhardt," Bernhardt said, his voice betraying nothing. "Give me status on *CC43*. CORE 326 is targeting it, and *CC43* is carrying a passenger. Where is our response?"

"We are responding now, sir. There is a full set of countermeasure modules on board *CC43*. We are deploying them now. But *CC43* is now over two hundred thousand kilometers from Earth. The speed-of-light delay . . ."

"Well, dammit, see that there are no other kinds of delay!" Wolf snapped. It was the first crack in his armor, his first display of emotion.

"Ah, ah, yes sir. But it takes some time for the countermeasures to deploy. We should see deployment start in about fifteen seconds."

"Stay on this line, Countermeasures." Wolf hit a touchpad and cut his microphone. "Beadle. Tell me. What are the countermeasures for this ship? What will happen? What will we see?"

"Well, sir, we will commence by firing chaff bombs."

"Chaff bombs? What are these, please?"

"Chaff is small strips of aluminized plastic, highly reflective to radar. A very old defense against radar systems. The ship launches the bombs, which move out ahead of the cargo carrier and explode, producing a cloud of chaff. That blinds the CORE's radar. Then the ship fires a cluster of decoys, each designed to display a false radar image that mimics the ship's. While the CORE is blinded, the decoys and the cargo craft all maneuver. The decoys try and draw the CORE off, get it to attack them instead of the ship."

"And this will work? This will protect the ship?"

Joanne looked at Wolf Bernhardt, looked him in the eye, knowing the expression on her own face was the answer he did not want. Just for a heartbeat, the mask fell. All the fear, the strain, the guilt shone through. Then, just as fast, all trace of emotion vanished. "We don't know, sir," she said. "In theory, it ought to. In practice, it's a rush job. We cobbled the system together in a hurry—and the COREs are fast and powerful. My guess would be that—''

''Yes? Yes? Your guess would be what?''

''That the CORE will be agile enough to smash the decoys *and* the ship long before the ship can get out of range. Even if the ship escapes for now, there's nothing to keep the CORE from making a second pass.''

The mask flickered once more, but this time it did not fail. ''Thank you, Beadle. I appreciate your candor. Now let us hope that you are wrong.''

Aboard CC 43
Deep Space

Yuri Sakalov woke from fitful slumber. Some sort of noise, some vibration transmitted through the ship's hull, had awakened him. There it was again, a muffled, far-off thud. Something being ejected off the ship, out into space? What the devil was—

Then an alarm sounded, and a mechanical voice blared out of the speaker at him. *''WARNING. WARNING. AC-CELERATION WARNING. RESTRAINT SYSTEM ACTI-VATION. MAKE SURE ARMS AND LEGS ARE IN RESTRAINT POSITION.''*

It took Sakalov a moment to remember that meant making sure his arms weren't pinned to his body by the airbags. His arms had been half-floating over his body as he slept, and he pulled them back to his sides just as the bags inflated, grasping him tight. The neck restraints filled, forcing him to hold his head straight.

He felt a new vibration and a sharp, high hissing noise. *The attitude control jets,* he realized. His head was pressed down into the padding, and slightly lighter pressure held his feet. *The aft port and forward starboard thrusters,* he decided. *Setting the ship into an end-over-end spin.* Then the hissing noise cut off, and the pressure stopped. Was that

what all the fuss was about? That one little tap on the jets.
There had been no need to—

But then the main engines roared to life, slamming him
down into the padding with incredible force. Sakalov
gasped, the wind knocked out of him. It had to be at least
eight gees. Why in the world would the ship need that hard a
kick? It took him a moment to realize the attitude rockets
hadn't fired a second time to counteract the rotation caused
by the first burn. That meant the ship was still under that
end-over-end spin. But firing the engines without the ship
being stable on all three axes meant it had to be corkscrew-
ing all over the sky. What possible reason could there be for
such an insane maneuver?

And then he knew. He knew. And in that moment, with
the engines still roaring, the acceleration still crushing him
into the padding, his body cocooned in the restraint airbags,
Yuri Sakalov was suddenly at peace.

Calm. He felt a remarkable calmness that surprised him
even as he felt it.

And then he understood. It was the *certainty* of the thing.
For the first time since the Charonians had appeared and stolen the Earth for their own mysterious reasons, there was
something certain, clear, definite, in his life. And that was a
great comfort. Even if the certain thing was his own death.

*Suddenly, a cloud of blinding-bright reflectance burst into
being in the Guardian's radar sense, dead ahead, just in
front of its target. The target itself vanished in the glare,
completely hidden from view by the shimmering mass as it
swelled to many times the Guardian's own size. For a brief
instant, the Guardian knew fear, thinking the cloud was as
solid as it seemed, that the Guardian would smash itself into
it, be reduced to a mass of useless rubble, dying wastefully,
accomplishing nothing. It decelerated violently, prepared
for evasive action.*

*But the cloud continued to expand, and began to dissi-
pate. The Guardian retuned its radar sense, in effect squinting at the cloud in order to see it better. It was nothing but*

a shimmering illusion, millions of low-mass bits of high-reflectance material. The cloud was harmless. But its target, its quarry, was hidden behind that cloud—and this deception made it clear that the target was controlled by the Adversary. It must be destroyed at all cost. The Guardian re-accelerated, diving straight for the center of the cloud and the target's predicted path.

The Guardian braced itself for impact with the edge of the cloud, but the flurry of tiny impacts was so slight as to be almost undetectable. With a feeling of triumph, the Guardian sped through, clearing the rearward edge of the cloud—

—To find seven targets, each presenting a radar image identical to that of the original target, each maneuvering in a different direction. Had the enemy duplicated itself somehow? Reproduced? Or was this another illusion, another deception?

No matter. If there were suddenly seven enemy targets, then the Guardian would simply have to destroy all seven. All were maneuvering, but none at even a tenth of the Guardian's normal acceleration.

The Guardian came about and aimed itself at the first of them. It rushed forward, gathering velocity, focusing its radar sense on the target, bracing itself for impact with an object large enough to produce such a bright radar reflection.

But then, at the last moment, just before impact, it refined its radar imagery once again, and discovered the astonishing truth—the target was a quite small object that somehow produced the radar image of the original large target. A decoy. Truly, the Adversary was full of cunning.

It smashed into the decoy, the impact nothing more than a slight jolt, a shudder.

But now. Now it had learned the subtleties of the Adversary's gambit. There were tiny differences between the false image produced by the decoy and the image produced by the true target. Now the Guardian knew enough to distinguish one from the other, even at a distance.

It examined the remaining targets, ignored all the decoys, and moved in on the true agent of the Adversary.

Kourou Spaceport
Earth

"The devil take it!" Bernhardt muttered under his breath, but Joanne barely heard him. She was staring at the same image he was, the same image the was being displayed on nearly every screen in the control room. The red dot that was CORE 326 was heading straight for Sakalov's ship, ignoring all the decoys that lay in between. "The thing learns too quickly," Bernhardt said, his voice weak and powerless. He pulled a chair out from the console and slumped down on it. He leaned his arms on the counter top and sat there, staring at the screen, shaking his head. "Too fast."

The Guardian brought its radar sense to maximum acuity, tightened the beam down as far as it would go. Yes. This was the real target, the one being shielded and hidden by all the Adversary's trickery. The target was maneuvering in a complex pattern, but the Guardian could shift course far more quickly and move much faster. It could catch the enemy in just a few seconds. Eager for the kill, it put on more speed.

Aboard CC43
Deep Space

The cargo ship fired its attitude jets again, even as the main engines continued to fire at maximum thrust. Dr. Yuri Alexandrovich Sakalov felt his tired old body being rattled about like a pea in a pod, despite the best efforts of the restraint system. It did not matter. True, if he survived, he would be covered with bruises from head to foot. But he was not going to survive. If there was any subject on which he was expert, it was the behavior and abilities of the Close-Orbiting Radar Emitters. And if a CORE decided to hit a ship, no amount of maneuvering was going to save it.

Yuri Sakalov tried, in the midst of the thundering chaos, to think through his life, as it ended. He had regrets, many of them. Things he had done, and had not, women he should have loved, mistakes he should not have made. And yet. And yet.

He was just about to die trying. Surely that counted for something.

The ship lurched suddenly, the engines cut out for a few seconds, and fired again. Sakalov frowned. What was the point of all these wild gyrations? It could not gain them anything but a few seconds of futile respite.

Soon now. He knew it would happen too fast for him even to be aware of it. The multi-megaton mass of the CORE would be moving faster than a bullet when it struck. There would not even be time for pain when it—

The Guardian smashed into the target, this time half-expecting another undetectable impact. But this time the Guardian struck a large mass moving at high velocity. Not enough to kill the Guardian, of course, or even to do it significant harm, but the impact was violent enough to stun it, confuse it, knock it off course.

Huge explosions ripped through the target, engulfing the Guardian in a shockwave of shrapnel and gas and heat and light that dissipated almost immediately. Debris of all sizes and descriptions tumbled through the sky.

And suddenly, where there had been two large bodies moving through space, now there was but one, surrounded by a cloud of wreckage.

Though still disoriented by the force of the impact, the Guardian felt pleased with itself.

It had destroyed an agent of the Adversary.

Or at least, so it thought.

Nineteen

CORE Feelings

"Gerald MacDougal and I had another argument concerning the nature of the Charonians tonight. (What *else* of comparable importance is there to talk about? Know thy enemy, and all that.) Gerald says we must be extremely wary of any tendency to consider any particular Charonian as an individual. Better to think of the COREs and Singularity Rings and Carrier Drones and other forms as different castes of bees or ants than as different species. Some of the MRI theorists say the Charonians are *less* individualistic than ants.

"I am not so sure. I have spent years observing and tracking various Charonians, and I have concluded they have a bit more individuality—a bit more personality—than a line of ants going after bread crumbs.

"Gerald has his own theories, needless to say. He says that the Charonians don't really seem to have the *idea* of the individual, but that this does not prevent them from *being* individuals. He says it is a mistake to regard the idea of the individual as being some sort of *opposite* to the idea of the group.

"I pointed out that one person apart is qualitatively, as well as quantitatively, different, from a group of people, and it is well established that group behavior in humans is fundamentally different from individual behavior.

"He said that each member of a given group, while conforming to group behavior, can behave *as an individual at the same time.* Five thousand people walk north along the crowded avenue, and five thousand more walk south, all more or less managing to give way and step aside and cooperate so everyone keeps moving. Yet each of those ten thousand cooperative beings regards himself or herself as a single person, wholly unaware of cooperating, each intent on his or her own business.

"Nor is the cooperation perfect. People run into each other, arguments flare up if too many people want to get in the same door at the same time. Groups compete within themselves.

"But the cells in the human body likewise cooperate *and* compete. Sometimes they react at crosspurposes to each other. Sometimes they will even attack each other. Certainly *that* is individual behavior. But is the cell aware of it?

"A talk with Gerald always leaves me questioning assumptions I never knew I had. In a way, it's a shame he never entered a seminary. He would have given the lecturers headaches.

"Groups and individuals. Another one of those damn dichotomies that seem utterly clear until you start looking closely at the borderlines. Do my cells know they make up a human being? If they do know, do they care?

"Maybe the Charonians are not a group, but a billion individuals who have self-awareness and don't know it. Or maybe humanity is a group-being, a mass mind whose individual units are unaware of their collective consciousness."

—Dianne Steiger, master of the *Terra Nova*,
personal log entry, April 23, 2431

Permod Three
Deep Space

Sianna Colette opened her eyes from a restless, dreamless, sleepless fog of unconsciousness. Her hands still hurt. She looked at the open palms of her hands, and the deep red welts in her flesh where her fingernails had sliced into the base of her palm. Clotted over now. Had she really done that to herself? She had bit her lip, too, somewhere in there. She ran her tongue over the bite, and it stung.

At least she was not bleeding anymore. Just as well. Tiny spots of blood were splashed all over the permod's interior and her clothing as it was. Her face must look a sight.

She shook her head from side to side, trying to clear it, and rubbed her face with a grubby, bloody hand. How long had it been? It seemed as if she had been in here for weeks at least, but that was not possible. The life-support system could not have kept her alive that long—unless they had been lying to her. Maybe they had hooked up some sort of supply module alongside her permod, once she was inside. But why? Why the hell would they want her to stay in space for that long? Some secret plan to send her someplace even worse than NaPurHab? Maybe they had diverted her craft, sent her on a direct path to rendezvous with *Terra Nova*.

No, she told herself. It was bad enough being claustrophobic. No sense getting paranoid into the bargain. No. The clock display must be right, and it had only been two days.

Was she running a fever? She put a hand to her forehead. She *felt* hot, and God knows her mouth was dry, but she couldn't really tell.

She felt as if she were recovering from a fever, an illness, in that gentle moment of recuperation where you knew you were getting well, when the illness was getting weaker and you were getting stronger.

She had conquered the permod, more or less unharmed. Horrible as it was, she had discovered that she could survive being sealed up in this damned box. Maybe being sealed in a coffin for a few days was all anyone needed to cure claustrophobia. Granted, it would never be a *popular* cure, and she still was not exactly enjoying herself, but even so, the fear had been burned out of her. Oh, she still wanted to get *out*. But all but the last bat's-squeak of irrational ravening fear was gone. After this trip, she wouldn't have the slightest concern about stepping into that elevator car at MRI.

Not that she ever would have the chance, of course. She was never going back.

Sianna blinked, gulped hard, and forced herself to accept it. She was never going back to Earth. Not with the COREs and SCOREs and whatever other space-monsters the Charonians could dream up blocking the way.

Unless, by some miracle, humanity found a way to open the spaceways, it would be death to try and go home. She was dead already, so far as anyone back on Earth was concerned.

She would never see her friends, her city, her books, her clothes, her bed again. All she had was what was with her now. And she had been able to bring so little. Her personal luggage allotment here in the permod was only five kilos' worth to fit into a space roughly the size of a large handbag. A few family photos, a pair of shoes, and a few changes of underwear. God only knew what sort of clothes the Purps would provide. Best to bring at least a *few* items that would allow her some chance at modesty and comfort.

We bring nothing into this world, and we take nothing out of it. . . .

No. Enough of that. It was time to look forward. Toward NaPurHab, toward the *Terra Nova,* toward the Lone World—the Lone World that she had unveiled, revealed for what it was.

Back home, back on the Earth that was lost to her, they were monitoring the Lone World, every antenna and detector they could manage aimed at it, listening for its commands. Her friends back there were scurrying around the archives, digging through all the old data, searching for whatever transmissions from the Lone World the detection hardware had recorded by chance over the years. The experts in Charonian notation and language were working night and day, struggling to squeeze meaning and understanding from the Lone World's transmissions. They were learning the enemy's language of command, thus the enemy's most powerful secrets. And she, Sianna Colette, had told them where the secrets were kept.

That was something to have pride in.

Now if she could get the hell out of this damned box . . .

Kourou Spaceport
Earth

Wolf Bernhardt sat at the water's edge, in the darkness, in the hot, fetid night of the South American coast. He stared up at the blackness where the sky should have been. Thick cloud cover hid the stars from view, and made the night as dark and blank as his heart.

Soon he would have to head back to the ops center and watch over the next phase of this bloody nightmare. He would have to be strong, and firm, ready to make decisions. Before then, he needed sleep. He knew that. He should go back to his quarters and try and rest. But not yet. Not yet. He needed the darkness, and the roaring surf, and the chance to be alone.

Wolf shifted on the park bench, some tiny fragment of his mind wondering why on Earth no one ever made such benches comfortable. They always seemed to cut into some part of one's anatomy. Thinking on trivial matters at such a time prevented one from thinking about so many other things.

The Atlantic lay before him, the water of the mighty ocean quite invisible in the darkness. But it was there, all right. The roar of the surf, and the salt air, and the glint of lights from the spaceport reflected off a whitecap all told him that. The unseen was still there. The hidden could be close, and powerful.

Half-mechanically, Wolf checked the glowing numbers of the time display on his wristaid. Two hours since Yuri had died.

But that was not strictly accurate. Better, more accurate to say, that it was two hours since Wolf Bernhardt had killed Yuri Sakalov by sending him off on a suicide mission.

And Sianna and Wally still were out there, just waiting to be picked off, the defenses on their ships just as useless as the ones on Yuri's.

And that was his doing, too. His. All of it. This whole mad, jury-rigged scheme to resupply NaPurHab before the SCOREs arrived. The hurried, improvised, idiotic, un-thought-out, comic-opera-heroics idea of sending Sakalov and the others to Captain Steiger and the *Terra Nova.* Others had thought of it, but he had agreed. He had liked the idea.

But no, damnation, *no!* It was not idiotic. It was right and proper to send those three to Steiger. MRI could beam all the information it wanted to the ship, but knowledge was not ex-pertise, or wisdom, or insight. Sianna Colette had proved that much. She had not discovered anything new—she had simply put the pieces together, and *made* something new out of the parts everyone else had already seen.

Sooner or later, *Terra Nova* was going to have to confront the Lone World, and when she did, she would need not just the data concerning the Lone World, but the minds that had lived with that data, talked it out, seen it from a dozen different angles.

He needed to talk. Never had he felt more alone.

He pulled his phone from his pocket and stared at it for a moment before he realized that it was, of course, Yuri that he wanted to call. Call and apologize for the very thing that made the conversation and the apology impossible.

But if not Yuri, then whom?

Time and events were rushing past, beyond all control. The crisis, the moment, was still unraveling. Early tomorrow, the first of the SCOREs would arrive in the vicinity of Earth, just about the same time Sturgis got to NaPurHab. That moment would give the first clue as to what the SCOREs—and perhaps the entire Multisystem—intended. Would they indeed attack Earth, land and use it for their breeding ground? And if so, could Earth survive?

Wolf had spent every waking moment of the last five years struggling to prepare for the time when the Charonians moved against Earth. He had gleaned every bit of data from every observation of the nearby Captive Worlds, attempting to analyze the nature of the attacks on them by the scars left behind. He had cajoled the United Nations and the rump national governments to prepare weapons to defend the planet, given a hundred speeches, written endless articles and reports urging this plan or that proposal, preparing these evacuation plans and those training programs.

Now the time had come and, across the world, armies and scientists and politicians were scrambling to be ready for the unknown, for whatever the SCOREs might do.

Perhaps the Battle of Earth would start tomorrow when the first SCORE made its closest approach to the Moonpoint Ring and then turned toward Earth. Perhaps tomorrow would mark a victory—or the beginning of the end.

But Wolf had already fought his battle. Either his efforts would be enough, or else they would not. There was nothing left for him to do. And perhaps it was too much for one man to imagine the fate of the world. Instead he found himself thinking about the fate of one child-woman, one frightened girl he had met but briefly and would never see again, a woman he had sent out into the void. Wolf glanced at his wristaid and figured the time. Thirty hours from now, Sianna Colette would either be dead, or just arriving at NaPurHab.

And maybe the SCOREs would move faster than expected, do something unimagined, get the job over faster, exterminate the local fauna immediately so as to clear the way for the Breeders. Maybe everyone on Earth would be dead or dying in thirty hours' time. No one could know. Wolf Bernhardt sighed and turned back from the sea. Time to get some sleep, before reawakening to the nightmares.

Multisystem Research Institute
New York City

Ursula Gruber, Ph.D., stared, unseeing, at the datapack in front of her. No doubt there were all sorts of useful—perhaps even vital—datapoints in the cloud of numbers and charts and statistics in front of her eyes, but she couldn't see them anymore. She rubbed her eyes and sighed. No point trying any more just now. Last night Yuri had died. Last night she had not slept a wink. She needed quiet and rest. Not that she was going to get it.

They had it wrong. She was becoming more and more certain of that. She did not know where, or how, but she knew they had it wrong.

The SCOREs were the key to it. But they didn't have that key in the proper lock. The SCOREs were headed toward the vicinity of the Moonpoint Ring, and not toward Earth. The conventional wisdom was that the SCOREs were going to perform gravity-assist maneuvers, do slingshot turns around the Moonpoint Singularity and come in for landings on Earth to commence a Breeding Binge.

But that made no sense. The Charonians had never used gravity-assist maneuvering before. Why should they? Even the most energetic gravity assist could only add ten or twenty kilometers per second of velocity change, and any Charonian could manage ten times that much velocity without any strain at all. Gravity assists made sense when you were short of energy but had lots of time, whereas the Charonians had all the energy anyone could hope for—and seemed to be in a desperate hurry.

Which led her to the conclusion that SCOREs were going toward Moonpoint not for gravassist but because the Moonpoint was their ultimate destination.

Now all she had to figure out was why the devil would they want to go to the Moonpoint. And there were the damned Ghoul Modules, to use the Naked Purple name, a name which seemed likely to stick. Sixteen of them had landed at equally spaced intervals on the inner surface of the Moonpoint Ring. No one had offered the least explanation for them. They seemed to be sending power through the system, but why?

This one little planet was far from being the chief concern of the Charonians. Granted, that was difficult to keep in mind as the huge fleets of Charonians swarmed about Earth. Similar fleets of SCOREs were headed toward between fourteen and twenty other Captive Worlds—but not toward all of them. Just some. Why?

Furthermore, on three Captives, the SCOREs had already arrived—but no one could tell what happened next. The worlds where the SCOREs had arrived were just too dim and too far off to see what was going on in detail.

About half of the SCOREs apparently went missing after arrival at the target planet. That would seem to support the assumption that at least some SCOREs were landing on the planet—but then why were the *other* half still detectable? Why didn't *they* land and commence breeding as well? Waiting for their turn?

It didn't quite hang together. With every passing minute, Ursula felt more and more sure that they had the whole Breeding Binge idea wrong. Yes, there was no doubt that the Charonians used planetary surfaces to reproduce, but why assume they were going to do it *today*?

But despite feeling they had it all wrong, she still had no idea what was *right*. She had no alternative explanation. What other motivation could there be besides a Binge?

Well, no point in wondering. There was enough else on her plate to keep her busy. The latest from the cryptographic section, for example, with a new analysis of the transmissions from the Lone World—

A discreet little beep tone from her calendar roused Ursula from her thoughts. Damnation. Time to phone in her report to Wolf Bernhardt.

Why couldn't he just accept a written report, instead of interrogating her twice a week? She hated his questioning. Of course, Bernhardt was not likely to be in top form today. Not after getting Sakalov killed the day before.

She reached out a tired hand and pushed screen panels marked PLACE SCHEDULED CALL and AUDIO LINK button. She hesitated a moment, then punched up the video link as well. Normally, she didn't like the additional intrusion of someone seeing her as well as hearing her, but *she* wanted to see what sort of shape the man was in.

Besides which, it might be no bad thing if *he* saw that *she* was nearly at the end of her tether. Wolf had a tendency to forget that people needed sleep.

"Yah. Bernhardt here," said a voice from the console, speaking before the video display had gotten his image up on the screen.

Then the announcement screen faded and she could see Wolf Bernhardt, sitting at what looked like a console station in some sort of command center. She could see a vague, mousy-looking woman just at the edge of the frame. Where was he? Still at Kourou, according to the infostrip across the bottom of the screen. She had assumed he would be back here in New York long ago. Ah, well, good thing the phone system could keep track of where he was. Ursula certainly couldn't.

Bernhardt looked drawn, tired, and pale, but not nearly so

much as she expected. The man never wore out—or at least he was determined to make it seem that way.

"Wolf. Good morning." Strange. She thought of him by his last name, but always addressed him by his first. Somehow, the two of them had always simulated intimacy, without actually having it.

"This morning is anything but good," Bernhardt replied, a hard edge to his voice. "Last night was nothing but disaster. How could this morning be good?"

Damn the man, kicking her in the head for a commonplace courtesy. As if she were to blame for Yuri's death. *She* had not sent him out in that death-trap permod. But still, she must say *something*. "I mourn his death as well, Wolf. I am sorry."

"Yah, yah," Bernhardt replied, ducking his head and running his fingers through his hair, avoiding eye contact. Ursula allowed the moment and the silence to linger.

But then it was over. Wolf cleared his throat, adjusted the papers in front of him, and moved resolutely to new business. "Now, your report and analysis. Have you got anything new? Any revised behavior analysis on the COREs or SCOREs?"

Ursula punched a panel or two on her menu screen. "Text and data on their way to you now. There is something new in it, too."

"New in what way?"

"Something a little hard to put down in numbers and charts." Ursula blinked, covered her mouth as she yawned. She felt the need to get up and stretch.

"Well, what is it then? A behavioral change in the SCOREs, perhaps?"

Ursula shook her head no. She was feeling restless, cooped up. She threw a switch that moved the image of Bernhardt over to the main wall display, and cut from the desk camera to the one over the wall screen.

She stood up, came around to the front of the desk, perched on its corner, and addressed the wall screen. "No change on the SCOREs, Wolf. We're still tracking them heading toward the Moonpoint Singularity.'' She hesitated, tempted to say something more about her thoughts on that. But no. Leave it for now. Talk about the rest of it instead. ''But I'm starting to see something else in all the data. Nothing I can define absolutely, nothing I can hang a number on, but it's there, all the same.''

Bernhardt gave her an odd look. ''What is where, please?''

Ursula gestured vaguely. ''The COREs, Wolf. They are becoming increasingly aggressive.''

Wolf shut his eyes and nodded. He was more tired than he looked. ''Yah. More intercepts.''

''I am afraid it goes deeper than that. They are not just more aggressive. They are more erratic.''

''What do you mean?'' Wolf demanded, looking up at the camera, his expression hard and sharp.

Ursula Gruber paced the floor. She knew that she was going in and out of the pan limits of the cameras, and knew how irritating it could be for Wolf when she wandered out of the shot, but she couldn't help it. She was too keyed up, too edgy.

''There are more attacks, but there is less logic behind any given attack. Launch-window constraints meant we had to send some cargo via high-risk trajectories—but the COREs aren't taking the bait. Cargoes we almost *expected* to be smashed are getting through—and the ones sent via the safest routes and launch windows are getting hit far more frequently than they should be.

''We have enough ships and routes and attacks to know it isn't just some slight skew in the numbers, a hiccup in the statistics. It's a real change. Based on the numbers we had a week ago, Dr. Sakalov's ship should not have been attacked.''

''And the other two, Sturgis and Colette, are still en route, in the middle of it, on those 'safe' trajectories,'' Bernhardt said in a bitter voice, a note of anger and blame there as well.

But one look at his expression made it clear he was blaming himself, not her. Well, if *she* felt guilty enough to think he was pointing the finger at *her,* no wonder. "I gave you the trajectory data, Wolf," she said. "His death is on my hands as well."

"Ursula, we are fighting a *war* here. Yes, one man has died, and two others might, but the fate of the planet is on the line. *We* made the mistake together, Ursula, if you like. But his blood is not on our hands. The *enemy* killed him. Not us."

"But the other two *are* on the same sort of safe trajectories. Now all my calculations turn out to be useless and we don't dare change their courses for fear of attracting the COREs' attention. I could get them all killed, to no purpose."

"Then they will be killed!" Wolf said. "*We* got them killed. I assure you, the nightmares came every time I lay my head down even *before* Yuri's death. Now they will come even worse. I know that. But we must move on. If the other two are on dangerous trajectories, it's too late now. There's no way to recall them, no way to save them. If at least one of them survives, then that will be enough. The knowledge, the experience we have here at MRI will get to where it needs to be."

"And if they both die? If the COREs get them both?" Ursula asked.

"If the COREs get them both—" Bernhardt began to answer, but stopped abruptly, as if to calm himself and collect his thoughts. "If the COREs get them both, I will review the situation and decide what to do. We may attempt to send someone else out. By that time it may no longer be within our power to do anything at all. It is not, thank God, a decision I must make now."

"Have you—informed—either of them?" Ursula asked. "Do they know what happened to Yuri?"

"No. They are not to be informed until they arrive at NaPurHab. No good purpose could be served by telling them now. Cooped up in those damned tin cans, what good would knowing do them? Besides, the panic could kill them.''

"You're right, I suppose," Ursula conceded, "but that doesn't make it *feel* any righter."

"No, it does not." Bernhardt was silent again for a moment. He just sat there, staring down at his hands. Ursula found it in her heart to pity the man, even if he did seem more than half robot most of the time. This was hard on him, harder than he ever let show. "But let us move on," he said at last, in a brisk, efficient tone of voice. "How goes work on the Lone World transmissions?"

"We're learning fast," Ursula said, trying to sound equally brisk and efficient. "We're seeing a lot of new syntax and vocabulary, but the underlying structure is very similar to the message traffic we've been reading for years."

"Excellent," Bernhardt replied. "That is going to be the key, Ursula. If we can read the Charonian's basic commands, perhaps we can still survive."

"We're working around the clock, I promise you. But there's something else that might be of more immediate concern. We have tracked what seem to be two incidents of— well, I am not quite sure how to describe it."

"Two incidents of *what*, Ursula?"

"Of what look very much like COREs attacking each other. And another of a CORE attacking a SCORE."

"Charonians attacking each other?" Wolf asked.

Ursula nodded. "Suicide attacks, in fact, but that much at least makes sense. An impact powerful enough to kill one would pretty much have to kill the other."

"But they are attacking each *other*?"

"We've seen it before, occasionally, in the vicinity of some of the other Captive Worlds. Never more than one at a time."

"Are you sure they were attacks? Might the incidents not be something else you are misinterpreting?"

"One CORE moves in on another, crashes into it, and both of them go dead in the water. No further movement or radar emissions, and a cloud of fragments and debris. What else could it be?''

"But that doesn't make sense," Wolf protested. "Why would they attack each other?"

"I don't know," Ursula said. "Why the hell do they do anything? Any explanation I can give comes down to projecting human emotions and motives onto a bunch of flying rocks and mountains. But something *is* different about the way they are acting. That much I can say for sure. A few incidents of one crashing into another could just be malfunctions or accidents, or a result of more traffic causing congestion. It's more general than that. Their movements are more sudden compared to even a few weeks ago. There's something rather *abrupt* in the way they move, something that wasn't there before. I've seen a few COREs start in toward a target and then abort, brake to a halt almost before they start. They're *jumpy*."

"But why?" Wolf asked. "What sort of orders could they be getting that would make them act that way?"

Ursula shrugged. "We're just at the beginning stages of being able to read Lone World command sets, but I don't think they *are* being ordered to do anything. Besides, the shift in their behavior is too subtle a difference to be caused by orders. It's a question of tone."

"Tone? Ursula, what the devil are you talking about?" Wolf said.

Ursula sighed. "All right. I think they're sensing panic from higher up, and the panic is spreading. That's the short form. They're trigger-happy because the Lone World is nervous."

"That's a lot to read into one asteroid crashing into another."

"Wolf, I *know* these particular, individual COREs. They've been in near-Earth space for years. I've been tracking them since they arrived, watched them the way a behaviorist watches herds of animals. And they do have individual behaviors. Certain COREs are more aggressive, others more cautious. If two COREs got within a certain distance of each other, one would give way to the other—and I could predict which one. I have files and data on every move they've ever made.

"These COREs are acting *scared.* Something has them spooked. The best I can describe it is that they are like hunting dogs who start acting nervous when their master is edgy."

Ursula walked back behind her desk, dropped into her chair, and stared up at Wolf's face on the wall screen. "Which, of course, brings us back to the old, old question. What is frightening enough to spook the Charonians?"

Boredway Car/Come/CarGo OpCent
(Formerly Broadway Cargo Operations Center)
NaPurHab

The top of the permod swung open and Wally Sturgis sat up, feeling more than a little pleased with himself. He knew for damned sure that you weren't supposed to be able to open the things from the inside. He counted the fact that he had managed it as a major victory.

His head felt a little funny, unaccustomed to any sort of movement after three days in the mod. He felt his stomach lurch just a bit as well, as he found out the hard way that sudden movement in a microgravity environment could be most disorienting. About a hundredth of a gee this close to the axis. Enough to tell him which way was down, more or less, but not much else. *Welcome to NaPurHab,* he told himself.

He took a deep breath to steady himself, and thus got a lungful of air that did not smell like Walter J. Sturgis, another novel experience after the last three days.

That led him to realize precisely what flavor Walter J. Sturgis had become in the last seventy-two hours. Perhaps a shower might be in order. Wally set to work detaching himself from the permod's plumbing attachments, and got out of the permod, moving very carefully.

"Hey! You there guy! Get outta that mod now-right!"

Wally looked around to see who was calling to him.

A small, peppery-looking woman bounced up to an overhead guideway about twenty meters away. She was dressed in rather grubby-looking purple-and-orange pants and a torn pullover with a tiger-stripe pattern. Her hair was shaved in a tonsure, and her skin was dyed, not purple, but a rather striking shade of yellow. "Get outta that thing!" she said again, pulling herself along on the overhead stanchions.

"I'm getting, I'm getting," Wally said, scrambling out of the mod, feeling more than a bit woozy.

"Those supplies are everybody's, buddy," the woman shouted, hurrying over, swinging along, arm over arm. "Cargo headhoncho don't want *no* lib'rating without his okay . . ." Her voice trailed off as she got close enough to get a whiff of permod. She looked down into the permod, took another look at Wally, and said, "Oh." She let go of her stanchion and drifted slowly down to floor level, landing after a leisurely five-second fall.

"You been in that thing?" she asked.

"Uh-huh," Wally said.

"Not sposed to be outgetting alone," she pointed out in a rather accusing tone, but with something less than crystalline clarity as to what she was accusing him *of.* Was she saying it wasn't allowed? Or unsafe? Or commenting on the fact that it was supposed to be impossible?

"Sorry," Wally said. "Should I get back in until you're ready?"

Twenty

Blood in the Sky

"There's an ancient, ancient joke in which a man has made a hash of his business and is being interviewed in the aftermath. 'Have you learned from your mistakes?' the man is asked. 'Yes,' he replies. 'I'm sure I could repeat them exactly.'

"This, when applied to the Charonians, sums up their response to our tactical and strategic failures—and successes. They will do tomorrow what they did yesterday. So long as they continue to follow this practice, we will have at least some whisper of hope."

—Gerald MacDougal, journal entry,
November 5, 2430

Terra Nova
Deep Space, Approaching Near-Earth Space

Slowly, slowly, the big ship moved in toward Moonpoint.

Dianne Steiger sucked on her bulb of coffee and considered just how much she hated zero gee. Not for herself, mind. After an adult lifetime spent in spacecraft of one sort or another, a shift from this gravity to that meant little to her. The medical problems caused by zero gee were no great challenge, either, if people paid attention and took care of themselves—and she made quite certain that everybody on a ship of *hers* took care of themselves. Zero-gee debilitation was to spaceflight as scurvy had been to sea travel five or six hundred years before—completely preventable, and fatal all the same, for anyone fool enough not to take precautions.

It was the headaches that zero gee caused in managing the ship. *Terra Nova* had been designed for operation either in zero gee or in roll mode, rotating along her long axis to produce artificial gravity via the centrifugal effect. The *TN* could function either way, but roll mode was preferred for almost everything on board, from drinking coffee to flushing the toilets, from pumping coolant to controlling the ship's thermal load. There were ways to *do* everything in no-grav, but most of them were awkward and inconvenient, workarounds rather than straightforward procedures.

To make it harder, they were trying to operate at minimal power. Every use of electric power, by definition, generated electromagnetic radiation of one sort or another, including radio emissions—not good around things like COREs, designed and built to detect radio frequencies.

So no hot food, no hot showers. Large areas of the ship were in darkness, while sections in active use were using half their normal lighting. It was getting damned depressing.

Nor did she greatly enjoy standing four-eight-four-eight watches, but she didn't see much choice in that matter, either. There just weren't enough command and ops personnel available to keep the ship running on alert status any other way. Four hours of general supervision where needed in the ship, eight hours on bridge duty, then four hours of dealing with whatever low-priority matters and office work had cropped up during the day. Then—in theory—eight hours to eat at least one decent meal, wash, and grab some kind of sleep before starting it all over again. Not that she had gotten eight hours of downtime since they had started the approach to Earth. Something always came up.

Last night, for example, she had spent half the time she was supposed to be sleeping sweating out the closest approach of CORE 219. *Terra Nova*'s course had taken her within six thousand kilometers of the CORE at one point. But the CORE had done nothing, and *Terra Nova* had drifted past it in the darkness of space.

All in all, a lot of trouble just to get the two surviving MRI specialists—assuming they did survive—and *Terra Nova*'s share of the supplies sent from Earth.

Ah, well. Back to business. Dianne started checking the repeater displays, in effect looking over the shoulder of her crew.

"Oh, hell." Dianne spotted something on her small repeater screens. "Tracking officer! What the hell is going on with CORE 219? I show a shift in aspect ratio."

"Wha—huh? What's the . . . just, just a moment, ma'am." Dianne looked over at the young officer. Who was it? Hamato. Dead flat tired, like everyone else. Exhaustion was getting to be at least as great a danger as the COREs. At least he was coming awake once she gave him a poke. "Ah, ma'am," he said. "Confirming aspect ratio shift. I read CORE 219 coming about, presenting itself broadside to us—"

An alarm sounded, and Hamato, now very much awake and alert, slapped at the cut-off button. "CORE 219 redirecting its radar, tight beam on *Terra Nova*."

"Battle stations!" Dianne shouted. "Stand by for evasive action."

"Trajectory change for CORE 219—219 coming out of

previous patrol orbit. Turning toward *Terra Nova*."

"God damn it! Defense Officer Reed, stand by for authority. I'll need to stay sharp." *Defense Officer!* How strange an idea, in this day and age. It sounded as anachronistic as a rigging master. "Tracking, give me a tactical display and verbal report. What is range to 219?"

"Current range 15,434 kilometers."

"Why are they moving on us now?" Dianne demanded. "We had closest approach hours ago."

"Unknown, ma'am. CORE 219 now accelerating toward us, acceleration rate climbing from twenty-five gravities. Thirty. Forty gravities acceleration. Holding at forty gees on a direct bearing for *Terra Nova*."

"Very well," Dianne said. "Let the datalog show that I am declaring an attack as of this time. Defense Officer, I authorize release of all weapons and defense systems. Stand by for chaff canister launch." It was the same tactic Sakalov's cargo craft had tried—blind the attacker, deploy decoys, and make a run for it. Dianne Steiger, however, had seen to it that the *Terra Nova* had a few more teeth than a cargo ship.

"CORE 219 has ceased acceleration," Hamato announced. "CORE 219 now on an intercept course for a broadside impact with *Terra Nova* in eighteen minutes, five seconds. Closing velocity thirteen kilometers per second."

It was tempting, damned tempting to try evasive action now, but there was no point to it. Not when the *Terra Nova* could just about manage three gees with the wind behind her and the CORE was barely clearing its throat at forty gees. No. No. They would not survive here by running away. Sakalov had proved that much.

They were going to have to kill this thing.

Dianne licked her lips nervously and tried to concentrate on her display screens as the bridge erupted into action, staff rushing to their battle stations, voices shouting out orders and questions.

Check the screens. Range to the CORE was dropping rapidly, at terrifying speed. But because the CORE had allowed the *TN* to fly past the point of closest approach, the CORE was coming in on a long stern chase, rather than head on. It was coming in from the rear and below and to starboard, on a direct heading, rather than circling around, getting into position, lined up nose to nose with the target, then barreling straight down for a head-on impact.

Was that good or bad? What did it mean, if it meant anything at all? Think! Think as the seconds ticked away. The *Terra Nova* had the means to fight back, but she was not going to get any second chances.

And if the *Terra Nova* had learned from the attack on Sakalov's ship, so too had the Charonians. The CORE that attacked his ship had no doubt sent a description of the event to every other CORE around Earth.

All right, you know that they know. But do they know that you know that they know? There were still endless arguments as to the nature of Charonian intelligence. No one knew for sure if Charonians were self-aware, or if so, if they *knew* they were self-aware. From there it descended into philosophical horseradish, but one thing Dianne knew for sure, at a gut level: the Charonians weren't much good at dealing with change. Nor had the Charonians shown any sign as yet of being aware of human intelligence.

Right. Good. But the clock is moving. What does that tell you? That the CORE coming up behind them was doing so on the expectation that the *Terra Nova* would behave exactly as Sakalov's ship had done.

Dianne jabbed at the touch panels, brought up the data beamed up from Earth. She ran the attack on Sakalov backwards and forwards from every angle she could find, one eye on the tactical display on the main screen, ticking down the dying minutes and seconds until impact.

She watched as *Cargo Craft 43* fired its chaff bombs, dispersed its decoys, and the ship and the decoys commenced maneuvering violently, hidden by the chaff. She saw CORE 326 burst through the sheltering chaff, smash one decoy, and then, it seemed, learn to tell the difference and barrel straight for *Cargo 43*. Run it again, from the top—

Wait. There. That was it. Good. Okay. The only way out is through. If they lived that long. She turned to Lieutenant Reed, sitting at the Defense Ops.

"Defense Officer Reed. Do not, repeat, do not, use pre-programmed or optimized spread on chaff dispersal. I want your initial chaff dispersal to be *identical* to what *Cargo 43* did. Same number of chaff cans, fired in the same pattern when this CORE is at the same distance. And don't tell me *Cargo 43* did it all wrong: I know that. You do it the same way and stand by for further orders."

"What's the plan?" Gerald asked, materializing at her elbow. How long had he been there?

Dianne realized she didn't know the answer consciously. She forced herself to put it into words, and found she was explaining it to herself as much as to Gerald. "The CORE is optimizing its attack," she said, "but it's basing that optimization on *Cargo 43*'s behavior." Her hands worked the tactical display controls as she spoke, overlaying the current tactical situation with the death of *Cargo 43*. "When the CORE came through the chaff, the real ship, the target, was well to the rear of the formation. *This* CORE didn't make its move until it was lined up for a perfect shot at exactly the same position."

She looked to Gerald, trying to tell if it made sense to him, if he saw what she saw. Not that it mattered. She was still in command—and there was no time to change the plan anyway. But still, to see that understanding would help just now. God, it would help.

He nodded, and allowed the slightest of smiles to crease his lips. "You're right," he said. "That's what they're assuming. They think we'll behave exactly the same way the cargo ship did."

Dianne grinned back, a hunter's smile. "That's what I figured. I thought we might want to encourage that idea."

"Defense Officer! Reconfigure decoy units to match the deployment from *Cargo 43*—but load an additional decoy and program it to duplicate *Cargo 43*'s own movements. Helm, prepare to come about to a course parallel to the CORE, two kilometers off its port beam and traveling in the opposite direction at maximum acceleration. Do not, repeat, do *not* bring ship to boost attitude until ordered to do so. Defense, be ready to load and fire additional decoys and chaff. All sections, stand by and prepare to execute.''

There. That was that. A guess, a hurried plan, and a flurry of orders. Already it was too late to turn back.

Dianne watched her bridge crew scrambling to obey her orders, watched the clock count down the moments until projected impact, watched another clock display with less time on it tick down the time left until action, until *Terra Nova* would begin the same dance that *Cargo 43* had performed—although, God willing, this time with a different end.

Cargo 43 had deployed its chaff at six minutes six seconds before projected impact. Every attack simulation Dianne had run told her that was far too late, and that the cargo craft had used the chaff badly, running in precisely the wrong direction.

What they had to do now was convince this CORE they were going to do the same.

"Coming up on one minute to chaff bomb launch," the Defense Officer announced.

"How long after launch will the bomb blow and spread the chaff?" Gerald asked.

"Optimal time would be two minutes, fifteen seconds after launch," the Defense Officer said. "However, we are matching the *Cargo 43* time of one minute twelve."

"Defense, the moment that first chaff bomb has the CORE blinded, fire a second one programmed for optimal chaff release time. And put countdown clocks for everything on the tactical view," Dianne said. "Helm, stand by for minimum-time throttle-up to maximum thrust on main engines," Dianne said.

"Stand by," the Defense Officer said. "Second chaff

bomb programmed for optimized dispersal pattern. Count-down clocks for launch and dispersal of both loads now on tactical.''

''Thank you, Lieutenant Reed,'' Dianne said. *This was it,* she told herself. *First blood, first attack. This was the first time the crew of the* Terra Nova, *indeed the first time any humans on Earth or in the Multisystem would fight back.* Hijacker *had tried to fight, but she had failed. Now they would avenge her.* Cargo 43 had merely tried—and failed—to do what humans had been forced to do against the Charonians every single time—retreat, run away, surrender in hopes of surviving.

But running wouldn't work anymore. *Cargo 43* had told her that much. *Terra Nova* had been little more than a passive observer for the last five years. That time was over. No more watching from a distance.

Now it was fight or die. Dianne had come to that decision in the last few days, half without knowing she had done so. The disastrous *Hijacker* mission had served to fix the idea of death in the minds of all aboard. Someone had scrawled *No one gets off this ship alive* in the wardroom head. Dianne had ordered it removed at once, of course, but she could not erase the sentiment—or the fact that it was probably true. Better to die fast and clean, fighting to live, battling their tormentors, rather than rotting in the dark.

''Helm, stand by to perform minimum-time attitude correction on my mark. We're doing this one by feel.''

''First chaff launch in thirty seconds,'' the weapons officer announced.

''Very well,'' Dianne said, her eyes on the tactical monitor, working the time-advance display, juggling all the predicted moves in her head. But which direction would it move, and how fast, once it spotted the decoys? Where would the *TN* be by then? Could they get safely inside the chaff cloud by then? Would the two chaff clouds be enough? Should she order a third chaff can? No, too late.

''Twenty seconds.''

Damn it, had she guessed right? What if the CORE decided to switch to thermal sensing and spotted them in the chaff cloud? There was no way to mask a fusion exhaust flame, after all. The fusion flame. Now *there* was a weapon. Was there any way to rake it across the CORE during the flyby? No, too late to set that up. Play it as it lies.

"Fifteen seconds to chaff launch."

Of course, the chaff wouldn't just hide the *TN* from the CORE. It would hide the CORE from the *TN*, at least on radar. No way around that, of course, and it wouldn't have any practical difference on the outcome, but even so it was a nuisance. "Tracking—can you give me a confidence level on visual tracking of the CORE once we're in the chaff?"

"No problem there, ma'am," Hamato replied. "We should be able to see it just fine on visual and infrared."

"Let's hope it doesn't think to look for us in something besides radar, then."

"No sign they ever have, ma'am," Hamato said.

"Your optimism is most comforting, Mr. Hamato."

"Ten seconds."

The tension built. Not that the chaff launch meant anything. Just a small canister cast free into space and lighting its engines. But it had to work. It had to. The countdown clock reached zero and winked off the screen. Dianne somehow was disappointed not to be able to feel or hear the launch directly, though of course she knew better.

"Chaff bomb away," Reed announced. "Good ejection, good engine light and attitude. Chaff bomb on proper course and heading."

"Here we go," Gerald announced. He slid into his station chair, strapped himself in, and pulled on his headset. "All stations, all hands. We will be experiencing high acceleration and rapid maneuvering. All hands secure for boost and maneuvering. Do not, repeat, do not leave boost stations after first burn. We may be doing repeated burns on short notice. Remain at boost stations until further notice. That is all."

"Chaff bomb engine shutdown on time. Chaff dispersal charge to fire in forty seconds at my mark. Mark, forty seconds to dispersal charge."

"Defense, prepare for manual launch of decoys and second chaff can on my order."

"Ready for second launch. First can dispersal in thirty seconds."

Dianne worked her displays, and brought up the forward radar image. There it was, dead ahead, glowing big and bright in its own radar emissions. And there was the chaff can, a bright and tiny dot illuminated by the CORE's radar. Almost into the same not-quite-optimum position that *Cargo 43*'s had been in. Almost ready to blow.

Of course, it would take time for the chaff to spread after the can blew. The artificers said it *ought* to expand out to a cloud of ten or twenty kilometers' diameter in something like a minute. Dianne did not like dealing with numbers that vague, but she had not wanted to risk testing the system, for fear of a chaff cloud attracting some CORE's attention. There was no way to know for certain how big the cloud would get, or how fast—and no way to know just how opaque it would be to the CORE's radar sense. Suppose this CORE was smart enough to have cobbled together a sensory system that could see through the chaff?

Suppose they all ended up dead in the next ten minutes? The bridges were burning behind them now. No way back.

"Second chaff canister ready for launch."

"Very well," Dianne said. "Decoy status?"

"Decoy programmed as per your orders."

"Very well. Will we be able to control the decoys from inside the chaff cloud?"

"No, ma'am. Our radio links will be jammed by the chaff."

"How are we going to order them to switch over to homing mode?" Gerald asked. "We don't know exactly when we're going to be shielded by the chaff. If they start moving in before we're out of sight, the CORE might figure it out and come after the one signal that's still running.''

"Yes sir. We've thought of that. We've programmed them to switch to homing mode twenty seconds after losing contact with us.''

"Excellent, Reed. Remind me to double your pay if we ever get to someplace where they use money.''

"I'll do that, sir. First chaff can detonating—*now*. Good detonation. Um, ah, cloud expansion looks somewhat rapid.''

Dianne watched on the radar screen. More than somewhat rapid. It was too damn fast. The faster the cloud expanded, the faster it would blind the CORE—but the faster it would dissipate as well, leaving the *Terra Nova* exposed. This was going to be a close run thing, that was for sure. But at least the CORE would be blinded fast. Any second now, the cloud would spread out, hiding the CORE from the *TN*'s sight—and vice versa. Any second, any second. Anticipate just a bit.

"Defense, reset that second chaff can. Set it for minimum lateral boost only, straight off the port beam. No forward boost. We're going blow its chaff right where we are now.''

"Yes ma'am.''

Dianne glanced at the countdown clock in the upper-left-hand counter, showing time to impact with the CORE. A bare five minutes left, three hundred seconds to live if the CORE had its way. How many of those seconds would they need? When would the CORE be utterly blinded, and how soon until it could see again?

No way to figure, not even time to set up the problem. Never mind. Do it by feel, by gut, by the heat of the sweat in your armpits—

"Dump second chaff can *now*,'' Dianne shouted. "Now, now, now! Helm, use attitude jets, translate hard to starboard, five-second burn. Give us some clearance. Give me a call-out at safe distance for main engines.''

The *Terra Nova* shuddered and slapped herself sideways, lumbering away from the chaff can.

"Safe distance—mark!" the helm officer called.

"Helm, correct attitude and bring us to CORE-parallel-negative course—NOW!"

The ship lurched harder, twisting end-over-end to come about, and Dianne could feel the vibration of the att jets. The jets cut, and then came another slap from the opposite side as the helm officer killed the rotation. "On attitude," he called. "Stand by for main-engine throttle-up."

The acceleration caught at Dianne, shoving her down into her command chair. Caught at her, and did not let go. A dull roar seemed to come up from nowhere as the engines' shuddering vibration began to fill the ship.

"Point five gees," the helm officer said, shouting to be heard over the increasing roar of the engines. "One gee. One point five. Two gees. Two point five. Three. Three point one. Safety limit at three point two gravities."

"Give us some leeway," Dianne shouted into her headset, watching the numbers on the tactical screen. "Throttle back to three point zero."

"Throttling back, three-zero."

"Intercept on chaff cloud in fifteen seconds," Gerald called. "We're going to take some impacts."

That was an understatement. The ship was going to plow into any number of the tiny, insubstantial bits of chaff, moving at thousands of kilometers an hour relative to the ship. The *Terra Nova*'s micrometeoroid shielding had been designed to protect the craft for a hundred-year trip between the stars. It would be able to take the strikes, but it was going to be a rough ride for all of that.

"Decoys running, armed and active!" the Defense Officer called out. "Second chaff can showing good telemetry and ready to blow as programmed."

There was a sudden new vibration and the ship seemed to lurch just a bit, as if had run into something—as indeed it had. They were in the chaff, and taking strikes on the hull.

"All stop on engines," Dianne called. The noise of the engines vanished, and the great weight lifted—the first mo-

ment she was even aware that it had been pressing down on
her. Now they could hear the clittering patter of the chaff
impacts on the hull, echoing through the ship's interior.

Dianne checked her radar display screen, now a perfect
fog of murky white, the chaff particles reflecting and back-
scattering the CORE's radar pulses in all directions. The
CORE had entered the chaff cloud itself by now, was passing through it on a course opposite to the *Terra Nova*'s and
just a few kilometers away. But you could not tell that from
the screen. It was impossible to get a radar fix on anything in
that bright cloud.

And if they could not see the CORE, then the CORE
could not see them. They were safe for the moment, barring
accidental collision.

For the moment. Never mind that. They had a fight to
fight. "Tracking Officer, what have you got on visual and
IR?"

"It's a little murky, ma'am, but clear enough for our purposes."

Dianne pulled up the visual image and was presented with
a cloud of murk, filled with shimmering bits of blur, the millions of bits of chaff shining by reflected light as they tumbled through space, the camera shuddering and bouncing as
its shielded housing took repeated hits from the chaff. In
short, the imagery was a mess. Good thing the Tracking Officer could make sense of it, because *she* couldn't.

"The CORE just went right past us," the Tracking Officer said. "No sign that it spotted us at all."

"Second chaff should be blowing *now*," the Defense Officer called out.

"Good. That will keep the damned thing blinded longer.
Just a few seconds longer," Dianne said. Of course, she was
damned near close to blind herself at the moment. She struggled to make sense of the visual display.

"Hamato, can you clean this imagery up a little? I can't
make heads or tails of it."

"What? Oh, ah, ma'am, you must have punched up the

raw data image. Pull up the NVIRTH screen.''

''NVIRTH being what?'' Gerald asked.

''Noiseless Visual-Infra-Red Tactical Hybrid,'' Hamato said. ''It subtracts the noise elements out of the visual and IR, pulls in the course projections from tactical and corrects—''

''Shut up, Hamato,'' Dianne said. Some of these kids got too involved with the tricks the hardware could do. Results were what mattered. She punched up the NVIRTH channel and was rewarded with a crystal-clear display, the CORE and the decoys neatly labeled. The CORE was moving at terrifying speed, the decoys rushing about the sky in all directions, just the way they had for *Cargo 43*.

Dianne leaned in and stared at the screen, holding her breath, knowing it was bare seconds now. Either it would work, and they would live, or it would fail, and the CORE skymountain, the CORE hunter-killer asteroid, would kill them.

''Decoys switching from evasive to homing mode,'' Reed called out, but Dianne could see that, too. They were turning, coming about, moving in on the CORE instead of running away.

The CORE had to go for the decoys. If it understood in time, it could escape, get away, turn and search for the *Terra Nova* just as the ship came out the other side of the chaff cloud. And then they were all dead.

The CORE came out of the first chaff cloud and moved straight on, deep into the second cloud. Maybe it was moving so fast it had no chance to react to the brief moment of clear skies. Damnation, that thing was moving fast! It was already out of the second cloud now. At best, two or three seconds to traverse it. Would that be enough? Would it confuse the CORE just enough that it would not think to look back the way it had come?

''CORE maneuvering! Diving down, negative y axis,'' Hamato called out, but Dianne could see it too. Turning, down hard about, almost at right angles, aiming toward the rearmost decoy, the one where *Cargo 43* had been.

Yes. *Yes.* They had won! Unless the blast was not powerful enough. Unless a CORE could take even *that* much punishment—

"CORE closing on Decoy Seven. Collision imminent—"

And the screen vanished in a flare of brightness, a dazzling glare. The proximity bomb in Decoy Seven detonated at the programmed ten meters from its target, and CORE 219 flew straight into a fusion explosion, a blare of stellar power tearing a hole in the middle of the darkness.

The CORE was lost to sight, stopped almost dead in its tracks by the force of the blast, but still moving slowly forward, into the heart of the explosion, into the furnace.

The other decoys moved in, accelerating toward the explosion, diving for the CORE.

"We are approaching edge of chaff cloud," Hamato said.

With the suddenness of someone snapping on a light, the *Terra Nova* came out of the chaff cloud, rushing away, quickly moving far enough off to get a clear line of sight on the death of the CORE.

For death it was. Now there could be no doubt.

Someone slapped a switch, and threw the imagery from the hi-res cameras onto the main screen, zoomed in on the fast-receding end of the battle. Another explosion, and another, and another, flared in the sky, blinding the screen. Then, out of the glare, tumbling end over end, lumbering through the darkness, the CORE emerged from the fireball.

Another decoy homed it, slammed into its target, and the darkness blazed again. The CORE cracked open, splitting along its long axis. A huge chunk of material sheared off, and a *something* squirmed free, a great grey oblong shape, surrounded by a cloud of lesser shapes—all of them, the big one and the small ones, shuddering, twitching, spasming in their death throes.

A cheer went up, the bridge suddenly full of people clapping each other on the back, shouting, laughing, yelling. Dianne did not join in. Instead she sat there, stock still, staring straight ahead, letting the celebration go on without her. *One* of them. They had got *one* of them.

First blood, she told herself. *The first tiny victory, the first time anyone in the Multisystem had managed to so much as muss the enemy's hair.*

Now all they had to do was do it about another hundred thousand times, and they'd all be safe.

The last of the decoy bombs homed in, and exploded, and the thing from inside the CORE vaporized. She turned and looked toward her second-in-command as he watched the death—not of an enemy, but of a complex and ancient life-form. She could see that in his eyes. All the Charonians were trying to do was stay alive, just like anyone else. That's what he'd tell her. Maybe there *was* something wrong about cele-brating a death—any death, even a CORE's.

"Gerald," she said.

"Hmmm? What?" He blinked, turned toward her, his face pale and quiet. He knew how close it had been, too. He knew it could have been the ship that died, probably would be the next time. "Yes, I'm sorry. What it is, ma'am?"

"Secure the ship from battle stations," Dianne said. "Prepare to return to previous course." She punched up the shipwide intercom circuit. "All stations," she said in a tired quiet voice. "Now hear this."

How to say it? What was it they needed to hear?

"Now hear this," she said at last. "We are still alive. Re-peat, we are still alive. That is all."

Twenty-one

Acceptable Losses

"When we repelled the attack on the Solar System, we destroyed Pluto and Charon as a way to save all the other worlds, and lost all contact with Earth as a consequence. We told ourselves that half a loaf—the seven surviving worlds of the Solar System—was better than none.

"But suppose you were part of the half a loaf that got sacrificed? For you, it wouldn't seem like that much better a deal."

—*Memoirs,* Dr. Jane Webling, Science Director, Gravitics Research Institute (retired)

The Ring of Charon Command Station
Plutopoint
THE SOLAR SYSTEM

The Autocrat moved his pawn forward to the third rank and leaned back in his chair. Sondra Berghoff did not react, did not lean forward, or rub her hand on her chin. Instead she stared, motionless, at the board. She had always regarded herself as a pretty fair player, but the Autocrat was head and shoulders above her. And yet there were flaws, weaknesses in his game. She had never met his equal for being able to think three—or five, or eight—moves ahead, and he was remarkably skilled in seeing the board as a whole.

But for all of that—perhaps *because* of all that—the Autocrat often failed to see the small details, the little things, sometimes even the obvious things. If it did not lead to infinite opportunities in five moves, he paid it little mind. The only times she had managed to beat him had been the times she had found the little moves that did not seem to lead to many possibilities—for sometimes one possibility was all that mattered.

She moved her sole surviving rook down the length of the board and set it down in the eighth rank. "Checkmate," she announced.

The Autocrat looked up in surprise. "So it is," he said. "So it is indeed. I must say it is a pleasure to get a real game out of someone. Almost worth the trip to Plutopoint all by itself."

"Why can't you get a good game of chess back on Ceres?" Sondra asked.

"People are afraid I'll execute them if I lose," the Autocrat said, in a calm, matter-of-fact way as he set the board up for a new game.

Sondra was not sure whether to laugh or to be shocked. Was he joking, or had he or some predecessor established a reputation as a terrible loser? She never quite knew what to make of the Autocrat. Well, she had to say something in reply, and somehow, professing shock did not quite seem polite. "Well, then," she said, in as light a tone of voice as she could manage, "I suppose it's lucky for me I'm outside your jurisdiction."

"Ah, but you are well inside it," he replied. "The Autocrat's jurisdiction has no set bounds or borders. I am required to see after the good of the Asteroid Belt and its people in all times and all places. I assure you that, if I ordered you executed, being outside the Asteroid Belt would be no defense for you at all."

"For the crime of beating you at chess?"

"For any reason, if I judged you to be a danger to justice or peace. On at least one occasion one of my predecessors executed a man for precisely the crime of winning at chess, under rather peculiar circumstances involving a dishonorable wager with a third party. Not a pleasant story, and not one with which to mar the present evening."

It was not the first time that the Autocrat had tossed a story of mysterious death and execution into the conversation, and Sondra could not help but notice that the Autocrat had never offered any assurance that *he* would not order someone executed.

Quite the contrary, she had been left with the clear impression that the crew of the *Autarch* was trained and ready to shoot holes in anyone at a moment's notice, should the Autocrat give the order. No doubt it was all meant to be very unsettling, and it certainly was.

But for all of that, she *liked* the Autocrat. There was something a bit sinister about him, but so too was there something warm and approachable. He reminded her of a strict but fair father, relentlessly firm with his children, quite ready to give them a dispassionate spanking if they needed it. "Another game, Autocrat?" she asked.

"No, I think not," he said, standing up. "You are improving a trifle too quickly for me," he said. "You are learning how to beat me, and I think perhaps I should give you a day or so to forget what you have learned." He crossed the wardroom and looked out the porthole to the huge and gleaming oval of the Ring of Charon, now almost edge-on as seen from the Command Station.

"Do you think I plan to take over this station?" he asked in a rather casual tone of voice.

"Sir?"

He turned and looked back at her. "You heard the question. Surely the possibility crossed your mind when a heavily armed and uninvited guest overstayed his welcome. I was supposed to leave here quite some time ago. *Do* you think I plan a takeover?"

"The possibility has occurred to me, yes," Sondra said, choosing her words very carefully. "Some of the staff are more than a little concerned. But I think you wish us to fear you, wish our backers on the Moon and Mars to fear what you might do. You want to show that you $cou'd$ take this station, control the Ring of Charon. But you do not—and did not—intend to carry out the threat."

"I see," the Autocrat said. "And why would I pursue this course of action?"

"To strengthen your hand at the bargaining table. To make everyone else a bit more eager to please you. To force everyone to come up with a solution to the problem of a monopoly source of gravity beams."

"Will your friends in the Inner System now come to the table before there is a crisis?"

"I think so. You certainly have their attention."

"And have I come up with a solution? Have I found a way to parcel out this resource?"

Sondra was scared, very scared indeed. Some games she did not wish to play with the Autocrat. "I don't know," she said. "I don't think so."

"You are quite correct," the Autocrat said. "I as yet have no solution. But it will come. It will come."

"So you don't intend to seize this station?" Sondra asked.

The Autocrat looked her straight in the eye and gave her one of his finest non-answers. "That is not my current plan," he said. "But that is of no consequence. I believe I have the answer to a more interesting problem. I think now I know why I came here," he announced, staring out the port.

"What? I'm sorry? What do you mean, Autocrat?" Sondra asked. She got up and went closer to him—but not too close. "I thought you were here because of the gravity-beam issue. I thought you came out here with some very specific political ideas in mind."

"Oh, yes, indeed. Quite so. And I have thought of some very promising avenues, even if I have not come up with an ultimate solution. But that is as may be. There are reasons and reasons for doing a thing, you know. Making sure that the Ring does not fall under unilateral control is important, that gravity-beam technology does not set off an interplanetary war is likewise vital. I think that my coming here has alarmed our friends on the Moon and Mars enough that we can now resolve those issues and keep you independent. Useful stuff—but it is not why I came. Not really."

"Then why *are* you here?" Sondra asked. But she barely heard her own words, her heart was beating so fast.

"To see this," he said, gesturing toward the Ring. "To be reminded what real power is, and how small I really am. I have the power of life and death over any number of people, but out there is the most powerful machine ever built by humanity—and it is as nothing compared to the might of the Charonians. *They* have the power of life and death over whole worlds—and yet they lay hidden here in the Solar System. They *feared* some other, greater power, and did all they could to hide from it. I knew all that, I suppose, and I've seen my share of Charonian power, but this—" he gestured toward the Ring "—this is *ours*. And it was powerful enough to destroy two worlds."

"But you knew all that before you came here," Sondra said. What was all this? He came out here, not to do a little saber-rattling, but as a tourist?

"I knew Earth was a place with fresh breezes and open skies and wild animals," the Autocrat said. "But I did not *understand* it, deep in my heart, deep in my soul, down at the level of instinct, until I had been there. Now I am as far as I can get from where Earth was and still be in the Solar System. I had to come here, too, before I could really understand.''

''You're doing better than I am, Autocrat,'' Sondra said. ''At least I know I'm never going to understand *you.*''

The Autocrat smiled at Sondra, a warm and open expression that nonetheless scared the hell out of her.

''Good,'' he said.

Dreyfuss Memorial Research Station
North Pole
THE MOON

Larry Chao opened his eyes to a room full of faces. Tyrone Vespasian, Selby Bogsworth-something, Marcia MacDougal, a nurse, Lucian Dreyfuss, all of them staring at him.

Wait a second—*Lucian?* That was impossible. Larry shut his eyes, shook his head, and opened them again. He was relieved to see the imaginary Lucian was gone—but also more than a little disappointed. Lucian. Lucian was going to be with him for a long, long time.

''Hey,'' Vespasian said. ''He's awake. Hey, Larry. You okay?''

''Yeah, yeah, I guess.'' Larry shifted position just a bit to sit up in bed, and instantly regretted it. His body was a solid mass of sore muscles. ''Well, I *will* be all right, anyway. Pretty stiff just now.''

''I'll bet you are,'' Vespasian said, his enthusiasm and sympathy sounding more than a bit forced. Clearly he was not here because he cared about Larry Chao's health.

Larry decided he was not much in the mood for small talk himself. ''So,'' he asked, swinging his feet around and putting them on the floor. A real, solid floor, and not a computerized pressure simulator. ''Did you get it all?''

''We got it,'' Vespasian said. ''But we're not sure what it

was. We were hoping you could tell us more about it.''

"I have the feeling you saw less than I did," Larry said. "Things got rather . . . strange . . . after Lucian and I started flying around. I don't think you could have gotten the feel of it off a simple video link. So what did you see?"

"A video sequence," Marcia said. "It showed something attacking a Sphere, and then what happens when the Sphere is shattered. It had the Shattered Sphere images we got five years ago in the middle of it. The Sphere dies, its gravity systems fail, all the Captive Suns go flying off into space. The old Shattered Sphere images must have been some sort of shorthand version of the sequence we saw today."

Larry nodded and stood up. A robe was hanging by the bed, and he pulled it on, wincing a bit. Lots of stiff muscles. Damn it, why couldn't they give him a few minutes by himself? A chance to go to the toilet, wash, get dressed? Well, it was important. He knew that better than they did. But he still needed a little bit of time *alone*. "Shorthand is about right," he said, trying to keep his temper. "If you showed the shorter sequence of a Sphere getting smashed to any high-level Charonian, it would know what it means."

"But what the hell *does* it mean?" Vespasian asked. "Why did Lucian show it to you? Was it history, or legend, or a warning?"

"All three," Larry said, a bit sharply. "But wait a second. That's all you saw? You didn't see the rest of it—what I saw?"

"No one's ever sure they saw what someone else saw," Selby said dryly. "I know I never am. But what was it *you* saw? Something different from the Sphere getting smashed?"

"Not something different," Larry replied. "Something more. Something like the answer to all of it."

"There were bursts of imagery and data," Marcia said, "running too fast for us to make sense of them. We've been doing playbacks, over and over again, but we still haven't been able to understand them."

"Yeah, those bursts of data," Larry said. "Though they sure weren't bursts to me. They were long and detailed—with Lucian, or whatever Lucian is now—whispering in my ear the whole time, *telling* me things. For me it seemed as if it took hours for the whole sequence to run. It sounds as if it all took just a few minutes for you."

"About five or ten," Marcia said.

"Then you *didn't* see what I saw," Larry said. "It all changed when Lucian led me up into the sky. I think the whole time I was with him he was looking for a way to do whatever it was he did then. But everything changed then. Before, it was a plain old TeleOperator setup. Very realistic and convincing, but I could tell I was in a simulation. And then . . . then Lucian took me into the sky and it was all *different*."

"Different how?" Marcia asked.

"It was like . . . like the difference between a live performance and a recording. When you're there, really there, there's layers, subtleties of . . . *presence*, of being there, of *touching*, of being inside looking around rather than outside looking in. I don't know. It felt like all my senses were brought together. Sight and hearing and touch and taste and smell all one. Maybe there was some sort of feedback through all the connections and electrodes that put me in synch with it. What you got as data bursts, I got as someone opening up my head and pouring information in."

"So what was the information?" Selby asked. "What the hell did you *see*?"

"The Adversary," Larry said. "The Enemy. The Charonians' enemy. The thing that killed the Shattered Sphere, and wants to try and kill the Sphere that's holding Earth."

Selby, Marcia and Vespasian exchanged glances with each other. "Look," Vespasian said, his voice more than a little patronizing, "maybe you'd better start at the beginning."

"Maybe I'd better," Larry said, a bit irritably. "In ten minutes. After I've had a chance to wash my face and get into some clothes. And someplace besides here, with you three clustered around my bed.''

Marcia looked at her companions, a bit uncertainly. ''All right,'' she said. ''There's a conference room just down the hall. We'll meet you there whenever you're ready.''

Selby seemed about to protest, but Marcia gestured for her to be quiet. ''We'll be outside,'' Marcia said.

Larry watched them go, more than a little surprised at himself. What had gotten into him? That was not the way he acted. But then it dawned on him. He remembered back to five years ago, to the way he and Lucian had bickered and argued. What had gotten into him, indeed.

That was the way *Lucian* acted.

Larry felt a little more settled—and quite literally more himself—when he came out and found the others in the conference room. It was rather satisfying to have the others being careful not to upset him again, treating him with a bit of fearful courtesy. It had clearly dawned on them that he had what they needed, and that bullying him might not be the best idea. They all got through an awkward series of pleasantries. Then Larry sat down at the head of the table, and started talking.

''I got a lot more from Lucian. Maybe even more than I think. It was like he was whispering to me as he showed me what we all saw. That's not quite accurate, because he still had a great deal of trouble talking—but I know he gave me much more than you got.''

He hesitated for a moment, trying to decide how to start. ''You have to go back a long time,'' he said at last. ''I don't know how far back. I got a pretty good feel for shorter time spans, but time spans of any length get pretty tricky because—well, maybe you'll see. It was millions of years ago, at any rate. Maybe five million, maybe a hundred and fifty million. The Charonians were already well established by then. They had spread across a large part of the galaxy, building their Spheres and collecting their worlds into Multisystems. Back then there was no fear and caution about them. They didn't have anything to hide from.

"All the Sphere systems were connected to each other by wormhole links, and the Spheres stayed in close contact with each other, trading worlds and life-forms and new information back and forth across the links. Maybe at the peak of it all, there was a network of a few thousand Spheres."

"So what happened then?" Marcia asked.

"What happened was they discovered they weren't the only ones using gravity and wormholes."

"These Adversaries you mentioned," Selby suggested.

"There's only one of them," Larry said. "It can subdivide itself and then remerge the divisions as it sees fit. Group and individual don't mean much to it. But it can and does split up into as many bits as it likes."

"What do these bits look like?" Vespasian asked.

"They're spherical. They have to be. Usually a dirty grey in color, but that's just debris that accumulates on the surface. They can be any size—but the ones that take on a Sphere might be the size of a CORE or an average asteroid."

"Why do they have to be spherical?" Marcia asked.

"They're pulled into that shape by the force of gravity," Larry said. "They're small, but they are extremely massive. I can't say for sure, because it wasn't in the memory store Lucian showed me, but I think they're made out of strange matter, with densities comparable to neutron stars. A blob of Adversary the size of a large dog would outweigh a good-sized asteroid."

"Strange matter? What the bloody hell is strange matter?" Selby asked.

"An alternative form of matter—or at least, an alternative form of heavy particles like protons and neutrons."

"Like antimatter?" Selby asked.

"No, no, not at all like antimatter," Marcia said. "Antimatter blows up if it touches matter, so it doesn't last very long. Strange matter could exist perfectly well in our Universe—if it existed. And it sounds like it does."

"So why so dense?" Vespasian asked.

"There are upper limits on the size of the atomic nucleus in normal matter," Marcia said. "Anything much above uranium is unstable—it decays. In theory, there *are* no limits on the size of an atomic nucleus made up of strange quarks. You could have a strange atom with an atomic weight billions or trillions of times higher than in normal matter."

"But no one has ever seen strange matter, right?" Vespasian said.

Marcia looked to Larry. "Not until now."

Larry sighed in frustration. "Look, I know it all sounds mad, but there it is. It's true."

"This is what Lucian told you, or showed you," Marcia said. "That doesn't mean it's *true*. He could be wrong, or insane, or you could have misunderstood."

"Or he could be exactly right," Larry said, feeling a bit annoyed. "I know it seems impossible for something that small to attack the Charonians, but hear me out, all right?"

Vespasian shrugged. "Five years ago, who would have believed that a monster inside the Moon was going to steal the Earth? You go on, Larry. Tell us."

"All right. Thank you. I don't pretend to understand everything about it, but the Adversary is the key to it. It is capable of action, organized action, but I'm not even sure we'd consider it to be alive."

"What sort of action are you talking about?" Vespasian asked.

Larry gave him a funny look. "Killing Spheres, of course."

"Wait a second," Marcia protested. "How could a thing that small kill a Sphere?"

"Look, let me tell this from the beginning and it might make more sense. We think the Charonians, the Spheres, evolved from some intelligent species, more or less like us, that sent out an automatic seedship programmed to modify the genetics of the life-forms it was carrying, adapting them to the planet it encountered—except the seedship took over, and the life-forms served it, and not the other way around. The Charonians merged biology and technology and guided their own development, their own evolution, until they got to the system of Spheres. As best I can understand it, the Adversary did the same thing, guided its own development. It's as if . . . I don't know . . . an amoeba, a very simple animal, evolved intelligence, and figured out how to make a new and better type of amoeba out of itself.''

"But an amoeba is nowhere near complex enough to have anything remotely like intelligence," Marcia protested. "All sorts of research demonstrates you need to reach a complexity threshold much higher than you can get in a single cell before you have the capacity for intelligence. You can't do it in one cell."

"Not if you build that cell out of carbon and hydrogen and nitrogen and oxygen. But the atoms building up this creature might each have more *particles*, more neutrons and protons, than there are atoms in an amoeba. The complexity is there, but it's at the nuclear level."

"Wait a second," Vespasian protested. "I thought Marcia said no one had ever detected strange matter. Where is this thing supposed to live?"

"On a neutron star," Larry said. "It evolved on the surface of it. Of course, on a neutron star, the gravity flattened it out of its spherical shape to a pancake shape."

"Oh, come off it!" Selby protested. "This is ridiculous. A giant one-celled pancake living on a neutron star? How the hell could such a thing come to be?"

"By evolving—or developing, or whatever—inside a massive gravitational field, and knowing how to feed off it," Larry said. "The Adversary uses gravitational fields the way we use electrochemical energy in our bodies. It gets its energy by manipulating gravity fields. Somehow—I don't know how—I think it uses gravity to convert normal matter into strange matter. It builds new pieces of Adversary out of some of it, and the rest it uses as an energy source, somehow."

Marcia was thinking. "It all sounds a bit outlandish, but *something* killed that Shattered Sphere," she said. "Even so, things would be a great deal easier for a species that was adapted to high gee. To us, a gravity field powerful enough to warp time and space is deadly, and nuclear physics takes place at a scale so small we can't even see it. But to the Adversary, high gee is normal, and the atoms it deals with are so big they might even be visible to the naked human eye. It would be as if we could create a wormhole with, say, a five- or ten-gee field, or do genetic engineering with genes the size of children's blocks. The threshold would be much lower."

"But the Charonians," Selby insisted. "What do they have to do with the Charonians?"

"The Charonians have a network of wormholes linking their various Spheres and systems," Larry said. "The Adversary developed a similar network. It put together a wormhole link and locked onto another neutron star, and colonized it. And then another, and another. Both nets grew out from the center."

"My God," Marcia said. "I get it. Now I get it. One side accidentally tapped into the other's wormhole net."

"Right. Exactly," Larry said. "But the thing to bear in mind is that the Charonians *use* high-gee fields and wormholes, but the Adversary *lives* in them, feeds off them. The Charonians use gravity very differently, but they make a living off gravity fields as well.

"High-gee situations and wormholes are still dangerous to Charonians. They still have to be careful around them. In that respect, we have a lot more in common with the Charonians than the Adversary. At least Charonians and humans inhabit the same experiential universe. The normal place for a part of the Adversary to be is on the surface of a neutron star. To the Adversary, a wormhole is just like home."

"If you look at it that way, then the size difference doesn't matter, either," Marcia said, "any more than it does in a fight between a swarm of crop-eating locusts and a group of humans trying to chase them off.''

"What's a locust?" Vespasian asked. Apparently, he hadn't spent a great deal of time on Earth.

"A voracious insect," Marcia said. "Be glad they never got to the Moon. Millions of them would descend on a field and eat it bare in a day. They were adapted to a certain sort of environment, and if they found that environment, they took it and used it. It didn't matter to them that humans created the crop field, or would want to use it for themselves. Crop fields were the ideal environment for locusts. They were better designed to exploit them than the humans who planted the fields. The locusts would gobble up the whole field, and the farmers couldn't stop them.''

"But that only works if you have millions of locusts that can overwhelm by sheer force of numbers," Selby protested. "We only saw one bit of Adversary in that video sequence.''

"One is all it takes. You saw the one that got through. The Adversary would force open a wormhole and enter a Sphere system as a single large entity. As soon as it was in, it would split up into hundreds of smaller units. Some would run interference and be destroyed by the Charonians. But only one Adversary bit had to make it all the way. It didn't matter if the rest get killed, because they're all the same.''

"And one of them—just one—is able to kill a Sphere?"

"Just one," Larry said. "The best way to stop them is to kill the parent just as it enters the Sphere's system through the wormhole, before it can split-breed. The way to kill the parent is to throw a planet at it. Adversary units are tough, and the big parent ones are tougher. Only the kinetic energy of a whole planet moving at relativistic speed can kill a large Adversary. Smash into it at a good fraction of light speed and you'll destroy the Adversary—and the planet. The Adversary will penetrate most of the way to the planet's core before it's destroyed. The Charonians kill one planet to save all the others. Acceptable losses. Half a loaf. Sound familiar?'' Larry smiled at his own unfunny gallows humor.

''Larry, there's something more,'' Marcia said. ''Something else you're not telling us. Lucian wouldn't have worked so hard to get you all this information unless it did more than clear up a mystery or two. It's nice to know who the Charonians are afraid of, but we don't *need* to know it.''

''No, no, we don't need to know all that. But . . . but . . .'' Larry turned his head away and looked at the wall. How to say it matter-of-factly? How to get them to believe? ''What we *do* need to know is the geometry of the Sphere system the Earth is in.

''When the Adversary comes for you, it comes through a wormhole link. And there *is* an Adversary coming for the system the Earth is in. That's what terrified the Charonians, set them into a panic. Somehow, it was the movement of Earth into that system that attracted the Adversary's attention. It's heading for the wormhole link with *Earth*. It might try for some other entry to the system, but the link it's most likely to come through is the one nearest Earth.

''And when a Charonian Sphere needs to throw a planet at an Adversary, it generally uses the closest one to hand.''

Twenty-two

Recalled to Life

"Source Matter: Dreyfuss Contact record

"Procedure: Thematically Keyed Recursive
Adversary/Charonian Translation
Routine, Pass #45,234 of 45,234.
Certainty Level circa 75 percent.

"Note: All Adversary units of measure and number
recast to rough scalar equivalents in
standard units. However, the accuracy of
these approximations remains variable and
highly uncertain. Furthermore, relativistic
effects, induced by both massive
acceleration and gravitational effects,
make measurement comparisons and
conversions even more problematic.

"We/I are the One. All touches each, and each, All. Time is our/my domain, space our/my prison.

"We/I travel up and down the milliseconds(?) and seconds(?) and the far-spanning hours(?) at will, and all times are as one to us/me. At need, we/I can send some of ourselves/myself into the transitways to times more distant still, to both past and future.

"But shall we/I boast of our/my current power, when once we/I sent ourself across duration-distances far longer? In truth, now are our/my transits short.

"Once were our/my sojourns in the paths of duration great, yet in this epoch we/I may venture but feebly to the domains of othertime(?) and otherplace(?). The distortions of masslessness in the other, lesser, dimensions hem us/me in, and keep us/me held close to our/my home at Allcenter, and our/my past ways of venturing are lost.

"The dark masslessness warps duration itself. In that cold and dark [domain?], time rushes by at such terrifying velocities that to venture but briefly into it is to risk loss of synchrony with the All, beyond all hope of recovery. [Darktime?] flares past a thousand, a million, times faster than does time in its natural state, shattering all links between the sojourner and the All, diminishing each of us that are linked into one.

"Yet in time far behind, far behind even as time is reckoned in the Dark, it was/is not so.

"In the beginning, deep in the [far back?] we/I [refined itself?] from the cold and ghastly chaos of the massless nether reaches and gathered close to Allcenter. This we/I did a full galactic rotation from the Now, a duration-distance so mighty that none of us/me could attempt a transit a thousandth so far without dooming the All. [Farback?] and [gonelong?] is the beginning, beyond all reach.

"We/I came to be, and came to growing. Long was the slowtime as we/I bred ourself, spreading across the surface and duration of Allcenter.

"Until the others came, with their questings and probings and jostling gravity waves, seeking to [subsume?] Allcenter into their web of space. But it was we/I who [subsumed?] them.

"Beyond all understanding, beyond All comprehension, they were and are and shall be. But great was the treasure of [power?] and [transit?] we/I took from them.

"Until they escaped. Deep was our loss and great our weakening. Grown great upon the energies of the others, the All lost all it had gained, and more beyond. Weak and low was our/my state. Long did we/I [search for them?] in all the transit links.

"And now we/I have found them again."
—Heritage Memory Transcript, Contact Archives, *Journal of the Dreyfuss Memorial Research Station,* 2431

Dreyfuss Memorial Research Station
The Moon
THE SOLAR SYSTEM

"Good afternoon," Larry said, looking out over the auditorium—a rather grand name for the rather scruffy-looking hall, but it was the only room at the station that could hold everyone, and everyone wanted to hear this. "We've come a long way very quickly, and I thought it would be smart to bring the whole team together to talk it through. The leads Lucian Dreyfuss provided have given us some guidance and some clues into what we should be looking for.

"Dr. Selby Bogsworth-Stapleton has made a tremendous contribution. Her expertise in reconstructing and interpreting old computer records has been invaluable. Thanks to Marcia MacDougal's work over the last five years, we had a lot of Charonian visual-symbol units translated already, giving us the basic vocabulary to move forward fast.

"The teams working on chronology and duration have found all sorts of measures and scales in the data bursts, and that right there is a breakthrough. We know more about *when* things happened than we ever have before. Dates back to about five thousand years we know with great precision. Everything before that gets more and more uncertain. Some of the older data could come from a million years ago or a hundred million. We don't know.

"Much of what I am about to tell you has been at least guessed at before. The difference is that now we have evidence and, in many cases, absolute proof that turns speculation into fact. We have filled in many—but not nearly all—of the holes in the story.

"Let me start from the beginning. Something like eighty million to sixty-five million years ago, a seedship Charonian, a large Charonian carrying the lifecodes and schematics for all the forms of Charonians, landed on the Earth and bred the various forms of Charonians, producing everything from smaller scavenger robots to things the size of asteroids, and producing them at a ferocious rate. The Charonian Breeders fed off terrestrial life—and picked up whatever odd bits of DNA they found of interest.

"At least one large Charonian lifted off for the Moon and started digging and burrowing and building itself into what we now call the Lunar Wheel. Other Charonians hid themselves in the depths of space, mostly by disguising themselves as asteroids and comets. Then the Lunar Wheel sent a signal to its parent Sphere that all was in readiness, and all the Charonians in the Solar System went dormant. They waited for a call that never came—until five years ago.

"Now, that original Charonian seedship that landed on Earth and started the Breeding Binge was one of thousands sent out by its parent Sphere system—the system in which the Earth now finds itself. Perhaps only one out of a thousand seedships would find a suitable star system. Each of those few would do as the Charonians did here—set things up, send a ready message, and then wait for a call. The parent Sphere might elect merely to order any usable stars or planets shipped into its system, or it might decide that it had enough surplus power and material to assist its offspring Charonians in tearing apart the star system they were in and helping them build a new Sphere system.

"Many are sent out, but few are called. For whatever reason, the Lunar Wheel was never called—until it was quite accidentally activated five years ago. Until I accidentally activated it." Larry paused to take a sip of water, and worked very hard at not making eye contact with the audience. Being forthright was all very well, but there was no sense in pushing his luck.

"In any event," he went on, a trifle too briskly, "the Sphere never called on the Solar System. Even for the Charonians, eighty million years is a long time. Our best guess is that the Sphere simply forgot about us, or found some other star system to be more useful. Or else the crisis I am about to describe made it impossible for the Sphere to deal with Earth and the Solar System.

"Sometime after the Charonian seedship arrived in the Solar System, bred, and went dormant, the Charonian network encountered the Adversary. The Charonians quite suddenly found themselves cast down—the lords of creation reduced to a mere food source for the Adversary.

"You have all seen the famous image sequence of a bright spot of light smashing through a Sphere and then smashing its way back out, taking a second bright spot of light with it. This is more or less the classic tactic of the Adversary. A single large Adversary unit gets into the system via a wormhole link, then splits up into as many smaller subunits as possible. Floods the Sphere system with large numbers of highly expendable Adversary units, all of them driving for the Sphere. Sheer numbers ensure that at least one or two get through for the kill. Whatever Adversary unit gets through seizes control of the central power source and smashes out of the Sphere with it.

"How, exactly, the Adversary uses the power source, or what, exactly, the form of the power source is, we haven't a clue. We assume that it was made out of the original star the Sphere was built around, but God knows what the Charonians might turn those core stars into. Maybe they convert the core stars into black holes, and use those to generate gravitational power. We don't know.

"Think for a moment how the Adversary experiences the Universe, what sort of place it is for it. Certainly it does not perceive the Universe as we do. Our senses would, of course, be completely useless to it, and yet it must be able to sense its environment. To it, what we regard as normal space must seem cold, dark, and disturbing. Should some sub-part of it move out of their high-gravity, slow-time world to the universe outside, little or no time will have passed there though they might have been gone years, perhaps centuries, as seen from out here. Neutron stars and wormholes are the safe, comfortable places. We think of wormholes as transits between two points in 'normal' space. They regard the web of wormholes as normal space, surrounded by cold, dark, and danger.

"In any case, once an invading Adversary had used a Sphere's power source to reproduce, it would send its—I suppose 'spawn' would be the best word—it would send its spawn down the network of wormhole links, on the hunt for other Spheres to consume.

"The Spheres fought back as best they could. One of their tactics was to perform a rather brutal kind of triage—killing a threatened Sphere and thus wrecking its whole system of stars, planets and wormhole links—so as to deny the power source and transit links to the Adversary. Sometimes a Sphere would commit suicide rather than be taken. You will all recall that the Charonians in the Solar System accepted the command to die that we sent to them. We wondered why they were programmed to take such a command in the first place, but now we know.

"It would appear that only a very few Charonian Spheres of that era survived. Those that did learned to hide themselves, conceal themselves from the Adversary.

"In theory, wormholes can be used not only to link two points in space, but as a means of time travel. We humans have never managed it, and there is no evidence that the Charonians ever used wormholes in this way.

"Be that as it may, we found indications that the Adversary *does* travel backwards and forwards in time.

"Maybe the Adversary was lying, or being poetic, or the Charonians misunderstood, or *we* misunderstood. However, there is one form of time travel we know the Adversary used. It is called waiting.

"As mentioned earlier, these portions of the Adversary— or constructs, or entities, or whatever you want to call them—live on the surfaces of neutron stars, where gravity is tremendously intense, and they can survive more powerful gravity fields than that. *How* they survive, we don't know. Perhaps they can manipulate inertia. Dial your inertia down to zero, and you have reduced your apparent mass down to zero as well. Give a mountain the inertia of a pebble, and you will be able to propel that mountain as if it weighed no more than a pebble.

"But back to the question of time. As we all know, as the strength of a gravity field increases, time slows down. This is not a trick, or an illusion, or a theory. It is a fact, part and parcel of the phenomenon of gravity itself. A massive gravity field will retard time tremendously—and, of course, a black hole stops time altogether.

"The Adversary cannot go into a black hole and survive. But it can get deep, deep into a gravity well without suffering harm—and there it can wait. A year for us might seem a day—or a minute—for an Adversary unit in a wormhole. This explains why the danger is not passed, although the Charonian-Adversary War ended—or seemed to have ended—millions of years ago. The Adversary has a tremendous capacity to *wait*. The Adversary may have some way of piloting singularities through interstellar space, living in slow time near the event horizon as its singularity moves. It would be a clever solution to the problem of long star journeys.

"One hundred and forty-seven years ago the Adversary, having worked its way through all the dead wormholes, or perhaps traveling through normal space for an extended period, found Earth-Sphere's parent.

"The Adversary attacked. That Sphere seems to have sent a warning, and either died or killed itself before the Adversary could make any wormhole link to other Sphere systems. The holes were slammed shut, and the tuning controls for the holes destroyed.

"When that Sphere died, its system was wrecked. Its Captive Suns, no longer held in their orbits by the Sphere's gravitic control, flew out into space. A few of those stars retained at least some of their planets, but many more planets were flung off. The Shattered Sphere rules no suns, no worlds. It is alone in space, with nothing but the corpses of spacegoing Charonians for company. The wormhole links to other systems were slammed shut when the Sphere died.

"In the meantime, the Adversary apparently went back down a wormhole and remained there, living in slow time. It was, in effect, asleep for most of the last 147 years.

"However, five years ago, the Abduction woke it up. Earth's transition through the wormhole between the Solar System and the Earth-Sphere system created a . . . disturbance . . . in the wormhole network. Without going into a great deal of mathematics on the subject of gravity-wave propagation, suffice it to say that the transition of a massive object through a wormhole would set up a resonance pattern—a gravitational vibration, if you will. When the Earth was stolen, its passage caused a disturbance that reverberated up and down the wormhole links, not unlike waves in a pond moving out from the point where a rock hits.

"This uncontrolled, unshieldable vibration was like a

blast of light, illuminating not only the position of wormhole links between the dead Sphere's system and the Earth-Sphere system, but the precise tuning and resonance setting for them. Then, we sent the kill command to the Charonians here. That kill command was loud and indiscriminate, and likewise may have served to illuminate the wormhole links.

"Thus the Adversary learned exactly where to find a new Sphere system. It will take some time for the Adversary to respond. It is possible it has not responded yet. But it will. It will emerge from its gravity well—unless it has already. It will move toward the center of the gravity-wave disturbance. It will go through that link, and attempt an attack on the Earth-Sphere system. It will do all these things—unless it has done them already.

"The Earth-Sphere must know all this better than we do. Once the Sphere is certain that it is to be attacked, it will set to work preparing to defend itself by every means it can.

"The Earth is in terrible danger. If the Sphere dies, Earth will almost certainly be ejected out into the depths of interstellar space, or smash into some other body in the Earth-Sphere system.

"However, the odds are poor that Earth would survive even that long. The best defense against an Adversary unit that has penetrated into a given Sphere system is to smash a planet into it at the highest-possible velocity, before the Adversary has a chance to split-breed. As the Adversary will be homing in on the wormhole exit that Earth came through, Earth is the most convenient rock. It is going to be smashed to rubble in the first few milliseconds after that Adversary gets through."

Larry hesitated and looked around the auditorium.

"That is what will happen. Unless, of course, it already has happened. With every day that passes, the odds are higher that Earth has already been destroyed."

Twenty-three

Boast of the Duck

> "By the time you understand the rules of a complex game, you will no longer be able to explain those rules to anyone who does not already understand the game."
>
> —*Hoyle's Law* (apocryphal attribution)

"What Hoyle sez to a sim gamester izzat inna a chinwag re a 'game' all hands need 2b playing with same deck. They need to be kneeding the same words for same things, need to capiche what they wanna do, have a handle on what secret rules say no 2 if you know, and a

"What Hoyle's Law says to a game theorist working in simulation is that a discussion of a complex system or situation—a 'game' in the parlance—requires a shared vocabulary of terms, a mutual comprehension of goals not clear from the outside, a concept of the limits on ac-

troo digging of the ground game stands on, air game breathes. Gag is, only after an outside geek can speak *all that weird backdoor info and whispertalk, will he-she comprende a peek at the rool book—but by then, won't half/have to look, and outgeek nomore. Everywhere thisiz troo, from groupmindwarp to nookspooking, from howto cheat at cards polite or ballbashing to who presumes to whom at a HiPurp All-Hands-Haftawanta Hands-off Gangbang.*

"Run through the numbercrunch and you'll nail down that the big prize of runaroundbusy gigs is mosttimes toughest to spot from outside. An outgeek will not spot the hiddenholes the player knows their cans can fall in. Outgeek might noknow lettle sidethangs on the gameplan, or be able to tell dodging from going ahead—and might not even able to scope what the big goal iz.

"Flipside, itza regular run for outgeek to peep game without digging rules and not make nohow know-

tion set by assumed and thus normally unstated rules, and an understanding of the system's environment. Only after a person absorbs all that data will an explanation of the game itself be comprehensible—but the background data is so complex, and contains so much contextual and implied information about the game, that by the time one absorbs it, the explanation is no longer needed. This phenomenon holds true in everything from political theory to nuclear engineering, from the etiquette of poker or the rules of baseball, to the pecking order at a High Purple Compulsory Volunteers' Celibate Orgy.

"It can be demonstrated mathematically that the ultimate goal of complex action is generally the most difficult thing to ascertain. An outsider will not be aware of obstacles or of subsidiary goals, and will not at first be able to discern between action taken to avoid or resolve problems, and action taken to move toward the goal. The observer will not, perhaps, even be able to

*ing noway of what the play-
ers doing at all.*

"*Boildown, shows why
we geeks to Charos, and
show they would noway
nohow capiche humyn
beans,*—*if Charo rools let
em notice wewas here to
hear.*

comprehend what the goal
is.

"To state the converse, it
is possible—indeed quite
normal—for an outsider to
watch actions guided by an
unstated rule set and not be
able to make heads or tails
of what seem to be utterly
inexplicable actions.

"This is why we don't
understand the Charonians,
and why it is doubtful they
would understand us—if
their rule set even allowed
them to be aware of us."

—Eyeballer Maximus Lock-on *NaPurno/Knowway
(The Naked Purple Way of Knowing)*, Datastreem-
dream Prezz, NaPurHab, published 100101111110
(A.D. 2430) (translation by the author)

Permod Three
Aboard *Cargo Craft 108*
Deep Space, En Route to NaPurHab
THE MULTISYSTEM

She had taken the pills at last, let the drugs take her under,
give her rest—but there was more to her unconsciousness
than mere sleeping pills could explain.

Sianna slept, slept *hard*, with a fierce intensity, the exhausted, unrestful sleep of fever and exhaustion, slept as if
some dark, denying corner of her mind were determined to
keep her under as long as possible, take her as deep as it
could, down away from her fears and her circumstances, as
if her subconscious were determined to hide from the gruel-

ing, mind-snapping reality of the permod for as long as possible.

And yet, her dreams were as harsh as any reality might have been—death, whirling darkness, the demons of fear and loneliness and loss made palpable, real, in the looming blackness that surrounded her. There were no true places, or events, or people in her dreams, but only distorted sensations, confused externals, threatening entities that seemed to fade away as they drew close and then remade themselves, over and over again.

She slept as her cargo craft fired its engines, maneuvered, guided itself in toward NaPurHab. Slept as the ship docked itself, and the hab's cargo handlers grappled the cargo modules into the hab and stacked the modules any way they could, helter-skelter, along Boredway on the long axis of the ship. Slept deeply, fitfully, as all of those things pushed and prodded and bounced at her, rattling her like a pea in a pod, and her mind wove the bouncing and jouncing into her dark, unknowable dreams.

And slept as she came to rest, in the microgravity of the Boredway, her personnel module stacked under one module full of emergency rations, and two others packed to bursting with ten thousand changes of underwear.

Inside the permod, nothing mattered.

She slept.

Boredway CarCome/CarGo OpCent
NaPurHab
THE MULTISYSTEM

Canpopper Notworthit got to the bottom of the stack, looked at the funny-looking mod at the bottom, and realized whatthehell it was. DamnNation! He glared at the permod, durn good and angry at the thing—and the offhabber inside—for having the bad grace to show up on his shift and in his section.

He hadn't popped a permod can for years, since wayback

before the Charos did the snatch, but he knew they were bad news. Remembered one bad time especial, tin can with a hellsmeller whacked-off offhabber of a Purple wannabe inside, bumping and thumping and banging and yelling from inside the permod. The fellow had been truly freaked-and-a-half long before the mod got to the hab. Had the gallopsing claustras, that fellow did. Upwoofed his lunch everywhere into everything. Had to strap down and dose him with heavy feelgoods to de-fruitcake him bigtime before anyone could deal with him.

Not blinked his rheumy brown eyes, stroked his scraggly, greying beard as he thought back to that nasty day. He shook his head sadly at the memory—and instantly knew to call the headshake mistake as his head tried to snap itself off.

Double dose of damitol, the *one* time this year the head honcho declared a compulsory bender, and Notworthit hadda be on duty next A.M. No justice. And just no ice for the drinks last night, either. Nor now not much he could do about the headbanging throb in his noggin nohow. No one was getting any breaks. The hole car come-go team had been slogging twenty-four-hours-plus everydamn day, humping all this freight, trying to get it packed into anywhichwhere.

Irony slap, this permod wuz. Only reazon, wayback, that he had took thiz job wuz so's he woodn't hafta deal with people alltime. Also course cuz Earth never sent no freight nohow, so the workload didn't make ya explode. Till now. More freight in last three daze than in the five years since the Charos did the Earthsnatch.

Never wooda signuped if heed knowed it half meant having to crack open cans with people in 'em. The smell alone was enough to drive a soul bendround. Plus besides—three daze inna can? *Can't* be good. Would be enough to flip Notworthit's brain, and even Not knew Not didn't have all that much to flip in the first place. Stood to reazon big brain would git more scrambled than a leetle one.

Plain fact wuz he not much wanted to deal with whooever whazzin the permod. Unpurple flipped-out bigbrain offhabber who wuz gonna smell like last year's recycle bin? Nohow.

Cept a job wuz a job, and Not knew the honcho would land like tunnabricks if he caught Not not doing.

Totally no justice putting him on thiz gig. No justice—just ice. Whatever that meant. Yeah. It sounded good, and that was all that really mattered.

Vaguely mollified by this sentiment for some reason, Not set to work opening up the permod. He checked the exterior read-outs. All scanned as cool on the inward side. He checked the seals, poppled the safeties, and braced himself for the smell as he undid the final latches.

The lid popped open and swung up about a centimeter or so, and the permod's air whooshed out into the OpCent. The smell warn't no better than Not'd figured it'd be, and then some. But that didn't even register fullways on him. Something else was dawning on him, the thing what *weren't* thar—noise. No hullbanging or muffle-shouts before he popped the hatch, and still no noiz now. Chick inside shoulda been cheering to get out, or cursing Not's head for taking so slow, or *some* such. Somewhat alarmed, he got his hands under the lid and pulled it open. It swung away easily, up and over.

Not felt another kind of knot in his stomach as he looked inside the mod. There she was, the lettlest slip of a thing, lying still, so still. There was blood spattered all over the permod interior, and on her face. Her hair was a tangled, wadded mess, her clothes along ago sweated through.

At first, Canpopper Notworthit thought she was dead, that the trip had killed her. But no. There. Her chest was rising, falling. Her eyelids fluttered. She was alive, at least sumwut.

Well, wut wuz wrong with her? Unconscious? Sick? Comatose? No—leastwise, didn't *look* like none of thoz. Just asleep, looked like.

Pretty lady, she wuz, even under alltha grime and stuff. Canpopper Notworthit at least knew *he* had no right to carp about someone else being a bit on the dirty side.

"*Heavy* dozer," he muttered to himself in admiring tones. The first half of his name was derived from his job, but Canpopper Notworthit had earned the second half by being sure nothing was ever worth the effort required. He was, however, a big admirer of sleep, with real respect for anyone who knew how to do it right. And this chick knew, for sure.

Help. Get her some help. That wuz thing todo. No. Waitasec. Not get. *Give.* For wunz in life, do tha thing self, notdoa handoff.

Not knelt down by the permod, looked over the plumbing connections, and undid them with a minimum of fumbling. He shifted his weight, got his arms under her, and lifted her up. He turned and started carrying her toward the medfixer, moving carefully in the microgee of the Boredway, down the closest gangway to the docshop.

Even down in the hi-gee decks, she didn't weight hardly nothing at all, nohow.

Windbag Central (Command Center)
NaPurHab

Eyeballer Maximus Lock-on had the fear sweats, and no surprise. There was trouble abubble, no doubt. There was a perfect torrent of cargo headed toward the hab, and every can of it carried a little bit of trouble.

Prob was simple. Every arriving cargo that was incoming at more than zero speed—which was all of them, of course—gave the hab a leetle goose. To put it a bit more formally, every arriving cargo unit added a microscropic velocity vector to the hab. Plus, were lots of cargo craft arriving, all from about the same direction, which meant that there were a lot of microvectors coming in and adding up. Plusmore, each time the Ghoul Mods tweaked the grav systems on the Moonpoint Ring, that perturbed the hab's orbit as well. Normtime, such tiny perturbs wouldn't matter—but no such thing as *minor* orbital perturbs this close to a singularity.

Sooner or later, Eyeball knew she was gonna hafta light the maneuvering engines on this mother and tidy up the hab's orbit—if she could. She had a nasty feeling that the cargo teams were not making her job easier. Couldn't light the engine with unsecured cargo floating allways about.

Eyeball decided to head on down to cargo and get a peek for herself, live up to her name. There wasn't much she could do about the SCOREs just now, and the hab orbit wouldn't destabilize for a while yet.

She powered down her station, got up, and moved out into the labyrinthine, and rather grotty, corridors of the hab. Put plain, the place wasn't looking so good these days—and the hab expecting guests, too. Those eggheads from MRI, coming in on permods. Strange thought, that: the idea they should spruce up because company was coming. Was that one of the pointless counteract instincts the Pointless Cause was supposed to whack out of the Purpfolk? Or was it a good thing, a "Troo Way," however the term was being spelled this week? The bigshot Purpthinkers were forever pronouncing contradictory Noo Ways and Troo Ways. What was part of firm and unswerving policy last week was out the window next. That wuz the Purpthinkers *job*—to keep the rules changing so's no one got too comfortable. It was hard to keep up, and that wuz the idea. Keep you on edge, alert, awake, thinking.

Eyeball threaded her way along the mazeways, the rat's nest of corridors and detours and vertical ways that made up the hab. Somewhere underneath the dark, Purple-built squatter's boxes and pseudo-art and dayclubs was the straight-out, linear, geometric corridors and passages laid out by the original architect of the hab. Prob if they cleared away all the Purpbuilt add-ons it would take half as long to get anywhere, and there would be more room in the place to boot. But no, that would spoil everything. Efficiency was not the be-all

and end-all. People did not join the Purple so's they could do
things the *sensible* way.

Eyeball spotted someone—closer to some*thing*, maybe—
coming her way. It took her a moment, but then she had it
locked: Canpopper Notworthit, repped as one of heaviest
goofers on the whole damn can. You wanted a job not done,
you sent the Popper to do it. A very popular fellow during
official work stoppages. But the Popper was *carrying* something, something big and heavy, an event about as common
as nudists wearing tuxedoes to bed. Whatthehey was he up
to?

Eyeball moved toward Canpopper and realized he was
carrying a who, not a what—and a who that was in no good
shape. Eyeball hurried down the corridor. "Jeeks, Pop.
Who-the-hell?" she asked. Young kid, a pretty girl in a bad
way.

"Outta a can," Popper replied, looking down on his bur-
den. "One of the science jaspers up from Earth. Just a baby,
huh?"

"Just a baby for sure," Eyeball agreed. "Where to?"

"Nearmost docshop," Popper said. "I *think* she's core
okay, just burned out. Gonna make sure."

Eyeball reached out, touched the young one's face. *This*
was what the Earthside eggheads sent? Was that a real special brain in there, or was she just a lamb to the slaughter?
Her skin was warm, *felt* okay, not cold clammy or burning.
Eyeball moved her hand down, found a strong pulse under
her jaw. Maybe *would* be okay. But nothing she could do
doc couldn't do better. Her job was getting the cargo untan-
gled, else they *all* in bad shape. "Get her down pronto to
doc," Eyeball said. "Good way, Popper."

"On it, Eyeball," Canpopper said, and went on his way.

Eyeball watched him go, and then recommenced toward
Boredway. She walked through the zones and turfs and operations sections and rand centers, her mind much more on
cargo handling than her route. She knew this part of the hab
by heart. She could still get lost in the Downways zone, or

Old High Bagdad, but then why would she ever wanna go those place? She went through Looparound, took the short-cut across Doubleback turf, up three levels to get around the blockage caused by the Funway, through hydroponics control, past two or three childcare bars, and then up the access-way to the low-gee and no-gee sections at the axis of the ship.

Eyeball came out onto Boredway, the huge long-axis passageway that would have been called Broadway on any other ship, an enormous, enclosed cylindrical space that ran the whole length of the hab. It was a bright, gleaming place, very much in contrast to most of the hab. Even the Purps knew to keep this sector nice and tidy and clean and linear, if they wanted to stay alive. A wise Purp knew there were limits to chaos, just as there were limits to order. And there had best be no chaos at all hereabouts.

Back before the Purps has started rerouting corridors into more aesthetically pleasing forms, you could get to any point on the hab just by taking a vertical passageway to Broadway, moving to the vertiway nearest your destination, and heading back down. Too simple. Too easy. Too boring, and hence the name.

But still and all, Boredway was a pretty exciting locale just at the moment. All the conveyors and tow-ways were crammed with containers moving this way and that as the cargo jockeys struggled to get everything to where it belonged, and any number of cargo-container clusters were just floating free, tethered in most haphazard fashion and hanging in mid-air until someone thought of what to do with them.

Eyeball shook her head worriedly. She had been sweating this possibility. There was no way she could do any sort of course-correction burn until all the unsecured cargo was lashed down properly and stored in such a way as to retain the hab's center of gravity somewhere within shouting distance of its centerline.

The hab's cargo crews hadn't *ever* had to handle this

much in the way of incoming gear and supplies, even back in the unweird old daze before the Abduction. Cargo ops had been down to skeleton crews for years—and those skeleton crews hadn't been worth much. There had been near no inbound traffic and total no outbound traf whasoev for years. Meantime, allthetime, bigtime great deal of work needed doing elsewhere in the hab if the place was to hang in there. Lotsa Purps had turned into big swinging engineers the last few years, improvising their way outta a zillion shortages and hardware dropdeads.

With so little demand here, and so much otherplace, twas understandable in the circs that cargo ops had become a haven for the real dreggers of Purple society—and Purple dregs were about as dreggy as they came, yabbos what barely came up to the min standards for being losers. Now the Maximum Windbag was staffing the cargo ops teams any way he could, yanking in teams from every other part of the station who didn't know a thing about cargo. The Maxbag had been forced to find retired cargo oldfogies, put the oldfarts in charge to keep things running. But plain to scope, oldies weren't whipping the losers into shape.

Eyeball swore to herself and moved along against the stream of cargo, toward the aft-end air lock complex. Time to bust some heads if she didn't want the hab busting up when she lit the engines.

Multisystem Research Institute
New York City
EARTH

CORE destroyed, Ursula Gruber read. *Probability of renewed attacks high, probability of surviving same low.* Ursula shook her head. Captain Steiger was not much for excessive optimism. The woman won a great victory, and yet her report states she expects to be defeated next time.

Steiger was only partly right. A lot of COREs were still out there, but now people knew they were vulnerable, that they could be killed. The *Terra Nova* had taught Earth that its enemies were not utterly invincible. That knowledge would give people some backbone. Battles are not won by people who are certain they will lose.

Of course, a whole Multisystem full of high morale was not going to be much use against a CORE that managed to dodge the exploding decoys and kill the *TN*. The *Terra Nova* would have to win *every time* in order to survive. The odds against that *were* long, to put it mildly.

For that matter, hope would not be much use against a Breeding Binge, should such occur. Ursula was more and more convinced that there would be no Binge—but try telling that to anyone. Word had gotten out, of course, and every imaginable official and private preparation was being made. Troops were being called up, attack forces prepared. People were getting instructions on shelters and evacuation. Of course, any number of end-of-the-world groups were springing up, and a few of the Sphere-worship cults had gotten into trouble. Suicides were up sharply—but so were marriages.

But all of it for nothing. There would be no Breeding Binge—at least not now. The SCOREs did not make sense as Breeders, and they were heading for the Moonpoint Ring, not Earth. But who the devil would believe that it was a false alarm, when Gruber could offer no plausible alternative?

Never mind. People would learn soon enough. But *Terra Nova* and NaPurHab were, as Captain Steiger knew, the ones up against the real long odds.

All right then. It was time to change the odds. But how?

Ursula stood up and walked to the window, looked down at the absurd, underground, inward-looking bubble-in-the-stone headquarters of MRI. She slipped open the window and leaned out into the air-conditioned simulated fresh air. The ducks were on the pond, the drake flapping his wings, rearing up out of the water. She could hear his quacking from here, faint in the distance, announcing to all the world that he ruled this patch of water against all comers. As if he had built the cavern, and commanded the humans to come down to the water and bring stale buns to his flock.

Compared to how much say humans had in the running of the Multisystem, it didn't seem quite so absurd. But if the drake failed in caring for his flock, only the ducks would die. If the humans failed, then all the Earth would suffer.

Steiger was right. The odds against her ship were high and getting higher. There was no hope—and no point—in the *Terra Nova* battling endlessly against COREs. That was playing the Charonian's game, playing to their strengths.

So what game could mere human beings play, and beat the Charonians at?

Ursula had the feeling the answers were just out of reach, just beyond the questions she was asking. Something else had to happen before she would understand.

The SCOREs. That had to be it. They weren't going to do what everyone expected them to do. She was sure of that now. She had not the slightest idea what they were going to do instead—but when she did, it would be time to change the game.

Kourou Spaceport
Earth

Joanne Beadle—and every other person in the ops center—watched as SCORE X001 made its closest approach to the Moonpoint Ring.

The Charonians had never bothered with closest-approach gravity-well maneuvers, but if the SCOREs were indeed headed for Earth, they would have to make their moves there. Whatever they were going to do, closest approach was the moment to do it.

X001 was the vanguard SCORE, the first to arrive. The betting was that whatever it did, the follow-on SCOREs would imitate. And whatever it was going to do, it was going to do *now*. It could do almost anything by maneuvering at peripoint—but which way would it jump?

"What's it doing, Beadle?" Bernhardt demanded, leaning over his chair, as if Beadle had some special knowledge, could see something in the display screen that Bernhardt could not.

"I can't quite say," she replied, her mind far more on the display tank than on the director's question. "There's no way to guess. This one is no simulation."

"Yah," Bernhardt agreed. "We're through with those for a while, thank the heavens. I was beginning to forget things could be real."

Joanne didn't see how it could be a good thing that the alien craft approaching Earth were real. It would have suited her just fine if the whole fleet of them were imaginary. Still, there *was* something to be said for getting on with it all.

She stared at the screen, tense, waiting.

It would, of course, have been sheerest folly to try and read a human craft's intent from this range. The distances were too great. Even the fastest of human vehicles would be moving too slowly for a course change to be observable at this distance.

But not the Charonians. They could accelerate at hundreds of gees if it suited them.

She leaned closer to the screen, willing it to give up the secrets. "Peripoint in ten seconds," she announced, quite needlessly. "In five. Four. Three. Two. One—"

And then X001's flight path snapped neatly around in a perfect ninety-degree turn—and set itself on an arrow-straight course straight for the Moonpoint Black Hole.

"What the devil is *that*?" Bernhardt demanded. "Why is it doing this thing? Beadle—time to impact on black hole, if you please."

"Ah, ah, yes sir. Stand by. Just a moment." What the hell was that thing doing aiming direct for the black hole? It was the one possibility they hadn't considered. Well, why should they have? Why consider the possibility of the SCOREs traveling tens of millions of kilometers just to commit a highly energetic form of suicide? Unless . . . unless . . . Yes,

it made sense. Beadle ran the numbers on tim
they would be the same no matter what happen
was right—

"Sir, assuming the SCORE does not chang
will hit the event horizon of the black hole in a
five seconds—but, ah, sir, I don't think it's going
think it's going to go *through*."

"But the Ring is dead!" Bernhardt protested. '
no wormhole!"

As if on cue, the visual-band image system fla
flashed with the strange not-blue-white of a wormhol
ing. Joanne gasped in surprise along with everyone
the ops center.

"My God, Beadle, you are a good guesser," Bern
said in a half-whisper.

"Thank you, sir," she replied, most disconcerted, "
I'm usually not *this* good."

"The hole," Bernhardt whispered. "Why the devil ar
they going into the hole?"

Twenty-four

Tremors

"Too many people fail to make the distinction between the concept of dichotomy and that of oppo-
sites. We assume that, if there are two possibilities,
the two are therefore opposite. This is in some cases
true: Black is the opposite of white.

"However, male is by no means the opposite of
female. There is nothing to prevent some other
planet developing three sexes, and certainly plenty of
Earth life gets by with no sexes at all. In a Universe
that includes unliving matter—like rocks—death is
not the opposite of life. Much that we declare dead is
truly alive—a rotting corpse is literally alive with the
micro-organisms that are consuming it. Much that
we regard as alive in some way—the weather, music,
laughter, literature—are in literal fact lifeless.

"And the human perspective of the Universe is

not the opposite of the Charonian perspective. They are not even two points along a one-dimensional spectrum. The two are merely two points. Other points—that is to say, quite literally, other points of view—could be charted anywhere in relation to these first two points.''

—Gerald MacDougal, first officer's log, published in *Aspects of Life*, MRI Press, 2430

Wheelway, North Pole Sector
The Lunar Wheel
THE MOON

Larry Chao had no business being down in the Wheelway, but he was there. He walked along for quite a while, lost in thought, with no real aim, but the going was easy enough that it did not matter, even once he had walked past the last of the overhead lights. His thoughts were quite unclear, even to himself. The talk he had given, the dangers he had discovered—and the unquiet ghost of Lucian Dreyfuss—all whispered in his mind.

His pressure suit's headlamps lit the tunnel tolerably well, and Larry was not much in the mood for a lot of light anyway. Besides, the lighted signs indicating the side caverns served well enough as beacons in the darkness.

At length he found himself near the sign for Chamber 281, the most famous of the side caverns. Larry had always wanted to get a look at it, and now seemed a perfectly good time to do so. He turned off the main Wheelway into a small antechamber that opened out onto a much larger inner chamber. A transparent wall was rigged up inside the antechamber, so this smaller room could serve as an observation platform for the big room. The air inside the big room was clear, the ambient atmosphere of the Wheelway pumped out and replaced with nitrogen gas. An airlock arrangement permitted access to the interior. Even though the site was deserted, the worklights were on.

Chamber 281 was where they had found the most spectacular collection of dinosaur remains. Even after four years of work, they were just beginning to learn what the room could tell them. Two skeletons and a rather ratty-looking dinosaur mummy had been propped up on huge display boards near the observation chamber for the edification of passersby. Larry was fairly certain the mummy was a tyrannosaur, but he had no idea at all what the others were.

He knew, intellectually, that the creatures had been down here for tens of millions of years, but still, somehow, it was hard to *believe* it at a gut level. The behavior of this being or that eighty million years ago hadn't seemed as if it had that much meaning for life in the present day, any more than the dynastic wars of 15th century England, or the imperial collapses all through the 20th century had any meaningful consequence to the life of Larry O'Shawnessy Chao in the 25th century.

Except they did, of course. It was easy to trace the strands back, show that if *this* king had not defeated *that* usurper, if this government had held together, then all of subsequent history would be changed.

But that was dry, academic theory. The past, the human past, was dead. It did not come alive from out of nowhere, full of dangers all had thought put to rest long ago.

Not so the Charonian past—or the Adversarial past. How could a race of beings from the time of the tyrannosaurs come back, come to life, today, now?

In one moment Larry was staring down at the monsters of Earth's past.

—And in the next the cavern was bucking and twisting, writhing like a live thing. The transparent wall bulged, flexed, and smashed open. Larry went tumbling through the air and was slammed into the side wall of the cavern as the whole room shook, spasmed.

Loose bits of rock and debris tumbled free all around him. Half-stunned, Larry wrapped his arms around his head, trying to shield the helmet of his suit. The display boards holding the mummified tyrannosaur bucked and swayed and then toppled forward, sending the head of the monster smashing down into the observation room. Larry pulled his legs back just before the razor-sharp teeth could come down on them.

He pulled back from the leering head as far as he could and hunkered down in the corner, as tools and gadgets and bits of dead Charonian and dead dinosaur tumbled down on to him. A scorp claw caromed into the side of his helmet and put a deep scratch in his visor.

Moonquake, Larry told himself, but even as he thought it, he knew it could not be right. He had ridden out a quake or two since he had been on the Moon, and this was different. The ground was not shuddering from deep below. The whole cavern was spasming, somehow. At last the bucking and heaving began to subside.

Larry got to his feet, moving carefully, cautiously. He made his way out of the cavern, out into the main corridor. The lighted sign over the chamber entrance was out. He switched his suit lights back on and a beam of light speared out into the darkness, the air filled with billowing brown dust. The walls, the floors, the ceiling of the Wheelway were still quivering. That was when it struck Larry. The corridor was not being shaken; it was shaking *itself*.

This was no Moonquake. Larry knew that, knew it down in his soul. This phenomenon was every bit as alien to the Moon as Larry himself.

The Lunar Wheel itself was coming back to life, somehow, a spasm of activity five years after Larry himself had killed the massive being by sending it the command to die.

Every indicator, every test, every probe had confirmed that the Wheel was utterly dead, that *every* Charonian in the Solar System, from the greatest to the smallest, had died when Larry sent out the death order.

But clearly, somehow, some part of the Wheel had survived. Somehow its corpse was still capable of action, of movement.

But why did it choose *now* to move?

And then he knew. He *knew*. And negotiating his way down a pitch-black tunnel to safety was suddenly trivial, meaningless. A door, a way out, was suddenly open. But the dangers of the past had returned, infinitely more deadly than the teeth of a tyrannosaur. He had to get to a comm center. He had to get word to the Ring of Charon, to Sondra Berghoff.

His mind was racing, his heart pounding with excitement as he thought it through. It meant danger, yes, that was clear. But it might mean hope, as well.

The second pulsequake knocked him off his feet, but that was of no consequence. He waited it out, clinging to the floor of the bucking, twisting Wheelway as best he could. When it stopped, he got up and moved on.

Kourou Spaceport
Earth
THE MULTISYSTEM

It did not make sense. Wolf Bernhardt stared at the screen, as if he could will the data to be logical and coherent. The SCORE had gone through the wormhole. What was it all about?

He looked toward Joanne Beadle, her eyes still locked on the display screen. "Very well," he said, in as brusque a tone as he could. "It has gone into the hole. So, where does that wormhole lead? Back to the Solar System?"

"I don't think so, sir. If our theories about what happened are right, the Ring can never be returned. The tuning adjustment mechanism has got to be huge and complex—and there's just no way it survived in any sort of reparable state."

"Then what are you saying?" Bernhardt asked.

Beadle licked her lips nervously and looked up at Director Bernhardt. "I'm saying that's a detuned hole out there."

"Detuned? So it goes nowhere? That SCORE just sent itself off into oblivion?"

"No sir. I'm not an expert, but as I understand it, a detuned wormhole drops back to a, ah—I suppose you'd call it a default mode. Every transit pair of black holes has its own natural resonances. Leave them alone and they will revert to that tuning."

"So why couldn't the Ghoul Modules tune this one?"

"The parts of the Moonpoint Ring that could do it are one big fused lump. Nothing can budge the Moonpoint Ring away from its default tuning, ever again."

"And you're sure that the default is *not* the same as that of the ring in the Solar System?"

"Couldn't be. The whole *point* of the Moonpoint Ring is to serve as a tuning system to force the black hole *off* its default tuning. Besides, don't forget the people back in the Solar System closed their end of the hole as well."

"If that is so, then where does that damn SCORE think it's going?"

Joanne shook her head. "I don't think *anyone* is that good a guesser, sir."

Terra Nova
Deep Space

The full staff was on the bridge, everyone hushed, quiet, tense. Not that there was much point to having anyone at all on the bridge just now. The ship was days away from being able to do much of anything besides watch.

The *Terra Nova* was moving toward NaPurHab at a crawl, well below the relative velocity that would attract the interest of the COREs that still circled the Earth—at least according to the Earthside theorists and their simulations. Dianne smiled to herself, but there was no pleasure in the expression. Sakalov. Sakalov had been one of those theorists—and had died for the crime of guessing wrong. Perhaps there was some justice in the theory spinners putting themselves on the line, but sometimes the price of justice was too high.

Besides, there was no justice if Sakalov died for being wrong. *All* the theories were wrong. No one had predicted the SCOREs heading *into* the singularity. So what the hell else had they got wrong?

"Talk to me, Gerald. What the hell is going on?" Dianne asked. "I thought the SCOREs were supposed to land on Earth and breed."

"Be thankful we were wrong," Gerald said. "But we may have other problems."

"What do you mean—"

"SCORE X002 coming up on closest approach," Lieutenant DePanna announced. She was the detection officer for the watch, and Dianne was glad to have her. DePanna knew how to interpret what she saw.

Dianne watched on the screen, ready to see this one follow the other into the wormhole.

"Closest approach in five, four, three, two, one—peripoint." DePanna checked her boards. "X002 is not, repeat, not, on a course into the wormhole. It is moving at a tangent to a wormhole intercept course. It is coming about. X002 has ceased maneuvering. Course projections running now. We show X002 now in a circular polar orbit of the wormhole, radius 2,231 kilometers."

"Now what the hell does *that* mean?" Dianne demanded.

"No idea, ma'am," DePanna said in a smooth, steady voice. "Stand by. Something more." She checked her instruments and looked up in surprise. "SCORE X002 radars cut off," she said.

"But the COREs never cut their radar," Gerald objected.

"Yes sir," DePanna said. "That's what I thought too—" Something on her displays caught DePanna's attention, and she started adjusting her detectors. "—and we were both right. Radars still active, but *redirected.* I am running backscatter and beam-leakage analysis. Stand by. Ah, Captain, as best I can tell, SCORE X002's radar is now directed in a tight beam, focused on the singularity."

"Oh, come *on!*" Dianne said, baffled and infuriated.

"This is ridiculous. Why aim it at the wormhole? They can't tell where it *is?*"

"I don't know, ma'am. But that's what it's doing. X003 coming toward closer approach."

"And what the hell is *this* one going to do?" Dianne demanded. "A song-and-dance routine?"

Gerald MacDougal rubbed his chin thoughtfully. "No song and dance," he said, "but if we consider that the primary function of a CORE is to detect and destroy spaceborne objects that threaten something the Charonians value, maybe we get toward an answer."

"What do you mean?" Dianne asked.

"I mean if we assume the SCOREs are behaving rationally, and further assume that their behavior programming is based on the COREs, that suggests that these SCOREs are getting into position to strike at something. Then if we consider what positions they are taking—"

"X003 has entered the wormhole. X004 is taking up an equatorial orbit."

"My God," Dianne said. "Half of them taking up parking orbits on *this* side of the hole, and the other half going through it. They're trying to stop something from *coming through the hole.* First line of defense on the other side, and the second line here on this side."

"Yes," Gerald agreed. "They're watching for something they expect will come through it."

"But why not just slam the wormhole shut?" DePanna asked.

"Because they can't," Dianne said. "Whoever is on the other side is able to force the wormhole open. What other answer could there be?"

"None that I can see," Gerald replied. "I've been thinking on this a lot. The Charonians are getting ready to *fight* something, even though we don't know what. Much of the evidence points toward their fighting something *stronger than they are.* It's hard to imagine that, I know, but there's more evidence of it right out there."

"My God," Dianne said. "If something on the other side of that hole can force the wormhole open against the Charonians' will, we are in deep trouble. It just takes *one* CORE to knock out a mid-sized asteroid, and hundreds of SCOREs are headed this way. What the hell can fight back against a hundred SCOREs crashing into it? If that's even the way SCOREs fight. We don't know."

"We don't know damn much of anything," DePanna said, showing a bit more emotion than she usually did.

Gerald stared at the display screen as another SCORE moved into a parking orbit. "We don't know much yet," he said, "but things are happening. We'll know more soon. But I don't think we'll enjoy knowing it."

Windbag Central (Command Center)
NaPurHab

From where Eyeballer Maximus Lock-on was sitting, twas no great deal sussing the slides of the SCOREs. Half the damnthings were heading straight for the hab, or near enuff. NaPurHab's orbit was so damn close to the singularity that anything heading for it *had* to slide rightby the hab. Eyeball could not help but whirry on the whatif re if the hab's orbit round the black hole carried it right into the path of one of those mothers. At a guess, the SCORE would just smash right through the hab and keep right on going likit hadn't hit anythang.

At least some SCOREs were scooting into various orbits around Moonpoint. Eyeball didn't have to worry bout dodging *them*.

But Eyeball had other things to sweat 'sides SCORE orbits—like incoming cargo and the stability of the hab's own orbit. Neither was in the greatest shape, and the two problems were more knit to the SCOREs than might seem at firstglance.

The *S* in *SCORE* might stand for "small," but them whizbangs was plenty big—and plenty massive. Their gravity fields were jogging the hab around just a bit as they passed. Likewise, the Ghoul Modules were popping the wormhole open and shut, and using gravity waves to do it. Lots of per-turbs coming at them.

She was gonna *hafta* boost this can into a higher, more stable orbit real soon, or hab was toast for sure. Cept no way to do it with the cargo still streaming in, and incoming SCOREs all over the place. The hab was a big old lump of a tub, easy to hit and hard to pilot. Chance of taking a major impact was way too high to risk maneuvering. Best wait until it all settled down, at least somewhat.

If ever did.

The Ring of Charon Command Station
Plutopoint
THE SOLAR SYSTEM

"We detected the second gravity-wave pulse eight minutes after the first," Sondra said, reading off her notes. "We picked it up as a harmonic of one of the sub-frequencies we were working on. Of course we immediately retuned to zero in on that frequency. Then the third pulse came about ten minutes after the second, and they've been coming at intervals of between five and sixteen minutes ever since."

"And you have never picked up anything like this before?" the Autocrat asked.

"No, never, not since we turned the Ring on."

"And what does it mean?" the Autocrat asked.

"Before I get to that, there's something else you need to know," Sondra said. "Just a few minutes ago, I received a high-priority signal from Larry Chao on the Moon, reporting a moonquake at *exactly* the same moment we picked up the first pulse, with a follow-on quake exactly when we picked up the second pulse."

"But don't gravity waves move at light speed? No gravity wave that the Moon detected could possibly reach us here at the same moment, unless the wave generator was exactly the same distance from both points, on a plane exactly between the two points, here in the Solar System.''

"You know your stuff, Autocrat. Except these gravity waves did not come from anywhere in the Solar System. They were from an external source.''

"But that's impossible,'' the Autocrat protested.

"Except for the fact that it's happening, I'd agree with you. Dr. Chao thinks he knows what is happening, and I am inclined to agree with him.''

"And what does he think is happening?''

Sondra hesitated a moment. "He thinks something— actually a whole series of *large* somethings—are moving through a wormhole link with a resonance frequency almost precisely the same as the Lunar Wheel's natural tuning frequency. The pulse is coming, not through normal space, but through the contiguous planar space adjacent to the Wheel in a wormhole stack.''

"I beg your pardon?''

"I'm sorry. Let me try that again. Somewhere out there, something big is going from one point in normal space to another by way of a wormhole. That passage is setting up gravitic-wave vibrations, and the Lunar Wheel's basal, default tuning is so close to the frequency of those vibrations that it is reacting. The automatic sensor part of the Wheel is trying to wake the Wheel up again, get it to respond to the pulse—but it can't, because the Wheel is dead.''

"And the Ring of Charon?''

"Is a gravity-wave sensor. It would be pretty remarkable if it failed to pick up a wave pulse this powerful.''

"This is all most interesting. But why is it as important as you say?''

"Because the pulse frequency is so powerful, and so close to the Lunar Wheel's default tuning.''

"So you think this all has something to do with where Earth is.''

"Yes. Yes I do. I think the Charonians are using the wormhole to send something into or out of the system where they have Earth—and I'd bet big money they're using the same singularity that Earth came through. The tuning is that close.''

''But why? How?''

Sondra shook her head. ''I don't know. But I don't think it is likely to be good news. It never is, with the Charonians.''

Dreyfuss Memorial Research Station
North Pole
The Moon
THE SOLAR SYSTEM

Tyrone Vespasian watched the last of the personnel come up out of the transit car, up from Wheel level to the lunar surface. Two dead, twelve injured. It could have been, should have been, a lot worse.

''Everyone accounted for?'' he asked the technician in charge, without moving his gaze off the transit car.

''Yes sir. Full roll call completed and confirmed.''

''All right then,'' he said, though damn little was all right. ''Seal it off,'' he told the transit technician. ''No one goes down without my specific written authorization until further notice. Until we know what the hell those pulses are, and until they stop, the Wheelway is off-limits. Period. Is that clear?''

''Yes, sir. Understood.'' The tech turned and hurried back to his post, though he might as well have taken his time. The Lucian Dreyfuss Memorial Station was quite suddenly out of business.

And what of Lucian Dreyfuss himself? Alone in the dark again, down in the Wheelway, still entombed by the Charonians, still hooked up to the simulator system, lost to them once again. Did *Lucian* understand what was happening? Had he even survived this latest disaster? Damnation, they should have set up the control system on the surface, rather than down in the caverns. Then they could have tried to wake Lucian again, ask him what it meant.

But as it was. . . . Lucian was gone again, lost to them once more. Sleeping still, or killed outright by the tremors, no one could say.

And yet Vespasian could not believe that Lucian was gone altogether. Not after coming so close to death, and yet returning, at least part of the way. No. Some part of what had been Lucian Dreyfuss was still down there, somewhere. He was lost to them for now, but not forever.

Unless, of course, everyone up here managed to get themselves killed by whatever the Charonians were trying now. Which thought brought Vespasian's thoughts to Larry Chao.

Larry Chao. He claimed to understand what it was all about. Tyrone had had just about enough of that fellow's ravings. Maybe everything he said was true, but somehow Vespasian could not quite believe any of it. Except. Except, here they were, with the Lunar Wheel bucking and heaving and word back from the Ring of Charon that it had something to do with wormholes and gravity waves. And gravity waves were what Chao did.

Tyrone turned his back on the Vertical Transit Center and went to find Chao.

Larry Chao was in his quarters in the temp worker section, working his main computer and a half-dozen interlinked notepacks all at once. Tyrone didn't want to interrupt him, but then Larry looked up and saw him standing in the doorway. Larry's eyes were bright, over-alert, and he seemed agitated, twitchy.

"So," Tyrone asked, not quite sure where to start. "What's going on? What's with the quakes?"

"They're not quakes," Larry said. "They're the Lunar Wheel reacting to large masses passing through a wormhole almost on its tuning frequency. If the Adversary can sense a pulse moving through the wormhole net, then why not the Lunar Wheel? But that's not the important part."

"So what is?" Tyrone asked.

"What it means," Larry said. "I think I know what it means."

"And that would be?"

Larry held his hands out, palms toward Tyrone, a small, cautionary gesture. "There's a lot we don't know," he said. "A lot. But we've got all the data on the Adversary—plus a lot of what Lucian fed to me directly that I haven't worked out all the way yet. But *if* the Adversary were going to move on the Multisystem, the Earth-Sphere system, it would head for the wormhole that it sensed in the first place. And if it sensed the arrival of Earth in the Multisystem, then it would be the wormhole Earth came through that it would have detected. And *if* the Charonians knew their cover was blown anyway, and *if* they knew which hole the Adversary was going to come through, maybe they'd decide to set up some kind of forward defense on the other side of the hole."

"That's a lot of ifs and maybes."

"I know. I know. But I think it hangs together. And if it's right, then the Charonians are getting ready to defend against an attack. And if the first line of defense fails—"

"Then the Charonians throw Earth at the Adversary," Vespasian said. "I still can't quite believe that. How could someone throw a *planet*?"

Larry smiled thinly. "How could someone *steal* a planet?"

Vespasian nodded. There wasn't much of an answer to that.

"I don't know if I'm right," Larry said. "But I might be. I might be. And if I am, then we have to get word to Earth."

"How?"

"Somehow," Larry snapped. "Somehow fast. Before Earth isn't there anymore. And I have an idea how."

NaPurHab
Orbiting the Moonpoint Singularity
THE MULTISYSTEM

Sianna Colette moaned, shifted in her sleep, and then woke up, her eyelids fluttering open most unwillingly. She tried to prop herself up on her elbows, but even that effort was too much. She slumped back onto the bed, and suddenly realized that she *was* in a bed, and not a coffin-shaped tin can.

She rubbed her eyes, realizing in the process just how stiff and sore her arms were. On the second try, she managed to prop her herself on her elbows, and from there to sit full up in bed.

She seemed to be in some sort of hospital room or infirmary, clean enough if a bit chaotic in the decorating department. The walls were covered with graffiti, most of it cryptic—and occasionally rather cheerfully obscene—get-well messages for past occupants of her bed. The furnishings were all rather tatty and run-down looking, but warm and safe and bright for all of that.

Wally was sitting at the foot of the bed, looking a bit thinner and paler, and dressed in an odd-looking outfit that seemed to be a cross between overalls and a bathrobe. He was staring at the screen of a datapack, and hadn't noticed her waking up.

"Wally?" she asked—or at least tried to ask. It came out sounding more like a grunt than a word, and Sianna found herself taken by a fit of coughing. Wally got up suddenly, got her a glass of water from the side table, and gave it to her, putting a hand on her back to support her. She took a big gulp of it, and grimaced just a trifle at the taste. Now she knew they were definitely on NaPurHab. Only a habitat would recycle water *that* many times.

"Wally," she said again, and this time her voice worked. "We made it."

Wally nodded and smiled, but there was something sad, something worried behind the smile. "Yes," he said. "We made it. They got you out of your permod about sixteen hours ago.''

"My God! That long. I don't remember anything at all about the second half of the permod flight. Have I been unconscious that whole time?''

Wally shrugged. "I suppose," he said. "The doc says it looks like you were running a pretty high fever for a while there.''

Sianna lay back down onto the pillow, and Wally let her down easy before sliding his hand out. "So," she asked, trying to keep her voice calm and casual. "Have I missed anything?''

Twenty-five

The Way Out

"One of our most cherished illusions is that we always have a choice, that there are always options. We seem to feel there is something unnatural about the inevitable. We like choices, even if they are meaningless. Most people are more willing to accept an unpleasant reality once they are convinced that there is an alternative—even if that alternative is nothing more or less than death."

—Dr. Wolf Bernhardt, Director-General, U.N. Directorate for Spatial Investigation, Address on the occasion of dedicating the *Hijacker* Memorial

Multisystem Research Institute
New York City
Earth
THE MULTISYSTEM

Ursula Gruber did not like the ideas she was getting. They were dangerous, grandiose—and yet, they smacked of surrender, somehow.

The Lone World monitors were coming into their own, pulling down all sorts of data, and that was the good part. The data teams were listening in on nearly every command the Lone World sent to the Ghoul Modules controlling the Moonpoint Ring. By now the data teams were confident they had correctly interpreted all the basic commands.

And they were at least fairly certain they could duplicate at least a few of them.

Well, maybe that was the way they would have to go. She was not sure she saw any other way out.

If "out" was the right word to use, all things considered. Ursula checked the time and sighed. Time for her call to NaPurHab, a chore she did not look forward to. She did not like dealing with those people. In a better world, she would not have to do so.

Of course, in a better world, aliens would not have kidnapped the Earth, either.

NaPurHab

Sianna Colette, still in her hospital overalls, slipped into the back of the MainBrainMeet Room. Wally was there, listening to the call from Earth with rapt attention. Sianna felt she ought to be in on the conference, even if she was too much in shock to pay much attention. After all the effort made to get her here, she felt something close to honor-bound to attend.

But effort expended was the least of it. Sakalov had *died*. Died to no purpose whatsoever, pummeled to death by an intelligent rock.

And there was something else she could not help realizing: they were stranded here, she and Wally. NaPurHab was supposed to be a way station for them, a place to wait until the *Terra Nova* came and collected them. But that was not going to happen anytime soon. Not with a sky full of COREs and SCOREs making everyone's life interesting. Maybe it would never happen.

But Dr. Sakalov. Would he still be alive, now, if she hadn't run into Wally that morning a few days and a hundred years ago? If she and Wally had not guessed at the nature of the Charonian command center and inspired Bernhardt to send them off to take a look at it? As best she could see, the only concrete result of that guess was Sakalov's death.

But no. At least try to listen. Ursula Gruber was on the screen, giving Eyeball an update. Gruber. Strange that the first thing Wally did upon arrival here was to phone in to *her*.

"Half of the SCOREs are heading through the revived Moonpoint Wormhole," Gruber was saying. "The other half are taking up positions around the hole. They are going into a layered spherical envelopment outside the perimeter of the Moonpoint Ring."

"And we be insideward too," Eyeballer Maximus muttered, too low for the mikes to pick it up. "Not likeworthy." Sianna had yet to make sense of the Purps in general, and Eyeball in particular. Eyeball was a smart, tough, clear-thinking woman. She *could* talk normally if she wanted to. Except, most times, she didn't. Sianna had met her when she breezed through Sianna's docshop room—in order to ask Wally something. Wally seemed to be fitting in awfully well around here.

". . . From what we are able to tell," Gruber was saying, "the SCOREs are directing their radar *toward* the hole. They appear to be watching for something coming *out* of the volume of space they are protecting, rather than trying to keep anything from going *into* it."

"Agree there," Eyeball said. "SCOREs notlooking at incoming cargo cans. And just had malf that told more, too. One cargo can missed NaPurHab, did a flyby instead of latching here. Flew on past, heading out of SCOREguard zone. SCOREs beat hellout uvvit. Can no more.''

Gruber image's on the screen listened carefully, and seemed to take a bit longer to reply than could be accounted for by just the speed-of-light delay. "Ah, yes. We saw that. A cargo vehicle that missed its docking pass was destroyed by the SCOREs as it moved out of the volume of space the SCOREs are watching.''

"Just *said* that," Eyeball said. "No echo need.''

"Ah, yes,'' Gruber said. Sianna suppressed a small smile. No one had taken the Purps seriously for generations. Now they had no choice: the Purps were the front-line troops, as it were. Five years ago Ursula Gruber would not have deigned to speak to someone named Eyeballer Maximus Lock-On. Now she was being as polite as she could, no doubt for fear Eyeballer would cut the connection and doom the Earth, or something.

There was the ghost of a smile in Eyeball's expression. Clearly she knew all that too, and was having a bit of fun with it. "Anyhow, can got creamed. Likewise, empty cargo cans get smashed by SCOREs. What uvvit? No noseskin of ours peeled off.''

"On the contrary," Gruber replied. "I think there's a lot of skin off your nose.''

"Say what?'' Eyeball said.

"You've got your maneuvering tanks just about filled now. What are your plans?''

"Kick orbit upward a bit, get away from black hole.''

"I don't think that would be wise," Gruber said. "In fact I think it would be extremely dangerous.''

"How so?''

"The malfunctioning cargo craft and the jettisoned cargo cans were *not* destroyed when they crossed out of the spherical volume protected by the SCOREs. They were attacked *at the first moment they showed any movement* out from the centerpoint of that volume of space. Anything that moves outward from the center of the protected area dies.''

''No how,'' Eyeball said, her disbelief plain. ''We boost the orbit just a tad, stay away from SCOREs, we okay.''

''I wish you were right. Check your own data. See when the SCOREs attacked.''

Wally already had a datapack out. Sianna looked over his shoulder as he pulled up the orbital tracks and attack playbacks. ''She's right,'' Wally said. Sianna took the pack from Wally and worked the data herself.

''Tricks!'' Eyeball said. ''Groundhog tricks to keep Purps down.''

''No,'' Sianna said. ''Why would they want to do that? They just jumped through hoops resupplying you. The actual impacts happen when the targets are near the periphery of the protected zone, but the SCOREs begin their attack runs the moment the targets start moving out from the center.''

Eyeball grabbed at the datapack and checked the numbers. ''Damn all,'' she half-whispered to herself.

''It's no trick,'' Gruber went on. ''You *must* not raise your orbit around the black hole—at all. *Any* raising of your orbit, by however slight an amount, would almost certainly cause the SCOREs to respond and attack.''

''But *hafta* fix orbit,'' Eyeball protested. ''Charos destabbing us something fierce. We do a spiral-down onto black hole less we goose the orbit.''

Ursula Gruber nodded awkwardly. ''Yes, yes. We know that. But there is another way.''

''What? Stabilize at current radius? Nohow. Unstab. Can't hold here for long.''

''We know. With all the perturbations your orbit has experienced, it's a wonder you're still there at all.''

''Good at job,'' Eyeball said, a bit aggressively. ''No damn miracle needed.''

''You'll need one soon,'' Sianna said. ''You can't hold out here forever.''

"She's right, Eyeball," Wally said. "You've managed with repeated microburst corrections. You're inducing as much instability as you're correcting. Even without any more perturbations, tidal effects alone are going to get you into trouble."

"Hey, boyo, don't yap at *me* on tidal effects. Been fighting to keep hab out of tumble for days now."

"And you don't think that's going to get worse?" Sianna asked. Eyeball turned and glared at her.

"You're out of options," Gruber said, her voice gentle, her words tripping over Sianna's just a bit, thanks to the speed-of-light delay.

"Not go *lower*," Eyeball said. "You're not telling me to drop to *lower* orbit, are you?"

"No, not exactly, ah, Eyeball," Gruber said. "*I'm* not on that habitat. *I* can't tell you what chances to take. But we've been learning fast down here. We've learned the Lone World's command set, and now we know how to send its form of commands ourselves. If we have to, if we want to, we can link direct to the Ghoul Modules and control the Moonpoint Wormhole. Open and shut it whenever we want."

Dead silence. All three of them stared at Gruber's image on the screen.

"Think about it," Gruber said at last. "Talk it over. It's a desperate, risky plan, but as best I can see, the only way out is through."

Two hours later, not much in the room had changed, except that Gruber's image was off the screen. Sianna was sitting in the furthest corner of the room, sitting on the floor with her arms wrapped around her knees, trying to force herself to think. *Think.* Being dropped down a black hole. There had to be another way. There *had* to be. So think, damnation. What was it?

"Do you think it would work, Wall?" Eyeball asked

Wally. The two of them were sitting at the beat-up conference table.

"It ought to." He thought for a moment and then nodded enthusiastically. "Yes. It will work. The mass density is different, of course, but that shouldn't matter. It's risky, of course, but it sure beats getting pasted by a SCORE or being accreted onto the singularity."

Sianna shut her eyes and took a deep breath. "Hold it," she said. "Pretend I'm stupid. What exactly are you talking about, from the top?"

"What Gruber said," he replied. "They play back the command sets that they've been capturing on Earth. They send commands to the Ghoul Modules, and order the Ghouls to open the wormhole for us. We go through the wormhole instead of piling into the singularity or getting smashed to pieces by the SCOREs."

Sianna looked from Wally to Eyeball. The two of them were actually serious. "You can't do that," she protested. "There are over nine thousand people in the hab. You can't drop it through a black hole just for the hell of it. There has to be another way."

"Then lay it on down," Eyeball said. "We got the ears, you got the words?"

"Yeah, Sia," Wally said. "You got a better idea?"

Sianna hated being called Sia. And Wally was ganging up on her, siding with this Eyeball lunatic instead of her. Suddenly, she got mad, blind angry. It would have been a perfect moment to come up with the brilliant solution, to have the blinding flash of inspiration that would make everything okay.

The trouble was, she couldn't think of a damn thing.

Ohio Template Windbag, the Maximum Windbag himself, sat in his comfortable, frowzy old armchair, his hands folded over his ample gut, watching Eyeballer Maximus Lock-on pacing back and forth, listening to what she had to say.

"I don't like it, boss, but I think the straights have it

nailed down right. Was gonna do a bigburn correction, get
our orbit up. But *can't* go high orbit—get clobbered bigtime.
We can't go low without destabbing like crazy, badnews
tidal effects. And can't stay where we is without orbit rotting
out.''

"Who you been yapping at?" Windbag asked.

"These two, some," she said, indicating Wally and
Sianna with a negligent flick of her wrist. "Been running my
own data. And on the horn to Gruber," Eyeball said. "She's
trying to square it up with the head hun Earthside."

"Who? *Bernhardt?* Gruber didn't sign off with him
first?"

"Not before she talked to me. Guess didn't want to push
me, just drop idea. Our call, not theirs. But the straights have
been picking the brains of that Lone World, tapping all its
signals. These two have shown me some sims and data, and I
buy it all. We *gotta* suck up what they spitting out. Nothing
else for it. Deal's real. Go in and through, not up and out."

"Want to get this solid. You and Gruber and these two all
asking me to okay dropping NaPurHab *through the wormhole?*"

"That's the deal," Eyeball said.

"You nuts for *good* this time? All anyone's said 'bout
that hole for sure is they sure it *ain't* home on other side."
He cocked his head toward Wally. "Ol' Windbag Max got
that straight?" he asked, clearly hoping to be told he was
wrong. "Noway the Moon and the Sun and Mars and home
on the hole flipside?"

"Ah, no sir," Wally said. "The hole is locked on its default tuning, and we know they had to retune it to lock on to
the Solar System. The Solar System is the one thing we
know *isn't* on the other side."

"Hmmph. So gimme guesses?"

Wally shrugged. "We don't even know if there *is* another
side, for sure. We *assume* there must be, because they're
sending the SCOREs into the hole. My guess would be another Multisystem of some kind, but I don't know."

"Any one of you have *any* idea past that?"

No one replied.

"Thanks for the bigtime info," the Windbag growled. "Could the Hab survive there? Would there be enough light to the solar collectors, or not too much? We can adjust some, but by enough? Stable orbit possible? Low enough radiation density?"

Wally turned his palms up helplessly. "No way to know."

"Can we even get hab *through* hole? This is a pretty bigtime tincan."

Wally nodded vigorously. "Oh, yes. We should be able to do it. It will take some very tight work, and some very good piloting, but it's doable."

"Um, sir?" Sianna said, struggling to find her voice. "There is another factor I think you really need to consider."

"Yeah? Like what?" the Windbag asked as he gave his beard a thoughtful scratch.

"The SCOREs are setting themselves up to keep something from getting out of that hole. What, we don't know. But obviously whatever it is has to be on the other side of that hole."

"You don't think we should do this, do you?" the Max Windbag asked.

"No, no sir, I don't. I think it's close to suicidal."

"Got any instead ideas? Something we could live through, maybe?"

"Not really."

"Thanks for the bigtime help," the Windbag said. He stood up and started pacing the compartment, not speaking for a while. "Time," he said at last. "We on the clock?"

"Ticking loud," Eyeball agreed. "Earthside numbers crunch to fifty hours, maybe sixty, sixty-five tops. I get near-same. Orbit won't hold past that. Practically every perturb is goosing us in closer. Past six-five hours max, we'll be too deep in the hole's gee-well to climb back out. High-speed orbital decay after that. And we pile it in."

"Can't stabilize where we are for lit-bit longer?"

"That's *with* us duking it out to hold orbit. Can't raise orbit without SCOREs doing for us. Can't hold orbit exactly, perfectly steady with all the grav action round here. Means we drift in, no mistake."

"Gimme some odds," Windbag said, with something close to a note of pleading in his voice. "What if we don't go down the tube? Say I put it all down on staying here. Gimme a bet."

Eyeball made a thumb-out fist and then turned thumbs down. "Near enough zip makes no nevermind. This crate can't dodge SCOREs. We stay, we pile it in. SCORE-splat or hole-smash. Dumpster locked."

"Fershure?"

"Nailed. No odds."

"No odds. No odds at all," the Windbag said. "Don't cut me much, does it?"

"Zip or less," Eyeball said.

The compartment went silent as the Windbag stood there, motionless, thinking.

"Odds not much better if we take the dive," he said. "Hole run deathride, otherside hostile, the scarything the Charos are trying to keep out. But zillion-to-one beats zero."

He sat back down in his chair, with his forearms on the arms of the chair, his hands gripping deep into the worn fabric. He stared straight ahead, at nothing at all, the distracted, far-off look of a chess player on his face. But a vein was throbbing at his temple, and his eyes were flat and hard.

"All right," he said at last. "All right. Gotta call a Purple Deluxe Meet. Pull in all the honchos and honchettes, tell them about it, get 'em close enough to realworld that they sign off on it. But that's *my* gig, not yours. You got work to do."

"Tell me straight," Eyeball said. "No mistakes, no say-whats later on this one. Go Code?"

"Go Code," the Windbag agreed, his voice a whisper. "Go Code it is." He looked up at Eyeball, at Wally, at Sianna, and the fear was plain in his eyes. "Do it," he said. "Gear us up and get us down that hole."

Twenty-six

It Goes In Here . . .

"Theory is a fine thing. But if it were the *only* thing, we would not need the real world. If we could rely on theory, then theory would protect us from everything else. When the experiment went wrong, we could simply hold a strong, well-thought-out, sensible theory up and show it to Mother Nature, and she would be forced to revise her policies.

"That, of course, is not how things work, though God knows there have been times when I wished it were. I have long since lost count of the number of people who have sent me letters or notes or datapacks that prove that the Abduction never happened. They have all sorts of numbers and data and formulae that prove the Earth was never stolen, that it was all a mistake or an illusion or a clerical error or a Belter plot.

"I would be delighted to find they were right. Mother Nature, the laws of the Universe, reality—whatever you call it—is not that cooperative. Things don't go according to plan. God knows I have better reason to know that than most. It remains true that we never know for sure if it will work, or what, exactly, will happen, until we try it. That, after all, is why they are called experiments."

—Dr. Larry Chao, unpublished essay

Terra Nova
Near-Earth Space
THE MULTISYSTEM

Dianne Steiger sat at the command chair on the bridge and tried to force the exhaustion from her mind. The news from NaPurHab. Incredible. Absolutely incredible. Into the wormhole. Nine thousand plus people, dropping through into the unknown. God help them all. By the time the *Terra Nova* arrived at NaPurHab's position, NaPurHab wouldn't be there anymore.

Dianne was frightened for the people in the Naked Purple Habitat, but she had something more than a humanitarian interest in the fate of NaPurHab. She had her own ideas, her own theories—and her own nightmares.

At least the COREs were giving them less trouble. Only a handful of close encounters, and no more actual attacks. But even that was worrisome. Dianne could not get rid of the irrational feeling they were being *herded*.

Soon, very soon, she would have to make a decision. Bail out, abort the mission, and head meekly off into the depths of space—or else press on, head for the rendezvous point, and then . . .

She had spent too many long nights staring a hole in the overhead bulkhead, brooding over what the Charonians were, and where they came from—and who or what it was they feared.

Fear. Charonian fear. *That* was the key that turned the lock, the question that would lead to the answers. Dianne had watched the SCOREs appear, watched the Ghoul Modules come in and commandeer the corpse of the Moonpoint Ring, watched the way things had turned hard-edged recently. Up until a few months ago, the system had reminded Dianne of a huge, lumbering beast that could go where it wanted and do what it would. Now it was moving in panicky fear. Something, somewhere had told the Sphere that some threat was suddenly near. Things were nearing their climax.

And she was damned if the *Terra Nova* was going to miss the party.

NaPurHab

Sianna Colette opened the door to her quarters and stuck her head out into the corridor. After the incident with the cleanup robot the night before, she was not going to venture into the hab's public ways without careful consideration. NaPurHab was a madhouse. But that, Sianna thought, was the normal part. What was remarkable was the degree to which it was managing to organize itself and prepare for what everyone was calling the Big Dive, a term that seemed to come out of nowhere.

But then *everything* around here seemed to come from nowhere. Nothing made sense. The Boredway Gang started a petition that protested not the Dive, but the existence of the wormhole itself. She had learned the fine old Purple tradition of signing someone else's name—preferably an outsider's name—to a petition when someone shoved a page full of scrawls, scribbles and *x*'s, all purporting to be Sianna's own signature, under her nose. She had signed Wolf Bernhardt's name.

But the hab did, after all, work. It kept its citizens alive, and managed to hold itself together. The Purp had to be doing *something* right. Certainly the manic enthusiasm with which the entire populace was preparing for the Dive was impressive. Even if the cleaning robots did chase people around now and again.

The coast seemed to be clear, more or less, except for the man editing the graffiti on the opposite wall. Sianna stepped out into the corridor, determined that, this time, she would find her way to the Eyeball Central—the navigation room—without getting lost. She made her way through the tangle of passageways turned into living spaces, and living spaces turned into found art, and lost art turned back into passageways.

At last she came upon the hatchway marked I-BALLS OWNLEE. She had made it this time, without needing to ask directions of a local who might improvise a fictional route, or send her in exactly the wrong direction, just to demonstrate the foolishness of linear thinking, or something. Or else tell her she was going to be given false directions, and then give exact, precise, and accurate instructions on how to get there.

She stepped inside and closed the hatch behind her with a distinct sense of relief. In here, things were relatively sane. More or less. After all, Wally was there.

Sianna had been working herself to exhaustion every night, dragging herself back to her cabin only when her eyes just would not stay open any longer. But Wally had always been there when she left, and there when she arrived the next day. Sianna didn't think Wally had left Eyeball Central in the last two days. He was right where she had left him last night, hunched over a video display, staring intently at something or other, not even aware she had come in. Sianna didn't even try to offer him a greeting. Just like old times.

Eyeball came in a minute or two after Sianna, and offered Sianna a smile, of sorts. A tricky woman, Eyeball was, and not too much interested in the Purple way of doing a thing if that way did not suit her. Her lab space was immaculate. No rubbish heaved in corners, no drawings scribbled on the walls. Wolf Bernhardt himself kept no tidier an office.

''Good morning,'' Sianna said.

''Morn,'' Eyeball said. ''Least morn or less. Losing track.''

''I know the feeling,'' Sianna said. ''But we're getting there.''

'' 'Less there's getting *us*,'' Eyeball said, rather cryptically. She sat down at a workstation and got back to work.

Sianna nodded, to herself as much as anything. Talkative group.

Of course, to be fair, Eyeball had to plan the precise trajectory through the wormhole, working off the numbers Sianna and Wally were developing on exactly where and when and what size the wormhole would be.

Analyzing the wormhole events that had let the SCOREs pass through was Sianna's job.

She had spent a good part of yesterday running playbacks of all the recorded passages of SCOREs through the hole, getting precise timings, positions and trajectories for all the events.

Well, back at it. Sianna told herself. She sat down at the console next to Wally's and punched up the recorded images of the wormhole events. She could have cued it up at the point she had left off the night before, but instead she ran it from the beginning, fast-forwarding through repeated blue-white flashes of the wormhole bursting open, the SCOREs heading through, the wormhole slamming shut behind them.

Sianna stared at the screen, watching the wormhole opening and shutting, at the stream of SCOREs heading into it. Opening, shutting, on, off, in, out, on, off.

Wait a second. Sianna had been a bit slouched down in her seat. Now she sat straight up. Wait a second. On-off, pos-neg, yes-no, zero-one, dot-dash. The most basic signaling system. *Signaling.* . . . Yes!

''Wally,'' she said, ''Wally!''

Wally looked up from his datapack, and turned to look at Sianna. He was clearly surprised to see her, but that was no surprise.

"Huh? What? What . . . what is it?" he asked.

Eyeball looked up from her own work. Sianna hurried on with her question before Eyeball could shush her.

"What would happen to an inert wormhole aperture with the same default settings as this one when this one opens up and something goes through? Like, say, the Earthpoint Singularity back in the Solar System. What would happen?"

Wally frowned and looked off into space for a second. "Well, if current theory is anywhere near right, in some dimensional domains, Earthpoint and Moonpoint are contiguous. Well, more than contiguous. They aren't just two adjacent planes in space, but two sides of the *same* plane, coplanar. Anything that affected one would *have* to affect the other. And of course the *other* side of the Moonpoint Wormhole is coplanar with whatever it's linking up with."

"Huh?" Eyeball asked. Straight or Purple, that seemed to be the standard response to one of Wally's explanations.

Wally looked around and found two sheets of scratch paper. "C'm'ere," he said. "I'll show you." The two women got up and stood over him at the console. He put one sheet of paper down on the counter top, then put a second sheet on top of it. "The sheets of paper are the wormholes, and the space between them is the plane of normal space that divides them." He lifted a corner of the top piece of paper and pointed to the one below. "Here's the bottom sheet, the first wormhole. The bottom side of it exits out to wherever the SCOREs are going. Top side opens up here in the Multisystem, in the middle of the Moonpoint Ring." He dropped the corner of the upper sheet back down on top of the first. "Top sheet. The bottom side of *it* also opens here in the Multisystem, but the top comes out from the Earthpoint Singularity back in the Solar System."

"Yeah, I got it," Sianna said. This much she knew.

"Almost," Eyeball said. "Go on."

"Well, you could think of it in generations. Call the point we're heading for Point X. Point X is the *grandfather* singularity, and it produced the Moonpoint Singularity. Moonpoint is the *father* to the Earthpoint Singularity back in the Solar System. Earthpoint would have to have similar resonance characteristics to its father and grandfather, Moonpoint and Point X. Sort of like genetics. Characteristics would be passed down, with some variance—though not much. There's probably no more than a fourth-power variance between them at best, enough to differentiate the Moonpoint from Earthpoint and Point X.''

''Great, good to know,'' Sianna said. ''But it doesn't answer my question.''

''It doesn't?'' Wally asked. Clearly he felt that the next stage in the reasoning was utterly self-evident.

Sianna looked to Eyeball and shrugged. ''Does it?''

''Not so I suss, nohow. Come on, Walls—what *would* be popping at Earthpoint ifwhen Charos drop SCOREs down Moonpoint tube?''

Wally had not ever shown the slightest trouble understanding Purpspeak. ''Earthpoint ought to ring like a bell, resonate in all sorts of gravitic frequencies. Sympathetic vibration. We've always assumed that a lot of the hardware on a Ring-and-Hole pair was to damp out that sort of vibration.''

''That's what I thought,'' Sianna said. ''Okay. Would the people back in the Solar System be able to detect that? If they were running any sort of gravitic detection gear hooked to the Lunar Wheel or the Ring of Charon?''

''They'd be lucky if it didn't blow every circuit breaker on the detector grid. Absolutely. In fact, I doubt they'd need detectors. The Lunar Wheel itself would react. No way they could miss it.''

''Charon Ring?'' Eyeball asked.

Wally thought for a second. ''*Maybe*. If they were running in the right sort of detection mode, they *might* pick it up. If the folks on the Moon warned them, they could certainly recalibrate and listen for the next one. Of course, we don't know for sure anyone is still running the Ring, or if anyone is observing the Lunar Wheel.''

"Okay," Sianna said. "Good. Great. There have been lots of openings and closings, lots of SCOREs headed through. Something like a hundred so far, and maybe another dozen to go."

"And they'd have been watching them," Wally said, getting the idea. "And they know reverb theory as well as we do. They'll know it means something is up with us."

"Holdit holdit holdit," Eyeball said. "*We're* going through, right? *We're* gonna send a command set to pop the hatch on that thing and dive in. That command set. *Has* to go through to your Point X so's the other end of the hole knows to open. Right?"

"Sure, right. We'll send the signal the same way the Charonians do. Earth will send a radio beam to the Ghoul Modules. The Ghouls will respond by sending out command modulations on a gravitic carrier beam," Wally said.

Eyeball leaned back, stared at the ceiling, and thought for a moment. "Now how 'bout folks back home in Solar, at Charon? They be able to detect commands, maybe read 'em and reap?"

Wally shrugged. "Read them, sure, but I don't know what they'll get out of them. All the signals are virtually identical. Without some sort of code key, like we got off the Lone World, it'll just be the same burst of noise over and over."

"No," Sianna said. "They have a code key, sort of. They knew enough Charonian visual symbol language to close the wormhole five years ago. They'll know it's a wormhole transit signal, and they'll have enough of the syntax to be able to get something out of it. Besides, the signals aren't precisely identical. There are timing variables and mass variables."

"Okay, they'll be able to parse the signal, work out the grammar. Maybe even mimic the signal. But there won't be anything in the signal they'll be able to read and understand."

Sianna stood up straight rather suddenly and put her hand over her mouth. "Wait a second. Wally, stick around. I get my best ideas around you. There will be nothing they can read in the signal—unless we put it there.''

''Say what?''

''There's a null sequence in the command set,'' Sianna said. ''Like a comment line. It's preceded by a symbol telling the Ghoul Modules' processors to disregard the following sequences. Probably it's a place to put in the Charonian equivalent of a manifest name, or an explanatory note. *We* could use it.''

''Could we put something *in* there?'' Wally asked, in a tone of voice that made it clear that he was not concerned with the technical challenge, but whether they would be allowed to do so, as if the grown-ups wouldn't let them fool around with the equipment that way.

Sianna nodded enthusiastically. ''I don't see why not. Wally, pull up that diagram of the signal syntax. I want to see how much room we have.''

Wally got out his notepack and worked the controls. He shook his head. ''Not much. About thirty characters, tops. Can't say much in that.''

''But enough to tell them it's *us,* '' Sianna said. ''Enough to say it's Earth, it's people going through.''

''What good would that do?'' Wally asked.

''At least it would tell them we're still alive,'' Sianna said. ''We've been out of contact for five years. They have no idea whether or not we're still here.''

''Could do more than that,'' Eyeball said. ''Would let them know they could use same command set on Earthpoint Singu—no, no, that fish ain't tunable no more. The Ring of Charon, though. Maybe they could tweak *it* up enough to scoot a ship, send it thru true to Point X.''

''Wherever that is. Is that going to be doing them any favors?'' Sianna asked. ''Suppose we all get killed the second we go through, just after we've sent them an invitation to join us?''

''Risk worth it,'' Eyeball said. ''Think 'bout it. We can't make passage to Solar Space nohow now. Suppose we find a real, perm way to get forth and back, use Point X place for long shortcut. Worth plenty, that." Eyeball thought for a second. "Risk they might miss it, though. Mebbe we could send own shout, longer message? Just talk, without sending something through?"

"Not now," Sianna said. "Maybe not ever. The only command set we know is the one the Lone World's been sending. We don't know any other way to do it, any other code set. And *I* don't want to mess with a wormhole if I don't know what I'm doing. Don't forget this whole mess started when that Chao guy accidentally switched on the Earthpoint-Moonpoint wormhole. We might send a text message that also told the wormhole to convert its mass into energy, or something."

"Could we do like that with this nullset thing, the comment line?" Eyeball asked.

Sianna frowned. "My God, I hadn't thought of that. Wally? Could we do any damage using the nullset area?"

Wally shook his head, serenely—and disconcertingly—confident. "No way. Impossible. That null sequence area is safe. That's the whole point of it." But then he cocked his head to one side, and thought about it a little more. "At least I don't *think* it could do any damage. Don't *see* how it could. But, ah, I'm not quite sure I can make any promises."

"Beautiful, Walls," Eyeball said. "Glad you cleared that one up."

"So? Well?" Sianna asked, looking toward Eyeball. "It's your hab, your home," she said. "You're the pilot. Your call."

"Yeah. Yeah. Wish weren't." Eyeball turned her back on the other two, and stepped over to the porthole. She looked out onto the depths of space, at the Moonpoint Ring, at the Multisystem beyond. "I got family Earthward," she said. "Sis and pop live, mom longdead. Never gonna seem 'em again, likeward. But let 'em know I'm alive, that we made it? *Gotta* do that. Be sweet to let 'em know we all reet. Risk so high on diving the Hole anyhoo, it ain't no nevermind to bet one more leetle chip.''

Sianna thought she had followed that, but she wasn't sure. She looked at Wally. ''She's going to do it?'' she asked.

Wally gave Sianna a strange look. ''Of course,'' he said. ''Isn't that what she just said?''

Multisystem Research Institute
New York City
EARTH

''This is madness,'' said Wolf Bernhardt, watching the displays in his office. ''I cannot believe that you agreed to this.''

''I didn't *agree* to it, Wolf,'' Ursula Gruber replied. ''I suggested it, as you know perfectly well. And, I might add, you approved it.''

''For which I should have my head examined most carefully,'' Wolf said. ''Was there no other way? No way for them to escape at lower risk?''

''No,'' Ursula said. ''Nothing. This is their last, best, desperate hope.''

''We are ready to send the command set?'' Wolf asked. ''You have the latest update?''

''Yes, Wolf, yes. Everything has been made as ready as possible. We send the wormhole command in approximately sixty-five minutes. And they are already very much committed. They did the first burn an hour ago, changing their course. They are spiraling in on the wormhole, and they don't have the power to pull out.''

''And the sensors and the cameras?''

''Up and running. We don't think we'll get more than about sixty seconds of transmission radioed back before the wormhole closes down. Maybe much less. With some luck, that will be enough to know what sort of place they are in.''

''And then the hole slams shut, and we know nothing more.''

''Precisely.''

"They could all die the moment after the wormhole closes, and we would not know. Any hope of reopening the wormhole afterwards?"

"Oh, yes," Gruber said. "So long as we have a mass—a large one—to send through it."

"Why should the wormhole care if we send something or nothing through?" Bernhardt asked.

"Because we don't think the Ghoul Modules are smart enough to do the compensations a full Ring can do," Gruber explained. "The amount of mass to be transferred is a major variable in a wormhole transfer. Get it wrong by any substantial amount, and the Ghoul Modules won't have the capacity to absorb the excess power. They'll burn out."

"So tell the Ghouls we are sending nothing—or something very small—through."

"The minimal mass is too high. We don't know any way of doing a zero-load setting on the Ghoul Modules. After all, the reason they are there is to manage mass transfers. Maybe we can find ways around that, but we don't know how yet."

" 'We don't know.' The motto for our era." Wolf stood up, turned around, and looked out his glass-wall window at the great city outside, the sun just setting over the gleaming towers. " 'We don't know,' " he said again. "Ah, well. We're about to start learning very quickly."

NaPurHab

Somewhere in the aft areas of the habitat, the main maneuvering thrusters cut off. "Second main trim burn complete," Eyeball announced. "We are in the groove. I think."

Sometimes talking—or thinking—in Purpspeak was not such a good idea, and more or less standard English was a wiser choice. Eyeballer Maximus Lock-On figured that piloting a habitat through a wormhole with groundhogs for assistants was just such a time.

And they were heading through, and no mistake. Of course, *with* a mistake, they would be heading in, not through. Either NaPurHab made it through, or the singularity at this end of the wormhole was just about to gain a little weight.

The hab was as battened down as it was ever going to be. They had spun it down to zero rotation, zero gee. The solar collectors were stowed, all the loose cargo was in theory strapped down, all personnel had been ordered to emergency stations until further notice—producing the usual number of protests from the kneejerker set—and all the docshops were standing by. Everything that could be done had been. But everything sure as hell wasn't much.

Closer, closer, drifting closer.

Eyeballer swallowed hard and tweaked back the attitude controls by just half a hair. She was not piloting by the numbers anymore, but by feel, by guess. They were deep inside the probabilities now, so tangled up in the variables that there was no longer time to set up the problem, let alone work through logical, mathematical solutions.

Too slow, Eyeball told herself. They were too slow, by the tiniest bit. What would happen if the wormhole slammed shut while the stern of the hab was still moving through?

"Stand by," Sturgis said. "Variable projection shows us coming up on another Ghoul pulse. Probability peak in ten seconds."

Eyeball glanced toward the prob display, absorbed the data on the display without really seeing it. "Got it, Walleye. Hanging." Had to hand to the groundhog—he was good.

Obviously, the Ghouls were adjusting for the mass imbalance caused by NaPurHab itself. At least that gave Wall some sort of way of guessing what they would do next. If the Ghouls followed the trim pattern he was predicting, then the hab would have to slow down its approach again—by almost exactly the amount she had just gotten through speeding them up. Damnation! This was getting out of control. The Ghoul Modules were doing their best to stabilize the wormhole, and Eyeball was constantly adjusting NaPurHab's trajectory, trying to move with sufficient precision to make it through the hole, even as the hab's movement destabilized the gravity patterns the Ghouls were trying to maintain. Two feedback loops combining to set up a meta-unstable synergy. Or something. She could write learned papers about it later. If they survived.

"Coming up on wormhole transit link activation," Wally said. "MRI will send the command sequence to the Ghoul Mods in five seconds. Four, three, two, one—MRI sending commands."

Eyeball felt her stomach turn to ice as nothing, nothing happened. The wormhole would not open. They would crash into the singularity. But no. Speed-of-light delay, command-activation delay. It would take a little time, just a few seconds before—

Eyeball took her eyes off her control panels and risked a look through the main viewport. The wormhole came suddenly alive, pulsing, swirling, a strange serpentine tunnel with walls of swirling not-blue. The begloomed black-grey sky of the Multisystem brooded in the background, set off here and there with the dull red glow of reflected Spherelight on a dust cloud.

The undead Moonpoint Ring was a ring no more, but a band across the sky, too close to see more than a small piece of it at once. But she had no eyes for the ring. She looked back at the growing power of the wormhole.

"Pray God to save us, pray God to save us, pray God to save us." A small voice at the back of the compartment was chanting the words over and over again, and, Eyeball realized, had been for some time. She glanced overshoulder. Sianna. Poor kid. How n hell had *she* got dropped into this mess? How *any* of them? Notime to thinkitall now.

Back to the transit calculations. Yawing just a bit, losing alignment, don't overcompensate, just the lightest of micropulses on the thrusters. Easy now. Easy.

flared across them.

ball looked up again, ahead, toward their destination.
rmous blood-black shape, far too large to be seen as a
, swallowed up half the horizon, its huge surface
ed and pitted and scored. And there, dead ahead, a wi-
little ruin of a world seen in half phase hung over the
lack-red form beyond.

Naked Purple Habitat moved forward, down into the
hole, toward the strange worlds on the other side—
nd then they were gone.

Terra Nova

''Tracking, tracking—the hab is closing on the singularity.
A great deal of interference is being produced by the Moonpoint Ring and its interaction with the singularity,''
DePanna said, as if she were talking about a little static during a call from her Aunt Minnie.

Dianne wished, not for the first time, that her detection
officer could be a trifle more excitable. That hunk of iron
and glass out there, with thousands of people on it, was
about to drop straight on through into the unknown. Yet
DePanna seemed more concerned by the fact that her display
screens were difficult to interpret.

Of course, if DePanna *had* gotten emotional, Dianne
would have relieved her of her duty. But being upset with
someone else's reaction helped keep Dianne from getting
too upset herself.

''They shouldn't have done it,'' Gerald said. ''It's suicide.''

''What choice did they have?'' Dianne asked. ''It was suicide to stay where they were.''

''I know,'' Gerald said. ''I know—but even so.''

All the Earth was watching NaPurHab's battle, its struggle to ride the rapids of gravity, the shoals of warping space,
fighting past doom and disaster—toward what?

A dozen screen displays were running at once, and Dianne
was trying to watch all of them. But the direct feeds from
NaPurHab's external cameras meant the most. They would
show what sort of place NaPurHab got to.

Assuming it got to anywhere at all.

NaPurHab

Getting closer, closer, toodamn close. The gaping mouth of
the hole was getting larger and larger—but was it large
enough? Did those straights back on Earth *really* think they
had a strong enough capiche on this thing to pry the hole

open big enough for something the size of a hab to punch through?

Back off. Bail out. Abort this. This is crazy. But there was very little point in listening to the panicked gibberings of her hindbrain. They had passed the point of no return long, long ago. *We're going to slam into that damned hole anyhow, anyway,* she told herself. Shush. Quiet, concentrate.

"Ghoul Modules commencing compensation," Sturgis reported. "Attempting to use gravitics control to pilot us in. Right on predicted schedule."

"Oh, good," Eyeball said. Wally had predicted that the Charos might try and manipulate the hab's course, setting it into the ideal transit path for a SCORE with the mass of the hab—which was not the right path for the hab. Eyeball would have to compensate for the attempted corrections as well.

"Confirming attempt at gravitic course compensation," Wally said.

Eyeball suppressed the urge to swear. The man sounded *pleased* that the Charonians were going to take another crack at killing them all. After all, it proved that he had gotten the problem right. Wally was *born* to the Naked Purple. "I'm getting the distortion now," Eyeball said.

Then the sounds started. The hab itself creaked, once, quietly, and then subsided. Too many shifting stresses were grabbing at the structure and the fabric of the poor old hab. Eyeball knew it was but a precursor of some truly *serious* noise. The tidal stresses were going to build up ferociously in the next few minutes.

The theory was that the hab could take it—but the damn thing was so old. NaPurHab had passed through a lot of hands before the Purps had taken possession. Eyeball was reasonably sure the original designers had not intended the thing to hold together for 150 years, let alone be dropped through a wormhole.

But none of that mattered now. NaPurHab had run out of choices long ago. A thousand things could go wrong, a

thousand ways they could all be destroy[ed]
hab crashed into the event horizon, was
SCOREs, was ripped apart by tidal stress, o[r]
by a clumsy pilot at the helm, the result wo[uld]
She could get this exactly right, and they c[ould be]
killed. Somehow, that made her feel better.

They were skewing to port just a tad. She
jets a trifle and took a deep breath.

"Tidal forces becoming significant," Wa[lly]
and, as if on cue, there was another low mo[an]
shifted its load.

Eyeball tried to ignore her fears. *Get it rig[ht,]*
no second chances, no apologies. An alarm b[e-]
hind her, and then another, and another. But th[ere]
an alarm drill since Eyeball had joined the r[anks]
breach? Power short? The galley out of coffee[?]
She had to pilot this thing and there was noth[ing]
do. Let the others worry about everything else
the alarms and silence returned, at least for a r[

Closer, closer. She could see the motion no[w]
effort, see the wormhole coming closer, swe[ll]
was the wormhole aperture actually expandi[ng]
hard jolt punched at the habitat, and the main li[ghts]
cut out. A sort of rippling shudder moved ov[er]
she grabbed at the yaw controls, fighting to k[eep]
the right course and heading, even as the mass
strained to tear it apart.

Closer, closer, the inner depth of the ho[le]
Eyeball looked up to see how far off the N[
was from here—and saw nothing but the
nothingness of the wormhole wall. They
swallowed whole by the hole, or maybe sw[
the whole.

But they *couldn't* be in or through, or ov[er]
yet. No. Eyeball could see nothing on th[
seconds felt like hours. A new, deeper, sh[
grabbed at the hab. Something wrenched

Twenty-seven

Pandora and the Tiger

"It's been said that a little knowledge is a dangerous thing. I've often wondered if there is a direct relation, or an inverse one, between the amount of
knowledge and that of safety. There are times, I'm
quite sure, when a *little* knowledge is dangerous—
while a large amount is positively *fatal*."

—Selby Bogsworth-Stapleton,
entry in personal journal

Dreyfuss Memorial Research Station
The Moon
THE SOLAR SYSTEM

Larry Chao waited until everyone else had gone to bed
before he went to see her, until there was no chance of being
interrupted or overheard. He had thought it all out very care-

fully, and it seemed to him that he needed Marcia MacDougal. He could do the flight alone, yes. But that was not the point. Well, not all of it, anyway. He had personal reasons to get back to Plutopoint, no question—but it was also his duty to go there. If they were detecting radio signals, Plutopoint and the Ring of Charon were where the action was. That was where he was needed. Get back to Pluto, and then . . .

No. Don't think past that, he told himself. *Don't get ahead of yourself.*

And he had the ship to get him there, get him there fast, if they would let him use her. The *Graviton,* the gravity-beam ship. The test program was nearly complete. They would have started piloted tests in another week or so anyway. If he could get flight clearance, the door would be open. Sondra Berghoff would back him, and provide the gravity beams for the flight.

But no one would let Larry Chao do a solo flight. Not if he had learned anything about people these past few years, and come to understand that he was close to halfway around the bend as it was.

But with Marcia MacDougal—sensible, clear-headed Marcia MacDougal, expert in Charonian visual symbolism—as part of the deal, it would work. He could sell it.

But first he had to sell it to her. And he thought he had a way to do that, too. Maybe not the straightest, purest way—but a way. And if Larry had it figured right, it was even fairly honest.

He got to the door of her room and knocked. There was a brief pause, and then a bump and a thud or two. The door came open a crack, and Marcia peered around the corner. "Larry," she said with a yawn. "What brings you around at this hour?"

"A proposition," Larry said, and suddenly the words were spilling out of him. "A proposition I think you're going to like. The odds on it are a little long, and a lot of things have to go right, but—"

"But what?" Marcia said, her expression halfway between puzzled and alarmed. "What?"

Larry paused, calmed himself. "Marcia, it's long odds and a lot of guesses, but . . . but I think they're going to be able to use the ring to punch open a wormhole link, and I think they're going to do it soon, very soon. When they do, they'll send a ship through and . . . and . . ."

"And what?" Marcia asked.

"And how would you like to see your husband again?" Larry asked.

The Ring of Charon
Plutopoint

Computers, Sondra thought, *are good at what is known and stays the same.* People *are good at what changes and becomes different.* Plodding through the pattern-recognition results files would have told her that much, if she hadn't known it already. The Ring of Charon's detectors had recorded dozens and dozens of wormhole passages by now. The computers had recorded reams of data about each and every event. The pattern-recognition software had massaged all the data, finding differences and similarities between the various events. The software had come to a rather unremarkable conclusion about the wormhole events: they were all pretty much the same.

But it was in the variance, the spread of values, the outliers, that Sondra hoped to find more useful data.

In theory, the team at the Ring now had enough tuning information to tune the Ring to the resonance patterns themselves, pump enough power into the Ring, and open up a wormhole link to the target location.

In practice, things were not so easy. There were hardware problems, for starters. Tech crews were working around the clock, finding ways to reconfigure the Ring so it could in fact form a wormhole link.

Sondra had confidence in her people. But hardware wasn't the only problem. Sooner or later—probably sooner—the

Ring would be capable of opening a wormhole link to whatever was on the other side of those tuning parameters.

But did they *want* to open such a wormhole? Large masses were being moved through a wormhole somewhere, but Sondra was nowhere as convinced as Larry Chao that Earth was involved. In her opinion, Larry was reading too much into the evidence. He *wanted* it to be Earth, and therefore it was.

All that being said, she'd be damned glad to get Larry the hell back here, if he could finagle the powers-that-be to let the *Graviton* make the run. She'd send all the gravity beams they wanted to get Larry back here. He might be one of the few people around who could actually give her some worthwhile advice.

But leaving Larry to one side for the moment, even if Earth *were* on one side or the other of the wormhole link, opening a link to the same target point might not be such a good idea. Did she, Sondra, really want to open a door that might let monsters like the Adversary loose into the Solar System?

If and when they got a hole open, what would they do? Merely look through it? Send a probe, or a ship? The Charonians knew how to make safe wormhole links—but did the Ring of Charon team? Might there not be, say, some unexpected source of radiation formed by the wormhole link? For that matter, could they be certain that the Ring of Charon itself would be safe? Might there not be some unexpected danger that could damage or destroy the ring? Granted, there were no such *known* dangers, but that really wasn't much comfort. Mother Nature loved surprises.

They would, therefore, take it slowly. They would slog through all the data, looking for the tiny clues, the microscopic hints, that might add up to some sort of idea about what was on the other side. Then she would decide.

She would decide. That was a startling thought. No one else had authority over the Ring of Charon, and the Ring was the only game in town so far as gravitics was concerned. The

Autocrat could try and impose a decision, with the bully-boys in his crew there to serve as enforcers, but the Autocrat seemed serious about keeping the Ring *out* of his jurisdiction.

Good God. *She* would make the call on what might be the most important decision for humanity since the Abduction. Should she leave Pandora's box closed, keep all the evils safely on the other side? Or was this the Lady or the Tiger? Was Larry right that Earth was in mortal danger even now? Suppose that danger was real, and there *was* something the Solar System could do to stop it? Leaving the wormhole shut could doom the Earth. Or opening the wormhole could bring the same danger to the Solar System.

Or suppose opening the wormhole *now*, in a hurried, un-considered rush, would bring some *other* danger home to the Solar System—or wreck the Ring of Charon beyond repair, and thus destroy the last hope of some future contact with the Earth?

Or suppose that this was *it*, the last best chance to use the Ring? Suppose this wormhole activity ceased, and the Charonians cut the link or destroyed it, and the Ring of Charon never, ever, detected another usable tuning frequency?

And *she* had to decide.

She was nearly at the last of the gibberish interpretations the pattern-matchers kept offering up, when something that seemed *orderly* scrolled past the screen, almost too fast for her to see it.

She frowned, and moved the scrollbar back. Forty zeroes and ones run together, repeated three times. The pattern matcher had broken the string out in various ways. Two twenty-digit numbers, four ten-digit numbers, eight five-digit binary numbers and so on.

Five digits . . . Not a very useful length. The largest number you could express in five binary digits was 11111, or 31. So why did the computer bother to break it out that way?

And then it hit her. Because of 26. Because 26 was

smaller than 31, and you only needed 26 numbers to express a certain rather useful symbol set . . .

She started working in her head—but no, this was no time to drop a digit and get confused. She punched a few mindlessly simple commands into the pattern matcher and the answer popped up on the screen.

01110	00001	10000	10100	10010	01000	00001	00010
14	1	16	20	18	8	1	2
N	A	P	U	R	H	A	B
01110	00001	10000	10100	10010	010000	00001	00010
14	1	16	20	18	8	1	2
N	A	P	U	R	H	A	B
01110	00001	10000	10100	10010	01000	00001	00010
14	1	16	20	18	8	1	2
N	A	P	U	R	H	A	B

And all of a sudden, her decision was much simpler.

Terra Nova
Approaching the Moonpoint Ring
THE MULTISYSTEM

Dianne sat at the captain's chair in the briefing room as Gerald MacDougal stood by the wall screen, using the wall controls to stop the playback again.

He locked onto one frame of the images sent back by NaPurHab, a slightly blurry picture of a small grey world lit in half-phase, hanging over a cracked and pitted red-black surface that filled the background. What looked to be a SCORE was visible toward the right edge of the frame. "Once they entered the wormhole, we only got about ten seconds of video and other data before we lost the signal," he said. "Earth didn't do any better. Nowhere near as much as we'd hoped for, and that's the single best image."

"Why so little data?" Dianne asked. "Five years ago, when the *Saint Anthony* went through the wormhole from the Solar System to the Multisystem, we got hours and hours of data.''

''They had time to set things up for a proper line-of-sight relay straight through the wormhole,'' Gerald said. ''NaPurHab didn't manage to launch a relay, or else the relay failed immediately. Without a relay, we had to have direct line-of-sight with NaPurHab to get a signal—and the moment the aft end of the hab entered the wormhole, the signal was cut off.''

''How so?''

''Think of the wormhole as a long thin tunnel. If the *Terra Nova* had been lined up with one end of it, we could have seen all the way down it, and we would have picked up NaPurHab's signal as the hab beamed it out of the tunnel. But we're well off to one side of the wormhole—and the moment they entered it, the tunnel wall cut off the radio link.''

''So the lack of data doesn't mean they were killed instantly, or anything like that?'' Dianne asked.

''No. All the telemetry was more or less normal up until the moment of cut-off. We were getting a lot of indications of structural stress, but that was to be expected, and it was well within tolerance.''

''So this is the best we have,'' Dianne said, getting up to look at the video frame. She stared at it for a long time, searching it, trying to pull meaning out of it—and succeeding. This *told* her things. Including things to do.

''So there's a planet in front of a Sphere like ours. One clear frame of video can't tell us much past that,'' Gerald said, after the silence had dragged on for a bit.

''The hell it can't,'' Dianne said. ''There are *lots* of dogs not barking in here.''

''I beg your pardon?''

''Read your Sherlock Holmes,'' she said. ''When a dog that always barks stays silent, *that's* a clue too.''

''Ah. Okay. So what don't you see here?''

''Shadows,'' Dianne said. ''No multiple shadows, no illumination at all in the darkened hemisphere of that little world.''

''Meaning?''

''Only one light source. If that red-black is the surface of another Sphere like ours, then it should have two or three dozen Captive Suns orbiting it, the way ours does. Any planet there would have seven or eight captive stars shining on it at any given moment. And yet there is only one light source here. That tells me this Sphere has lost nearly all of its captives.''

''Okay, I guess. What else?''

''The surface of the Sphere. It's banged up as hell. *Lots* of impacts on it. It's not protecting itself against debris.'' Dianne stabbed a finger down on one of the larger features. ''And *that* looks like a wide-angle crack going all the way through the surface of the Sphere. It's much darker than the bottom of the other cracks and craters.'' She shifted her finger to point out a pair of straight lines crossing at right angles, almost out of the frame toward the bottom. ''And *that* looks a hell of a lot like one of the 'latitude' lines intersecting a line of 'longitude' on our Sphere, seen from damned close-up.''

Gerald stared at the image himself, stepped back from the screen for a minute to get a better look. ''You're right,'' he said. ''I was just seeing that as two long straight cracks, but you're right. Hey—wait a second.''

Gerald thought for a minute, then turned to the table and grabbed a datapack. ''We've got the optical data on the cameras NaPurHab was using,'' he said. ''Let's see. Factor in the focal length of the lens, assume those lines are the same width as the ones on our Sphere, and that gives us a scale. Get the *apparent* width of the lines and we'll have a range to the Sphere in the picture.'' He measured the line width and punched the numbers into the datapack. He looked at the answer, then ran the problem again. ''I don't believe it,'' he said. ''It *couldn't* be that close.''

''*How* close?'' Dianne asked.

"Twenty-two million kilometers," Gerald said. "NaPur-Hab came out twenty-two million kilometers from the surface of a Charonian Sphere."

"A *dead* Charonian Sphere," Dianne said. "A Sphere that can't hold onto its stars, that can't prevent impacts on its surface. And to hell with being close to the Sphere. Remember what Sturgis and Colette figured out, that the Lone World here, in *our* Multisystem, was Charon Central, the brains for the whole operation."

She stabbed her finger down on the video image again. "*That* is the Lone World, Charon Central for the system NaPurHab is in. It is orbiting the Sphere directly. *It is the place from which the Charonians controlled this system.* Maybe it's the *Last* World in that system, too, the only one left.

Gerald looked at his captain with something between fear and excitement in his eyes. "It makes sense," he said. "I think you're right." He looked at the image again, and worked it all through, nodding to himself. "Yes," he said. "It's got to be."

"So," Dianne said, "There we have it." Suddenly she knew what to do. "So now what?" she asked.

"I beg your pardon?" Gerald asked, turning away from the image.

"What next?" Dianne asked again, leaning in close, her eyes intent. "We were supposed to rendezvous with NaPur-Hab. Now what?" If Gerald saw the same answer, then there was at least some rational basis for it.

Gerald's eyes lit up. "I think," he said, "that we should give serious consideration to proceeding with the rendezvous—at an alternative location."

"You thought it was too dangerous for the Purps to try the passage. You said so yourself. Why would it be safer for us?"

"The circumstances are different. Because they went through, *we* know there's another side. *And* we know there is

something over there that can kill Spheres. That's knowledge we need.''

"But we don't even know if the Purps survived. They
could have been destroyed the moment after we lost contact.''

"The *Terra Nova* can take more punishment than they
could. And, we can't survive here that long ourselves. Beating one CORE was a triumph. We can't make a career out of
it. Sooner or later, one of them is going to get us.''

"We could shift our trajectory away from Moonpoint,
and regroup,'' Dianne suggested. "Get well away from all
the planets and all the COREs and SCOREs, take a month or
a year to think it through.''

"No,'' Gerald said. "What would wasting time change,
except that the Ghoul Modules could shut the Moonpoint
Ring down again? We go in after them. That Last World
alone ought to tell us more about the Charonians than anything else we've ever seen. A month or two ago we were
hoping to learn more by boarding a CORE. Now, maybe we
have the chance to explore the mind of a Charonian Sphere.
Compared to exploring an unguarded Command Center and
a Sphere, what is there for us here?''

Dianne took a deep breath and then let it out. Now the
idea, the mad idea, was out in the open. "Good,'' she said.
"I needed to hear you say it. I wanted to be sure I wasn't
crazy.''

"What about the SCOREs on the other side?'' Gerald
asked. "Won't they try and stop us?''

"I don't think so,'' Dianne said. "Not if we've got the
rest of this figured out. They're trying to keep something
from coming through the hole going the other way. The
SCOREs on this side are blocking anything coming *out* of
the hole. That only makes sense if the SCOREs on the other
side are there to block anything going *in*. We ought to be
safe enough heading outward.''

Gerald nodded his head abstractedly. "Ordinarily, I'd say
that was mad optimism. The risks are far too high. But with

all the other chances we'd be taking, that one seems almost trivial.''

Dianne smiled sadly. ''When the chance of getting smashed to atoms by SCOREs on the other side of a wormhole seems trivial, then I say things are in a pretty bad way.''

Gerald laughed. ''Let's you and me get to work, and maybe we can find some way to make them better.''

Twenty-eight

... And It Comes Out There

"One of the tricky things about researching NaPurHab's arrival in the Shattered Sphere system, and what happened afterward, is that neither the people in the Solar System nor the people in the Multisystem knew the whole story. It's hard, now, after the fact, to remember the appalling ignorance we all suffered under. Everyone had holes in their knowledge. Big enough holes that, for all intents and purposes, no one knew what the hell was going on.

"Come to think of it, the Adversary and the Charonians knew even less than we did."
—Larry Chao, transcript of interview for *Gravitics Research Station Oral History Project,* Charon Datapress, 2342

Another attacker came at the Adversary, and it dealt with the assault as effortlessly as always. The Adversary smashed through its multi-megaton assailant, emerging unscathed, its course unchanged, and leaving another cloud of debris in its wake.

The immediate threat dealt with, the Adversary extended its senses outward and noted a different disturbance in the vicinity of its main target. It focused its attention there. Some odd sort of mass, quite different from the others it had seen, had come out of the link from the living system. Had the Adversary entertained any lingering doubts at all that this was the real target and that all the others were decoys, then the arrival of this strange object would have put those doubts to rest. The Adversary's kind had long experience of the Charonians, and how they behaved. The unique link locus, the one with something, anything, different about it, was the real one. The Adversary was well pleased to have its previous conclusions confirmed. It moved smoothly on, toward the link and the rich feeding grounds beyond.

NaPurHab
Transiting the Wormhole

Sianna held on as the habitat bucked and kicked like a live thing, and she promptly put any thought that she was cured of claustrophobia right out of her head.

You bloody idiot, what the hell are you doing going down a wormhole down a wormhole down a wormhole?—They were trying to send the hab through a tunnel of infinite length, and that tunnel was inside a hole that took up absolutely no space whatsoever. Sianna's fear of being closed in rose to new heights, took on new meanings, as NaPurHab headed deeper into the hole, the ride getting progressively rougher as Eyeball fought to keep them moving down the centerline—and as the gravitation fluxes and tidal pulses struggled to tear them apart.

After an especially sharp bang and a thud, the overhead lights cut out and came back up and then went out and stayed out. A dozen new alarms started up, hooting and beeping and ringing, and Sianna could smell something burning.

At least the exterior monitors stayed on, even with the cabin lights out. The sideview cameras showed an un-blue-white tunnel wall of flailing storm, seething with power, rushing past the habitat, and that was bad enough. But the forward cam showed the view looking straight *down* the wormhole, down, down, down the seething, glowing tube, toward the tiny black pinprick that was the way out, the only way out, impossibly far off and getting no closer. Sianna clutched at the arms of her scruffy old crash chair and tried to tear her eyes away from that seething tunnel.

The passage seemed to go on forever in time and space, taking them further and further away from the Universe, deeper and deeper into the tunnel and the depths.

And then, abruptly, it was over—gone, all at once. The wormhole swept past the forward view, and the Universe beyond came into view, and they were up, and out, and through.

But through into what, and where? The forward camera showed a huge, sullen-red globe, a tiny, dried-up grey lump of a world, the black of space—

Suddenly the habitat was pitching over, starting to tumble, end over end.

"Damnation!" Eyeball called out. "Aft boom caught wormhole side. Sheared right off. Morons failed to retract or what?"

"Can you correct?" The Maximum Windbag had to shout the question to be heard over the alarms.

"Dunno!" Eyeball shouted back. "Shut up and stand by!"

Something broke loose behind Sianna's head and went windmilling across the compartment to smash into the far wall. The lights on a whole bank of terminals flared and went out, and the hot smell of burnt insulation was suddenly stronger and more pungent. Wisps and tendrils of smoke filled the compartment. *Air. They were going to run out of air and suffocate and die in the darkness.*

Sianna shut her eyes so as not to see the darkness. She prayed to someone, anyone, she didn't care who, to get them out of this get them out of this, now, please God now—

A whole bank of circuit breakers slammed shut with a bang, and the overhead lights came on. The ventilators kicked back in, and Sianna was desperately glad she hadn't noticed them cutting out. The air cleared, and the control thrusters cut. Eyeball worked the conn, slowing the tumble, bringing the hab around to a steady, stable attitude. Eyeball let out a sigh of relief and leaned back in her crash couch.

The ops boards were still more red and amber than green, and new alarms seemed to be going off every time an old one was silenced. But they had made it. They were here, wherever that was, and they were alive.

At last all the alarms were turned off, and the command center was still, and quiet, for a moment.

"Well," Wally said, speaking into the silence, "let's not do *that* again."

NaPurHab
The Shattered Sphere System

Sianna held the carrybag with one hand and started climbing the ladder, making her awkward way up to the zero-gee levels. It was four days since the hab had come through the wormhole, but the reality of it all hadn't set in yet, at least not for Sianna.

What do we do now? she wondered. No one knew. They were surprised enough just to find themselves alive. Most of the Purps weren't yet thinking clearly enough to manage a state of shock.

Sianna found herself busying herself with small details. Make the tea—one the way Wally liked it, and the other for her. Make the sandwiches. Pack them in the carrybag. Go to where Wally was.

It might have been possible to think no further than lunch if she had been allowed to hole up in her cabin with her pil-

low over her head. Unfortunately, Eyeball had put Sianna
and Wally in charge of charting the big picture, making it a
trifle harder to escape.

Sianna reached the top of the vertical shaft and stepped
into the horizontal corridor that led to the ob bubble. She
swung her legs around and kicked off from the end wall, in-
tending to send herself sailing smoothly down the corridor.
Unfortunately, the weight of the carrybag in her left hand
threw off her balance. She overcorrected and sent herself
tumbling through the air, bouncing off the corridor wall. She
caught at a handrail, bounced once or twice, and then stead-
ied herself before making her way along the corridor in a
more controlled fashion.

She shifted the carrybag full of lunch to her other hand,
opened the hatch, and moved into the observation bubble.
Wally, as usual, did not notice her arrival. The autoscan
scopes had been working overtime since their arrival in-system, and he was busily pulling the data off them and logging
it in to his simulator datapack.

Eyeball had just told them to get some sort of inventory of
the system. Wally was way past that, already hard at work
using his knowledge of the Earth's Multisystem as a rough
working guide to setting up a dynamic model of this system—and of what this system had once been.

"Wally," Sianna said. "I brought back lunch." She sat
down, opened up the carrybag, and handed Wally a bulb of
tea.

"Hey, great," he said. "Keep forgetting to eat."

"I know, I know. And I keep remembering to feed you,"
she said, handing over a sandwich. She dug out a sandwich
for herself and looked out the observation port.

There it was. Huge, brooding, smashed and dead, an overwhelming sight. The Shattered Sphere had named itself. Not
even the Purps could dream of calling it anything else.
Sianna could see a dozen craters of various sizes, and one or
two impacts that had punched holes clean through. The

Sphere was covered with a jagged, broken network of cracks.

The Last World hung close in the sky, still in half-phase, appearing somewhat larger now than it had when NaPurHab had first arrived. Sianna had named it Solitude, and it seemed as if the name might stick—a fact that gave her immense pleasure. Not many people got the chance to name a world.

She looked down on it, and was surprised at her own reaction. She felt sorry for the poor thing. A lone world, a last world, a lonely world. An airless, waterless, lifeless lump of rock, all that was left of the control center for a mighty stellar empire. "Sorrow" might have been another name for the place.

It had taken the slightest of burns on the maneuvering jets to put the hab into an elongated elliptical orbit about Solitude. Eyeball might well decide some other orbit would be better later on, but this one at least kept them from crashing into the planet, which was the main thing for now.

Well astern of the hab, and getting further away by the minute, was the wormhole portal, a Ring-and-Hole set very much like all the ones back in the Multisystem. That was no surprise. Most of the SCOREs that should have been in orbit around it seemed to have gone missing. Only nine or ten were on station, their radars aimed _out_ from the wormhole, clearly watching for something on its way in.

But the hab's radar center had detected signals from at least four or five other clusters of SCORE radars, and visual checks showed that each cluster surrounded its own dormant Ring-and-Hole set. It would seem that the SCOREs the Multisystem Sphere had been sending through other wormholes back on the other side had been reinforcements for a number of sites on _this_ side. But the SCORE counts were low at the other Ring-and-Hole sets as well. That was a good-size mystery right there—where were the rest of the SCOREs that had been streaming through the wormholes?

No doubt plenty more mysteries would crop up before

some answers presented themselves. "So," Sianna asked. "What's the state of play?"

Wally took a swallow of tea and a bite of the sandwich. "Well, this place looks like what the Multisystem would look like if our Sphere stopped using gravitics to hold the place together. First, there's the Sphere itself, and presumably a black hole of about one solar mass inside it."

"Why do you assume the black hole?"

"No gravitic controls means Solitude has to be in a natural orbit, and that means something with enough mass to produce that much natural gravity. If the Dyson Sphere was built out of disassembled planets, it can't have that much mass on its own—not by a factor of a thousand. So there has to be something massive inside it."

Sianna nodded. "Right. I should have seen that. And it has to be a compact dark mass like a black hole. If it were a star, we'd see its light shining from inside the Sphere through the holes, and be detecting lots of heat energy."

"Exactly. Aside from the Sphere, we've got Solitude, of course, and one Captive Sun that's still around. It might have been in a natural binary relationship with the star the Charonians built the Sphere around."

"Any more tracks on the other stars and their planets?"

"Plenty of them," Wally said enthusiastically. "It's going to take *months* for me to build up a simulation of the momentum exchanges that ejected them from the system. So far I've tracked seven definite ejected Captive Suns moving away from this system. Working backwards from their current velocity tells us it happened something like one hundred fifty years ago."

"What about the Captive Worlds?" Sianna asked. "Are they still with their stars?"

"Not most of them," Wally said. "But then you wouldn't expect them to be. I just ran a quick-and-dirty simulation of the Multisystem, to see what would happen if the gravity control system shut off *there*. One or two planets per star stay anchored in their orbits. The rest are thrown around by

momentum exchanges caused by various close passes between the Captive Suns. The planets in those pseudo-stable
orbits go sailing off into space, or impact with other planets,
or spiral into their suns. Some of them end up in extremely
eccentric orbits of the Sphere. Two or three impact on the
Sphere—including Earth.''

Sianna shivered at that thought. Wally could put it all in
terms of hypotheticals, theory. But this place was death, and
it was real. Suppose whatever killed this place went through
the wormhole and visited itself on the Multisystem. ''How
did it die, Wally?'' she asked. ''What *did* all this?''

''I haven't the faintest idea,'' Wally said. ''Right now,
you know everything I know. No, wait, there *is* one other
interesting thing. As best I can tell, the co-orbital wormhole
ring loop is still more or less intact.''

''Hmmm? What?'' Sianna blinked and looked back toward Wally.

''Just like back in the Multisystem. There's the Lone
World, and then a whole system of modified and oversized
Ring-and-Hole sets spaced at equal intervals along the same
orbit. It looks as if there used to be sixteen—and all but two
are up and running. The only damn things in this system that
still are.''

''How can you tell which ones are operational, or how
many there are?'' Sianna asked. ''We can't possibly see
more than two or three of them from here. The Shattered
Sphere gets in the way of line of sight.''

''Yeah, but I rigged a whole set of alternate-mode gravity-
wave detectors, the ones based on Charonian technology.
The ones we built have never worked real well, but believe
me, even on a bad detector, an active Ring-and-Hole set
shows up very nicely, no matter how many Spheres are
around.''

''They're active?'' Sianna asked.

''Makes sense they'd be the last thing to go,'' Wally said.
''They served as communications relays and cargo conveyors. Even if everything else went, as long as the wormhole

ring loop was intact, Solitude could still maintain radio communications with the system, import new stars and worlds from other systems and move raw materials around this system.''

"But once the wormhole ring loop goes, you're dead."

"Right. So you set things up so it keeps running, no matter what. That's why there are so many rings in the loop. You only really need three or six, but this system had sixteen—and fourteen survived whatever killed the rest of the system."

"But what the hell are they using for power?"

"*That's* the other thing," Wally said, suddenly grinning. "I finally cracked one of the mysteries about the Spheres that's been bugging me from day one. Remember how we figured out the longitudinal lines were huge accelerator rings, super-big versions of the Moonpoint Ring? But we could never figure out what the latitudinal lines were?"

"Yeah, so?"

"So with this Sphere dead, all the other power systems aren't masking the readings. I nailed them. The latitude rings are power-storage rings, holding reserve energy. About thirty percent of the rings on this Sphere are still intact and carrying a charge."

"And the wormhole ring loop is tapping into them?"

"At real, real, minimal levels. But I doubt they'll last much longer. Everything's decaying."

Sianna looked out the viewport again, at the dead Sphere and the dead Last World of Solitude. "Very impressive work, Wally. Find any other surprises out there?"

"Not really," Wally said. "There's the little stuff, of course. Asteroids, impact debris, dead COREs, other dead Charonians, and random skyjunk. This Sphere's taken impacts from all kinds of stuff."

"So this is what happens when a Sphere dies," she said. "Sounds like that old poem, doesn't it? 'This is the way the world ends,' " she whispered. Though there was little as gentle as a whimper in the violence that had been wrought here. Smashed, broken worlds, stars flying off in all directions, planets being flung off into the frozen interstellar darkness. Sianna shook her head, staring out into the void with unseeing eyes.

"How did it happen, Wally?" she asked again. "What killed the Sphere?"

He shrugged. "I'd love to know. We have that three-dee clip from five years ago, of something smashing into a Sphere and pushing through, but that still doesn't *tell* us anything."

Sianna stared out at the dead world she had named. "This is a sad place," she said at last. "Death, decay, collapse."

They had all thought of the Multisystem Sphere, of the Charonians, as the enemy, and that was right as far as it went. But it did not go far enough.

There were enemies that human, Charonian, all life battled against: Death. Entropy. Collapse. Life of any sort reversed entropy, brought order to the Universe, and made a haven for more life. The lesson of the Shattered Sphere was slowly dawning on Sianna: *this was Earth's future if humanity somehow succeeded in defeating the Charonians.* Like it or not, willing or no, the Multisystem was now Earth's haven, and it had to be protected. But that was too much to say to Wally, too much to express.

Besides, he was already done with his sandwich, and back at his work. He had already forgotten she was there. Sianna sighed and turned her back on the viewport. She sat down and got back to her own work.

Actually, her own work was a trifle on the undefined side, as Wally was doing the whole job that had been assigned to both of them. Sianna knew damned well that it would be all but impossible to pry any part of it away from him, and, worse, that the two of them working together would probably do the job less well than Wally working by himself.

Wally saw the Universe as a species of wind-up toy to be taken apart, figured out, and put back together. Once the puzzle was solved, he lost interest and moved on.

Sianna liked to think she had the imagination to find the problems in the first place, the ability to step outside and see things no one else had. She could *interpret* the puzzle, take the pieces Wally put together and make them into more than the sum of their parts.

But to do that, she had to at least get a look at the pieces. The hab's databanks were already full to bursting with images and readings of all sorts. Sianna had taken on the job of looking at all of it, feeding the raw data to her skull, knowing it all from the ground up.

She fired up her terminal, called up the scope log, and started scrolling through it. More small objects of debris located, more of the Sphere's surface mapped, higher-resolution images of Solitude. All good, important data, but none of it new, unexpected, nothing that made her ask questions.

But then something caught her eye. Not an object, but an event, about two hours back. According to the log reports, no one had reported at the time, which was not surprising, given that things were more than a little busy about the habitat.

Sianna called up a full data playback and was rewarded with the image of a brilliant flash of light, along with a hell of a lot of radio-frequency, gamma, X-ray, and infrared radiation. Sianna frowned. What the hell could have produced that much radiation all over the spectrum? A nuclear explosion? Some black hole absorbing a huge amount of mass all at once?

How big had it been? How far away? The autoscope had logged the sky coordinates, but it had no way of reporting a range.

She brought up the radar ranging data, going back to the moment when NaPurHab had arrived in-system, and cross-linked it against the coordinates for the energy flash.

NaPurHab's radar system had been meant for use in a traffic-control system, and it had certainly done good service with all the incoming cargo vehicles not so long ago. The Purps had pressed it into service as an early-warning system against spaceborne debris, as the Shattered Sphere system seemed to be even more full of skyjunk than the Multisystem.

Like all active radar systems, the hab's gear sent out timed bursts of radio signals. Some portion of a given signal would reflect off a target and bounce back. By measuring how long the signal took to make the round trip, radar systems could compute the precise distance to a given target. Of course, the further off a target was, and the smaller its reflecting surface, the weaker the returning signal would be.

Local-traffic control systems didn't need to be all that powerful. The hab's hackstaff had done their best to hot-wire their traffic radars into a debris detector, but NaPurHab did not boast the most gifted technicians in the known Universe, and they had moreover done the job in a hurry with rather limited resources.

Sianna had no idea what the energy burst had been, or whether it had come from ten thousand kilometers away or ten thousand light years. Sianna was not really expecting to get any useful data at all out of the cobbled-together system.

She certainly wasn't expecting to be astonished one more time.

Let alone terrified.

Twenty-nine

Incoming

"What is our struggle with the Charonians about?
That I can tell you in one word. There is something
they stole from us, something we want back again.
Something that has been at the bottom of every quarrel, every battle, every war in human history.

"In that one word, we fight to get one thing back
from the Charonians.

"Power."

—Wolf Bernhardt, private signal to the master of
the *Terra Nova*, 2429

Multisystem Research Institute
New York City
Earth
THE MULTISYSTEM

Dusk was falling, night settling over the city. *Herr Doktor* Wolf Bernhardt, Director-General of the Directorate for Spatial Investigations, Chairman of the Governing Board of the Multisystem Research Institute, stared down at his folded hands, at his empty desk, and faced the fact that, for the first time in years, there was nothing for him to do. At the end of the day, nothing demanded the attention and the authority of Wolf Bernhardt. And worse, much that he had done had proved to be of no use whatsoever.

"All of it for nothing, eh, Ursula?" he asked.

Ursula Gruber let off pacing back and forth along the length of the room and turned to look at her superior. "I beg your pardon?" she said.

"I said it's all for nothing. All of the effort to rescue NaPurHab and *Terra Nova*. All the struggle to resupply them before the SCOREs could come and cut them off from us. All the panicked effort to get three scientists to the *Terra Nova*. Now Sakalov is dead, and if they are lucky, Sturgis and Colette are merely stranded with a habitat full of buffoons on the other side of a wormhole. Unless they are dead, too. And all of it based on guesses that were dead wrong, too. The SCOREs weren't the least bit interested in Earth, just the Moonpoint Ring. All our preparations have been utterly wasted."

"It's not over yet, Wolf," Ursula replied. "And there's no question that you *did* save NaPurHab—or at least gave it a fighting chance. Perhaps that won't do us much good here in the Multisystem, but the people on the habitat are still alive. If nothing else at all, your spacelift got enough propellant to them so they could adjust their flight path and make it through the wormhole. They'd have been smashed by the

SCOREs or have crashed into the singularity if it weren't for you.''

"Perhaps. Perhaps. If they even survived the passage. But now we are to lose the *Terra Nova* as well. What good can come of Steiger going down the wormhole?''

"A great deal," Ursula replied. "What more could they accomplish here in the Multisystem, at lower risk than the wormhole transit?''

"I know, I know," Wolf said. "And they may be able to learn a great deal, *do* a great deal, on the other side.''

"Except?" Ursula asked.

"Except," Wolf said, "except we have utterly lost control of events. We, here, on Earth, we in this institute—you and I here in this room, have lost the initiative. Now we must merely watch from the sidelines, wait, hope that word will come.''

Ursula smiled. "There may be hope for you yet, Wolf. Not many autocratic, authoritarian leaders would be willing to admit that.''

Wolf looked to Ursula, but did not return her smile. "Indeed? So, very well, I admit it. But I find it remarkably small comfort.''

He stood up from behind his desk and turned around. He looked out, up into the sky, to where the great ship was preparing for its passage. "Now," he said, "it is up to them.''

NaPurHab
Orbiting Solitude
THE SHATTERED SPHERE SYSTEM

"There, there, there, and there," Sianna said, stabbing her finger down on the display screen with each word. "Debris clouds, all lined up nice and neat, one right after another. You can run a single track through all of them. And there, there, and *there,* bright radar images, what *have* to be SCOREs running with their own internal radars turned off. One flight of twelve SCOREs still fairly close in, and others further enough out that we can't get a precise count. Each flight of SCOREs on a precise intercept course with the projected sky track you get by running a line through the debris clouds. We figure the debris is what's left of the SCOREs that tried and failed to smash whatever is moving in on that track.''

"We can't see it?" the Maximum Windbag asked.

"Either it's too small, or too nonreflective, or it's using some sort of stealth technique," Sianna said. "And I don't think it's stealth."

"What for why not?" Eyeball asked.

"That thing's moving in a straight line right for the SCOREs that are moving to intercept it," Sianna said. "It's not trying anything evasive or tricky, just barreling right through. Besides, it's obvious the SCOREs can see it, even if we can't. It's not hiding. It just doesn't care."

"How *they* see it?" Windbag asked.

"I haven't the faintest idea," Sianna said. "Obviously some sort of sensor *we* don't have."

"What's more important is where the object is heading," Wally said.

"Wherzat?" Windbag asked.

Sianna pointed at the display again. "Right there. Straight for the wormhole we came through. In other words, straight for Earth—and Earth's Sphere—on the other side. It's coming for us, Charonians and humans."

"Say what?"

"We've got to assume this—this *object* is what's been scaring the hell out of our Sphere," Wally said. "We've got to assume this thing, whatever the hell it is, killed the Sphere here. It's going to try and kill the Sphere in the Multisystem. And that will kill Earth."

Windbag stared at the screen and nodded thoughtfully. "You know," he said, "this isn't good."

Terra Nova
THE MULTISYSTEM

Dianne Steiger sat down in the pilot's control station and started working through her checklist. Normally, the bridge team sat at their consoles, fed commands to the computers, and watched the computer fly the ship. Not this time. Too many uncontrolled variables. Too many unpredictables and imponderables. Computers could react faster than humans could, of course, but the ship's computers could not *think*, and quick thinking might be necessary to get them through this. If something went wrong, she would have to be ready to take over *fast*.

It had been a long time since Dianne had flown the *Terra Nova* manually, and she was more than a little nervous. But she was a pilot first and foremost, trained to fly spacecraft long before she had been called upon to command a crew.

She powered up the navigation display and confirmed the flight path. Manual thruster controls on-line. Auxiliary engines at go. No need for main engines on this one—just a few light taps on the thrusters and the auxiliaries and they would be on the beam.

It wasn't *necessarily* a one-way trip, of course. The folks back on Earth were learning a lot about manipulating the Charonian command system. NaPurHab's passage showed that the folks at MRI knew how to open and shut a wormhole. Sooner or later, humans might well be able to shoo the COREs and SCOREs out of the way and pass freely through the wormhole to whatever lay beyond. Ursula Gruber's cryptographic and linguistics staff seemed quite confident about the matter.

But confidence was no guarantee. After all, the *Terra Nova* had cast off from Earth five years ago, eager to explore the Multisystem, confident of return, never dreaming that she would not make planetfall in all that time.

No. They had to assume this was to be a one-way trip. No looking back.

The relay satellite had been launched. It was programmed to perform highly precise station-keeping, keeping in exact alignment with the wormhole aperture. If all went well, they would launch an identical relay on the other side. The two relays were equipped with radio and comm lasers. In theory, they would be able to contact each other whenever the wormhole was open. With a fair amount of luck, Earth and the *Terra Nova* might be able to retain at least some sort of intermittent contact.

Dianne checked the countdown clock. Almost time.

Just a pilot, she told herself. *You're just a pilot moving a hunk of iron around the sky. Just get it where it's supposed to be. Don't think about all the people aboard, or that you've got their lives in your hands. Don't think about what you might see on the other side, or how you got into this mess. Just fly this thing.*

The clock moved down, moving too fast and too slow, both at once, the way all countdown clocks did. But then the numbers got to zero, and it was time. Back on Earth, some computer sent the commands to the Ghoul Modules, and the wormhole bloomed into being, dead ahead.

Dianne fired the engines, and the *Terra Nova* moved in.

Thirty

Rubicons

Terra Nova
TRANSITING THE WORMHOLE

Gerald MacDougal watched the wormhole getting closer, surprised at how calm he was. He should have been terrified, his pulse pounding, the sweat thick on his body.

And yet he was not. Was he serenely confident they would make it? Was he so certain they were doomed that he had given himself up to death with calm and dignified resignation? Or was he so terrified that he could find no other reaction than absolute, blanket denial?

As the blazing un-blue-white circle of the wormhole aperture swelled forward, rushing toward them, like a wall in space they were just about to slam into, Gerald braced for the impact, his instincts telling him the ship was about to crash into the barrier that was not really there.

Gerald glanced up at the status displays. Dianne was flying at a much higher velocity than NaPurHab had used. Maybe that was wise. No sense remaining inside any longer than necessary. Or maybe it was downright suicidal.

But then they *were* in. No turning back. They had crossed their Rubicon; they were committed. The ship hit the un-blue-white, and dove into the wormhole. Gerald felt a sudden thrill of excitement. At last, at long last, the *Terra Nova* was living up to her name. She was off in search of New Worlds indeed.

Dianne Steiger drove the ship in, her whole attention, her whole soul, focused on the job of getting her ship in and down and through and out. The ship bucked and jittered as the complex tidal and gravitational forces inside the wormhole grabbed at it. Dianne was flying by the seat of her pants, the joystick in a death grip. *Easy now,* she told herself. *No heroics. Just get it done.* But hell, getting it done would *require* heroics.

A secret part of her knew that, and gloried in it. She had been here before, after all. She had been in space when the Abduction struck, just inside the zone that the Charonian wormhole had swallowed up, flying a little cargo shuttle. A hundred meters further out from Earth and she would have been left behind in the Solar System. And she had brought her ship home, back to Earth, in a spectacular crash landing at Los Angeles Spaceport she had no right to have survived. She had lost her left hand in the crash, and had long since forgotten that her new one was a sprint-grown bud-clone. It didn't matter. Because she had lived. She had beaten them all.

The secret soul of a certain kind of pilot lives for the thrills it does not get. It wants to fly to and past the ragged edge of disaster, to bring its craft through the greatest of perils, and yet escape. Pilots who flew winged craft back from orbit wanted to come to a smooth rolling stop right on the centerline, knowing that, by all rights, they ought to be part of the gooey dead slime in a fiery crater a kilometer short of the runway.

Pilots of that sort live to cheat death. Dianne had tasted that forbidden thrill back then, and God forgive her but she wanted it again. And she was getting it now.

Back then, she had flown through a wormhole because she had no choice. The Charonians had had it all their way. But now, today, was her chance to use their own damn wormhole to save her ship, the ship the Charonians were trying to kill.

So here she was again, up against a wormhole, the sweat standing out on her forehead, a strange, fierce anger in her heart, battling the forces that wanted to destroy her ship.

They were going to have to try a lot harder if they were going to kill a ship with Dianne Steiger at the controls. She could feel it. They were going to make it!

There. There, dead ahead, was the exit from the wormhole. Closer, closer, closer—

A shuddering thump and bump, and they were through. The wormhole snapped out of existence behind them, and they were there.

Wherever they were.

Ring of Charon Gravitics Research Station
Plutopoint
THE SOLAR SYSTEM

"We picked up the signal twenty minutes ago," Sondra told the Autocrat. "Same pattern as with NaPurHab. The words TERRA NOVA TERRA NOVA TERRA NOVA coded into the wormhole activation command."

"Interesting. Most interesting," the Autocrat said. "It seems reassuring to know our friends on Earth were willing to send a habitat *and* a ship through."

"Somewhat. Not all that much. Autocrat, once again, I must ask you to reconsider. You are a head of state. Do you really feel it is wise for you to leave your people, your nation behind? The odds are very good that we will die on the other end, or be stranded there.''

''But *you* are going,'' the Autocrat said.

''It's my job,'' Sondra said. ''I couldn't send anyone in my place if I were unwilling to go myself.''

''My feelings exactly,'' the Autocrat said. ''I do not think any more need be said.''

Sondra nodded. ''All right,'' she said. ''I know when I'm beaten. Not that it matters, of course.''

''Why not?'' the Autocrat said, a little startled.

Sondra grinned, delighted to finally find a break in the man's armor. She couldn't resist pressing home her advantage. ''You forget,'' she said, ''we've never done this before. You can't go through a door you can't get open. The only way this ship is going anywhere is if our team can successfully establish a stable wormhole link to the proper coordinates and tuning frequency on the first try. What do you think our odds are?''

The Autocrat smiled. ''Actually,'' he said, ''I'd say they are rather good. And they can only get better if your friend Dr. Chao manages to get here. Do you think he'll make it?''

Sondra frowned. ''I hope so, Autocrat. I sure as hell hope so. Because I know Larry. If he doesn't make it, he's sure to die trying.''

Graviton
Departing the Vicinity of the Moon
THE SOLAR SYSTEM

Larry Chao tried to look calmer than he was. ''All right,'' he said, ''three minutes to beam reception.'' *If* the Ring had actually sent the beam, long hours before. That was one slightly nerve-wracking thing about gravity-beam propulsion. The beam had to come from the Ring of Charon. From lunar space, your power had to come, at the speed of light, from a little matter of forty astronomical units, or just under six billion kilometers away. In theory, the Ring had fired the beam five and a half hours ago. In three minutes—no, two now—they would find out if they had done it right. They could abort *now* by slamming on the rocket engines and blasting out of the beam's path—but once the beam hit the ship, the *Graviton* was committed. No one had ever tried shutting off a gravitic-beam system from the shipboard side of things, but theory indicated the attempt would destroy the ship. Once the beam touched them, there was no turning back.

The *Graviton* had lifted off the Moon eighteen hours before, and done pretty good time under old-fashioned rocket power getting to the safe-distance point. A nice, smooth, routine flight. But now. Now they had turned their crash couches around, and they sat in the ship's backwards control room, with the floor where the ceiling should have been. Now came the interesting part.

Larry looked over to Marcia. "I'm scared to death," he said, "but I'm maintaining a brave front. How about you?"

She smiled feebly, but did not take her eyes off the countdown clock. "Just about the same. Three days to get there," she said. "I know it's much shorter than the old transit times, but is it fast enough?"

"They won't leave without us," Larry said, with more conviction than he felt. "They've had just as many glitches reconfiguring the Ring as we had getting the *Graviton* ready. Probably they'll still have half a dozen snags that will need me to sort out when we get there," he said, trying to make a joke out of it.

"I still can't believe it's happening, finally happening after so long," Marcia said. "Gerald. I'm going to see Gerald. Maybe it really isn't happening. Maybe the *Terra Nova* went through the wormhole from place A to place B, and we're just going to place A. Is it possible we have it backwards?"

"I doubt it very much," Larry said, watching the last of the seconds fall away.

TERRA NOVA TERRA NOVA TERRA NOVA. Not much of a message, but it was all the Ring team had gotten during the last wormhole passage, a week ago. They knew the *TN* had gone through the wormhole. Marcia's fears to the contrary, they knew which set of coordinates it was moving toward. But they did not know if the ship had survived.

"Here we go," Larry said. The clock reached zero—

And nothing happened. Not at first. But then the meters twitched and starting crawling upwards. The *Graviton* creaked and groaned a time or two as the ship's structure took up the new stress load. It was happening. The *Graviton* was taking the gravity beam and using it to create an imaginary mass just ahead of the ship's nose, under their feet. One that was pulling her forward at forty gravities. Larry felt his weight returning as the acceleration-shielding system tapped some of the gravity field to produce a little resistance, just enough to give them an interior one-sixth gravity. It was working. It was *working*.

Thirty hours accelerating, nine hours in zero gee, and thirty more hours slowing down. They were making history. They were the first people ever to ride a human-built gravitic spacecraft. But that was a trivial point, almost beneath notice. What did such things matter, compared to the fact they were going to get there in time?

Thirty-one

The Autocrat Departs

*The Mind of the Sphere felt a second strange pulse move
through the wormhole web, a rough, crude movement
through the net. Then, shortly thereafter, a third pulse—this
one coming from outside, somehow, from a wormhole aperture no Charonian had ever formed. But like the first two
illicit wormhole transits, this one terminated in the default
link station in the dead system—the same link point the Mind
had sent its own forces through, the same link point the Adversary was driving for.*

*Were these passages some strange new scheme of the Ad-
versary? The Mind's fears were instantly aroused. It examined the records of the link in more detail. No, no. This was
not the Adversary. It was all too coarse, too crude, too awkwardly done, too cautious.*

*But it was something. Something to do with the strange
troubles that had surrounded the last world brought into the*

Multisystem, such a brief time before. For a moment, the Mind considered the idea of destroying that world now, as a precaution, and expending the massive energy needed to bring another planet forward to serve as a projectile weapon.

But no. That would drain its energy reserves to dangerously low levels. And these were such small and weak interlopers. Certainly there had to be more frugal means to defend against them, if need be. Surely it would make more sense to conserve its projectile planet, keep it for its intended use.

Besides, the Mind could always destroy the troublesome planet later, after all this was over.

Terra Nova
THE SHATTERED SPHERE SYSTEM

There was a lot going on. Communications to establish with NaPurHab, navigation settings to work out, observational procedures to work out, once they figured out what they were looking at. But Gerald was happy to let the captain and the comm officer dicker and bicker with NaPurHab and sort out the rest of it. He had a ship to manage.

He quickly confirmed what he had been hoping for—the ship was safe, at least for the moment. No damage from the wormhole transit, none of the handful of SCOREs in the neighborhood showing any hostile intent, and no other danger on the immediate horizon.

He punched up the intercom and set it to general announcement. "This is the executive officer," he said. "All sections, secure from special shifts and resume normal shift rotation. Resume normal watches. Everybody get some rest."

They had made it. They had gone through the wormhole, and not so much as a scratch on the paint job. Gerald glanced toward the main screen as the tracking officer put up a live feed of NaPurHab. It was little more than a sharp-edged spot in the screen at this range. Dianne already had headphones on, no doubt talking to the Maximum Windbag himself.

The passage must have been much tougher on the hab. It had to take some real courage to take her through, Gerald told himself. *We had it easy.* The *Terra Nova* was much newer and smaller and more compact, built more robustly and maintained with much more care than the hab.

Gerald smiled to himself. The *Terra Nova* and NaPurHab had just crossed into the unknown, and he was thinking about comparative maintenance schedules. But after a passage like that, it was time to get things back to as near normal as possible as fast as possible. *To every thing, there is a season, and a time to every purpose under heaven,* Gerald reminded himself.

But they were suddenly some unknown number of light-years from Earth, and some rather disturbing questions appeared, unbidden, in Gerald's mind. This far from home, were they indeed still under heaven? And unto what purpose—unto whose purpose—was this time to be given?

NaPurHab
THE SHATTERED SPHERE SYSTEM

"Okay, that's a lock," Windbag said to the commlink. "See your team in our maxmeet shop, twentyfour from now." The Windbag cut the commlink to the *Terra Nova* and sighed.

He punched up the stern exterior camera shot and was rewarded with a view of the *TN* with the Charonian wormhole control ring behind it. Nice looking ship, but that was not exactly the key factor here. The Windbag found himself wishing bigtime he did not have to deal with a ship full of straights just now. He knew he shoulda been slap-happy glad to get 'em. Like to get heavily lonesome in these parts, and NaPurHab could use all the help it could git. The *TN* had all kinds of hardware and braintrust types who knew how to run things. Evenso, now wuz not-time for distractions. He had enough on his plate without the *TN* screaming for attention.

But still they had to have a maximum meet, all the honchos and honchettes. They had to slap together some way of surviving out here, and plain-fact-one was that they were gonna need each other.

But that didn't make it fun.

Sianna looked around herself and realized that she had blundered onto the Boredway again. How many wrong turns could one person make? Quite a few, as it turned out. The whole hab was a madhouse.

Boredway was anything but boring at the moment, as tangled in frantic activity as an overturned ant heap. The air was filled with the smells of burnt insulation, sweating bodies, hot metal, and bonding chemicals, a tech crew just down the way trying to repair something while a cargo crew was struggling to make sense of the cargo canisters that had been strapped in any which way in the aft sections of Boredway. A few hundred meters forward, some sort of protest group was forming up. God only knew what they were protesting—or whom they were protesting to.

Sianna decided to risk a shortcut through Loopaway turf. If she could avoid any more wrong turns, it would cut twenty minutes off her trip.

She remembered the old joke about time being nothing more than nature's way of keeping everything from happening all at once. For a while, it seemed as if it didn't work this side of the wormhole. It had been a busy few days.

The captain of the *Terra Nova* and her executive officer had come aboard, looking more than a bit disoriented—understandable, considering they had both spent the past five years aboard one ship. Of course, NaPurHab would be disorienting no matter where you came from.

There had been another energy burst the day before—a multiple one this time—as the ''object'' slammed into a half-dozen SCOREs at once, with every scope on the hab and the *Terra Nova* watching it. The object was tracking closer and closer, heading right for the wormhole.

The object. It was coming this way, at high velocity. And when it got here, it was going to force open the wormhole and kill the Multisystem, and that would kill the Earth.

Oh God. How to stop it. How to stop it? Or were they just going to have to sit here and watch it happen?

At least life was chaotic enough to take her mind off things. Somewhere in the swirl of comings and goings, in between Purpgroups of this or that philosophy, while the frantic repair crews were rushing to patch up the systems that had been damaged in the passage of the wormhole and the tech teams were juggling like mad to keep the hab working with the solar collectors suddenly delivering a third less power than before, it had all turned from strange to familiar. Sianna had gotten used to it all, and that scared her.

Sianna stopped at the turning that always got her muddled and hesitated a long moment before taking the middle way. Yes, this was the right way. She recognized the stain on the wall. Straight along this way, then down two levels, and she'd almost be there.

Oh, it had been a time, with all the big events seeming to produce little ones in their wakes. A riot or two had broken out, a sit-in had been staged in the Maximum Windbag's office. Meantime, certain residents of both ship and hab had decided on a change of scenery. Two dozen Purps had applied for crew positions on the *Terra Nova*, while twice that number of the *TN*'s crew had applied for Naked Purple citizenship, which was a great nuisance, as the Purple Citizen's Council had ruled there was no such thing as a Purple Citizen three years before and then disbanded.

Ah. Here it was. I BALLS ONLEE. Someone had changed the spelling again. She pulled open the hatch and went in. Wally was lost to the outside world, buried in some sort of elaborate simulation of the incoming object. It seemed to be running on every screen in the room, from a different viewing angle on each one. Eyeball was on the comm to someone, cursing them out with alarming skill and virulence as

she compulsively neatened her immaculate work station.
There were Solitude and the Shattered Sphere out the viewport, glaring down on them.

Sianna sighed happily and sat down at her own station.
Scary to think that a scene like *this* could be the most comfortable and familiar thing in her life—but then, you always
had to work with what you had.

Autarch
Docked to Gravitics Research Station
Plutopoint
THE SOLAR SYSTEM

Sondra Berghoff was scared, and trying not to show it. Plans
and theories were all very well, but reality was a bit trickier.
Hanging in space, the nose of the *Autarch* pointed straight at
the Plutopoint black hole, she could no longer see the slightest logic to sending a ship through the wormhole. Yes, they
had some important information. Couldn't they have just
scribbled a note, stuck it in a bottle, and tossed it through the
hole?

She sat strapped into her chair on the main deck, right behind the ship's pilot. She didn't even know the man's name,
or the names of any of the *Autarch*'s five crew members. All
of them were nameless, faceless, utterly taciturn, and sworn
to unquestioning obedience to the Autocrat.

She had not seen any of them show any facial expression
except something midway between a poker face and rigor
mortis. Robots showed more in the way of reaction.

Suppose they couldn't immediately dock with the *Terra
Nova* or NaPurHab for some reason, and she was stuck with
these guys for a month or two? Suppose the Charonians or
the Adversary had destroyed the big ship and the hab, and
she was marooned with these guys for *life*?

Well, at least the crew members weren't the only ones on
board. She turned and looked to her right, to the Autocrat.
There were at least some signs of life and thought in his face.

A strange man, to say the least, but at least he was capable of conversation.

She looked over to Marcia MacDougal, and Larry. A miracle they were here. No doubt if anyone survived long enough to write history books of the period, the books would record how those two had come along because they were experts in gravitation and Charonian language. That was even accurate, as far as it went.

But it wasn't true, of course. They were here because they *had* to be. Look at the expressions on their faces. Both staring straight ahead, tense, alert, expectant. Marcia was going in search of her husband. And Larry. Larry was going in search of what he always sought, and would never find. Absolution.

Sondra turned back to the main viewscreen and watched what the others were watching—the image of the Ring of Charon. They were face-on to the Ring, its running lights a hoop of blue diamonds in the dark, the Ring itself a perfect circle in the sky. No change yet, but it would come soon.

Too soon. Why in the hell had she felt so honor-bound to go along on this ride? Why wasn't she back on board the research station where she belonged, feeding numbers to the computers?

The Ring's running lights dimmed, went out, and re-lit in blood red. Stand-by. Almost ready. The team would be loading the last of the command strings to the Ring. A faint patch of dimness appeared at the centerpoint of the Ring, just barely visible at first and then almost fading out. Were they having trouble getting the lock? But then the luminous spot grew brighter, larger, stronger, rippling with power. Yes, yes, it was working.

The center of the nimbus grew darker, harder, more focused—and then flared over into a strange un-blue-white and settled down, rock-hard and solid.

The *Autarch*'s engines fired, and the ship moved forward, straight for the hole in the sky and whatever lay beyond.

Down a wormhole, Sondra told herself. *Down a human-*

made wormhole. Good God. She could not even begin to sort out the emotions that washed over her. Fear, excitement, pride, astonishment, panic, and half a dozen others all mixed up together. They were going in. They were going in.

Just before they reached the wormhole, the Autocrat turned to Sondra and smiled. ''I expect,'' he said, ''that it will be an interesting trip.''

NaPurHab
THE SHATTERED SPHERE SYSTEM

The Windbag stared out the viewport in his office, not at the Shattered Sphere or at Solitude, but at the Ring that ran the wormhole they had come through. The wormhole was where the action was, no doubt. The Windbag was worried, and getting more so. What the hell to do? Colette and Sturgis's objectional ''object'' was on a collision course with the wormhole. Leetle invisible thing was killing every SCORE in its path. Could it really kill Sphere? *Sounded* loony, even if their charts and graphs looked real, even if Eyeball said they were on the money.

But what to do about it even if the ''object'' wuz real deal? How was a hab full of headbangers scraped off the walls of every town on Earth gonna stop an invisible object that converted SCOREs to guacamole?

The Windbag was at that melancholy point in his reflections when there was a flare of un-blue-white light from the wormhole. The Windbag frowned. Another SCORE? Thought the last of them had come up. Too damn far away to get a visual at this range. Maybe the radar johnnies could tell him something. He had his hand out to punch up the codes and ask them, when the screen blanked and presented a live radar image. The caption line reported that the imagery was coming from the *TN*.

His intercom warbled, and the Windbag slapped at the accept switch, knowing who it had to be before he heard a word. The woman had been checking in about a million times a minute.

"Bossman, you got eyelock on screen?" Eyeball asked.

"Eyeball," he said. "What a nice big old shock to hear your voice. Yeah, I got it up and I see it. 'Nother SCORE?"

"Nope," Eyeball said. " 'Nother *ship*." There was something in her tone of voice, something strained under the wiseguy tone.

"Say again? What the hell other ship could Earth send to join the party? Some cargo craft they goosed through?"

"None of above, big guy. Ship from Solar Area. From *Pluto*. Ring o' Charon, ifyawanna believe their ID codes."

Windbag stared at nothing at all for a good five seconds, trying to deal with that information, but somehow it just couldn't get inside his head.

"Say again?"

"I say it's a god-damned ship from Pluto with the god-damned old Autocrat himself along for the ride."

"Autocrat? *Ceres* Autocrat? The Big Cold Fish himself?" None too surprisingly, the Naked Purple movement had never gotten along well with the Autocrat of Ceres.

"Stand by, Wind. Yeah, you bet. Got him on the viddy now, wriggling on the slab with his gills flapping."

"He *sick*? Hurt?" Windbag asked, suddenly alarmed. No one wanted to be the guy in charge when the Autocrat keeled over. His followers might take a dim view.

"Huh? Naw, he's okay. But he's sure a Fish outta water. Who's gonna do what he says *here*?"

"Ah. Oh. Got it." Sometimes Purpspeak was a bit *too* colorful.

But a ship from Pluto, from Solar Area? How could that be? What did it mean?

Well, one thing fershure. Had to *talk* to these people.

Gerald MacDougal stood by the entrance to the lock, and nothing in the Universe mattered but the fact that the lock was about to open. Marcia. Here. Now. Alive.

Shattered Spheres and invisible objects that killed SCORES and wormhole transits to habs full of lunatics. None of it was of the least importance. Marcia. Here.

It was impossible, it couldn't be true, and it was happening. Five years and more since he had last seen her, since he had touched her. Five years since the Charonians had torn them apart—and now the *Autarch* of Ceres and NaPurHab were bringing them together. It made no sense at all, but that didn't matter either.

The airlock hatch swung partway open, and then paused for a moment. Gerald stepped forward, his heart slamming in his chest.

And then the hatch swung clear, and she stepped through. Marcia. Here.

They were in each other's arms before either of them knew it. His body remembered the feel of her close and warm against him, and some part of himself that had been lost for far too long was suddenly there again. He breathed in the smell of her hair, wrapped his arms around her and held her. Never again. Never again would they be separated.

They let go of each other just enough so that they could take that quarter step back to look in each other's eyes, and he knew that he was seeing what she saw. An age line or two, a grey hair that had not been there before—but none of that mattered either. The last five years had not happened. They had always been together, and they always would be.

She reached her hand up and caressed the side of his face, pulled him close, and they kissed.

They drew back again, after a time, and looked at each other again. "Hello, Gerald," Marcia said, her voice warm and low. "Did you miss me?"

Sianna Colette sat and listened, sat and watched, as the meeting lumbered on. There he was. That was *him*. Larry Chao, the man, the monster, the ogre who had caused the Abduction. She—or at least her subconscious—had been expecting someone nine feet tall with fangs. But not a man, a rather ordinary, shy, gentle-looking man with dark hair and a haunted look in his eyes.

But there were other matters in hand. "There is no doubt in my mind at all," Chao was saying. "The object that Miss Colette and Mr. Sturgis have been tracking is the Adversary, the danger that terrifies the Sphere that holds Earth captive. The danger that could kill Earth and everything on it. The Multisystem Sphere will not hesitate to throw Earth at the Adversary in order to kill it."

"How canbe that?" Eyeball said. "Can't quite believe it'd take Earth-smash to clobber that thing. Wally, Adversary is what size, tops?"

"No way to know," Wally said. "My *really* rough guess is that it is about the size of a very small asteroid. Say, less than a kilometer across. Maybe a lot less."

"How massive is it?" Captain Steiger asked.

"Well," Wally said, "We've tracked a bunch of debris within orbits perturbed by near passes of the Adversary. We can work from there directly into a computation of its gravitation, and thus its mass. It comes out to something on the order of a lunar mass."

"It weighs as much as the *Moon* and it's too small to *see?*" Steiger asked.

Wally shrugged and smiled. "Strange matter is pretty strange," he said.

"There is not much funny about this, Sturgis," Steiger said. "A mass the size of the Moon striking the Earth is not a joking matter."

"But would it even work?" MacDougal asked. "I mean, would it kill the Adversary? It seems to me that this Adversary has taken a lot of punishment."

"Should work great," Eyeball said. "Charos accelerate Earth to high-nuff speed, you bet. Force equal mass times acceleration. Big enough mass, enuff accel, no prob."

"Nuff to zap strange matter?" the Windbag asked. "Turn it to normal matter or mebbe energy? E-equals-MC-square it?"

$E = MC^2$. That phrase tickled something in Sianna's memory. Not the formula itself. But sometime, somewhere, when someone had said it. What had it been about? Suddenly this meeting seemed very familiar, as if she had been through all this before. Some other meeting, or bull session, or whatever, when someone had not been believed and that equation had come up in conversation.

"Don't *think* so," Eyeball was saying. "But you can kill *me* without turning my body into energy pulse. High-speed impact with Earth oughta benuff to break bonds *between* strange atoms, reduce Adversary to thin cloud of by-themself atoms. Kill it bigtime."

"Sides, if it don't work, Earth death anyho," the Windbag pointed out. "Adversary kills Sphere, Earth loses orbit, and whammo."

"That's getting just a bit off the point, isn't it?" Steiger said. "I really don't care how Earth would die. I don't want Earth to die in the first place."

"Which brings us," the Autocrat said, "back, once again, to the question of alternatives. Is there anything we can *do*?"

"How about wrecking the wormhole?" Sondra Berghoff asked. "We could blow up the Ring around the black hole so it couldn't be used to tune and amplify the wormhole signal."

Gerald MacDougal shook his head. "If that would do any good," he said, "then the Charonians would have done it long ago."

"The Ring's dormant anyway," Sianna said. "We can detect a few trace signals to show it *could* be activated, but it didn't power up at all when the SCOREs or our ships came through. The other side provided all the power and control." Something in her own words teased at the idea in the back of her head. *Dormant. Not dead. Dormant.*

"And presumably the Adversary would do the honors for its own transit," Captain Steiger said. "Besides, I don't know that we could rig up powerful enough bombs to be sure of destroying the ring—and the SCOREs on guard duty around the wormhole aperture would take out our missiles anyway."

"How about shooting some sort of particle beam at the Adversary?" MacDougal suggested. "Something with enough directed energy to do some damage. Maybe induce the strange matter to reform into normal matter."

"Sure, no problem, if we had a twenty-year research schedule and an unlimited budget and a hell of a lot of luck," Steiger replied. "Besides, none of us are particle physicists. Where would we even begin?"

"Could we be diverting?" Eyeball asked.

The Autocrat frowned and turned to look at her. "I beg your pardon?"

"Divert it. Shunt the Adversary some other way 'sides through the wormhole?"

Yes. Yes. That was it. Or at least it was close. Sianna looked from one face to the next. One more hint, one more notion from the outside, and she would have it. She *knew* she would.

"How?" the Autocrat asked.

Sianna looked hard at Eyeball, willing her to give an answer that would set free the idea Sianna was trying to have.

Eyeball shrugged. "Dunno."

Oh, hell. No joy there. All illusion anyway. There was no idea—just the wish for one, so strong it made her think she was really close to something.

"Could we divert to the Solar System?" the Autocrat asked. "Find some way to retune the wormhole so the Adversary came out there instead of the Multisystem?"

There was a moment's shocked silence, no one quite sure what to say. But then Eyeballer Maximus Lock-on found words. "You cold fish or loonie? Set that thing loose in *Solar Area*? How many it kill there?"

"I see no reason for it to kill anyone at all in the Solar *System*," the Autocrat said, rather primly. The Purps obviously irritated him deeply. For some reason, their determination to call it the Solar Area seemed to be the thing that grated most on him. "It is in search of the sort of energy source the Charonians' Spheres contain. There is no such there."

"But what's to stop the Adversary from using the Ring of Charon or the Lunar Wheel and the Earthpoint Singularity to link back to the Multisystem?" Sondra asked. "It knows where the Multisystem is now, and it doesn't seem like the sort to give up easy."

"And it's awfully optimistic to assume it would do no damage in the Solar System. How do we know that it wouldn't decide it could dine on the Sun in a pinch? Suppose you're wrong?" Captain Steiger asked.

"Then many people might well die, including many of my own citizens—but far fewer than if the Earth were destroyed. But let me ask again. Do we have the capacity to change the coordinates on the wormhole aperture, and send the Adversary to some other location?"

"Well, yes, I suppose," Sondra Berghoff said. "We can't shut it off altogether, but we might be able to change the settings—but only to a valid tuning. And the only tuning we know is the Ring of Charon."

"With all due respect," Gerald MacDougal said, "that's not a solution. It's gambling with mass murder. Suppose we divert the Adversary to the Solar System and it wreaks havoc there, and *then* it heads for the Multisystem. Your solution might result in the last surviving humans being those of us here in the Shattered Sphere system."

The Autocrat's face grew stern and angry, and he nodded rather curtly. "Your points are all well taken. But these are desperate times, and we may well be forced to make desperate choices. I will withdraw my suggestion—for now."

There was silence again in the room, and the definite feel of tension rising. Tempers were starting to fray.

"*I* still have trouble believing in the damned Adversary," Steiger said, in a tone of voice that suggested she was speaking as much to change the subject as anything else. "Is there any chance that we've got this wrong? That there's something else going on? Something we've missed?''

Sondra Berghoff shook her head. ''Not that I can see. Believe me, I want to be wrong. Up until we got here and heard about this invisible object smashing SCOREs to dust, we didn't have any direct proof besides the data Larry got out of the Lunar Wheel. But everything here corroborates those images.''

''But the idea that it would take impact with a *planet* to stop something that small. How could that be?''

''How could something that small kill a whole Sphere system?'' Sondra replied. ''But it did. Look around you.''

''But that's not proof—''

''Please! Please!'' the Autocrat called out. ''Come now, we have covered all this, and time is short. We can't spend time going around and around in circles.''

And that was it. Good God, that was it. Sianna sat stock still, holding her breath, working it through. Yes. It would work. Right now, if they started this minute. Everything they needed had come together. It would not have been possible before the *Terra Nova* and the *Autarch* arrived, and it would be too late all too soon. But now. Now the tide was at its crest. It could be done.

She stopped listening to the conversation and grabbed Wally by the arm, digging her fingers deep in. ''Wally,'' she whispered, leaning in close to him. *''Around in circles,''* she said. ''We can send it *around in circles.''*

Wally turned and looked at her, clearly puzzled. But then it clicked. She could see it in his eyes, the way his eyebrows twitched. ''Yeah,'' he whispered back. He thought for a minute, and then frowned. ''At least I *think* we could. Maybe. There's a lot we'd have to—''

''Mr. Sturgis. Miss Colette. Is there something you'd like to *contribute* to the discussion?'' the Autocrat said, cutting into their private conversation in the classic, sarcastic tones of a pompous teacher chiding an unruly student.

Sianna looked up at him, and opened her mouth, but the words jammed up in her throat. Every trip to the principal's office, every social and scholastic disaster of her childhood suddenly flashed through Sianna's mind all over again. She swallowed hard and wished she could just slide under the table. It was absurd. She had a good idea—a *wonderful* idea. But the Autocrat's sarcasm had her rooted to the spot, as helpless as a jacklighted deer in a hunter's sights.

Fortunately, however, Wally wasn't much for noticing sarcasm. He grinned and nodded. "Yes, sir," he said. "I think we've got plenty."

Thirty-two

Once Around

> *Hotspur:* . . . I tell you, my lord fool, out of this
> nettle, danger, we pick this flower, safety.
> —Shakespeare, *Henry IV, Part I*

Terra Nova
Docked to NaPurHab
THE SHATTERED SPHERE SYSTEM

Dianne Steiger turned and grinned at Sianna and Wally as they hustled through the accessway and came aboard. Marcia MacDougal and Larry Chao came through the hatch right behind them. "Welcome to the *Terra Nova*. Take a good look around," she said.

Sianna nodded nervously. "It's funny. I'd almost forgotten this was where we were going in the first place. I guess we finally got here," she said. "Even if we aren't going to stay long."

"Let's hope not," said Gerald MacDougal. "We can't afford any delays. Speaking of which—" He turned and slapped down an intercom panel. "This is the executive officer. All personnel and cargo now aboard. Cast off at will. All hands to maneuvering stations."

Sianna followed the others out of the airlock complex, moving hand over hand through zero gee. They came to what was clearly a main passageway running the length of the ship and stopped.

Gerald turned toward Captain Steiger. "I might not see you again until it's over," he said. "Good luck." He raised his hand and offered her a salute. Salutes had to be rare on this ship, after five years of day-to-day living. Much as Steiger and MacDougal were trying to pretend otherwise, this was a special occasion indeed.

Steiger returned the salute. "Wish I could join the party," she said.

"Should have thought of that before you let them make you captain," Gerald said, smiling.

"Guess so," Steiger said, her face set and determined. "Good luck, Gerald."

"Good luck, Captain." MacDougal turned toward Sianna and the others. "All right then," he said. "Let's get going."

The five of them—Gerald, Marcia, Larry, Wally, and Sianna—headed toward the aft end of the ship as Steiger went forward. Gerald MacDougal set a stiff pace, moving along on the handholds. Sianna had a bit of a time keeping up, and Wally, who was not exactly in the best of shape, was flat out of breath almost immediately. *Too bad*, Sianna thought. *No time left to lose. Not if there was going to be a hope in hell of pulling this off.*

MacDougal led them into the hangar bay, a huge compartment filled with landers that had been meant to touch down on whatever worlds *Terra Nova* found at the end of her voyage to Alpha Centauri. But today, the biggest craft was being put to a somewhat different use.

"We've hardly used any of the auxiliary craft in all this time," MacDougal said. "Not much point, when the COREs would have smashed any lander that got near a planet."

"Maybe that's all about to change," Sianna said. "If this works, and we make it—then we ought to have learned enough to call off the COREs."

"And the ways shall be open to us," Gerald said. "Maybe. We're not there yet. Come on. We're on that boat over there, the biggest lander we have."

"What's her name?" Larry asked.

A shadow crossed MacDougal's face for a moment, but his voice was calm as he answered. "She used to be the *Scott*," he said, "but we rechristened her this morning. Now she's the *Hijacker II*."

Wally was looking up at the lander, and hadn't noticed MacDougal's reaction. *"Hijacker?"* he asked. "Strange name."

"I'll explain some other time," MacDougal said. "Come on, everyone else should already be on board. We'd better join them."

Two hours later, the *Terra Nova* was well away from NaPur-Hab and, her main engines having fired, was heading down toward a low polar orbit of Solitude. Dianne Steiger watched the view from the exterior hull cameras as the outer doors of the hangar deck opened and the newly christened *Hijacker II* moved out into space.

It was a good name, a proper name, for a ship about to be dispatched on much the same mission as the first *Hijacker*—on a somewhat larger scale, of course, but even so.

The *Terra Nova* moved in on Solitude, closer than she had been to any planet in all the long, lonely years since she had boosted out of Earth orbit. This was her moment, her time. This was the day for which the *Terra Nova* and her crew would be remembered—if there were any left alive to remember.

The *Hijacker II* cleared the hangar, drifted away from the ship, and lit her engines. They were on their way.

NaPurHab

Sondra Berghoff set the last of the controls. There. That should do it. She pushed a button to send the first-level wake-up command to the dormant ring that had once controlled the wormhole link to the Multisystem. Thank heavens this ring had been built—or bred—to accept straight radio signals. If it had only taken gravitic commands, they would have had a much tougher job on their hands.

She watched her sensor board, looking for signs that the signal had been received and accepted. It would take a few seconds for the signal to cross the distance to the ring, and for the ring to process the signal and respond.

Focusing on the sensors, she could try to ignore the latest dustup at the far end of the compartment. Eyeball and the Autocrat made an odd pair—one could not even imagine using the word *couple*—to put it mildly. The absolute symbol of authority, and the absolute rebel. They shouldn't have been in the same compartment together, even with a referee. Sondra briefly considered shooing the Autocrat out and letting Eyeball and herself get on with it—but no. The Autocrat had every right to see the last act of what he had helped to set in motion.

Besides, being in a black mood did not seem to have much effect on Eyeball's competence or capacity for work. If anything, she seemed to perform better when she was good and angry.

Sondra and Eyeball were going to have to manage one of the most delicate phases of the whole operation. Their timing was going to have to be superb.

There. Good. The ring had taken the signal. The long-dormant ring began to awaken.

Maybe they would pull this off after all. Of course, up here, they had the easy job.

Sondra knew enough of the Charonian language now that she had no real doubts that they could control this one ring. The team heading down to the surface of Solitude had the tough job.

After all—how the hell did you wake up a *planet*?

Hijacker II
On Final Approach to Solitude

Twelve hours later, the *Hijacker II* lit her engines for the final braking maneuver. The lander slowed, came to a halt, a nice, even hover. The pilot eased the craft to port and a bit forward in search of flatter terrain, and then gently moved back the throttle. A smooth, perfect landing, the first landing by any human spacecraft on a planet outside the Solar System—but everyone was too busy sealing their suits and getting to work to worry about history. Almost before the engines were cut, the airlock was open, and the first team members were on the surface, the first steps onto the new world going quite unrecorded.

But then, if this didn't work, who the hell was going to be around to write the histories in the first place?

Three days. They had three days before the Adversary arrived.

All Wally Sturgis knew for sure was that he was one of the last ones down to the surface. The whole situation seemed quite unreal to him. It was, after all, the sort of thing he did in simulations, not in real life. If it had all been hypothetical, if he were controlling a computer model of a landing on Solitude and the rest of the plan, then he could have believed it was real.

This, though. Strange. Very strange.

Wally followed the last of the crew to the airlock and cycled through with Larry and Sianna. The inner doors of the lock shut, the air was pumped out, and the hatch opened out onto Solitude.

"So this used to be the Moon?" Larry asked. "Or like the Moon?"

Sianna nodded. "We ran the simulations of how a world like this would come to be. This is what Earth's Moon would have become, if the Charonians had succeeded in taking the Solar System apart and building it into a Multisystem. The Lunar Wheel would have grown up and out from a single band deep under the surface, reaching out in all directions, building itself up into a control center, into the brains of the operation, into—this."

They climbed down the exterior ladder, stepped away from the lander, and looked around. They were near Solitude's north pole, and the *Hijacker II* was sitting on one of the few pieces of real estate in the area that was still dirt and rock, one of the few areas that the Charonians had not turned into . . . something else.

Once Solitude had been like any of the cratered, airless worlds that Nature seemed so fond of creating. It was about the same size and mass as the Moon, just a trifle larger and denser.

All around the lander, the surface was covered with low, misshapen domes, antennae, boxy metallic shapes, odd mushroom-shaped protuberances black as obsidian, and other forms even harder to identify or describe. No, strike that. The surface was not *covered* with the strange devices— the surface was *made* of them, their bases all merging one into the other, or else linked together by a brownish material that was dried up and flaking.

Larry knelt down and peeled a bit of the brown stuff up. "Wheelskin," he said. "Same stuff the Lunar Wheel is made out of."

The skin did not cover everything. Some spots were formed out of fused soil and bits of slumped-over rock. Small, half-melted craters were still discernible in spots. Wally crouched down to get a look at the brown skin of the—the *machine*, if you could call it that. He was facing a low, five-sided obelisk, and reached out a hand to touch it. What the hell was it, and what was it for?

Wally looked up at the sky and drew in his breath. The Shattered Sphere swallowed up half the sky, a black-red wound that reached from horizon to horizon, its smashed, ruined face broken and terrifying. A huge crack staggered across its surface from behind the horizon. Giant craters marred its surface. That *thing* was big enough that Earth's old orbit could fit comfortably inside. And they were trying to take it over, to use for their own purposes.

Keep your head down, Wally told himself. Look at the surface, not at the sky.

Wally put his back to the Sphere—and spotted a red claw, just peeking out from behind a stand of the black mushroom-shapes. Was it still alive, somehow? His stomach tightened just a bit, and he stood up, went around the side of the mushrooms, and took a look.

A small mobile Charonian, about a half meter long, beetle-shaped and fire-engine red, flipped over on its back, ten legs in the air, its manipulator claws dangling uselessly. It was, to Wally's relief, very clearly dead. A repairman? Larry and Sianna followed him over to take a look.

"Looks like a relative of the scorps we got in the Solar System," Larry said.

Sianna turned and looked farther out into the odd field of machinery. "They're all over the place," she said. Wally looked around, and immediately started spotting more of the repair bugs, all of them bright colored, and all of them dead, scattered all over the surface. Color-coded repair bugs?

"Hey, over here," Larry said. Wally and Sianna walked to where he was standing. A repair bug seemed to have succumbed with its front end dangling over the edge of some sort of hole. Wally pulled the handlight from his suit and pointed it down the hole. It was a long vertical shaft about twenty-five centimeters across. Far too narrow for a human to go down, but just the right size for the shocking-pink bee-

tle that had keeled over at its entrance. The shaft had ladder
rungs set into one side of it. His light was not powerful
enough to reach the bottom.

"Down below," Larry said, "this has got to be just like
the Lunar Wheel and the Moon, only much further along in
its development. The Wheel here has built clear up to the
surface, and built all this."

Wally looked around again, studying the shapes of the objects that covered the surface. What was all this stuff *for*?
And then it came to him. "So," he asked, "is this an antenna farm?"

"I'd say so," Sianna replied. "At least some of these
things look like detectors and signaling systems. The Wheel
down below would pipe its commands up to the surface
here, to other centers elsewhere in the system."

"But how the hell are we going to tap into it all?" Wally
asked. He started walking again, looking for something.
What, he did not know.

Three days, he told himself again. How the hell could that
possibly be enough time? Never mind that. Concentrate.
Solve the puzzle. Analyze. The dish shapes were clearly
some sort of radio-band antennas, and the spike-shapes
probably omni-directional antennas. But not everything
Charonian had a clearly functional shape. He couldn't guess
what everything was just by looking at it. That cable, there
for example, running between two of the pentagonal obelisks. It could be anything.

Wait a second. "Um, ah, Larry? Larry, come here a second."

"What is it?" Larry asked as he headed toward Wally.

"This cable. I saw some photos of Lucian Dreyfuss in
suspended animation. This cable here—"

"Yes!" Larry said. "It's the same stuff as the tendrils the
Wheel had plugged into him."

"Thought so." Wally traced the cable back down to one
of the obelisks and knelt down in front of it. "Access
cover," he said. "There has to be an access cover."

"How come?" Sianna asked. "Why couldn't it be sealed for good?"

"Wally's right. There are dead maintenance bugs all over the place," Larry said. "What good is a repair team if it can't get to the hardware?"

"There," Wally said. "Look." He pointed at a narrow gap between two faces of the pyramidical top. He pulled a flat-bladed screwdriver off his suit's tool belt and stuck it into the seam, working it back and forth.

"Careful," Sianna said.

The seam resisted for a moment, and then one face of the pyramid popped back just a bit, leaving a gap wide enough for Wally to get his gloved fingers in and bend it back. Wally put away his screwdriver and put his hands around the side that had popped free. "Gimme a hand, Larry."

Larry got in next to him, and the two of them pulled.

It took some pretty hard pulling, but they managed to bend it back to get a look inside. Wally aimed his handlight into it and peered inside.

"Bingo," Wally whispered to himself.

"Yes indeed," Larry said. "The same sort of tendrils as on Lucian." The tendrils terminated into various points in a sort of honeycombed surface inside. "I'll bet you whatever you want we can use the same tapping techniques as they used on Lucian Dreyfuss."

"It's only fair," Sianna said with an evil grin so wide Wally could see it through her helmet. "The Charonians used those tendrils to hook a dead man up to their machines. What do you say we return the favor?"

"Sounds good to me," Wally said, his mind already on test probes and circuits. He took another look inside. Three days? Hell, with the datasets they had now, and the hardware they had brought along, he'd have a link into the main wormhole loop center in three hours.

NaPurHab

Sondra Berghoff awoke, her eyes snapping open all at once. Four hours' sleep. The longest rest she had had since the *Terra Nova* had cast off, two and a half days before. Sleep. A guilty luxury, and one that she could ill afford. There was so much to *do*. But it would do no one any good if she could not see straight to run the controls. One chance. That was all they would get. One chance to stop it, or else the Adversary would get through.

She lay still, just for a moment longer, trying to savor the moment. After all, they were dealing with major energy sources and powerful entities. If things went wrong, this could easily be the last time she awoke, the last time she got out of bed.

Or even if things went right.

The Mind of the Sphere felt new disturbances up in the network, feeble twitchings and quiverings from places that had been dead long years. As a person with an amputated limb, so too the Mind felt sensations from parts, not of itself, but of its ancestor, that were no longer there. Something strange was going on, something disturbing, and the sensations had been growing more powerful. They had started shortly after the mysterious transits through the wormhole net.

But the Mind had no time to worry about such things. Not with the Adversary so near. No doubt the strange sensations were some sort of sensor malfunction. It would repair the flaws later.

If it lived.

Sakalov Station
North Polar Region
Solitude

Sianna Colette walked back from the *Hijacker II* toward the bubbletent, trying to convince herself she was ready.

Though how could anyone be ready? *Years* would not have been enough time to prepare, and they had had only a handful of days. But now the hour had come.

The last seventy-two hours had passed in a blur. Somewhere in there, they had wired into the datataps, assembled the bubbletents, moved in the equipment, and started linking into Solitude's control system. The bubbletent was half-buried in equipment hooked up this way and that to the tendrils and cables and components that made up Solitude's control system. But now the bubbletent had a name. She paused by the entrance and read it again.

Sakalov Station. Gerald MacDougal had thought of it, and painted the words over the tent entrance, so everyone could see them whenever they came back from the lander. After all, Yuri Sakalov had spent five years—and given his life—in the search for Charon Central, the command center for the Multisystem. Now, in part thanks to him, here they all were, at the command post of *a* Sphere system, albeit not the one he had searched for. He would have loved to be here.

Sakalov Station. It sounded good, right—if "station" wasn't too grand a name for a pressurized tent in the middle of an alien antenna farm. She headed into the airlock, cycled through, and took her suit off. She found herself working a bit more carefully than usual, stowing her suit, the helmet, the gloves as if doing so were some ritual of preparation. As indeed it was. She stopped to check her appearance in the mirrored visor of an empty suit, tidied her hair, straightened her collar. This was it. This was it.

Sianna took three deep breaths, and then told herself she was ready. She left the airlock section and threaded her way through the forest of hardware back to the main control panel at the far end of the bubbletent.

The rest of them were there already, busily testing all the connections one last time, reviewing the command sequence for errors. No second chances.

Larry Chao, his face intent and hopeful as he checked over the last of the displays: this was his chance to pay some of it back. Wally, running a test on the comm system that had hotwired into Solitude's hardware. It all seemed to be working, from what Sianna could see.

Gerald and Marcia MacDougal stood a few steps back from the main control system, hand-in-hand, the same looked of anxious worry on both their faces. Sometimes the two of them seemed like one person, the way they stayed together every moment of the day.

Sianna took her seat, between Larry and Wally, and started checking her board. Get all the details right. No simulation this time. No dreams of the dead. No assumptions as to what the enemy was up to, or guesses as to who and what the enemy was. This was it.

She set to work, commanding the dead and ancient circuits of Solitude to bring the Rings of the wormhole transit loop up to standby power, getting them ready, linking them one to another.

Fourteen Ring-and-Hole sets, each linked to the others, co-orbital with Solitude, forming a great circle about the Shattered Sphere. They were controlled by the planet beneath her feet. And Sianna, *Sianna*, was controlling the planet. Her fingers started to tremble even as she thought of it, but she forced herself to settle down.

"All right," Larry said, his voice and manner calm. "We're coming up on it. Everybody, look sharp and take it one step at a time."

And suddenly, gradually, they were no longer preparing, but *doing*. It had started. Sianna looked up at the right-hand screen, hooked into the long-range cameras, and spotted a dark blob moving through the darkness.

The Adversary had arrived, had drawn close enough to be visible.

"All right," Wally said. "Here we go."

Every eye was on the right-hand display as it showed the Adversary moving in, closer and closer to the wormhole aperture, moving fast enough that its motion against the starfield was noticeable even at this range.

"Doesn't look like much, does it?" asked Gerald Mac-Dougal.

The Adversary was a dark, lumpen sphere, pocked here and there with small, low, dimpled craters—all the evidence there was of the SCOREs' previous attacks.

"There go the SCOREs," Sianna said, needlessly. The left-hand tactical display showed the movement quite plainly.

The SCOREs moved in to make one last, desperate attempt against their ancient enemy. Sianna hoped with everyone else that they would succeed, and knew they could not. But if, somehow, the SCOREs could kill this thing, then all the risks and dangers of their own plan could be avoided.

The Adversary came in, moving fast, diving straight for the wormhole aperture. The eight surviving SCOREs moved in, rushing toward it, closing in from all directions. Then, in the space of a heartbeat, they appeared in the same frame as the Adversary. All eyes shifted to the right-hand screen just as the SCOREs reached their target. There was a brilliant, ravening flare of light, an explosion that seemed to go on and on, a ball of flame and fire that bloomed out into space, flared up, setting the sky alight—and the Adversary moved out through the burning cloud, its surface glowing just a trifle from heating effects, but for all intents and purposes, unchanged.

Sianna found she had been holding her breath, and she let it out in a sigh of disappointment and frustration. In a minute or less, the Adversary would reach the wormhole, force itself through, come out the other side—and then, it would happen.

Would the Sphere use the Earth as a kinetic impact weapon immediately, or would it first launch the cloud of SCOREs about the Moonpoint aperture in another futile attempt to stop this thing? Or would it send Earth and the SCOREs crashing in all at once? What difference could it make if Earth were destroyed two minutes from now, or two and a half minutes? All of it, gone. The oceans vaporized, the forests incinerated, the cities and towns smashed and shattered, a world of corpses and shattered, ruined bodies flung out into space—*Don't think about it,* Sianna thought. *Keep it from happening. Don't think about it.*

''Ready for shunt reception,'' Larry said. ''NaPurHab reports they retain control of the wormhole ring. They are ready to change the transit coordinates. So far so good.''

So far so good? This was the most dangerous moment of all. This was the moment when the Multisystem might act in some unexpected way, when the humans would begin to show their hand, when the Adversary might begin to realize something was wrong, when some bit of dead Charonian hardware might not respond in quite the way Wally expected.

''Sending link sequence command,'' Sianna announced. Now the wormhole transit loop was waking up in earnest, drawing energy from the surviving power storage rings on the Shattered Sphere, keying into each other. They were ready. As ready as they were going to be, anyway.

Terra Nova
In Close Orbit of Solitude

Dianne Steiger sat in her captain's chair and glanced over at where Gerald should have been. He was down there in the thick of it. And she was up here, orbiting this damn lump of rock, nothing more than a spectator. No, not a spectator. A warrior on a stretch of the battle line that had gone quiet for the moment. None of them would be down there, ready for the final battle, if not for her.

She had done her part, she and her ship, and her crew. Five years ago, before the Abduction, the ship had been in mothballs and Dianne's career had been as close to over as made no difference. Then the Charonians had attacked, and everything had changed. Now here they were, Dianne Steiger and her ship, about to save the world, maybe.

Not bad, she thought. *Not bad for a couple of mothballed has-beens.*

NaPurHab

They could see it, as it happened, with the naked eye. The Solitude Ring flickered awake, and the strange un-blue-white of a wormhole link came to life. The Adversary had activated the link, forced it to connect with the Moonpoint Ring in the Multisystem. It was heading in.

"Thirty seconds," Eyeball said. "Show time. Fire up automatics."

Sondra Berghoff reached over to set in the automatic sequencer, but then she swallowed hard, and thought of the button. Five long years ago, Larry Chao had set things so that *he* would send out the first pulse of collimated laser energy, not the computer. *He* had pushed the button that had made it happen, not some damn machine.

That beam of graser power had awakened the slumbering Lunar Wheel, and it had stolen the Earth. His finger on the button. No one else's. That was what history would remember.

What if they failed today? What if the computer guessed wrong in the next twenty seconds, and Earth died as a consequence? No. It was not *right.* If Earth died, let there be someone to blame. Let it be a human decision, not that of a microcircuit.

And if they succeeded, let it be penance, of a sort, for her friend Larry's finger on that button.

"I'm staying with manual," Sondra said.

"What!" Eyeball shouted. "You *nuts*?"

The Autocrat stepped forward, about to speak, but then Sondra caught his eye. Their eyes locked for a heartbeat or two, and then he stepped back. He would not challenge her. Sondra looked back toward her partner on the controls.

"Shut up, Eyeball. No time to argue. *Manual.*"

Now it was close. There was no time. The Mind of the

Sphere could sense the Adversary coming close, unstoppable, uncontrollable. It made ready to do what it must, to sacrifice one world in order to save all the others. It gathered power unto itself, drawing down reserves from the storage rings, preparing to send the raw, massive burst of gravitic energy that would slam down on the luckless planet and accelerate it nearly to light speed, straight at the Adversary. Now was the time.

Sondra checked her switches, watched the display, the timers. Too late, and there would be no time to make a full link over to the wormhole transit loop coordinates. Too soon, and the Adversary might sense the changeover and do something about it.

The autosequencer's countdown clock was still active, still counting down. Ten seconds. Nine. Eight. Seven. Six. Five. Four.

Yes, she had been right. Too far off. The Adversary was slowing for the transit. It was going to be too far off when the sequencer hit zero. Three. Two. One. *Zero.* Minus One. Almost there. Another second, let it draw in closer. But not too long. Not too long. Minus Two. Minus—

Sondra *felt* the right instant. She stabbed down at the button and sent the new coordinates on their way.

The un-blue-white of the wormhole link flickered and shifted, and then settled down again.

"Linkage!" Eyeball shouted. "We have solid link to the first wormhole aperture in the wormhole loop."

Sondra slapped another button, and sent a lockout command, ordering the Solitude Ring to take no further changes until after transit. The Adversary would not be able to change the setting back.

"Damnation!" the Autocrat said. "It's spotted the change."

The Adversary did not understand. Something was wrong. Something had shifted the wormhole coordinates. But that was impossible. It could not be. But it was happening. Stop.

Stop. Whatever had happened could not be right. Stop. Stop. Stop—

The Adversary was braking, trying to come to a halt before it went into the hole. Slowing, but not stopping. It had too much momentum, too much velocity. Closer. Closer.

And then, miraculously, it went in.

The wormhole winked shut behind it.

But had they done it? Had they really diverted it? Or had it made it through to the Multisystem? Had the Earth already been reduced to slag?

The overhead speaker came alive. "This is Sakalov Station," Gerald MacDougal's voice announced. "We got it," he said. "We have the Adversary."

The Mind of the Sphere braced itself, steeled itself against battle, and watched as the wormhole opened—and then shut again.

Nothing. Nothing had come through.

Astonishment did not even begin to express its reaction.

Sakalov Station

"We have it, but we won't keep it long," Sianna said, triumph in her voice. The Adversary in a stasis orbit, held inside a pinched-off wormhole moving at the speed of light, a hugely complex wavefront trapped inside the wormhole transit loop. The same way the Multisystem had held the Earth during the Abduction.

There was a difference, of course. The Sphere had some place to *put* Earth, some way to get it back out of the wormhole loop. But Sakalov Station didn't want to put the Adversary anywhere at all.

She remembered the conversation, back when all such things had been mere idle lab chat. Wally had been explaining how the Multisystem's wormhole transit loop had held Earth in a stasis orbit for thirty-seven minutes.

"Just out of curiosity," Wolf Bernhardt had asked,

*"what would happen if the Sphere was unable to provide
enough power? Would the Earth have dropped out of the
stasis orbit?"*

"Well, yes, that would be the problem," Wally had said.
*You'd get an uncontrolled spontaneous evaporation of the
pinched wormhole."*

"And what would that mean?" Bernhardt had asked.

Wally had tried to make light of it. *"E = MC squared.
Earth's mass would be expressed as energy."*

Yuri Sakalov had been there, still alive. *"Which would of
course be a great inconvenience to us,"* he had said, his tone
quite sarcastic. *"However, it would almost certainly be
enough to destroy the Sphere, and probably vaporize most of
the planets of the closer-in Captive Suns as well."*

And there it was. The Adversary had much lower mass
than a planet, of course. One lunar mass was about an eighti-
eth the mass of the Earth. But that was still a hell of a lot of
mass to express as energy.

The team on Solitude had no way to do a controlled release from the pinched wormhole, even if they had wanted
to. No way to turn the damn thing off at all. The Adversary
would stay in the transit loop until it ran out of power. The
effort of holding was already a substantial drain on the small
reserves in the Shattered Sphere's power storage rings.

Sianna watched her power indicators, and tried to work
against the clock. With the Adversary moving at the speed of
light, if they could hold out a full nineteen minutes, that
would give the Adversary time to go halfway around the
Sphere before it blew.

But that was wildly optimistic. The power levels were
dropping like rocks. They'd be lucky if it lasted five minutes
and got around the limb of the Shattered Sphere before it
blew.

And if it went off too close to Solitude? Too close to the
Terra Nova and NaPurHab? *We'll be dead, obviously,*
Sianna told herself. *Good way to go, saving the home planet.*

There was no way to *control* something this big. Not with

the speed-of-light delays involved. The command to shut down, to cut the power, would not even arrive at the other side of the transit loop for those nineteen minutes. Hell, the other side of the loop could have blown out or shut down already, and there would be no way of knowing it.

"Power levels reaching critical," Larry warned. "We're going to start losing Ring-and-Hole sets real soon now. Might have lost 'em already, 'cept we don't know it because of signal delay."

Sianna checked the display board. There was a strange little flicker in the main power ring energy-level display, a dip and a spike that shouldn't have happened.

Wally frowned and peered at the display. "That's funny," he said. "I wonder if—"

The skies lit up as the station went dark.

For a thousandth of a second, between the moment the wormhole loop collapsed and the moment when its very being was converted into a blast of light, the Adversary struggled to escape, straining against the very fabric of space to break out of the impossible trap into which it had fallen. But there were things beyond even the capacity of the Adversary.

Throughout the galaxy, other units of the Adversary, deep inside wormholes, nestled safely on the surface of neutron stars, felt the death of part of themselves, and were astonished.

Such a thing had never happened before.

A torch of light, a flarepoint of energy, ripped out from the transit loop as the fourth Ring-and-Hole set failed, its structure too weak to maintain a wormhole link. The mass of the Adversary, folded into a pinched wormhole, was distilled back out into the Universe as a gout of thundering flame. It burst out, swelled into a searing-bright ball of fire, blasting the failed Ring into nothingness. The blast bloomed out and touched the surface of the Shattered Sphere, smashing a huge new hole in it, doing massive new damage, mutilating the corpse of the once-powerful Sphere.

Tongues of flame shot up into space, vaporizing whatever bits of space debris came near. The blast of light and power expanded out into space.

It was over.

Thirty-three

The Way Back

"In a mechanistic, deterministic universe, the same reaction to the same situation will always produce the same result. A living thing confronting a dead universe will quickly learn that a certain set of actions *always* works, while another set *always* fails. This is not the case in a universe full of living things. A mouse might learn that one falling rock acts much like another, but one circling hawk will not always act like the next. One hawk might be looking the other way, another not hungry. Still another hawk might attack in response to the mouse's own actions—something a falling rock would not do.

"We humans, confronting a living, ever-changing universe over which we had but little control, have learned to make it up as we go along. The Charonians, on the other hand, learned eons ago which rules worked in their unchanging, utterly controlled habitat, where they were the only living things of any consequence.

"I believe that this goes far in describing the difference between Charonians and humans, and is the reason that the Adversary defeated them, while we defeated the Adversary. To put it another way, human intelligence is opportunistic, while Charonian intelligence is algorithmic. If this is so, then we must take every opportunity in future to change the circumstances, rendering Charonian algorithms worthless."

—Larry Chao, *Operations on the Shattered Sphere: Conclusions and Recommendations,* Datastreemdream Prezz, NaPurHab, 2432

Solitude
THE SHATTERED SPHERE SYSTEM

They were in their pressure suits, getting a look at the damage to the station. Gerald and Marcia walking hand-in-hand even in their suits, Larry and Sianna walking a step or two behind.

Up in the sky, on the leading limb of the Shattered Sphere, a huge new crater sat at the center of a massive scorch mark. There was already talk of launching an expedition to the Shattered Sphere, getting a look at a dead one before having much more to do with a live one.

"Well, the Charonians didn't much care for parasites," Gerald MacDougal said, pointing to Adversary Crater, as it had already been named. "I wonder how they'll feel about symbiotes."

"*That's* a strange way to look at it," Sianna said.

"How so?" Gerald asked. He stopped and turned toward her, his broad smile plainly visible behind his visor. "We saved the Multisystem Sphere, didn't we? We kept it alive."

"Yes, but not because we *wanted* to," Sianna protested.

"Because we wanted to save ourselves and our planet."

"That's what all good symbiotes do," Larry said with a smile. "Take care of their hosts to take care of themselves."

"I suppose," Sianna said, her tone a bit doubtful. "I don't much like thinking of the human race in quite that way." She turned around to look at Solitude Ring, hanging off in the middle distance. It had taken a bit of damage from the Adversary blast. Prize crews from the *Terra Nova* were already seeing about getting it up and running again. They expected to have working wormhole links to the Ring of Charon in the Solar System, and to the Moonpoint Ring in the Multisystem, within another week or two. They wouldn't be stranded here for long. A lot of people were going to be on their way back. There were going to be quite a few reunions.

Gerald and Marcia had walked on ahead, leaving Sianna and Larry alone. Sianna was glad enough to give them some privacy—but also glad that she and Larry had a little of their own. She didn't know him at all, but she wanted to. Not to conquer her schoolgirl fears of him, either. She wasn't a girl anymore. Not after the last few weeks. She couldn't have survived them without doing some very fast growing up.

But she could see a lot of herself in Larry. Both of them had been forced to deal with fear and loneliness. Both of them wondered about the Universe. And neither of them was ever going to fit in very well.

"You know," she said. "We have a lot in common, you and I."

"Really? I don't think anyone would like to think of themselves as being like me," he said.

"*I* don't mind."

"Thanks very much," Larry said. "But seriously, I like talking to you, too. You're the first person in a long time who didn't treat me like a sideshow freak, or come to me just because you needed something. It's nice."

"So," she said, turning to him, "what happens now?"

"What do you mean?" Larry asked, moving back a step or two.

Sianna reddened. That was *not* what she'd meant. "I mean, what happens with the Earth?"

"Huh?"

"Wally says he's doubled what we knew about Charonian command codes since we got here. He says he should be able to rig as many ships as we like with beacons that will tell the COREs and SCOREs to leave them alone. And we know a hell of a lot more about running wormholes than we did. Pretty soon we'll know how to make them sit up and beg."

Larry shrugged, exaggerating the gesture because of the pressure suit. "I suppose that's true," he said. "So?"

"So tell me, what do we do about *Earth*?" Sianna asked. "I came to you because you're the expert on moving planets."

Larry looked at her, hurt and startled. Then he realized she was teasing him, and relaxed. "I don't know about expert," he said, "but what did you have in mind?"

"Well, do we leave Earth where it is, or take it back home? If we can get to the other worlds in the Multisystem, really get out there and explore those worlds, maybe colonize them, there's a lot to be said for leaving Earth right where it is. Or do we take it back home to the Solar System, just for sentimental reasons?"

Larry seemed surprised by the question. He gave her a funny look, as if he weren't sure whether she was serious or not. At last he burst out laughing, a long and joyous sound that sounded good to Sianna. "I don't have an answer for you," he said. "But if *that's* our most serious problem, I'd say we were in very good shape indeed."

Wally Sturgis could not resist. Simulations were all very well, but here he was on the actual control panel, running the system that operated a planet-sized mind—and he had used it to destroy a real-life menace. It would be hard to go back to imaginary worlds after that.

Besides, there was so much he could *do* here. There was still lots of functioning hardware, and lots more that it ought to be possible to fire up. Lots of ways to get the network reconnected. And they were learning more and more Charonian command code all the time. Which brought Wally back to the idea that he could not resist.

It was obvious that the Multisystem had retained some sort of link with the Shattered Sphere system, if only through the sensors that had allowed it to monitor the movements of the Adversary. It hadn't taken Wally long to find those sensors—or find a way to subvert them.

A carefully crafted message, in carefully written code, ought to do the trick. It would almost be a post-hypnotic suggestion—unless you wanted to think of it as a computer virus. All it had to do was plant the idea in the Sphere's head. Except of course the Sphere didn't *have* a head. Never mind. The important thing was that the Sphere would not even know that it had received an instruction. Let the thing think it was its own idea.

Wally worked long hours before he had the code just right, was absolutely certain it would work—and even then he hesitated. He really ought to check with someone first, get someone's permission. But no, that would spoil the fun of the thing.

He set up the link, calibrated his equipment, and sent the execute command.

He couldn't resist.

The Mind of the Sphere did not understand what had happened. Clearly it all had something to do with the last world it had captured, the one that had come to it unexpectedly. Somehow it, or some unnoticed, insignificant creatures on it, seemed to have fended off the attack that the advent of their world had caused. Very strange. Very strange indeed. The Mind decided to pay more attention to that world in future. But for the present, the danger was past. It could withdraw its Special Guardians and rebuild them to suit other purposes. It sent out the word. All across the Multisystem and the Portal, the Special Guardians began their long journeys home.

Thinking on it further, it occurred to the Sphere that the new planet had managed to kill at least one regular Guardian—and it might not be wise to trifle with a world that could defeat the Adversary. And why waste precious Guardians to protect a planet that was perfectly capable of taking care of itself? Surely a world that could protect itself against the Adversary would have no trouble defending against incoming skyjunk. Almost by way of experiment, the Sphere decided to withdraw its regular Guardians from the new planet. It could always return them later, if need be.

Multisystem Research Institute
New York City
Earth
THE MULTISYSTEM

No word. No word at all from NaPurHab or *Terra Nova*, and now this. There had to be a connection, somehow. Wolf Bernhardt stepped out of the elevator onto the main level of MRI's underground headquarters. He rushed across the quadrangle to the auditorium. The word had come just a few minutes before. Wolf could have watched the video of the telescope images just as well from his office, but he felt the need to be with people, to join together with others.

Practically the whole staff of MRI was there, watching it on the big screen. The images from the terrestrial telescopes were grainy, and more than a little hard to make out, but they were the most beautiful thing Wolf had seen in a long time.

They were leaving. The SCOREs and COREs that had kept humanity bottled up on Earth for all these years were pulling out, departing their orbits, heading off across the sky.

Wolf looked around and spotted Ursula Gruber standing in the rear of the room. He hurried over to her, and she took him by the hand, her eyes shining and bright. ''It's wonderful, Wolf. Just wonderful. But what do you think it means?''

Wolf shook his head and looked up, past the auditorium ceiling, past the caverns of MRI, past the towers of Manhattan and the skies of the Multisystem, out to the unknown place, somewhere out in the Universe, where NaPurHab and the *Terra Nova* had gone. And past there as well, to Earth's own Solar System. Surely the rest of the human family was waiting as eagerly for news as Earth itself was. And surely news would come soon. The departure of the COREs was a message to that effect, all by itself.

"I think," he said, "I think it means that our friends out there have done rather well."

THE END

Notes on the Charonian-Adversary War

(Information on the Charonians and their life cycles can be found in *The Ring of Charon* by Roger MacBride Allen, Tor Books, 1990.)

It is important to realize that nearly every term in the discussion that follows must be regarded as an approximation or as poetic license. Paleontologists often speak of, say, a giraffe evolving a long neck, as if that were some sort of deliberate policy decision on the part of the giraffe. Clearly, this is merely convenient shorthand used instead of a more precise—and necessarily laborious—description of the process.

Just so, here we must discuss a "war" that moved at glacial speeds, over astronomical distances and tremendously long periods of time, between two belligerent parties that quite likely never regarded each other as the "enemy," so much as mere forces of nature. Both sides quite likely viewed it as a "war" only in the sense of a war against the weather, or an untamed territory, or a plague of locusts. It is likely that, for long periods of time, the two sides were not consciously aware of each other.

It was a conflict between army ants on the one hand and a flock of vultures on the other. Conscious decision-making played little if any part in shaping the conflict.

Like ants and vultures, the two sides had ways of life so radically different, and experienced their portions of the Universe in ways so wholly different from each other that they might as well have lived in separate universes.

Their worlds scarcely ever intersected—until, of course, their interests came into conflict.

Many details of our ant-vulture analogy are quite obviously at odds with reality, but the most skewed is perhaps that of physical scale. The Charonians—a differentiated species, with many non-reproductive individuals who labor to support those of higher castes—bear several resemblances to termites, ants, and bees. They modify their own environments extensively, develop and harvest their own "food" supply (in the form of various energy and gravitic resources), and invest significant resources in establishing new colonies.

The Adversary does not develop resources, but merely exploits such resources as become available. As an opportunistic feeder, the Adversary must range far and wide in search of energy sources, while the Charonians must remain in close proximity to their manufactured resources.

In short, the Charonians' behavior resembles that of social insects, while the Adversary's behavior closely parallels that of a free-range scavenger, such as a vulture. On Earth, the smallest scavenger birds are far larger than the largest insect. Even though the Charonians and Adversary reverse that pattern out in space, being of such disparate scales has exactly the same effect, no matter who is the larger: it is difficult for the two life-forms even to be aware of each other's existence, let alone perceive the other as an opponent, rather than a food source or an obstacle.[1]

Somewhere in the distant past, the Adversary broke into the Charonian wormhole network and cut a massive swath of destruction, smashing into Spheres and

---

[1] Indeed, the question of scale accounts for much of the Charonian difficulty in being able to perceive humans.

feeding on their energy sources, leaving wrecked Multisystems in its wake. After the first horrific onslaught wiped out most of the Spheres, the Charonians learned to fight back—and to hide. But the war did not end so much as peter out. The Adversary still feeds on Charonian Spheres whenever it can.

One hundred forty-seven years before the book opens, the Adversary found the Shattered Sphere and ate it. The Shattered Sphere, parent to the Multisystem that holds Earth, gave a warning, then killed itself before the Adversary could make a link to other systems. When the Shattered Sphere died, its system was wrecked. Dead planets, rogue stars, and dead Charonians wheeled through space.

After killing the Shattered Sphere, the Adversary unit responsible for the attack withdrew to a truncated wormhole and remained there. The Adversary unit lived in slow-time conditions where perhaps one year Adversary time is equivalent to a century of our time. It was "asleep" for most of that 147 years, inert, as seen from the outside Universe.

However, the Earth's arrival in the Multisystem created a disturbance in the wormhole net that stimulated the Adversary to wakefulness. Then, the human-caused interference was loud and indiscriminate. It served to illuminate the Shattered Sphere system links to the Multisystem, making the revivable wormholes clearly visible.

This gave the Adversary a wonderful guide to a new system to invade, a trail which it is following as *The Shattered Sphere* opens. The Adversary is preparing to make a transit of normal space heading straight for the main, default wormhole link, the one that produced the most clear and powerful signal—that is, the link between Lone World of Solitude to the Multisystem. The Adversary has taken five years to awaken and now is preparing to attack. The Multisystem Charonians laid low until there was no question that an attack was coming. Once there was no doubt, they prepared to meet it.

Glossary of Terms, Ship Names, and Locations

Abduction The event and time period during which the Charonians stole the Earth and placed it in a new orbit around the Sunstar in the Multisystem. There is a natural tendency to divide things into pre- and post-Abduction.

Amalgam Creatures *See* **Lander**

ArtInt (Artificial Intelligence) Typically refers to a machine or subsystem smart enough to do what should be done without being told.

Autarch The personal ship of the Autocrat of Ceres.

Autocrat of Ceres The absolute ruler of the largest asteroid, and the only effective instrumentality of law or justice in the Belt Community. A reputation for draconian justice has served to prevent most from daring his wrath.

Breeding Binge Those times when large Charonians land on the surface of a living world and use it as a breeding ground, often wrecking the planet's natural ecosystem in the process. It might take hundreds of thousands or millions of years for a planet to recover. Though no human has witnessed a Breeding Binge, the damage caused by them is plainly visible on many of the Captive Worlds nearest to Earth.

Captive Suns or **Captive Stars** Those stars that have been captured and held by a Charonian Sphere to serve as suns for its Captive Worlds.

Captive Worlds Life-bearing planets that have, like the Earth, been abducted into a Charonian Multisystem. They are placed in orbit around Captive Suns, at distances and orbital periods that will maintain their climates. The Charonians, in effect, use the Captive Worlds as breeding cages to reproduce certain subspecies during certain parts of their life cycle.

Carrier Bugs Any of the lowest-level Charonian types, capable of only the simplest fetch-and-carry duties.

Central City Formerly Central Colony. The principal city and capital of the Lunar Republic.

Ceres Largest body in the Asteroid Belt. The de facto capital of the Belt.

Charonians Named for the Ring of Charon, the Charonians are the aliens responsible for the Earth's Abduction. There are many species and subspecies of Charonian, ranging in size and complexity from Carrier Bugs to Spheres. They are partially living, partially mechanical. Though their ancestors were creatures not completely unlike humans, they have now guided their own evolution into forms so completely changed that it is often difficult to recognize them as living. The form and degree of Charonian intelligence are quite unclear.

Conner A citizen of the Lunar Republic. Derived from *colonist* and/or *con-artist*.

Consortium of Spheres Charonian term for the now-ruined network of linked Spheres and Multisystems connected by a web of wormhole links.

COREs, Close-Orbiting Radio Emitters Any of a large number of identical objects in various orbits, not all close, around all the worlds of the Multisystem. Their powerful radio signals—emitted over a wide range of frequencies—serve as an effective jamming mechanism. *See* **SCOREs.**

Directorate of Spatial Investigation (DSI) The organization charged with studying—and ultimately defeating—the Charonians. Wolf Bernhardt is the director. DSI works closely with **MRI.**

Dyson Sphere A huge sphere built entirely around a star, so as to provide huge surface area (hundreds of billions times greater than the surface area of Earth) and/or to capture all of the star's radiated power.

Earthpoint That point in space, relative to the Moon and the rest of the Solar System, where the Earth once was. The Earthpoint Black Hole, a.k.a. the Earthpoint Singularity or Earthpoint Wormhole, occupies this space. *See* **Moonpoint.**

Event Horizon The minimum distance from a black hole required before time or light can escape—or, to put it another way, the minimum distance required before events are possible. The stronger a gravity field, the slower time moves. Make the field strong enough, and get close enough, and time slows to a complete stop. Also defined as the point at which the local escape velocity equals the speed of light.

Event Radius The distance, usually measured in light-minutes or light-hours, between two points. So called because no event can have any effect at a given distance until light (or radio waves or other electromagnetic energy) has had time to cross that distance. Referred to as a "radius" because light expands out spherically. Not related to **Event Horizon.**

Fast-Time Space Normal space, as seem from the Adversary's point of view. Used to high-gravity, high-energy, slow-time environments, the Adversary views normal space as a strangely distorted—and hostile—place.

Ghoul Modules Large Charonian forms that docked themselves to the dead **Moonpoint Ring.** So called because they apparently brought the dead ring back to life.

GIGO, Garbage In Garbage Out A slang version of the obvious rule that inputting bad initial data will produce unreliable results. However, the primary usage is as a description of data that is known to be bad. "We can't run the simulation. All we have is that GIGO data."

Graser Gravity laser—a focused beam of gravity power.

Graviton An experimental ship using cannibalized Charonian equipment to generate a gravity-beam propulsion system, riding gravity beams sent by the Ring of Charon.

Guardian Charonian term for CORE.

Heritage Memory In effect, the collective race memory of the Charonian race. Each significant new experience of an individual is recorded and stored by at least one other individual, usually by a higher-level being capable of evaluating it. Copies of the appropriate sections of the heritage memory are placed in each newly made or manufactured Charonian. Each higher-level individual possesses a significant fraction of the race's history, in the form of individual memory. As nearly all Charonian behavior is based on precedent, the Heritage Memory is of tremendous importance. A Charonian facing a situation outside the experience of its Heritage Memory will have no guide for its actions.

Hijacker The small stealthship destroyed in the first attempt to board a CORE.

Hijacker II Formerly the *Scott*. The *Terra Nova*'s largest lander, used in a key action against the Adversary.

Lander One of many huge creatures, long hidden in dormant stages inside asteroids, which move through space under broadcast gravity power radiated by the Lunar Wheel.

Leftover A mildly derogatory term for a citizen of Earth stranded in the Solar System by the Abduction.

Lifecode DNA, or any extraterrestrial equivalent of DNA. Any means of passing and storing an instruction set for a life-form.

Lunar Wheel A huge, toroidal Charonian structure deep inside the Moon. It circles the Moon's core, and is aligned precisely with the border between the Lunar Nearside and Farside.

MG Wave Modulated gravity wave.

Moonpoint, Moonpoint Ring That point in space, relative to Earth, that occupies the space where the Moon once was. The **Moonpoint Ring,** a massive gravity-generator, holds the space now, with the Moonpoint end of the Earth–Solar System wormhole at its center. The Moonpoint Ring was killed in the battle for the Solar System. *See* **Earthpoint.**

Multisystem The huge artificial stellar system in which the Earth is placed. At its center is the

Sphere. It includes a number of G-class stars, around each of which large numbers of life-bearing planets orbit.

Multisystem Research Institute (MRI) A think-tank associated with Columbia University in New York City, and with the DSI. A major—and rather moribund—center for study of the Multisystem and the Charonians.

Naked Purple Movement Also known as the Point-less Cause. One of a number of odd social and political movements. Its belief structure is kept deliberately obscure and conflicted. Owns NaPur-Hab, the Naked Purple Habitat, and Tycho Purple Penal on the Moon.

NaPurHab (Naked Purple Habitat) A large and rather shabby orbiting habitat owned and popu-lated by the Naked Purple Movement. Originally in a figure-eight orbit between Earth and the Moon, NaPurHab is, as the book opens, in an in-creasingly unstable orbit around the black hole at the center of the Moonpoint Ring in the Multisys-tem. Its orbit is actually interior to the Moonpoint Ring's circumference. Population ten thousand.

Permod, Personnel Module A self-sufficient life-support unit about the size and shape of a coffin. It can be stacked and packed like a cargo module and flown in a cargo vehicle.

Plutopoint The point in space formerly occupied by the now-destroyed planet Pluto and its satellite Charon. Both worlds were totally absorbed into the Plutopoint Black Hole. The Plutopoint hole was then used to defend the remaining worlds of the Solar System against the Charonians.

Rabbit Hole The vertical shaft leading from the Lunar North Pole to the Lunar Wheel, forty kilometers below.

Ring of Charon Huge human-made gravity research tool, formerly orbiting Charon, Pluto's moon. It now holds the Plutopoint Singularity at its center. *See* **Plutopoint.**

Ring-and-Hole Set, R-H Set The combination of a gravitic singularity (such as a black hole) and an accelerator ring (such as the Ring of Charon). Together, the two can be used to generate gravity waves and beams, and to form wormhole apertures. The Charonians use R-H sets extensively.

Saint Anthony The automated relay probe dropped through the Earthpoint-Moonpoint wormhole just after the Abduction. It provided the last exchange of information between Earth and the Solar System. Named for the patron saint of lost objects.

Solar Area or Solar Space Naked Purple terms for the Solar System. The distinction is an ideological one: "system" implies order and control, whereas the chaotic, uncontrolled randomness of nature dictates against order. "Area" and "space" do not imply order.

SCOREs Small COREs. A new form of spacegoing Charonian. As the book opens, many of them are moving toward Earth at great speed. *See* **COREs.**

Scorpion A fairly sophisticated Charonian type, capable of dealing (though not necessarily dealing well) with unexpected situations. The term is applied not only to the scorpion-shaped Charonians, but to all creatures of its approximate ability.

Seedship A robot starship that carries fertilized ova, or the equivalent, to a new planet around a new star. The seedship lands, grows the ova to adulthood, and thus colonizes a new star system without the need of transporting a complex life-support system.

SubBubble Subterranean bubble—a standard type of Lunar construction. Consists of a large excavation under the Lunar surface, usually formed by melting an area of subsurface rock and then placing the interior under pressure. Much of Central City is composed of interconnected SubBubbles.

Sunstar The star in the Multisystem around which the Earth orbits.

Terra Nova (TN) Earth's only surviving major spacecraft in the Multisystem. Dianne Steiger is her captain.

TeleOperator A remote-control device, generally resembling a humanoid robot, but without a true robot's capacity for independent action. Instead, a T.O. is controlled by a human operator in a control harness at a remote location. As is the case with most virtual reality devices, the sensations reported by the T.O. to the operator can seem real.

T.O. *See* **TeleOperator.**

Virtual Black Hole (VBH) Currently a theoretical possibility only. In concept, a VBH is formed by an artificial massless gravity source sufficiently focused that a microscopic black hole forms. If a VBH of a sufficient gravity gradient survives long enough, in the presence of sufficient mass, it should be able to absorb that mass and thus become self-sustaining.

Virtual Reality General term applied to any technology that makes a non-local environment (real or imaginary) seem utterly real to an observer-participant. *See* **TeleOperator.**

VISOR, Venus Interim Station for Operational Research A large station orbiting Venus. Planned as the headquarters for the terraforming of that planet.

Worldeater Charonian, and, later, human terminology for the massive life-form known to humans as Landers. *See* Lander.

Wormhole A link between two points in space, formed by creating two identically tuned black holes. The wormhole in effect renders the two points contiguous across a flat plane, no matter how distant they actually are from each other.

Wormhole Transit Loop A ring of equally spaced **R-H sets** that share an orbit around a **Sphere.** They serve as relay stations for communications and transport.

THE BEST IN
SCIENCE FICTION

☐	51083-6	ACHILLES' CHOICE *Larry Niven & Steven Barnes*	$4.99 Canada $5.99
☐	50270-1	THE BOAT OF A MILLION YEARS *Poul Anderson*	$4.95 Canada $5.95
☐	51528-5	A FIRE UPON THE DEEP *Vernor Vinge*	$5.99 Canada $6.99
☐	52225-7	A KNIGHT OF GHOSTS AND SHADOWS *Poul Anderson*	$4.99 Canada $5.99
☐	53259-7	THE MEMORY OF EARTH *Orson Scott Card*	$5.99 Canada $6.99
☐	51001-1	N-SPACE *Larry Niven*	$5.99 Canada $6.99
☐	52024-6	THE PHOENIX IN FLIGHT *Sherwood Smith & Dave Trowbridge*	$4.99 Canada $5.99
☐	51704-0	THE PRICE OF THE STARS *Debra Doyle & James D. Macdonald*	$4.50 Canada $5.50
☐	50890-4	RED ORC'S RAGE *Philip Jose Farmer*	$4.99 Canada $5.99
☐	50925-0	XENOCIDE *Orson Scott Card*	$5.99 Canada $6.99
☐	50947-1	YOUNG BLEYS *Gordon R. Dickson*	$5.99 Canada $6.99

Buy them at your local bookstore or use this handy coupon:
Clip and mail this page with your order.

Publishers Book and Audio Mailing Service
P.O. Box 120159, Staten Island, NY 10312-0004

Please send me the book(s) I have checked above. I am enclosing $ _____
(Please add $1.50 for the first book, and $.50 for each additional book to cover postage and handling. Send check or money order only — no CODs.)

Name _____

Address _____

City _____ State / Zip _____

Please allow six weeks for delivery. Prices subject to change without notice.

MORE OF THE BEST IN SCIENCE FICTION

had built the cavern, and commanded the humans to come down to the water and bring stale buns to his flock.

Compared to how much say humans had in the running of the Multisystem, it didn't seem quite so absurd. But if the drake failed in caring for his flock, only the ducks would die. If the humans failed, then all the Earth would suffer.

Steiger was right. The odds against her ship were high and getting higher. There was no hope—and no point—in the *Terra Nova* battling endlessly against COREs. That was playing the Charonian's game, playing to their strengths.

So what game could mere human beings play, and beat the Charonians at?

Ursula had the feeling the answers were just out of reach, just beyond the questions she was asking. Something else had to happen before she would understand.

The SCOREs. That had to be it. They weren't going to do what everyone expected them to do. She was sure of that now. She had not the slightest idea what they were going to do instead—but when she did, it would be time to change the game.

Kourou Spaceport
Earth

Joanne Beadle—and every other person in the ops center—watched as SCORE X001 made its closest approach to the Moonpoint Ring.

The Charonians had never bothered with closest-approach gravity-well maneuvers, but if the SCOREs were indeed headed for Earth, they would have to make their moves there. Whatever they were going to do, closest approach was the moment to do it.

X001 was the vanguard SCORE, the first to arrive. The betting was that whatever it did, the follow-on SCOREs would imitate. And whatever it was going to do, it was going to do *now*. It could do almost anything by maneuvering at peripoint—but which way would it jump?

"What's it doing, Beadle?" Bernhardt demanded, leaning over his chair, as if Beadle had some special knowledge, could see something in the display screen that Bernhardt could not.

"I can't quite say," she replied, her mind far more on the display tank than on the director's question. "There's no way to guess. This one is no simulation."

"Yah," Bernhardt agreed. "We're through with those for a while, thank the heavens. I was beginning to forget things could be real."

Joanne didn't see how it could be a good thing that the alien craft approaching Earth were real. It would have suited her just fine if the whole fleet of them were imaginary. Still, there *was* something to be said for getting on with it all.

She stared at the screen, tense, waiting.

It would, of course, have been sheerest folly to try and read a human craft's intent from this range. The distances were too great. Even the fastest of human vehicles would be moving too slowly for a course change to be observable at this distance.

But not the Charonians. They could accelerate at hundreds of gees if it suited them.

She leaned closer to the screen, willing it to give up the secrets. "Peripoint in ten seconds," she announced, quite needlessly. "In five. Four. Three. Two. One—"

And then X001's flight path snapped neatly around in a perfect ninety-degree turn—and set itself on an arrow-straight course straight for the Moonpoint Black Hole.

"What the devil is *that*?" Bernhardt demanded. "Why is it doing this thing? Beadle—time to impact on black hole, if you please."

"Ah, ah, yes sir. Stand by. Just a moment." What the hell was that thing doing aiming direct for the black hole? It was the one possibility they hadn't considered. Well, why should they have? Why consider the possibility of the SCOREs traveling tens of millions of kilometers just to commit a highly energetic form of suicide? Unless . . . unless . . . Yes, it made sense. Beadle ran the numbers on time to impact—they would be the same no matter what happened. But if she was right—

"Sir, assuming the SCORE does not change course, it will hit the event horizon of the black hole in about forty-five seconds—but, ah, sir, I don't think it's going to *hit* it. I think it's going to go *through.*"

"But the Ring is dead!" Bernhardt protested. "There is no wormhole!"

As if on cue, the visual-band image system flared and flashed with the strange not-blue-white of a wormhole opening. Joanne gasped in surprise along with everyone else in the ops center.

"My God, Beadle, you are a good guesser," Bernhardt said in a half-whisper.

"Thank you, sir," she replied, most disconcerted, "but I'm usually not *this* good."

"The hole," Bernhardt whispered. "Why the devil are they going into the hole?"

Terra Nova

"Tracking, tracking—the hab is closing on the singularity. A great deal of interference is being produced by the Moon-point Ring and its interaction with the singularity," DePanna said, as if she were talking about a little static during a call from her Aunt Minnie.

Dianne wished, not for the first time, that her detection officer could be a trifle more excitable. That hunk of iron and glass out there, with thousands of people on it, was about to drop straight on through into the unknown. Yet DePanna seemed more concerned by the fact that her display screens were difficult to interpret.

Of course, if DePanna *had* gotten emotional, Dianne would have relieved her of her duty. But being upset with someone else's reaction helped keep Dianne from getting too upset herself.

"They shouldn't have done it," Gerald said. "It's suicide."

"What choice did they have?" Dianne asked. "It was suicide to stay where they were."

"I know," Gerald said. "I know—but even so."

All the Earth was watching NaPurHab's battle, its struggle to ride the rapids of gravity, the shoals of warping space, fighting past doom and disaster—toward what?

A dozen screen displays were running at once, and Dianne was trying to watch all of them. But the direct feeds from NaPurHab's external cameras meant the most. They would show what sort of place NaPurHab got to.

Assuming it got to anywhere at all.

NaPurHab

Getting closer, closer, toodamn close. The gaping mouth of the hole was getting larger and larger—but was it large enough? Did those straights back on Earth *really* think they had a strong enough capiche on this thing to pry the hole open big enough for something the size of a hab to punch through?

Back off. Bail out. Abort this. This is crazy. But there was very little point in listening to the panicked gibberings of her hindbrain. They had passed the point of no return long, long ago. *We're going to slam into that damned hole anyhow, anyway,* she told herself. Shush. Quiet, concentrate.

"Ghoul Modules commencing compensation," Sturgis reported. "Attempting to use gravitics control to pilot us in. Right on predicted schedule."

"Oh, good," Eyeball said. Wally had predicted that the Charos might try and manipulate the hab's course, setting it into the ideal transit path for a SCORE with the mass of the hab—which was not the right path for the hab. Eyeball would have to compensate for the attempted corrections as well.

"Confirming attempt at gravitic course compensation," Wally said.

Eyeball suppressed the urge to swear. The man sounded *pleased* that the Charonians were going to take another crack at killing them all. After all, it proved that he had gotten the problem right. Wally was *born* to the Naked Purple. "I'm getting the distortion now," Eyeball said.

Then the sounds started. The hab itself creaked, once, quietly, and then subsided. Too many shifting stresses were grabbing at the structure and the fabric of the poor old hab. Eyeball knew it was but a precursor of some truly *serious* noise. The tidal stresses were going to build up ferociously in the next few minutes.

The theory was that the hab could take it—but the damn thing was so old. NaPurHab had passed through a lot of hands before the Purps had taken possession. Eyeball was reasonably sure the original designers had not intended the thing to hold together for 150 years, let alone be dropped through a wormhole.

But none of that mattered now. NaPurHab had run out of choices long ago. A thousand things could go wrong, a thousand ways they could all be destroyed. Whether the hab crashed into the event horizon, was smashed by the SCOREs, was ripped apart by tidal stress, or was destroyed by a clumsy pilot at the helm, the result would be the same. She could get this exactly right, and they could *still* all get killed. Somehow, that made her feel better.

They were skewing to port just a tad. She tweaked the att jets a trifle and took a deep breath.

"Tidal forces becoming significant," Wally announced, and, as if on cue, there was another low moan as a support shifted its load.

Eyeball tried to ignore her fears. *Get it right*. No excuses, no second chances, no apologies. An alarm bell sounded behind her, and then another, and another. But they hadn't held an alarm drill since Eyeball had joined the nav team. Hull breach? Power short? The galley out of coffee? Never mind. She had to pilot this thing and there was nothing she could do. Let the others worry about everything else. Someone cut the alarms and silence returned, at least for a moment.

Closer, closer. She could see the motion now, without any effort, see the wormhole coming closer, swelling wide. Or was the wormhole aperture actually expanding? A sudden, hard jolt punched at the habitat, and the main lighting system cut out. A sort of rippling shudder moved over Eyeball, and she grabbed at the yaw controls, fighting to keep the hab on the right course and heading, even as the massive tidal forces strained to tear it apart.

Closer, closer, the inner depth of the hole now visible. Eyeball looked up to see how far off the Moonpoint Ring was from here—and saw nothing but the not-blue-white nothingness of the wormhole wall. They were inside it, swallowed whole by the hole, or maybe swallowed hole by the whole.

But they *couldn't* be in or through, or over, or across—not yet. No. Eyeball could see nothing on the other side. The seconds felt like hours. A new, deeper, shuddering vibration grabbed at the hab. Something wrenched at them, pulled at them, flared across them.

Eyeball looked up again, ahead, toward their destination. An enormous blood-black shape, far too large to be seen as a whole, swallowed up half the horizon, its huge surface smashed and pitted and scored. And there, dead ahead, a wizened little ruin of a world seen in half phase hung over the huge black-red form beyond.

The Naked Purple Habitat moved forward, down into the wormhole, toward the strange worlds on the other side—

—And then they were gone.